THE EDGE

To: Debbie

Hope you enjoy!

C. Bryan Cotton

8-10-01

THE EDGE

By

C. Benjamin Lattimore

This book is a work of fiction. Places, events, and situations in this story are purely fictional. Any resemblance to actual persons, living or dead, is coincidental.

ISBN: 1-58721-359-1

This book is printed on acid free paper.

1stBooks – rev. 6/26/01

About the Book

What if the anathema of Cocaine became a vigilantes waste management project? My novel, *THE EDGE*, tackles the all too familiar question of how to rid communities of Cocaine dealers and the scourge of Cocaine.

In *THE EDGE,* the actions of the *Just* border on anarchy in their attempt to regain communities lost to bandits who deal in the Cocaine enterprise. *THE EDGE*, on one side of the scale of Justice, is about love, understanding, trust, friendship and adoption. On the other side of the scale, *THE EDGE* is about rape, murder, fear, compromise and illiteracy. *THE EDGE* is a diabolical, demeaning, vicious and humiliating tale. It also has positive redeeming qualities that balance the scales of Justice. In *THE EDGE*, Justice—as we know it—is abandoned; the verdict is always the same!

DEDICATION:

To my loving wife, Marisa. To my two best girlfriends, my daughters—Monica and Courtney. To my "main man" Travis, my gentle man of a god child and to Boobie, Darryl & Gene, Aunt Viola, Aunt Carrie, Aunt Dot and to Gina, my Mother-in-Law. Especially to Isaiah, my new and precious grandson!

Ethereally to my parents Mary Alice and Walthro and little sister—Barbara Ann.

Thanks Scottie for your review.

INTRODUCTION

Like a recurring dream, the headlines from all over the country read the same:

"GUNMAN KILLS TWO CAMDEN TEENS." "FIVE FOUND DEAD IN DRUG DEAL GONE SOUR IN EAST L.A." "MAYOR OF WASHINGTON D.C. ARRESTED IN STING; VIDEOTAPED SMOKING CRACK COCAINE." "BIG-TIME AUTOMOBILE DESIGNER CAUGHT TRYING TO SMUGGLE COCAINE." "N.E. PHILADELPHIA MAN MURDERED WHILE TRYING TO BUY CRACK." "WHAT HAPPENED TO THE DRUGS, SHERIFF?" "BENNETT CALLS FOR ALL OUT WAR AGAINST DRUGS." "MODEL CITIZEN IN HIS COMMUNITY; DRUG BARON IN OURS." "COME TO OREGON AND GROW POT—200 ACRE FIELD UNCOVERED BY D.E.A." "THE WAR AGAINST NORIEGA: DRUG KING OR TYRANT?" "$6 MILLION IN CASH--$100 MILLION IN COCAINE FOUND IN ABANDONED TRUCK IN MIAMI." "WATCH OUT, THE POSSE IS IN TOWN; CHICAGO SAYS THEY ARE WANTED." "WOMAN PROSTITUTES HER 4 YEAR OLD FOR $5 WORTH OF CRACK COCAINE; CHILD DIAGNOSED AS HAVING GONORRHEA OF THE THROAT." "DALLAS DOES DRUGS—8 DIE AT PARTY FROM COCAINE LACED WITH ARSENIC." "IS YOUR BROKER FLYING HIGH WITH YOUR MONEY?" "LARGE CACHE OF DRUGS AND GUNS FOUND IN HOUSE ON LOWER EAST SIDE." "DEMOCRATS WANT TO ALLOCATE MORE FUNDS TO HELP DRUG USERS." "MOTORIST VIDEOTAPED BEING BEATEN BY L.A.P.D— THEY SAY HE WAS HIGH ON PCP AND UNCOOPERATIVE." "SOUTH CENTRAL BURNS AGAIN—OFFICERS FOUND NOT GUILTY IN BEATING OF MOTORIST." "CAR JACKINGS: THE LATEST WAY TO MAKE MONEY FOR CAINE." "WOMAN IN VIRGINIA

MURDERED AND HER 8 MONTH OLD CHILD IS KILLED WHEN THROWN FROM CAR AFTER CAR JACKING." "PHILADELPHIA MAN KILLED FOR HIS CAR—HIS NINE MONTH OLD BABY PLACED IN AN ALLEY." "THE DENTIST, THE DOCTOR AND THE ANESTHESIOLOGIST— THE METHAMPHETAMINE KINGS."

AND THE HEADLINES GO ON AND ON AND ON!

CHAPTER ONE

It was 3:30 p.m. on March 16, 1993 when Rashida Brooks felt the most horrible pain she had ever experienced. Rashida, a pretty girl of 15 years of age, was beginning to feel the benefits—or the agony—of her frivolous night of nine months ago. It was then, after spending a total of eleven hours with a 19-year-old, that she decided he was indeed the man for her for life. Malik, a tall, handsome young man, had spent many a night with girls like Rashida, promising them a full and faithful relationship. Rashida met Malik while shopping for clothes at a downtown mall. He approached her, offered to buy her lunch and give her a ride home in his new 300E after she had finished shopping. She thought he was cool, showing off his gold chains and expensive watch, while sporting the latest in leather attire.

The ride home was just what she imagined it would be. Malik offered her some caine. At first she refused, but later decided that he was cool and everything was going to be all right. They rode around the city with the sunroof open and the music at ear-piercing levels. Malik asked, "Do you want to hang for a while or do you have a curfew?" She responded, "No, I can stay out as late as I like." Malik shouted, "Cool, baby! You're just the kind of lady that I've been looking for and I can tell that we are going to be together for a long time." Rashida smiled and took another hit of the caine he had offered. This was only her second time experiencing caine, but she knew that she had to act like she was hip.

Meanwhile, back at Rashida's ranch on the ninth floor of the public housing building, her mother, a woman of 33 years, was busy banging her brains out for a vial of crack with the local caine dealer, a young man of 18 years of age. By her 18th birthday, Ms. Brooks had already given birth to twins, Rashida and Muhammad. She also had one miscarriage and two abortions. Muhammad never reached the teenager state—he overdosed two nights before his thirteenth birthday.

In thirty-three years, Ms. Brooks worked two jobs: one as a maid, from which she was fired for stealing $2.50, and the other as a cleaning woman, where she was also caught stealing. She had one never-ending message to her children, "Never tell a lie and don't do no kind of drugs." The old adage "Do as I say, not as I do" never was so true as when it came to Ms. Brooks. Ms. Brooks had a good teacher when it came to doing as I say, not as I do, because her mother was no angel, and even if she were, she was definitely from the dark side of the equation. Grandma Brooks was thirteen when she had her first daughter, Rashida's mother. As the story goes, she liked the so-called "good life"—a life of cheap champagne and pickled pigs feet. At the age of ten, she experienced her first sexual relationship with a man old enough to be her father two or three times over. No one really knew who the person was, but as rumor had it, the old man next door who was always giving her nickels and dimes was the culprit. Everyone remembers when she started to get big, he started packing his things. Nevertheless, Grandma was the perfect person to teach what should not be taught to the young.

After finishing sex for caine, Ms. Brooks began begging her young lover for the vial of short but sweet euphoria. The first cardinal rule for a pusher is never use what you can sell and never accept sex for dope, because in the long run, when it's time to pay the price, the sex can only spell trouble. Ignoring the rules of the street, the young stud began to snort the caine with Ms. Brooks, who had a nose like the intake valve at a hydroelectric plant and, to his dismay, had a tolerance level equal to three very large adult males.

"Slow down, baby. We got to make this shit last—at least until you give me some head."

"Baby, I don't give no head for this little bit of shit and besides, if you want head, you had better find me a pipe so that I can smoke me some adult shit."

"Ah, come on, baby. You sucked up your nose at least $100 worth of my good shit."

"Let me tell you something—it was all right, but I wouldn't invite none of my girlfriends over for this shit." Ms. Brooks knew that she was talking shit and realized that maybe she had pushed her new young lover too far. It was time to make some kind of gesture to appease him as well as to consider pleasing him with her tongue.

"Okay, pipe head. You want the pipe, then you gonna suck me until I cum in your ragged ass mouth."

"Fuck you! Who do you think you're fooling with? One of those little teenagers that you push this shit on?"

Realizing she had gone too far with her new supplier, Ms. Brooks felt that she was placing herself behind the eight ball. She knew this guy was a good screw and she realized what the other dealers would make her do for a hit. She thought she had better make amends with her potential new supplier. "Sometimes when I get high I say things that I ought not say to people. Come here, Daddy. Please, Daddy, don't make me beg for it. You're real good to me and I need to show you how much I appreciate what you do for me. Please Daddy, please, let me make you happy with my mouth. Please, Daddy."

The young stud was thinking, *who in his right mind would turn down an opportunity to get sucked off?* So, back on the sofa with his pants down, the young lover began to get the treat of his life, because without a doubt, Ms. Brooks could perform this surgery like no other woman on earth.

For twenty-five minutes, Ms. Brooks sucked and licked and sucked and licked. When he was about to climax, she stopped and said to her young lover, "Not yet, Baby; make it last just a little while longer."

"Baby, I got to go, so come on finish it."

"Turn on your stomach."

"What for?"

"If you're going to be my Daddy, then do as I say." As she began to shower her young lover with all the tricks she had learned over the years, she realized that she wanted another hit. She said, "Daddy, I need another hit." Realizing that he had now spent all of his profits on sex and that he was still hard, he thought, *what's a man to do in this situation?* They doped for a little while longer and then she took a little of the caine and put it on the tip of his penis. "What the fuck are you doing?" He asked, his eyes widening.

"Relax, Daddy. Now when I suck you it will tingle and make my mouth feel like sucking you all day."

Again the young lover was amazed at what his new thing could do with her mouth. He finally exploded, his cum pooling in the curl of her tongue, and she loved every minute of it. She had missed the feel of mammoth explosions because most of her partners were older men. She thought to herself as she was swallowing, I never again want to sleep with an older man. Besides the doping, she was convinced that there was no feeling like the sensation of a young lover filling her with his love juices. The young lover's name was Larry Holland. He was called "Larry the Wanderer".

CHAPTER TWO

The debutante showed up in the neighborhood only when she needed caine to entertain herself and her friends. As her brand new 500SL pulled up to the corner, she yelled out the window, "Hey, Larry, what you got for me?"

"I got what you want and what you need, Ms. Ann." "Ms. Ann" was the name most commonly associated with white females of means.

"Hey, Larry, I need $5,000 worth now and maybe another $5,000 tonight. Can you handle it?"

"Listen, why do you insist on coming down to the hood? I told you a thousand times, you know the man is watching between his naps."

"Hey, Larry, listen to me you little fuck. I just dropped off $1500 to those motherfuckers so that they won't bother me or the jig that supplies me. Now quit the shit. Can you handle the deal?"

"Listen, Ms. Ann, I'll be at Thursday's on City Line in 30 minutes. Be there and I'll have all of your shit."

"Don't fuck up, Larry. You know you still owe me one for getting those two Mafia types off your ass."

"Ms. Ann, don't worry. I'll take care of business and maybe before you get the second batch, we could, like have a conversation about something that has been on my mind for a long while." In the interim, Larry rubbed his inner leg, just enough not to be vulgar and just enough to illustrate or give a hint as to what he was talking about. "Larry, just bring the stuff. You know I don't do black."

"Hey, Ms. Ann, we all have a change of heart, don't we? You remember when you would only do weed? Now look at you. You've acquired the high-priced taste of the good old white witch. And you know what? I know you love the shit."

"Larry, don't be late."

CHAPTER THREE

Malik and Rashida were having a wonderful night out, something she had never ever done before. After many hours of mindless wandering around the city and snorting large hits of the caine, Rashida became an easy prey for even a small-time hustler like Malik.

"Baby, I know this place where we can go and have some champagne and get to know each other better."

"What kind of place is it?" Rashida asked.

"It's the kind of place where people dwell, baby. It'll be like our home for the night, if you can stay out all night like you said you could."

Feeling a little brave and wanting to keep her newfound friend interested, Rashida said, "If that's what you want to do, it's okay with me."

"Baby, we're going to be together for a long time. I can feel it, can't you?"

"You make me feel carefree and wonderful, Malik."

"That's the way a woman like you should feel, baby. I just want to make sure you're happy, that's all."

Malik pulled into his favorite sleazy roadside motel. Entering the registration area under the hum of the neon marquee, he requested a room for a couple of hours.

"That'll be $15 per hour plus $3 for two towels and two face cloths," said the cigar-smoking, pot-bellied attendant.

"I only need one towel."

"That'll be $2."

Malik gave the attendant a look and said, "Call me in one hour. I got business to take care of and I don't want to spend any more time or money on this broad than I have to."

7

"Understood. I'll give you a fifteen-minute warning call, but it'll cost you $2.50."

Malik handed him $4. "Keep the change and give me the key."

"Don't eat no soup without a spoon," the attendant said wryly.

Rashida and Malik entered the room. Malik took out his little drug stash and told Rashida to have another hit. Rashida didn't hesitate for a moment before beginning to snort the caine up her nostrils. The rush of feelings and euphoria she thought she was about to experience for the first time would only turn out to be a few minutes of dolorous activity.

After hugging, kissing and feeling all over Rashida's ripe body, Malik began to take off her clothes, with no resistance from her. Down to only her bra and panties, Malik struggled to remove the bra because he was unaware of the mechanics of the front snap. Half-dazed and high, Rashida lent him a helping hand and two of the most voluptuous and tender-looking breasts fell out of her undersized bra. Malik began to caress her, kiss her breasts and feel her in an area that no man had ever touched before. Rashida flinched at first, but was overcome by his sheer strength and determination to conquer her love zone. Malik, after removing her panties and hurriedly removing all of his clothes, told Rashida to suck him. Rashida looked at him and said, "I don't do that." After many slick and powerful words, Malik finally got pissed off and tried to force the issue. Rashida, now completely high and crying, begged him not to do it because she had never done it before. Malik responded by saying, "Bitch, the way you sucked up my caine, I know you can suck some dick." Rashida started crying louder and as Malik looked at his watch, he knew that the call would be coming in about fifteen minutes. He finally turned Rashida on her stomach and tried to penetrate her anus. Rashida yelled for him to stop. Malik, intent on his own satisfaction, didn't realize that the natural area was of virgin origin. Rashida continued to plead

8

with Malik not to hurt her. He finally turned her over and ramrodded her love zone. Rashida recoiled, but to no avail, because he now had her legs pinned up behind her head and was pumping and fighting for position while trying to beat the clock. The entire act lasted five minutes and Malik patiently waited for the call from the attendant so that he could "get busy," as he called it.

The call came through and Malik said to Rashida, between her sobs, "Come on, bitch, we got to go. That was my man. He has a deal for me to make some cash." Rashida entered the bathroom and noticed that she was bleeding all over the place. She asked Malik to come to the door, and he said, "I know, bitch, you're bleeding. Put some toilet paper in your panties until you get home. You'll be all right." Rashida looked in the mirror and decided that she had truly made a big mistake listening to all his bullshit. She once again started to cry, while the new jerk in town was yelling, "Come on, bitch, we got to go. I got to make some cash to pay for the shit you sucked up your nose."

After leaving the roadside motel, Malik turned to Rashida and said, "Oh, baby, I'm sorry about the way I treated you, but I was expecting some head from you." Rashida never said a word and somberly continued to cry inside and out for the terrible misjudgment of character she had made.

As the car continued towards the projects, a black, four-door Ford passed the 300E and made a screeching U-turn in the middle of the street. Malik looked into the rearview mirror and said, "Oh shit, them motherfuckers aren't going to catch my black ass." He hit the accelerator on the 300E and the car lunged forward and took off. A siren from the black car began to whirl and the red light began to turn. Malik knew that he was in trouble. Rashida turned to him and said, "Why are you running from the police? You didn't do anything wrong."

"Shutup, bitch, and hold on. Those motherfuckers are always after me for some bullshit that I didn't do."

9

"By speeding away like this, they're for sure going to think that you've done something wrong."

"Do me a favor please and shut the fuck up, you dumb bitch. I know what I'm doing."

As the car sped around corners on two wheels, barely missing other cars not to mention pedestrians, the officers in the unmarked car reported that they were in pursuit of a green 300E suspected of being stolen. Two additional police units joined in the chase and Malik was now without an escape route. As they continued to turn corners at racecar speeds, Rashida yelled at Malik, "Stop the car and let me out!" Malik backhanded Rashida right in the mouth, and in the process of taking his eyes off the road, ran broadside into a parked car. Rashida's face slammed into the windshield and knocked her out cold. Boyfriend, on the other hand, opened his door and took off like a bat out of hell. The police pursued him down several dark alleyways, but the slippery little rat was able to find a hole and crawl into it until the coast was clear.

After reviving Rashida and calling for an ambulance, the police officer read her the Miranda Act. A policeman asked, "What is your name?" She responded, "Rashida Brooks." Still groggy and not sure what had just happened, all she could tell the officer asking her questions about the driver was that his name was Malik. The officer asked Rashida, "Malik what? Do you know his last name?" Feeling rather foolish and realizing that she had just lost her virginity to an asshole whose full name she did not know, Rashida started crying. A sympathetic officer said, "The poor child was probably just out riding with that jerk."

The ambulance arrived and the attendants began to ask Rashida a lot of questions about how she was feeling and was there anything hurting. Rashida indicated that nothing was wrong. The thing that was wrong with Rashida would not be revealed because she was too embarrassed to discuss her current problem. As the crowds began to close in to satisfy their

10

curiosity, one girl said to her friend, "Isn't that Rashida Brooks?" Her friend responded, "Girl, that sure is, and she looks as usual—like shit."

"Man, they gagged that Benz! Look at that pretty 'E' all fucked up."

CHAPTER FOUR

At the police station, officers kept asking her the last name of the driver, and Rashida swore up and down that she didn't know his last name. They questioned her concerning when she met him and what they did. Rashida once again started crying so hard that her shortness of breath appeared as though she was about to have an asthma attack. The officers kept insisting that she would be all right and for her to tell them the truth. Rashida finally gained her composure and began to relate the events leading up to the chase, the accident and the subsequent abandonment by Boyfriend. She told them how she met him at the mall and he seemed nice at the time. She even admitted that she used cocaine with him, but swore to the officer that it was only the second time in her life she ever used the drug. The officer asked her, "Why did you do the cocaine?"

"I was trying to be big time and all. But really I was trying to impress him."

"Did he have a lot of caine with him?"

"All I saw was the little vial that he had when we were at the motel. I must have did the drugs twice or maybe three times with him—that's all."

"What was the name of the motel?" the officer asked.

"I don't know the name, but it's on Roosevelt Boulevard."

"Was it going towards the Northeast?"

"I guess so."

"Did he make any calls or get any?"

"He got one call."

"Did he say what it was about?"

"He said the call was from his man and that he had a deal for him to make a lot of cash."

"Frank, get a car over there and see if we can come up with the place, and if so, question the clerk and see if he will volunteer a copy of his register for us."

13

"Okay, Sarge."

"Now, Ms. Brooks, back to you. How old are you, young lady?"

"I'm fifteen."

"Fifteen? You look a lot older than fifteen."

"I hear that all the time, but I'm only fifteen."

There was a pause, and Rashida began to cry again. She finally got up enough nerve to tell the male officer that she had been hurt.

"What's wrong, young lady?"

Between sobs and deep breaths, Rashida said, "I had sex with him and he hurt me."

"How did he hurt you, Rashida?"

"He was just rough and I'm still bleeding down there." The Sarge called out, "Hey, Carl, get Ieisha and get this little lady over to the hospital in a hurry. That jerk we're looking for may have just added another charge to his biography when we catch him. Don't worry, Rashida, we'll take care of you. Please stop crying. I have to call your parents and make them aware of what has happened. Is this the correct phone number that you gave me?"

"Yes, Sir."

"Okay people, let's move. I have a sick young lady on my hands and we don't want anything going down here now do we? Okay then, let's hear that siren disappear. Rashida, I will come over later to check on you personally. Is that all right with you?"

"Please come, because I feel like I need to talk to someone," she stated between sobs.

CHAPTER FIVE

The sergeant tried to make a call to Rashida's mother but received a busy signal on each attempt. He finally called the operator and asked her to interrupt the conversation on the other line. The operator indicated to the Sarge that the line was out of order. He thanked her and hung up the phone.

"Hey, Smitty, get your stick. We're taking a little ride over into the hood."

"Okay, Sarge, but I hope you're wearing a vest tonight, because I sure as hell am going to put mine on."

"Boy, you worry too much about your muscles. If you get it, it'll probably be in your brainless head." As they were leaving the station, Smitty turned to the Sarge and said, "So what's the deal with that pretty little girl?"

"I think the child was just out to get some attention and bought the wrong kind of friendship."

"How do you plan on handling the paperwork on this one, Sarge?"

"I'll have another conversation with Rashida later and then we'll decide what has to be done. Frankly, I think she's a good kid who just got caught up with the wrong jerk."

"You want to know something, Sarge?"

"Are we going to play a game or are you going to say something relative?"

"No games, Sarge. I just want to say that I like the way you do police work. You realize that things are not always just black and white and that there is some gray in there sometimes. You ever wonder when you ask for someone to go somewhere with you why I always volunteer?"

"No, I don't, but I believe you're about to tell me why. I hope it's not because you are gay and you want to be close to a real man."

"Cute, Sarge, but not cute enough. I like the way you treat people, especially the criminals who are innocent until proven guilty. Some guys come in and say that they saw this kid running and therefore he robbed the little old lady eighteen miles away. But you—you take time to feel the pulse of the situation and then you do the police work according to their books, or in this case, according to your books."

"Smitty, you know that I have been criticized about doing it my way, don't you?"

"So what? Two out of four hundred times you made the wrong call. Shit, I'll take those odds any day of the week!"

"What's that address on the clipboard?"

"It looks like 903 South 2nd Street."

"It must be the second project building on the left hand side. Do you want me to call for a car to just cruise until we're out of the place?"

"Good idea, Smitty. The one thing about making your judgment calls is that in some cases, it's best to follow the instinct that says this is not such a great neighborhood and therefore we need an additional cruiser to protect the one we have to leave." Smitty got on the horn and called for backup. Within a matter of four minutes an unmarked car appeared on the scene with two uniformed patrolmen.

"Hey, Sarge, what's up?"

"Nothing much. We've got to go in and want to make sure that we can get out and away in a hurry if necessary."

"Anything heavy? Do we all need to go?"

"No, we have to inform a parent that her child is being questioned by us, that's all."

"Okay, we won't cruise. We'll wait until you guys get back."

"Smitty, put your box on channel 88 so that the boys here can monitor the situation. Okay guys, we'll be back in a few."

"You guys had better take some light. You know the Housing Department doesn't put light bulbs in the hallways but once a month."

"Hey, why don't you guys go and do this and we'll just watch your car."

"No thanks, Sarge, just trying to be helpful."

"Hey, don't go and get sweet on me now. I was just jiving for a minute. See you when we get back."

Once in the building, the officers were met by the Housing Department security man. "Gentlemen, what can I do for you?"

"We need to talk to a Ms. Brooks, the mother of Rashida Brooks."

"Damn, that kid ain't in no kind of trouble is she?"

"We don't know yet, but she is in the hospital with some female problems right now."

"Out of all of the kids in this place, she is the smartest, most respectful and always helps the old people who live here." The Sarge and Smitty just looked at each other and smiled as they both remembered the conversation about operating according to the book of instinct.

"Well, guys, I wish you luck when you go up to see the mother. She's a no-account, dope-doing, whoring bitch. She'll fuck an alley rat for that caine."

Smitty asked the guard, "Does she get violent?"

"Only if you got what she wants and you won't give it to her."

"Thanks, guy, we'll see you on the way out."

"Oh, by the way—I hope you're in shape. The fucking elevators are broken once again."

"Just what I need—to climb steps at my age," the Sarge said.

"Oh, it's not that bad. You only got to go to nine."

"That's eight more than I expected, buddy."

After climbing the steps and taking several philosophical breaks to discuss good police procedures, the Sarge finally admitted to Smitty, "This shit is killing me. I need to get from behind that desk more often and do some foot patrolling to keep

17

this old body of mine in some kind of pursuit and defensive condition."

"Sarge, you're doing okay. I work out every day and I'm just as spent as you are."

"Thank you Jesus!" the Sarge exclaimed as they reached the ninth floor. "Smitty, I know you white boys aren't used to the smell of stagnant piss that's contributed to on a daily basis."

"Sarge, I was born in one of these motherfuckers in Detroit."

"No pun intended Smitty, I guess I spoke in bad taste."

"Not at all, Sarge. No one can get used to their home being violated by assholes who refuse to use water closets."

"Water closets! What in the hell are you talking about?"

"Sarge, a water closet is a toilet. Or if you're in Europe in most places it's called the loo."

"Thanks for the lesson, Son. I see why I like to have you volunteer on these missions with me now. Okay, let's inform this woman and get the hell out of here."

KNOCK—KNOCK—KNOCK!
KNOCK—KNOCK—KNOCK!

"Ms. Brooks, this is Sergeant Beckmire with the Police Department. I would like to have a word with you about your daughter, Rashida." They could hear the ruffling of papers and the moving of objects and voices from inside whispering. Finally, a voice from within said, "Just a minute."

A minute or so later, the door opened and there were three sets of night chains on the door. A woman appeared apparently loaded and wreaking of cheap booze and said, "Where is my daughter?"

"Ms. Brooks, she was involved in an automobile accident, but prior to that had apparently experienced some rough sex with a fugitive who was driving a stolen car."

"Is she hurt?"

18

"She survived the car accident okay, but she sustained some kind of injury from her sexual experience. We took her to the hospital, where I am sure she is being treated at this moment. We tried to call you on the telephone, but it was off the hook. May we come in and ask you some questions?"

"I can't talk right now. I have company. What hospital is she in?"

"She's in County General, ma'am."

"Okay, I'll go over there in a little while and make sure that she's all right. Okay, I have to go now. Thank you. Good-bye." The door was slammed and they could hear voices discussing something other than the state of her daughter.

"With a mother like that, it wouldn't take long for a good kid to go bad, Sarge."

"You're right, Smitty. What do you think they were doing in there?"

"Probably drugs. Did you see the way her eyes kept going back into her head? She could barely stand straight up."

"Yeah, I noticed that, Smitty. It's a damn shame that kids have to be subjected to that kind of parenting. Let's get the hell out of here."

As the two officers entered the stairway there appeared to be a struggle in progress on one of the lower floors. They looked at each other and the Sarge put one finger to his mouth, signaling Smitty to be quiet. As they quietly descended the steps, the Sarge looked over the railing and saw tennis shoes and legs stretched out on the stairway. "Smitty, tell the guys in the cruiser we need backup on the stairway and to stop anyone trying to leave the building."

"Okay, Sarge." Smitty told the officers what was going on and that they needed backup. As Smitty and the Sarge reached the fifth floor they could see that someone was bleeding profusely and that two other people were rifling through his pockets. The Sarge yelled out, "Halt! This is the police!" From behind the two officers, a lookout man aimed his machine pistol and began firing at the two officers. Smitty caught two rounds in the chest and tumbled down the balance of the flight of stairs. Several more shots rang out. He fell onto the Sarge, and Smitty caught two more rounds in the back. The Sarge at this time was able to reach Smitty's weapon and returned the fire. The Sarge could not reach his own weapon because the unconscious Smitty had fallen on him. The 9mm rang out fifteen times and the gunman fell down the steps with at least eight hits covering his body. The Sarge then moved Smitty and secured his own weapon in the nick of time as the two individuals who were rifling the pockets of the bleeding man ran up the steps. The Sarge's reactions were automatic—he caught a glimpse of the individuals trying to escape and began to fire on them. Both individuals were hit by his gunfire. The two officers who were performing backup duties ran up the steps and yelled, "Police officers!"

"Watch it! They're on the fourth floor landing and they're armed," the Sarge cautioned.

"Okay, Sarge. We called for backup when we heard the gunfire. Are you guys okay?"

"I think Smitty caught a couple of rounds, but I'm not able to help him until I know the status of those two below me."

"Okay, just hang on and stay where you are."

"Police officers! Drop your weapons and put your hands where they can be seen." There was no response. One officer said to the other, "Fuck'em. Give them the procedure one more time and then we'll just shoot the shit out of them."

"Police officers! Drop your weapons and put your hands where we can see them."

"Okay, but no more shooting," the voice said. "We need an ambulance. We're both bleeding."

"Just keep your hands high where I can see them and there will be no more shooting."

"Okay, okay. My hands are in the air."

"Where is the other guy? I don't see his hands. Tell him to put his hands in the air or I'm going to blow his fucking head off."

"He's bleeding real bad, and he's not moving."

"Just keep your fucking hands in the air where I can see them." As the officer shined his light on the suspect, the guy who was allegedly bleeding real badly said, "Fuck you motherfuckers. Take this!" An automatic pistol rang out and two rounds caught the first officer in the arm and leg. The Sarge targeted the shooter and put a single round into his head and another round into the chest of the second suspect.

After asking the backup officers how they fared, one officer said, "My partner's been hit twice." At the bottom of the stairway, they could hear footsteps and then a voice that shouted, "Police officers, hold your fire!" The Sarge looked at Smitty, who was out like a light. He did not see any blood and said, "I thank God you wore that horrible vest." Sergeant Beckmire didn't realize that he had taken a round in the upper part of his shoulder. It turned out to be a grazing wound. Two of the gunmen on the other hand didn't fair too well; they died in the pissy corridors of Public Housing building # 903. The third gunman sustained three hits, and it didn't look as though he would live through the night. The victim on the stairway was dead from a knife wound to his throat.

Sirens whirled, lights flashed and the residents never came out of their doors. It seemed that these shootings occur often between rival caine dealers for this virgin territory. The wounded on both sides of the law were taken to County General for treatment.

CHAPTER SIX

At County General, the ambulances kept coming with victims of the latest drug war. Sergeant Beckmire rode in the same wagon with Smitty, who was still unconscious, but otherwise alive and doing well. Smitty was whisked off to one room and the Sergeant to another. The attending doctor said to the Sergeant, "You're one lucky ass. Where's your vest, man?"

"I hate those things."

"They're designed to provide protection, be they ever so cumbersome and uncomfortable," the doctor remarked.

"I know, Doc. After seeing what happened to my partner, you can bet your ass that the next time I go out, I may even have two of those damn things on."

The doctor told the attending nurse to hold a compress against the Sergeant's shoulder until he returned. The doctor went to the other room to see if there was serious injury to Smitty. "He was one lucky sonofabitch," remarked one of the nurses. Smitty had endured five shots, any of which would have been fatal without his vest.

After being revived, the first thing Smitty asked was, "How is the Sarge?" The doctor who treated Sergeant Beckmire said, "He just received a superficial wound in the shoulder. He should be leaving here in about an hour or so. Had he worn his vest, he wouldn't even have had that." Smitty said that they had joked about the vest prior to leaving the station and that he thanked God for not being macho, and for wearing the damn thing.

Further down the hallway, the officer who received the two gunshot wounds, one to his arm and the other to his leg, also shared a bit of luck. Each bullet went clean through. No arteries or muscles were injured and he would be as good as new in a couple of weeks. All in all, the police, deservedly, fared well that evening. The young, would-be lawbreakers on the other hand, would never see the sun again.

CHAPTER SEVEN

"Well, there you are, just like new," the doctor indicated to Sergeant Beckmire.

"Thanks, Doc. You do good work."

"Sergeant, you could make my work a lot easier if you wore your vest."

"Not to concern yourself, Doctor. It's as good as done from this day forward."

"Good man. Then the next time I see you it should be in the leg, right Sergeant?"

"Doc, the next time you see me, I hope it's at the theater or dinner."

"Yes, I see the inappropriateness of that last statement. I hope you didn't take it literally?"

"Not at all, Doc. Do you think it will be okay if I looked in on my partner?"

"I don't see why not. He's quite all right, unless the x-rays show a bone break somewhere."

Across and down the hall, the Sarge entered Smitty's room and said, "Hey, Smitty, how ya doing?"

"Sarge, other than feeling like I got hit by a sledgehammer, I'm okay. How's your wound?"

"Barely a scratch. But you know something—I thanked God that you had the sense to wear that vest, even after I gave you shit about it. You won't have to remind me next time as well, because it's now a part of my body from this day forward."

"Good! Forget those macho bastards who think the vest is a joke. The doctor tells me that I got hit five times, any of which would have proven fatal had I not had my vest on."

"Well, you get some rest. I think I'm going to look in on Rashida Brooks and see how she's doing while I'm here."

"Okay, Sarge. I'll talk to you later." As he was walking out into the corridor, an officer said, "Hey, Sarge, the Lieutenant wants to talk to you when you have a chance."

"Okay. Tell him I need to check on a patient and then I'll be right there."

"Excuse me, Nurse, but can you tell me where I can find Rashida Brooks? She should have checked in here about three hours ago." After checking the log, the nurse said, "She's in room 2304 East Wing."

"Thank you."

Knock—Knock! "Rashida, it's the Sergeant from the police station. May I come in?"

"Oh yeah, come on in. I'm dressed. Oh my God! What happened to you?"

"Oh, it's just a scratch, that's all. We went to tell your mother that you were in the hospital and on the way out of the building there were some problems."

"Did she start trouble?"

"No, it wasn't your mother, but some guys on the stairway who were looking for trouble."

"I could have told you before you went over there that my mother would probably be busy. She probably has already forgot that you came by to tell her that I was here."

"Well, let's not talk about mothers and trouble. I came by to see how you were doing and to see if there was anything that you needed." There was a long pause, and the Sarge knew that when this young lady paused, the next thing was going to be tears. So right he was. Rashida broke down and started crying like a baby once again.

"Okay, what's the matter now?" Between her sobs and erratic breathing, she managed to say, "I don't wanta go to jail."

"Who said you was going to jail?"

"No one, but I know I was in that car and I heard a cop say it was definitely stolen. And besides, I confessed to using caine and I know what happens to people who do caine."

"Rashida, you're not going to jail. I wouldn't let that happen to you unless you don't take charge of your life and get back on the right track. The guard at your building told me some very positive things about you that only confirmed my hunch that you're a good kid who needs some positive direction. No, dear, there will be no jail in your future because I have decided that Smitty and I are going to be your friends and mentors. Now how do you like that idea?" Rashida just started to cry more and harder and gave the Sergeant a wonderful hug of friendship. She did manage to say, "I really need a good friend right now, because I have nothing at home except drugs and my mom's lovers trying to seduce and rape me all the time."

"Don't worry, Rashida. We'll try to do something about that as well. Now you get some sleep and give me a call at this number tomorrow, and I'll see to it that you get home okay. I'll drop by and see your mother soon and have a long talk with her and see if we can't do something about the problems in your home."

"Thanks, ah—what do I call you?"

"Call me what all my friends call me—Sarge. I'll talk to you later, okay? And remember, don't you think about jail, because it just ain't going to happen. I'll see to that and you can hold me to it."

"Thanks, Sarge. I'll call you tomorrow."

As the Sergeant was leaving the room, he decided to inquire about Rashida's physical condition. "Nurse, my name is Sergeant Beckmire and I'm kind of a friend to the young lady in 2304 E. I would like to ask her doctor about her condition. Can you tell me who he is?"

"I most certainly can, but you must first of all stop thinking that all doctors are men. I'm the doctor who examined the young lady."

"A thousand apologies. I don't know what possessed me to think in that sexist manner. Please forgive me."

"It's okay, but anyhow, she is doing fine and from what I can tell at this point, she is just ruptured and swollen. Her boyfriend must really be an animal of sorts. The poor child has had her womb displaced and will probably be in pain for a few days. Until the swelling goes down, we can't determine if there was any real damage to her."

"Thanks, Doctor. I appreciate the information. It would be a service to the police department if you make sure that whatever she needs is provided. I think that she is a kid that we can save from the streets and I want to help her as much as possible."

"You could help her a lot by keeping her away from the animal who tried to sexually kill her."

"When we catch up with Boyfriend, he'll have to take a vacation. Maybe that will take care of the problem. Thank you again, Doctor."

Down the hall once again, the Sarge dropped by Smitty's room and said, "Hey, Smitty, anything I can get you before I get out of this place?"

"Naw, Sarge, I just want to sleep and reflect on tonight. I really feel like crying."

"Then that's what you should do, Smitty. There is nothing wrong with a man being happy to be alive. I certainly am going to go to church on Sunday and thank God for all of his blessings. See you later, trooper."

As the Sarge was working his way slowly out of the hospital, he stopped by Mack's room, where Clyde was standing in the doorway.

"Hey, Clyde, how's Mack?"

"Sarge, he's doing fine."

"I need to thank you guys for saving our asses back there. It really meant a lot to me to hear your voices on that stairway. I

28

love being a cop and love working with good and honest cops as well. I think I'll put my head in and say thanks to that old buzzard in there." In a rather subdued voice, the Sarge said, "Hey, Mack, how you hanging?"

"Man, I'm so glad that you and the kid are doing all right."

"Listen, Mack, we needed you back there and you came through for us. You know that little problem that you and your partner have been having? Tomorrow I'll give a call to the Commissioner and see if I can't call in some chips that are owed to me. But if I do that, you and your partner had better stay on the up and up. Is that a deal?"

"Sarge, I don't know nothing but police work. My family depends on my job. Just between you and me, we made a mistake and I think that we're willing to pay the price. But if there is anything you can do to help us out, it would be greatly appreciated."

"Okay, you get well and let me handle the deal. I'll talk to Clyde on my way out and make sure that I have his commitment as well. Again, Mack, we needed you guys back there and you came through for us. I can't forget that and I won't. Take care and I'll see you tomorrow."

As the Sarge was leaving Mack's room, he ran into Clyde. He said, "Hey, Clyde, I told Mack if you guys stay on the up and up, I'll see if I can intervene in that little problem you guys have. But you got to promise me that you people won't make that kind of bad judgment again. And let me say this—I am neither judge nor executioner. Right now, I'm just a cop trying to help a cop who saved my ass. I'm not accusing you of anything. But you and I both know what the deal is. So you guys hang clean and I'll see if I can't call in some points that are owed to me."

"Hey, Sarge—man, we need all of the help we can get. We acted poorly and we got an advantage. But we know we did wrong and just want to get back in the family of clean cops."

"Okay, buddy. Tomorrow I'll see if I can work some magic."

CHAPTER EIGHT

The following morning the Sergeant was at work early—at least three hours before his shift. He had established two goals for the day. One was to find a last name and location of Boyfriend, and the other was to help out the officers that helped him and Smitty the night before. The first goal was not going to be an easy task.

The Sergeant asked the lab and fingerprint specialists whether or not they had an ID of the driver of the stolen vehicle. The response was, "Absolutely." A very energetic female officer said, "It's the same guy who was ID'd at that bank robbery that went bad three weeks ago. His name is Malik. We have a last known address for the suspect, but officers sent to that address said that it was an abandoned building."

"Do we know his last name?"

"All they could come up with was Malik."

"Do we have a picture of Boyfriend?"

"I beg your pardon, Sir?"

"I'm sorry, Officer Wilson. I referred to him as Boyfriend because he also hurt a nice little lady who I befriended last night."

"Oh, I see. Well, the Feds have sent us a picture that was taken at the scene of the bank robbery, but I think it's less than perfect."

"What do you mean by less than perfect?"

"Well, Sir, the dummy didn't even try to hide his identity. As a matter of fact, the Feds said that he gave the camera the bird, but the light and film didn't hold his image."

"What a society we live in. Okay, circulate his photo and make sure that everyone realizes that I have a special interest in this one."

At his desk, the Sarge pondered his next move. After a few moments, he dialed the Commissioner's telephone number.

"Hello, Commissioner. May I come up and talk to you for a minute?"

"Sure, Sarge, but you had better come now. I'm expecting the Mayor in a few to discuss the rising crime problems in our district."

"I'm on my way, Sir."

A few minutes later, the Commissioner's aide told him that Sergeant Beckmire was here to see him. As the Sarge entered his office, the Commissioner said, "Hello, Beckmire. I hear you had a close scrape last night. Now maybe you'll start to wear that vest."

"Well, Sir, last night I learned a lot about human nature and the need for good backup, as well as witnessing how the vest protected my partner from five gunshots."

"Beckmire, are you telling me that you are going to start to wearing the vest?"

"Sir, I have it on right now."

"Smart move, smart move. Now what can I do for you?"

"Sir, I know that two of our men have been accused of doing the dirty with drug dealers. It appears that all of the information is circumstantial and would not hold up in a court of law."

"Just a minute, Beckmire. Let's leave that up to the lawyers."

"You're right, Sir, but I have a special favor to ask of you."

"Sarge, I already know what it is. When are you going to save one for yourself?"

"Sir, these are good men. If they have been dirty, and I'm not saying that they have been, I just think that it may have been poor judgment. But frankly, Sir, we've all used poor judgment at one point in time or another. I'm not asking for special consideration for these guys, but they saved my partner's ass last night, not to mention my own."

32

"Sarge, if you go too far this will be considered close to a conspiracy. Just shut up and let me think about it for a while and I'll do whatever I can. But you and I will not discuss this matter any further."

"Commissioner, you are who you are because you are a fair man and a policeman's policeman."

"Beckmire, cut the shit and get your ass out of here."

"Have a powerful day, Sir."

CHAPTER NINE

The ride to City Line Avenue was uneventful for Larry the Wanderer. As he slowly made his way up the little driveway in the borrowed wreck, he saw a lot of police cars and decided to drive to the rear where a hotel was situated. From his vantage point he could see plenty of jackets that read POLICE on the back of them. Sitting there with $5,000 worth of caine, Larry began to wonder if he had better get his ass far from this place. He left his vehicle and went into the lobby of the hotel and called information. "Oh yes, can you give me the number to Thursday's on City Line Avenue?"

"Just a minute please," was the response. A second or so later a voice said, "Your call can be automatically dialed for thirty cents."

Larry deposited the thirty cents and when connected he asked for Caroline Smith. The voice at the other end of the phone said, "Hold on, please."

A few minutes later, a voice said, "This is Caroline."

"This Larry. I got your shit, but what's going on over there?"

"Some guy and his girlfriend got into a big argument. Just stay where you are and come over here in about ten minutes. I'm sitting at a table in the back with one of my girlfriends."

"Okay, but I'm not coming near that place as long as all those cops are hanging out. Why would they send that many cops for a fight between two people?"

"Somebody said he had a gun."

"That's plenty of reason. Okay, I'll see you in ten minutes."

Larry had a bad feeling about this deal. He knew he was now $10,000 plus another $3,500 in debt to a man who would rather slit his throat than say hello. But his reservations were more centered on the police and Ms. Ann. He knew that he had done many a deal with her and had relative trust in her for making good on her payments, but this time everything seemed

35

out of order. He realized that he had never met her in a public place before and that most of their deals had been done while riding in her car and even at her apartment. He reasoned that all of those cops had made him a little gun shy and that he had to act like he was the man; nothing could keep him from cutting a good deal. Larry also recognized the fact that it was he who suggested Thursday's.

Ten minutes went by and Larry decided to give her another ten, just for comfort's sake. He made two additional calls: one to a dealer's pager number and one to his so-called girlfriend, who had a nose for the caine like an anteater. After the usual bullshit, he decided to go and do the deal. He left the hotel and watched for a long time to see if there was any indication that the cops were still in the area. Satisfied that they had all left, Larry the Wanderer started his little pimp walk to his car. He made the short drive down the parking lot and parked his car. He got out of the car and felt pretty good that there was no heat around and that the deal was just about done.

"May I help you?" the hostess inquired.

"Naw, I'm looking for someone—and I see her."

"Hi, Larry. Did you hook me up?"

"You know I did, Ms. Ann."

"Jennifer, this is Larry. He tends to make sure that I come out on top in terms of quality merchandise."

"Pleased to meet you, Jennifer. How's it going?"

"Everything is fine now that I know we are going to have a ball tonight."

Larry was scanning the place like radar and began to get bad feelings about the situation. Caroline asked, "Is everything cool, Larry? You look a little worried. We've been here all day and besides those jerks who were fighting, there are none of those other jerks around."

"No, Ms. Ann, I'm fine. I just like to take a survey of sorts before I get down to shoughnuff business."

"This is your lucky day, Larry. I'm going to, or rather we're going to give you an opportunity to make some real money. Do you think you can get your hands on $75,000 worth of product in the next two days?"

"That's a lot of product, Ms. Ann. What are you going to do with that much product?"

"Larry, don't worry about the results. The question is can you handle that much?"

What's a guy to do, when he is sitting in front of two good-looking ofay women who apparently have lots of cash? You're right. There was only one thing for a stud like Larry to do and that was to be macho.

"Ms. Ann, I could get you ten times that much if you needed it. All you have to do is have the cash, up front. It will cost you seventy-five percent up front and the balance on delivery."

"Fifty up front and fifty at time of delivery."

"Ms. Ann, you always run a hard bargain, but I think we can meet at the middle of the road. Sixty-five up front and the deal is done."

"Deal, Larry. Now go and see if your man can get his hands on what I need. When you come back, we'll do the little deal and be on our merry way."

Larry got up from the table and went to the phone booth. He dialed the number and said to the person on the other end, "Hey, this is Larry. I need seventy-five dollars by tomorrow. Can you handle it?"

The voice on the other end said, "Repeat that number."

"The number is seventy-five. Can we do the deal?"

"Call me back in ten."

"Talk to you later."

Larry was so confused but yet so greedy that he did not follow any of his instincts. When Larry returned to the table, the waitress was taking drink orders. "Larry, do you care for anything?" Ms. Ann inquired.

"I'll just have a Coke." Everybody except the waitress thought it was funny.

"Well, what's the deal?"

"I'll let you know in ten minutes."

"Good."

As the small talk continued, Larry excused himself and decided to make the call. "This is Larry. What's the deal?"

"The deal is simple. Seventy-five percent up front and the balance on delivery."

Larry cringed when he heard the numbers. "It's for a good customer, very reliable. I told them sixty-five up front and the balance on delivery."

"You want to make deals or be a roadster?"

"I never make the deals. I'm just the roadster."

"Good. Then the deal is seventy-five up front and the balance on delivery. Since you made a side-deal, then I'll hold you responsible for ten percent. Let me know when and where later. Larry, don't fuck up. I would hate to kill your entire family and then cut off both of your legs and arms."

"The deal is solid. I'll work out the details and get back to you."

Sweating as though he had just come out of a sauna, Larry decided that he had to do the bathroom thing and regain his composure. He entered the stall, shut and locked the door. He pulled the toilet seat down, sat on top of it and put his head in his hands. Watching the sweat run down his face, he realized that this shit was becoming too dangerous. He said to himself, *I've got to go straight. This drug dealing shit has a short and unhappy ending to it.*

He washed his face and looked at himself side-to-side and said aloud, "That sonofabitch is crazy. I've got to distance myself from all this shit. After this deal, I'm out of this fucking business. There is no future and I'm sick of the threats and the evil white bitches that prey on me only because I can satisfy their needs with a relatively good product."

Back at the table, Ms. Ann casually asked, "What's the deal, Larry?"

"The deal is done, Ms. Ann. Just have the numbers and you'll get the product."

Ms. Ann was surprised that he was able to pull it off. She knew that a roadster didn't make those kinds of decisions, especially about front and rear payments, unless he was the man himself. The very thought caused her to shiver. She knew that if he could make a deal like this, he could surely have her hurt. With a cracked sound to her voice, she said, "Okay, Larry, I'll let you know where and when."

"I've got to get out of here. Let's do the deal on the little game and we'll talk tomorrow about the Superbowl. Where's the cash?"

"It's all here. Hand it to him under the table, Jennifer." Larry reached and felt the envelope in Jennifer's hand and said, "I hope it's all here. You know you shorted me a couple of weeks ago by eighty."

"I must have made a mistake. Here—take this extra hundred and we're all even. Now where is the product?" Larry scanned the place once again, reached down in his pant leg and pulled the product out of the top of his boot. He handed the package to Jennifer, who put it in her bag and smiled. She unlocked the plastic bag and tasted the caine. She smiled and said to Caroline, "I see why you deal with him. He gives good shit." As Larry was saying his goodbyes, one of six women who were celebrating a fake birthday party jumped up and yelled, "Nobody move—Police. You are all under arrest for possession of a suspected narcotic for distribution and sale." Larry's heart fell right to the floor, and as he looked over at Jennifer, she had a pistol in one hand, her badge in the other.

"Sorry, Larry, I didn't have any choice. It was either you or I. I didn't have any choice." Caroline said. Larry just looked at her and remembered what a friend had once told him about them and us. Jennifer read Larry his rights and cuffed him. He was led away to an awaiting patrol car. He put his head in his lap and began to cry. One of the patrolmen said to Larry, "Save those tears. When the boys get your pretty ass in jail, you'll be crying for another reason."

CHAPTER TEN

At the police station, Larry was fingerprinted, photographed, and given an identification number. The lucky thing for Larry was that he had never been in conflict with the law and had no charges pending against him. His major problem was the size and value of the illicit caine that he attempted to distribute to Ms. Ann. After he was booked, he was led to the desk of Sergeant Beckmire.

"What is your full name, date of birth, social security number, address and telephone number and any aliases or nicknames? Now let me make it very clear to you—you have been charged with breaking all kinds of laws governing the use and distribution of illicit drugs. Don't make it any harder on yourself by giving me false information."

"My name is Larry Holland. I was born April 17th, 1975." Larry gave the Sarge his social security number and address. He also told the Sarge his telephone number. "Sometimes people who know me call me 'Larry the Wanderer'."

"I have a series of questions to ask you, but before I do that, I want you to see yourself in action."

The Sergeant showed Larry a video of himself arriving at the hotel and then making a series of telephone calls. It also showed Larry in the bathroom talking to himself and making the statement about getting out of the business. A tracer had been placed on the phone number he dialed from the restaurant and the line was tapped. Larry realized everything he had done was either on video or audio.

"Now that you've seen that wonderful piece of film, let's have the name of the person who you made contact with."

"Listen, I need an attorney. I can't give you the name of the person I contacted unless I want to sign my own death warrant.

41

Seems to me that with all of that fancy taping you cops did, everything else should be rather effortless. There is no way I'm going to give the name of the Man."

"Listen, Mr. Holland, you are in deep shit. Have you ever been arrested before?"

"No, Sir. This is my first time conflicting with the law."

"How long have you been selling drugs?"

"Not very long."

"According to the woman who you call Ms. Ann, you've been her supplier for some time now."

"If you can believe a person who sets people up to save their own ass, then you should be interrogating her, not me. I'm sure she has plenty of information to place the blame of her addiction and everything else all on me. Listen, Sir, I need a lawyer. This is all new to me."

"Do you have a lawyer?"

"No, Sir."

"Can you afford an attorney?"

"No, Sir."

"Mr. Holland, you were arrested carrying $5,000 in drugs and made a verbal, recorded deal for another $75,000 worth of drugs and you say you can't afford a lawyer?"

"Yes, Sir, that's correct. As you may know, I'm just a roadster. I don't make deals."

"Mr. Holland, you not only made the deal but you set the price and payment terms. That makes you more than a roadster. That makes you a dealer plus supplier. So as you can see, and as I indicated to you earlier, you are in deep shit."

"Sir, I know what the unwritten rules say about making deals and delivering goods. I'm just a roadster and right now I need an attorney."

"Okay, we'll see what we can do for you, but in the meantime, you had better try to figure out what you can do for yourself. Hey, Charlie, come over here a minute."

"What's up, Sarge?"

"Book Mr. Holland on possession of a controlled substance with the intent to sell. The paperwork is almost completed. Put him in a cell so that he can get a feel for what he's up against."

"Okay, Sarge. Let's go, Holland. I hope you like your new quarters, because as I see it, you may be in a place like this one for at least twenty years. Young man, that's hard time, especially with those older perverts trying to stick you in the ass every time you turn around. Let's go, son."

Larry was taken to lockup and placed in his first jail cell. As the officer locked the door behind him, an inmate among the twelve or so said, "That's my bitch, and the first motherfucker that looks at him will have to deal with me." Larry turned around and saw his fellow brethren—the scum of the earth. He had no idea who was making eyes at him, but remembered hearing from some friends that if you ever have to go to the cage, the first sonofabitch that looks at you more than once, knock the shit out him with anything that you can get your hands on.

Larry found a little unoccupied space and placed his back to the cell bars. He stood there scanning his fellow cellmates and tried to figure out who had made the call on him. As time went by, there seemed to be no action from the other side. Larry wondered if he had been forgotten or something. Three hours later, a guard came by with a rolling tray of sandwiches and fruit drinks. He handed each prisoner a sandwich and juice, then proceeded on to the next cellblock. Larry looked at the sandwich and decided to just hold it while he drank his juice. The guy next to Larry said, "If you don't want that, I could sure use it. This is the first thing I have had to eat worthwhile in about a week." Larry looked at the sandwich again and handed it to the guy without saying a word.

It was approximately 9:00 p.m. when Larry heard the sound of a crash. As he looked around to see what was happening, he saw a young white boy's pants being pulled down and his shirtsleeve being tied around his bleeding mouth. Larry said to

43

himself, what the fuck are they doing? He watched as a big burly black guy started pumping the white boy as if he were a woman. After he finished with the kid, three more dudes followed him and nobody used a rubber. Larry's first instinct was to call for help. He abandoned that idea and realized that the risk was too great for him. Another convict looked around the room and said, "I don't want to follow-up behind you dirty motherfuckers. I need some fresh ass." The guy looked at him and smiled. Larry's heart began to race. As the guy approached the area where Larry was standing, Larry dropkicked him right in the dick and then began to beat the living shit out of him. The guards heard all of the commotion and came running.

"What in the hell is going on here?"

Larry just looked at the guard and said, "The dude had the wrong idea about my sexuality and was trying to advantage me."

"You mean rape you?"

"That's exactly what I mean. That white boy over in the corner has been raped and this asshole thought he was going to rape me. I should have killed his fucking ass."

"All right you freaks! Get your asses over to the other side of the cell. Hey you! Put your pants on and come with me. You had better come also, because that guy is a killer."

"That's good cause if he ever looks at me again, he'll be a has-been."

Later, as Larry reflected on this incident, he realized that this time he got over. It was the next time and the time after that, began to worry Larry. As he felt a tear come to his eye, he said to himself, *can't show any weakness.*

At approximately midnight, Larry was taken before the judge where he, at the behest of his court-appointed attorney, pleaded not guilty to the charges of possession with the intent to sell a controlled substance, income tax evasion and other drug-related crimes.

BOOK TWO

CHAPTER ONE

The voice on the other end of the telephone asked, "May I speak to Sergeant Beckmire, please?"

"Just a minute. Who's calling?"

"My name is Rashida Brooks."

"Just a minute."

"Hello, Rashida. How are you doing today?"

"I'm fine, Sergeant Beckmire."

"I see you forgot already. You're suppose to call me Sarge, aren't you?"

"I guess I did forget."

"So how's my favorite little criminal? Just joking, just joking."

"I'm fine today. I feel much better than I did last night."

"Did your mom come by to see you yet?"

"Sarge, you saw her. Did she look like she was going to go visiting?"

"I'm sorry, dear. Well, just think, had it not been for last night, you and I would not be friends. So you see, there is some good that came out of all of this. Did the doctor say when you could be released?"

"She is so nice to me. She even told me that she would act like my big sister and help me whenever she had the time to. She even said that she finally found a policeman that she liked."

"Oh really. Who was he?"

"Sarge, she was talking about you. She said that you were genuinely concerned about me last night and she liked that in a man."

"Well, that's a nice compliment and she's right—I am concerned about what you do with your life. So many African Americans are trapped, like you, in a pool of never-ending poverty, despair and crime. All of these things lead to other social illnesses in the community like school-dropouts, drug-dealing, girls having babies out of wedlock and the perpetual drain on an already over-drained welfare system. Not to belabor the point, but something has to be done about the education system in this country. People leave high school with a diploma and can't read the directions on a transit schedule. Yes, she is correct, I have to find a way to help you and thousands just like you to escape the constant fear of drugs and poverty."

"Sounded like a sermon, Sarge, but one that I need. Never stop reminding me of my mistakes. Although my body feels good, my mind is all messed up."

Rashida started to cry. The Sarge interrupted her and said, "Don't be too hard on yourself. You got me now and I'm not going to let you turn into some sorry excuse for a lady. Now you get some rest. By the way—you never did tell me whether or not they were going to let you go home today?"

"The doctor said she really had no reason to keep me, but that she wanted to have more time to talk to me and this was the safest and best place for her to come in and get to know me."

"Sounds to me like you're going to have more friends than you bargained for. Well, if you get a chance, call me before too late. My shift ends at midnight. Okay?"

"Sarge, I can never thank you enough for being the father that I never knew, even if it was just for one night and one day. I think I needed to have someone to talk to."

"Don't worry, dear, you can't get rid of me that easy. I may drop by there on my break, but don't hold me to it. Talk to you later."

The Sarge hesitated a minute before hanging up the telephone and daydreamed about a daughter he never had.

"Yo, Sarge, you all right?"

"Yeah, I guess I was daydreaming. What was all of that noise back there in lockup?"

"We had a rape occur in the cell, but nobody saw anything and the victim ain't saying who did it."

"Was it the kid we sent back there a few hours ago?"

"No, it wasn't him. But he beat the shit out of some dude who was going to try to rape him."

"Can't we stop this shit? I mean, right here in our own lockup, a man gets violated and nobody has seen a damn thing. One day, we're going to get in a lot of trouble for this shit happening right under our noses."

"Sarge, look around the room. Every living ass is busy doing his job plus three others who were cut from the force because of budget reductions. I agree with you, but there's no way we can keep the pace with things going on in here when we are stretched so thin. I feel bad for the kid that got his cherry busted, but I can't take full responsibility for it. He has to take some of the responsibility, as well as society in general that says we are over-funded and provide lousy services."

"Charlie, did I ask you for that sermon?"

"I guess not, but I'm as frustrated as you are when it comes to trying to manage and operate this place efficiently, as well as watch and make sure that rapes don't happen under our noses."

"Charlie, I have an idea. Tell Peter down in maintenance to bring one of those surveillance cameras up here and put it on the cellblock. That may deter some activity, even though it won't be hot."

"Sarge, you're always thinking and that's what I love about you, dude. You're always making it better for everyone. By the way, how's the wound?"

"Charlie, it's just a scratch, and believe me, I could have put one of the bandages from the first aid kit on it. Tell Peter to get that thing hooked up."

Charlie started to walk away when the Sarge rang out, "Hey, Charlie, come here."

"Now what, Grandma?"

"Smartass, look I have a question for you. What was your opinion of that young man named Larry Holland?"

"Now he's a smartass. I mean, he seemed real smart, you know what I mean?"

"You mean smart in the positive sense."

49

"That's it. I mean he didn't seem like a criminal and all. He seemed very sad, not because he was caught, but I get the feeling that he really didn't want to be involved in that shit. It's as though it was the only thing that was available to him. You know what I mean, Sarge?"

"That's the exact feeling I got from him. I listened to him talk to himself in the bathroom at Thursday's and he said, 'I've got to quit this shit and get out of this business'."

"Oh, I didn't know that. That might set good with the judge when he hears it."

"Okay, Charlie, thanks. Be sure to take care of that other thing for me."

"Sarge, I know that look and that sound. You're about to try to save the world again through that kid, aren't you?"

"I wish I could save that kid, but we'll see what happens."

Charlie once again started to walk away when the Sarge rang out, "Hey, Charlie, one more minute."

"Sarge, why don't I just sit here a while until you remember everything that you want to say to me."

"Listen, before you tell Peter about the camera, go into lockup and bring that kid to me."

"I knew you were going to say that. Consider it done."

CHAPTER TWO

"Mr. Holland, I hear you had a little trouble in lockup."

"Just a little."

"Mr. Holland, I want to have an off-the-record conversation with you prior to your being taken to the prison. Everything that we discuss will remain between the two of us and there are no recording or video devices in place anywhere. Do you think that we can have a frank and honest conversation?"

"That depends on if you will put everything that you just said in writing and sign it."

"Fair enough."

After about three minutes of writing the information on official police stationary, the Sarge handed the document to Larry and said, "Will this do?"

After reading the memo to the file, Larry said, "I guess this will do, but I really don't feel very good about anything that anybody says to me today."

"I understand. You seem to have had a bad day yesterday full of not-so-good surprises, and I don't blame you for not trusting a cop. As I said earlier, I want to have a frank and off-the-record conversation with you, about you. May I call you Larry?"

"That's fine."

"You may call me Sarge. Now, Larry, you are about to face some big time in the big house. You have several conspiracy charges, possession, possession with the intent to sell and a whole host of other charges, not to mention the federal charge of income tax evasion. I don't want to know anything about your supplier or anybody else for that matter. The only thing I want to know about is you, Larry Holland. Give me some idea of who you are, where you come from, your parents and friends and anything else that would make me understand you better."

"Why do you want to know about me?"

"Let's just say that I have an interest in trying to help you for some odd reason, but you have to help me understand who I may be trying to help."

"Are you saying that you are going to try to help me keep from going to jail?"

"Larry, your crimes mandate a jail sentence. The question is whether or not it's a long sentence or a short one. I may be able to help you with the short sentence. The long one—well—frankly depends on you and what you have to offer the courts. That is not our conversation and I do not wish to discuss it. My concern is with you as a young African American male, who I believe is smart enough to do well in college, not jail. So help me help you. Let the information flow that I need to hear."

After twenty minutes of soft information, the Sarge said, "Don't waste my time, Larry. Let's start with your parents. I presume you do have those things, don't you?"

"If you really wanta know what makes me tick, then I would have to say it was my father—if he was my father. That dude ripped off a drug dealer when I was thirteen. He was the dumbest person I have ever known. You know, he broke into this old lady's house and robbed her. Two nights later he went back, robbed her again, but this time he raped her. On his way out, she put a butcher's knife in his back. The cops caught him bleeding half to death and got him patched up. Before he could stand trial, the old lady died of a heart attack and his story was that she was his girlfriend and that she was jealous because he was seeing a younger woman. The case was dismissed and he walked. Two weeks later, he ripped off the drug dealer for three-dime bags of caine and thought that he could get away with it. They found him the next day with six bullet wounds to the head and thirty cents in his mouth."

"So what does that have to do with you and the way you tick?"

"He tried to teach me to break into houses with him. When I told my mother, he beat her so bad that she had to be hospitalized for two weeks. After beating her, he hit me in the head with a baseball bat that he kept behind the door. The man hated books and said that any son of his caught with a book would be kicked out of the house and disowned. His real problem was that he was illiterate. The sonofabitch couldn't read or write. And for that, he was determined to make sure that I led the same kind of life style as he did."

"Where's your mom now?"

"She died about four years ago. He beat her so many times her brain was damaged. She died in the streets, not having a place to go or anybody to help her. At the time, I was staying with my grandmother when we heard that she was found in an alleyway, half frozen and hemorrhaging from the constant blows to her head."

"You seem very bitter towards your parents."

"I'm not bitter. People make choices and the results of those choices are not always good ones. In the case of my mother, she could have done a lot better than my father. He was shit—pure unadulterated shit. It was only a matter of time before his ass was going to be mine. I had made myself a promise that the next time he hit my mother, I was going to put a knife in his heart while he slept, all drugged and drunk."

"Well, thank God you didn't do that. Tell me more about your attitudes towards your parents."

"Well, my grandmother was my saving grace. Had she not died suddenly, I probably would have gone on to college. When she died, I was basically out there on my own. I had to steal to eat, rob to buy clothes and cheat and lie to survive. I've done a lot of bad things; some I dream about every night."

"What kind of things, Larry?"

"It's better that I not mention them, Sarge. You might decide to compromise my already existing situation."

"Larry, where did you learn to command the language so well?"

"Sarge, my grandmother told me if you talk like and act like a dumb nigger, then that's exactly what you'll be in life—a dumb ass nigger. She insisted that as long as I stayed with her, I would read until my eyes fell out. My granny was a character. She never went to school but could read her ass off. She learned by attending night school at the Opportunities Industrialization Centers, (OIC) but wasn't satisfied with that. That woman would spend countless hours in the library just going through that big dictionary. She would look at a word, learn how to pronounce it, and learn the meaning and use of the word almost immediately. She had a book with most of the Shakespeare writings in it, and we would spend time reading aloud to each other into the smallness of the night. She loved Shakespeare and would often equate his works to the suffering of the African American. She had a sense of wisdom and fairness that could only lead to success." Larry paused for a minute and a tear came to his eye. He said aloud, "Show no weakness. Sarge, I've got to go."

"Larry, you are not going anywhere except to jail."

"Sarge, I'm already in jail. Where I got to go is to the head."

"Oh, I see. Hey, Charlie, take Mr. Holland to the john."

After about five minutes, Charlie and Larry came back and both of them were laughing. The Sarge asked, "Did you two fall in love or something in the john?"

"Cute, Sarge. I told Mr. Holland here a joke I heard the other night."

"Why don't you tell me? I could use a good laugh."

"Okay, Sarge. Name the four animals that every woman should have in her life."

The Sarge paused for a minute and finally said, "I don't know. Why don't you tell me."

"Well, Sarge, she needs a mink on her back, a tiger in her bed, a jaguar in her garage, and a jackass to buy the other three."

"Go do some work, you moron. Where do you come up with these things?"

"Sarge, you have to be among the living to hear good jokes."

"I guess you needed that laugh, didn't you Larry?"

"I guess you're right, Sarge. Even though my ass is on the line, it was good to be able to laugh at something silly and not be judged based upon it."

"Yeah, I know what you mean, Larry. Let's go back to some of the bad things that you have done. I am particularly interested in those things that you dream about nightly."

"Sarge, you asked me to level with you. If I level with you any further, I might place myself in jeopardy."

"What does that mean? I gave you a written document stating that this conversation is off the record. I swear to you, nothing will be revealed about this conversation."

Larry stared at the Sarge and said, "I made a lot of mistakes yesterday and I hope that I'm not about to make more mistakes with you today. A year an a half ago, I offed this guy who robbed me on two occasions. He took the Man's drugs and money and I had to make good on the loss. I told him on the second time that his ass would be dead by morning. He laughed and stabbed me in the chest. Four weeks and $14,000 worth of medical bills later, I saw the asshole riding in a car. I waited until he got out of the car and said, "Hey motherfucker, you stab a guy for $140.00 and take $100.00 worth of drugs and you expect to live?" He said to me, "Fuck you, faggot," and reached in his pocket and pulled out a pistol. He fired two shots and missed and I fired one shot and luckily hit him right in the head. I took off and ran like hell. It seemed like I ran for hours without stopping. The next morning, I read in the paper that a drug dealer was shot and killed defending his turf."

"Damn, Larry, that's a big one. My word remains—this conversation never took place. I have just one more question, Larry. Earlier, you made reference to the fact that there may be some doubt in your mind about who your real father is. Would you care to enlighten me on that issue?"

"Not really. It has no relevance to this situation."

"Are you sure, Larry?" After a minute of soul searching, Larry looked at the Sarge and said, "Why am I giving the hangman all of this private information?"

"The hangman, as you call him, happens to be the only potential friend that you have in this place."

"Since you put it like that, then let me tell you a dark secret belonging to my mother. My mother worked as a domestic when she could find work. As a domestic, she was accustomed to cleaning the undergarments of white people. I guess she also found herself in situations that gave her some satisfaction and enjoyment out of life. Anyway, my father was a very fair skinned man, and during the winter months, he actually looked white. One night after he had severely beaten my mother, she said to me, "Don't you ever worry about being like him. He is not your real father. Your real father is a white man with good brains, but don't you ever tell your father that, or he'll kill me as sure as I'm sitting here." Well, needless to say, after time I forgot what she had said to me and always lived as though the wife-beater was my father. I did find out from my mother later that my real father was a financial wizard and he treated her with respect and always gave her extra money. So you see, Sarge, I really don't know who my real father is, and I'm afraid to try to find out. Either way, my mother got the bad end of the deal because the man she lived with eventually beat her to death, and her so-called lover never lived up to any honor. So I guess I'm just a bastard kid who doesn't know his real father."

"I wouldn't go that far, Larry. Your mother apparently did what she thought she had to do to get just a little enjoyment out of her days on earth. Remember the sacrifices that she made for you, and your memories of her will be forever special. Until you come to that crossroad, don't judge her, son. She apparently died in pain, so at least your memories can bring her soul a little comfort. Souls that die in pain wander until harmony is restored. I have a great-grandmother whose soul is aimlessly wandering around a place called "Dreamtime." Don't ask me about it—you don't know me well enough yet to inquire."

"Sarge, you are one strange dude. I thank you for the wisdom and I'm sure I'll have plenty of time to think about it where I'm heading."

"Hey, Sarge, telephone. It's a Rashida Brooks."

"Hi there. You doing all right?"

"I guess so. Doctor Harris wants to release me tomorrow morning."

"Well, that should be good news. Don't you want to leave that place?"

"I guess so, but it's so clean and nice here. I hate going back to that place where there is only trouble."

"Okay, do me a favor. When you see Doctor Harris, give her my number and ask her if she would please give me a call."

"Okay, Sarge. I'll talk to you later."

"Sarge, you know Rashida Brooks?"

"Yeah, why?"

"Just wondering. She is a real nice girl. If she weren't so young, I would have been all over her. What I mean is, all over her in a gentlemanly fashion."

"How do you know Rashida?"

"Like I said, I use to fool around with her like a big brother thang. I had other intentions, but couldn't come to the point of dealing with someone young. I mean, Rashida is the smartest girl in that building and is quite respectable, too. Her mother, on the other hand, is a stankass bitch. Everybody in the building has done her. I did her the day I got caught and she did some pretty weird things to me. Sarge, how do you know her?"

"Yesterday, she was a rider in a stolen car that was banged up."

"Naw, Sarge, you're lying. That girl wouldn't ride in a stolen car. I mean her mother's a caine head, but that girl has her head in the right place."

"Larry, not only was she riding in the stolen car, but she used caine. She also went to a motel with this dude and he hurt her through aggressive sex."

"Is she all right?"

"She's fine now, but when I saw her, she was bleeding like a plucked chicken down below."

"Who was the dude?"

"The only name we have is Malik."

"That piece of shit! Sarge, he is so dumb. He tries to sell caine, rob banks, liquor stores and anything else. He and I got into it one night outside of this club. He said, 'Hey fag, who's that dike with you? At first I just gave him the bird, which pissed him off, and then he had to show how big and bad he was. He ran over to me and tried to sneak me, so I beat the shit out of him in front of his friends and lover. He's just a pussy, Sarge."

"Larry, I know we are off the record, but I would really like to put my foot up his ass. Will you give me a name?"

"Sarge, that's against my code of ethics. I can't squeal on a guy even if he's punk."

"Well, then do it for Rashida."

Larry hesitated for a minute and then bellowed out, "Henderson."

"Thanks, buddy, I owe you one. On another note, let me tell you why I really want to know about you. The other night when my partner and I were leaving Rashida's house after telling her mother that she was in the hospital, we got into a gun battle with some well-armed thugs. My partner took five shots and I got this little scratch. He was wearing his vest and I got lucky."

"Yeah, I heard about that. Three dudes wasted another guy and you and your man wasted two of them and the third is about to die."

"That's what happened. Anyway you're probably saying to yourself, what's that got to do with me? Well, I have a plan for getting the drugs out of public housing and out of the neighborhoods in general. That's where you come in. You know what I'm up against and you can sort of school me. I've not completely thought this thing through yet, but if I decide that it's a go, then I'm going to get you involved. It won't require that you dime on people—just that you make me aware of the problems I'm going to have with my plan. Are you with me so far?"

"I think so. But if your plan falls short of being radical, then I don't want to know about it. The plan has to be very aggressive or it won't even jump off."

"I got you. Now the sad thing is that I must return you to your cell. I'll have the guys hold you over here for a few days until I can talk to some of my contacts and see what we're up against."

"Hey, Sarge, why are you trying to help me, man?"

"Hey, Larry, I'm tired of seeing young African American males come here to be processed to go to the big house. I'm sick and tired of putting you misguided assholes in jail. I know that there must be another way. But if you fail me, you'll wish that you were dead."

"Hey, Sarge, that's no way to start a partnership—threatening me and all. Let's wait until we see how much time I got to do and then whether or not you can help me. I really want to get away from that business. I hate peddling that shit. Do you want to know something? The assholes at two fast food places told me that I didn't have any experience. Can you believe that? The next thing I did was to contact my local dealer and ask for a job as a roadster."

"Larry, we'll talk later or tomorrow. I may spend the night in this place because I'm really beginning to understand what this shit is all about and how best to overcome the odds. I'll see you later. Oh, one more thing—about that dude that you offed—I wouldn't worry about it. Your secret is safe as hell with me. Talk to you later."

CHAPTER THREE

"Hey, Sarge, there's a Dr. Harris on line eight for you."

"Dr. Harris, what a pleasure. I'm so glad you called."

"Sergeant Beckmire, Rashida said you wanted to talk to me."

"That's correct. I need to ask a big favor of you, Doctor."

"What is it, Sergeant?"

"I need for you to find a reason to keep Rashida Brooks in the hospital for a few more days, until I can get an opportunity to see her mother and see if the child would be better off somewhere else."

"I thought it was important, Sergeant. I've already decided to keep her, but it's still going to cost you."

"Cost me what, Doc?"

"A dinner very soon. See you later." Click—and then the dial tone. The Sarge just looked at the telephone and thought to himself, what a marvelous idea.

"What did the doctor want, Sarge?" Charlie asked.

"Dinner, meathead."

"What does she look like?"

"Charlie, she looks like every other doctor who is female that I've seen."

"Gee, that bad eh?"

"Charlie, tell the guys to keep an eye on my new friend Mr. Holland. I have plans for that kid and I don't want any perverts trying to advantage him."

"Don't worry, he's in a penthouse all to himself."

CHAPTER FOUR

The reason Larry opened up to the Sergeant was because it seemed like the right thing to do. He felt that the Sarge, other than the information on Malik, never asked him who he worked for or how much caine he had been selling. Larry smiled to himself and thought, *if he were my Pop, I wouldn't be in the shit I'm in now.* Larry thought that the Sarge was easy to talk to and to be honest with—a pleasure that he had never shared with his own father. Time after time he remembered his father saying, "The only way to make it in this white man's world is to have a hustle. The jobs they give black folk aren't worth a damn." His favorite story was about his friend that went to college and got two degrees and couldn't find a job because they told him he was overqualified.

As the night began to really set in, Larry's predicament became increasingly real. He calculated the amount of time he would have to serve for selling the caine. He was not familiar with the details of the federal law concerning income taxes because he had never filed a return. His only awareness of the Feds was that when they bust you, your ass went away for a long time. As he reviewed his new and soon-to-be permanent home, Larry began to cry like a baby. He knew that he had fucked up big time and there was no way out. The very thought that he was locked up and caged like an animal was more than his fragile persona could handle. He rationalized that his best bet for a clean break was through the Sarge. He prayed that the Sarge was not just warming up to him in order to obtain the information needed to put the Man away. As he lay there with the tears streaming down his face, Larry the Wanderer knew that his ass was in for a tough time; there was no escaping whatever came down the pike.

As Larry drifted off to sleep, he was awakened by the sound of muffled screams. He knew that only men were in this section and that someone was being raped—a fate that he knew would confront him time and time again. Appalled with the idea of being violated, Larry began internalizing possible solutions, including suicide.

CHAPTER FIVE

The morning began quite early for the individuals in the cellblock. Many were strapped with leg irons and wrist cuffs and led off to a waiting bus for their rides to the holding institutions. Larry wondered when his name would be called but it never happened. The Sarge had left specific orders for Larry to remain at the precinct until he had finished with him.

The Sarge's day began with a pleasant surprise. "Good morning, Sarge."

"Smitty! How the hell are you doing? I thought you would be out for at least a week or so."

"No sense sitting around the apartment while all of those bad guys are out there in the streets."

"Just what I like in a cop—dedication to ridding the world of criminals. Anyway, I'm going to give you an assignment here in the precinct with me today. All you'll have to do is process the bad guys who are caught by the other cops."

"Sarge, just the same, I would prefer to be in the patrol car."

"Not today, Sonny. You're going to spend your time doing real police work for a change. At lunchtime, I'm going over to the hospital to visit Rashida Brooks. If you like, you can tag along with me."

"That's better than just sitting in this damn place all day."

"Are you having any pain or anything?"

"No, Sarge. Just where I was hit is still sore."

"Boy, we were lucky that night."

"I'll say so. I hope to hell I never get shot again, wearing a vest or not."

"Me too. Just the same, get over to that desk and start processing the bad guys."

65

As the day rolled on, the bad guys kept coming in. Smitty realized why he didn't want a desk job and wondered how on earth the Sarge enjoyed his work—day in and day out.

"Hey, Smitty, go back to lockup and get Larry Holland."
"Okay, Sarge."

Smitty escorted Larry to the Sarge's desk and said, "Here he is."

"Did you rest well last night, Larry?"

"I guess as well as could be expected considering the confines of my new home."

"Well, not to be smart or sarcastic, but I think you should start getting use to the confinement. It's obvious you're going to do time."

"Yeah, I know, but I don't have to get used to living like that, do I? Sure, I'm going to do the time, but I will never get used to living in a cage like that even if I'm there for twenty years. No, I'm not going to get use to this lifestyle."

"Good points, Larry. No matter what, don't let this place, or wherever you go, break your spirit. If that happens, you'll be in jail for the rest of your life. You see, prison life grows on some people, and they feel it's the best place for them. Of course they bring all of the excuses about the Man not giving them a chance and therefore they had to commit another murder or robbery. I have a couple of tough questions for you, Larry, but first I have to tell that officer over there something. Sit tight." The Sarge walked over to Smitty, looked on his desk and said that he was moving very slow. Smitty never replied. The Sarge didn't expect him to either. He just wanted to give Larry some time to think. Larry in the meantime was wondering what was this guy up to. Little did Larry know, the correct response could get him the break he needed.

"Larry, yesterday I said that everything you said to me was strictly off the record. Today, everything that you say to me is for the record. Is that understood?"

"Sure, Sarge. I knew it was too good to be true."

"Larry, I want you to dime on your supplier."

"Sarge, you may think very low of me because of what I did for a living, but I will not sink any lower and dime on anyone other than that punk Malik."

"Son, I can get your sentence reduced to almost nothing. In other words, you may have to do a little time, but you won't be looking at ten to twenty plus the federal charges. All you have to do is give me the Man's name and you can walk from here. I'll get your bail set and you're out of here. It's just that easy, Son, but you have to give me the name of your supplier."

"Sarge, you might as well have me taken back to the cell. I'm not going to sink that low and give up the one person who made sure that I had money coming in, no matter how dirty the money."

"Okay, Larry. I gave you the chance of a lifetime, but Son frankly, you blew it. You'll be shipped out of here on that bus that's leaving in about fifteen minutes, and where you're off to, it's going to be rough on you. Those guys will bid for your body as soon as you walk into the prison. You can't fight them all. That guy the other day was a pussy in comparison to the guys who are in there for murder, rape and hard time. Look at you, Son—you're a good-looking guy. Those guys are going to make you grow that pretty straight hair of yours until it's the length of a woman's. Then you're going to be someone's girlfriend."

"Sarge, you can't scare me. I'm already scared. I appreciate your offer, but it's against my moral code to squeal on someone."

"Hey, Smitty, get Mr. Holland's paperwork and give it to the driver. He's out of here. I wish we could have made a deal, Larry. I hate to see you go down to where hell begins. Take care, I hope you survive the scene."

Larry was shackled and led to the awaiting bus. It would be an hour's ride before he arrived at his new home.

"Okay, Smitty, let's grab some lunch. Some free lunch, I hope, from over at the hospital."

"Sarge, let's just stop somewhere and grab some real food for a change."

"Stop whining and let's get out of here. Do you have your vest on?"

"You know it. Do you have yours on?"

"Absolutely," replied the Sarge. As the two men rode down the street, Smitty asked the Sarge, "What happened with Mr. Holland?" The Sarge just stared at the road and said nothing. "How about this place, Sarge?"

"Looks good as any to get food poisoning. You know my requirements for eating out."

"Yes, I do. This place looks like you could sue them if you got sick."

"You know, Smitty, Mr. Holland is really a good kid. I asked him to dime on his supplier and told him that if he did, I would have him out of jail immediately. I told him how pretty he was and that he was going to be someone's girlfriend. You know what he said to me?"

"No, Sarge, what?"

"Mr. Holland said, 'You can't scare me, because I'm already scared'".

"Damn, Sarge, that takes guts to admit."

"I know, Smitty, but I have to let him run the gauntlet at least for a few days. I put a protective veil around him. It's just enough so that he can experience what it's going to be like in prison unless he comes forth and dimes on the guy."

"Sarge, do you really want him to dime on his supplier?"

"Smitty, sometimes I think you play with half a deck. Let's order."

After the meal the two officers proceeded to the hospital to see Rashida Brooks. The Sarge wanted to see the young lady, but he was also straightening his attire just in case he ran into Doctor Harris. The first thing they did when they entered the hospital was to go by and see the officer who was shot helping them out. As they entered the room, he was surrounded by his wife and father, and everyone seemed a little solemn. The Sarge, in his own inimitable way said, "Is everyone alive here or did someone die?" The wife looked at the Sarge and said, "Someone's spirits are dying."

"Well, show me the devil so that I can bring him or her back around."

"Hi, Sarge. I just told them how rotten I feel about that trouble that's on its way."

"Listen you jackass—excuse me, Evelyn—I told you that they owed me downtown and that I would go and see what could be done. Well, I did my part. Now let's wait and see how the chips fall. I can't believe you're giving up so early. There's been nothing official, just rumors. And rumors, my friend, have to be substantiated. Everyone in that station knows that I don't play that rumor mill shit. Excuse me, Evelyn, for cursing in front of you, but this jerk needs to get real. Don't go and waste my chips. I told you guys I wouldn't forget what you did for us. I meant it. Now I came here to see how you are doing—not to discuss police business. Now, how the hell are you, Mack?"

"Sarge, you are just what I needed. Give me a kiss you big, old, ugly sonofabitch."

"Let me work my magic before you go committing suicide and worrying these good folks here. Evelyn, I haven't seen you at church in a while. Come on back, kid. There's salvation in that place."

"I know, Sarge, but with the kids into so many things, it's tough to get to church."

"It's tougher getting to heaven, lady. See you in church soon."

"Okay, Mack, don't screw this up. I've planted the seed. Now let's watch and see if it grows. Okay?"

"Sarge, I owe you."

"Mack, you paid Smitty and I in full the other night. See you guy."

As Smitty and the Sarge were walking down the hallway, they passed by a room and a voice said, "How soon we forget." The Sarge and Smitty turned around and there was the voluptuous Dr. Harris, with a grin on her face befitting a lottery winner.

"Hello, Dr. Harris. You remember my partner, Smitty, don't you?"

"Hello, Smitty. How are you, Sarge?"

"The doctors I had the other night took real good care of me, my friends and my new little friend as well."

"Sound like very busy doctors."

"I'll say so. By the way—Smitty, didn't you want some water? Well, there's the fountain."

"I didn't say I—oh yes, I am thirsty as hell."

"Very subtle, Sarge. I was going to call you today and see what you wanted to do with Rashida."

"Has her mother been here?"

"I don't think so. At least no one has said anything to me about visitors. I'll walk you down there to see her. I presume that's where you were heading?"

"Once again, Doc, you're right. Was that the only reason you were going to call me?" Looking a little embarrassed, the doctor said, "Why frankly, no. I was wondering if you would like to have dinner with me tonight? This is one of the few nights I'm not on call and I would like to have your company if you know how to act like a gentleman. But before I officially ask you out to dinner, there is one question I have to ask. Are you married?" The Sarge looked around the hospital corridors and he could see by the look on her face that she was disappointed. The Sarge then said, "No, as a matter of fact, I haven't been on a real date in over a year."

"Is there a problem or you just don't like women?"

"No, Doc, I'm a widower. My wife was killed in a head-on collision." Realizing that she had just put her foot in her mouth, she stood there for what seemed an eternity, embarrassed by the Sarge's revelation in response to her feeble attempt at humor.

"Please forgive me," the doctor said. "Maybe we should try this in a couple of months or something if it's all right with you."

"Why should we wait that long to have dinner?"

"I just feel like a total idiot. Here I am trying to protect my own selfish and delicate feelings, and you have suffered the ultimate sacrifice. I just feel stupid, that's all."

"I'll feel stupid if you don't have dinner with me tonight."

"You run a convincing game, Sergeant. Here's my address. Is seven too early?"

"Seven's fine." As they both caught up with Smitty, he said, "That must have been a helluva conversation. I haven't seen this guy smile this way in years."

"Just take care of your own smile, Smitty. Leave mine alone, please."

As he entered Rashida's room, the Sarge said, "Rashida, how are you darling?"

"Hello, Dr. Harris. Hi, Smitty. Sarge, I was beginning to think that you had forgotten about me. I'm so glad you're here. I really missed seeing you."

"I've missed you too, Rashida. Has your mom been to see you yet?"

"No, and I don't expect that she'll get off of that pipe long enough to visit me either."

"Let's show a little more respect, young lady. I'll go by there and see if there is a problem."

"I'm sorry, I didn't mean to be disrespectful, but she's a trip. She won't come here—I bet you."

"If you bet me, you'll lose. I don't bet unless I'm sure that I can win, Rashida."

"How's your wound? Has it healed?"

"Thanks to your friend and mine—Dr. Harris—everything is all right."

"You two look good together."

"On that note, young lady, I'm going to visit the rest of my patients. See you later, Smitty, and I will definitely see you later, Sarge."

"Okay, Doc. Talk to you later."

"Do you have a date with her, Sarge?"

"Now, Rashida, dating is something personal and private. I'm sure that if the doctor wanted you to know that she had a date with me, she would have told you. But I didn't come down here on my lunch hour to talk about my dates. I came to see about a special little friend of mine."

"I'm sorry. I was just hoping that you two would get together because both of you are decent human beings. I don't see many good people together Sarge, so I guess I overstepped my boundaries."

"It's okay, but like I said, enough about me. How are you feeling?"

"I'm fine. The doctor said that I could go home anytime I wanted to, but I told her I never want to go back there."

"Smitty, take a walk. Now, Rashida, be it good, bad or indifferent, that is your home and your mother is your mother. You'll have to learn to make the best out of a bad situation until you can get out on your own. That's where school plays an important role. There are a lot of people just like you who are not born into wealth and good families, but they work their butts off to get a better life for themselves and their families. I want you to make up your mind that you want a better life, and that it does not include the fast life. You have to determine that you are somebody and that you're going to be somebody. When you realize that everything people make of themselves comes from hard work and sweat, then you'll realize what you have to do in order to live another kind of life."

"I know, Sarge, but it's really hard living in that hell each day. You never know when a bullet will hit the window or the door. I just hate living like that."

"I know you do, Sweetie. That's why I'm going to make sure that you work hard and go to college and that way, you'll give yourself a fighting chance to succeed in life."

"Dr. Harris told me that she once lived in a place called South Central Los Angeles. She said that the gangs were as thick as the grass on the ground. Dr. Harris also said that I have no idea what poverty was. She said that they were so poor that her mother did things with men to buy food for the family. She said her father was in jail for murder and was nothing but a small-time thug who couldn't grow old enough to leave the gangs alone. I think that between being able to talk to both of you when I have a problem, I should be able to do what's right and not make the mistake I made a few nights ago."

"That's my girl. Don't let anything break your spirits. Now I'm going to arrange for Dr. Harris to let you stay one more night here. I am personally going to pick you up and take you home. But for your remaining time here, I want you to think about a few things. First of all, I want you to think about the mistakes that you made the other night. Secondly, I want you to think about what you need to do in order to get back on the right track. And third, I want you to think of ways to make Dr. Harris and me proud of you from this day forward. Do we have an agreement?"

"You bet, Sarge, and if you bet me, you'll lose this time."

"That's my girl. Now rest and think and then rest and think some more until you can't think any more. You take care and remember, I am counting on you to do what is right and to make me feel happy and proud to know you."

"Okay, Sarge I won't let you down because you're the closest thing to a father that I've ever known. You're special to me and I won't let you down. See you later."

"No, I'll see you later first."

CHAPTER SIX

Sergeant Beckmire was a proud and powerful man. His pride stemmed from the fact that unlike Larry or Rashida, he had made a choice in life that gave him total fulfillment. Being a police officer was a goal that he had set for himself as a ninth grader in high school. His power came from his ability to persuade people to do the right thing. As a youngster, he had his problems. Poverty in the forties for black people was obvious and ignored. Also, unlike Larry and Rashida, his parents were caring, loving and demanding individuals. They insisted that their kids did well in school and attend church because they believed that if you believed in nothing, then nothing you were. The family was traditional in a sense when he was a youngster. There was abject poverty, but there was also stability. The family would discuss issues and make joint decisions about the little funds that were available to them for important activities as well as frivolous ones.

His father believed that punishment was best given by the rod. If in fact one of his kids had been extremely bad, his father would have them hold out their hand. He would then take his hand and smack their hand as hard or as soft as the incident warranted. If they jerked their hand away and he missed, the sentence would double. Each time he punished his kids, he would always remind them what jerking would cost. The girls were always punished with his left hand and softly at that. Mr. Beckmire could make them want to sever their hand rather than get hit by him.

The Sarge was a husband who watched as his wife died on the operating table from a head-on collision caused by a freaked-out LSD user. The one thing he would never realize in life was that twins were developing in his wife's stomach. She was seven months pregnant when she was killed. The culprit in the accident got off on a technicality. The Sarge's last words at his wife's burial indicated that one day he would avenge her death. It was not the kind of statement that a devout policeman would make. Nevertheless, the Sarge has honored his badge and oath, and has never once pursued the guy who ruined his life forever.

After primping for an hour or so and trying to figure which outfit would illustrate his true power and charm, the Sarge settled on a traditional blue blazer and contrasting gray slacks. He also donned a Lazo shirt with rising button down collars and a Format necktie. All in all, he looked more like a playboy than a cop.

Later across town, the Sarge rang the doctor's doorbell.

"Just a minute—Hello, Sarge. My, my, my...you look absolutely handsome."

"Thank you, Doc. You look as beautiful as the rising sun. I didn't know that your hair was that long and pretty."

"Well, now you see it. How about a cocktail?"

"That's a great idea. Do you have any Grand Marnier?"

"Why, Sarge, that's all I drink. At least we have one thing in common so far."

"I hope that before the night is over, we find other things we have in common. I made reservations at an Italian restaurant. Is that okay with you?"

"I would have preferred Chinese food, but Italian's okay."

"We can go to a Chinese restaurant if you like."

"Stop being so accommodating, Sarge. I might learn to expect it."

"As good as you look, you can expect almost anything from me."

"Why not everything?"

"Being that it's our first date, I would prefer to give you only half the world and see if you deserve the other half."

"You dear boy how sweet. I never thought about owning the entire world, but I guess I could get used to the idea."

They sat and chatted for a few minutes and enjoyed their cocktails. After about fifteen minutes or so, the Doc asked, "Shall we go?"

"Absolutely. By the way, you have a nice house and it's well appointed."

"Thank you."

At the restaurant and throughout dinner, small talk prevailed along with the usual compliments that follow when two people are having their first event together. They were both curious about each other's hobbies, and likes and dislikes, and were joyful when they agreed on a particular prescription for handling any given situation. Dr. Harris was flowing and glowing like a woman who had searched and found the one treasure in life that you couldn't mine or buy—love and understanding. The Sarge, on the other hand, was more like Anthony and his obsession with Cleopatra.

The Sarge had not been out on a date for a long time and felt a little uneasy when questioned about it. Dr. Harris was consistent in her conviction that the time wasted trying to find someone to share things and events with was cumbersome and often resulted in a total waste of energy and emotions. The two agreed that dinner—so far—was a success and they owed it to the misfortunes of one Rashida Brooks.

"Would you like dessert, Doc?"

"Sarge, would you like to call me Courtney instead of Doc?"

"Courtney, what a pretty name for a pretty woman. By all means Courtney it is. Courtney, would you like to call me Ben?"

"I like calling you Sarge."

"Then Sarge it is. Now back to the question that led to the subject of names—would you like dessert?"

"I stopped on the way home from the hospital at my favorite bakery and picked up a strawberry cheesecake. I thought that if we didn't fight or argue tonight, I would invite you over for dessert and coffee. Is that all right with you, or do you suppose I'm being a little too forward?"

"No, not at all. I like the idea. I would like the idea even better if you allow me to make a fire when we get to your place."

"Cheesecake, coffee and a fire to warm our exploration of each other's interests and feelings. Sarge, so far this night has been very special to me. Please don't destroy it."

"What do you mean by that?"

"I mean, I like you and all, but please don't go getting macho on me later."

"I would have thought by now you'd realize I'm a gentleman."

"I do—and for that statement, I could kick myself. Please forgive me. Later on, after the fire is going, I'll tell you where that statement came from. Agreed?"

"Courtney, I'm just happy to be here with you and that's all that's important to me at this moment."

"Sometimes in self-defense, I make a real fool out of myself. Can we go now?"

"Sure, as soon as the waiter comes back with my receipt."

The drive to Courtney's place was full of discussion concerning the decline of the neighborhoods. As they watched the countless number of homeless people crouching around subway vents, the Sarge rhetorically said, "Something just has to be done about this."

"About what, Sarge?"

"I was just thinking how awful it must be to not have a place to go to at the end of the day. Just look at all of those people, some not knowing any better or not having the mental faculties to improve their lot, and others just victims of rampant racism, ignorance, illiteracy or poverty. God, I wish I could make a difference."

"Sarge, somehow I think that you do make a difference. I saw it for the first time with Rashida Brooks. You had no reason to befriend her based upon what she was involved in. However, you not only called and checked-up on her but you visited her as well. You put yourself and your partner at-risk by going to her mother's house to inform her that her daughter was in the hospital. Now Sarge, you know as well as I, you would have generally just said that the phone was out of order and you couldn't make contact. So as I see it, you do try to make a difference and you will make a difference."

"Here we are."

"Yes, my little castle in the city. Do you know when I first moved in here, I was burglarized on three occasions? One night, the bastard came right into my bedroom."

"What happened?"

"I fired a round into the wall and he took off like a bat out of hell."

"Doctor, you are supposed to be in the life-saving business."

"I know, but he had another second to make a move, then I was determined to put ten shots in his ass. Excuse the French, but that's where my head was. I haven't had any problems since then. You know, I think I ran into him in the supermarket one day. This good-looking kid came up to me and said, 'Have you learned to shoot yet?' I just looked at him and he walked away. Are you going to start the fire now?"

"Oh yes, by all means. Is that coffee I smell?"

"Yes, I set the timer before we left and it seems as though it's almost finished. Would you like a piece of cheesecake with your coffee?"

"Absolutely, but not too big. Dairy products sometimes wreak havoc on me."

"Interesting. I have a slight problem with dairy products also, but I normally take the lactate substitute."

After more small talk and after devouring the cheesecake and coffee, Courtney asked the Sarge if he would like to have some Grand Marnier. He indicated, "I would love to have a drink about now." The two sat for a moment and toasted to health and watched the fire roar. Courtney rested her hand on his. As he gently held it he remembered the moments of yesteryear when he was holding the hand of his wife. Courtney, was recalling yesteryear as well, but with the many men whom she thought were the right ones.

The Sarge broke the stillness by asking Courtney about the macho statement. She went on to explain, painfully, the series of bad relationships and acquaintances that had plagued her life. It was as though she was too pretty to be trusted and too smart to be understood. In essence, her problem, which was not her problem at all, was that men found her incredibly beautiful and overwhelming when it came to the deployment of the brain. The Sarge told her that obviously the men were weak and superficial and not willing to risk knowing everything about her. He rationalized that most women like her generally face that issue— most men don't like to feel inferior to women. Courtney also went on to say that by expressing her feelings of the moment, such as holding a hand or even asking for a hug, she had led a few people to try to take advantage of her. The Sarge indicated that dating was a first step for him and that if he intended to move forward, a stronger proposal would then be articulated. The Sarge was a smoothie. He knew he had her thinking and decided that he would take this opportunity to say good night.

"Courtney, I have had a most memorable evening with you, and I thank you for having dinner with me. I enjoyed your company and your hospitality, but I'm afraid I must head on home. I have a big day tomorrow and need to do some homework."

"Well, Sarge, all I can say is ditto." The Sarge extended his hand and Courtney accepted it. He kissed her hand and turned and walked out the door. Courtney closed the door and gave out a silent scream of joy. She felt the Sarge's total persona all over her and loved the very notions that were swirling around in her head.

CHAPTER SEVEN

"Good morning, Sarge. How was your night?"

"It was wonderful."

"Excuse me?"

"That's right, Smitty, I said it was wonderful. Now let's get to work. Do you have a report on my friend Mr. Holland yet?"

"There was a breakdown in communications. Mr. Holland is now in the infirmary. He took a hell of a beating last night. A couple of the guys there wanted to make him their personal bitch."

"Dammit, I gave explicit instructions that there was to be an attempt, but I didn't want him hurt."

"Sarge, trust me, it was a mistake. There was no deliberate attempt to go against your wishes. The good thing is, Mr. Holland beat the shit out of one of the guys and broke the other guy's jaw. He's a tough little character."

"Good, I want you to arrange for him to be brought here this afternoon. If you can't get a bus, then have one of these office types get a vehicle and go and get him. I want to work with this kid, and I can't work with him if he gets his butt busted open. He'll lose all confidence in me and my ability to protect him."

"Sarge, you never said that you would protect him. You told him that if he doesn't serve up his supplier, then what happened to him was predicable."

"You're right, but just the same, I don't think I can save him if he gets raped. That kid would probably commit suicide rather than live with the fact that he had been violated."

"Sarge, I'm sure Mr. Holland heard the stories on the streets about what happens to guys when they get busted. I know he knows that there are no girls in jail and men will be men. When in Rome, do as the Romans do—anything or anybody and close your eyes and imagine it's whoever turns you on."

"Pretty graphic, Smitty. You seem to have some experience with this subject."

"None whatsoever, Sarge, but I do remember the kid I tried to save who got his ass busted in prison and the next day got raped twice by two different guys. He stabbed one in the eye with a fork and another in the throat before he cut his own throat."

"Damn, Smitty, we have got to find a way to save these first timers from suffering the indignities of prison."

"You're off to a good start, Sarge. Just don't abandon your quest. If you do, then who else is going to take care of the Rashidas and the Hollands who have just made a mistake?"

"Smitty, get someone over to the prison. Now! Get Holland over here by noon. I need to talk to that kid."

The Sarge knew one or two things probably resulted from the potential attack on Larry. The first he considered, was that Larry may get the feeling of invincibility and that would only get him slaughtered in prison. The other—which was more plausible—was Larry realized that in four days he had two attempts on his body. The Sarge also thought maybe Larry realized someone might succeed next time or the time after. Maybe, just maybe, Larry's spirits were a little low and he may want to play the Sarge's game.

As the Sarge was busy doing paperwork, he realized he needed to call Rashida and check on her. This was the day that she was going to go home. He dialed the phone number and the voice on the other end said, "Hello."

"Is this Rashida Brooks?"

"Hi, Sarge. I was about to call you and see if you were going to give me a ride home."

"Are you all ready to go?"

"Just waiting on you."

"Have you seen Courtney—I mean Dr. Harris today?"

"Now she's Courtney. I see. Did you two go out to dinner yet?"

"Rashida, you sure are nosy."

"You're right. Now I see why she was floating around here as though she was on drugs or something. You know, she even came in here this morning and gave me a kiss."

"That's only because she likes you."

"Right, Sarge, but she likes you a lot more."

"I'll see you when I get there, Rashida. It does me no good to try to change your mind. Goodbye, darling. See you in a little bit."

"Hey, Smitty, get dressed. We're going back to the hood."

"Hey, Sarge, I'm already dressed. How about you?"

"I'm dressed and ready. Have someone process Larry Holland when he arrives and keep an eye on him. Tell them to isolate him as much as possible."

"Okay."

"Let's go. I have to swing by the hospital and pick up Rashida Brooks and take her home."

"I figured that out, Sarge. But what I haven't figured out is what happened to you last night to make you feel 'wonderful', as you put it."

"Now that's none of your business, Smitty. Can't a man feel good one morning out of 365?"

"I guess so, but I called your house last night to see if you wanted to have a beer with me and there was no answer."

"Damn, Smitty, I went out for a little while. Next time I'll check in with you before I leave my house. Okay?"

"Cute, Sarge, but you still haven't told me anything."

"Yes I did. I told you it was some more of your business, didn't I?" Smitty just looked at the Sarge and shook his head. "Since you feel so wonderful, why don't you drive today?"

"Okay, Smitty. Ain't no thang," the Sarge replied. During the drive to the hospital, Smitty noticed the shit-eating grin on the Sarge's face. After entering the hospital, the two officers noticed a small disturbance between a doctor and a patient. It was a bit loud for a place where people come to get help and healing. The Sarge asked the doctor if there was a problem. The doctor indicated to the Sarge that the man refused to pay his bill.

"Sir, is there a reason why you won't pay your bill?"

"Yes, there is, and it's pretty damn simple, but too complex for this asshole."

"Okay, now, watch your language and tell me what the problem is."

"The problem is I don't have the money to pay him."

"Well, Doctor, if he doesn't have the money how do you expect him to pay you?"

"Listen, Officer, I'm tired of treating these people and not being paid for my services. I trained hard to be where I am, and these people keep coming here in need of service but won't pay their bills."

"Doctor, I think you need to talk to whoever is in charge and see if there is another way for you to handle your collection process. I don't believe it does anyone any good for you to be having this kind of discussion with a patient in the corridors of the hospital. Now I suggest that you both be a little more understanding of the other's predicament and try to work out a solution that makes everyone happy. Just keep the noise level down, that's all I ask of both of you. Come on, Smitty, let's go."

"Sarge, do you believe that shit? That doctor is out of his mind, beating up on that old guy for money he doesn't have."

"Hospitals are getting like jails, Smitty—easy to get in, but hard as hell to get out unless you have plenty of cash. You ever wonder why they always have their faces covered when they have you on that slab cutting all over you?"

"No, but why?"

"When they stick you up, they don't want you to see their faces. You might be able to identify them in a line-up for robbery."

"Cute, Sarge."

"Oh, Sarge, there's that pretty doctor." A smile lit up the Sarge's face as though he was at the altar. The doctor was smiling as if she had just swallowed the canary. "Hi, Courtney—I mean Doctor Harris. How are you?"

"I'm fine, Sergeant, how are you today?"

"I'm doing okay." Smitty, watching the dynamics, deduced that this was the reason why the Sarge was doing wonderful that morning. He interrupted the conversation and said, "Hello, Dr. Harris. The Sarge is not just doing okay. This morning he said he was wonderful."

"Smitty, you talk too much out of school."

"Sarge, will you call me later?" Courtney asked.

"Of course—ah, Smitty, there's the water fountain. Go and get yourself a drink. Courtney, he's been trying to find out all day what has me glowing so. Now I guess he knows for sure."

"Are you ashamed of me or something?"

"Why would you say a thing like that?"

"Well, because I'm not afraid to tell people here that I had a marvelous evening with you. As a matter of fact, I just finished telling Rashida about our evening."

"Oh well, I guess I'm in for it now. She asked me, but I didn't tell her anything. I have to pick her up and take her home now. I have a prisoner being delivered to me this afternoon and I need to be there when he arrives. I'll call you later if it's okay with you."

"If you don't call, I'll come and find you and tear you apart with these little hands. I can't wait to talk later. Maybe you can come over for a little homemade meal. But anyway, let me know."

"I'll call you first chance I get. Talk to you later."

Further down the hallway and around the corridor, a waiting Smitty was standing outside of Rashida's room. "Is she ready?" inquired the Sarge.

"I don't know. I just got here and was trying to remember the room number."

"Well, meathead, you're standing right across from it." Knock—Knock! "Is there anybody in there?"

"Hi, Sarge. Come on in, it's open."

"Okay, give Officer Friendly a big hug."

Rashida responded and tears came to her eyes. "Now why are you about to cry?"

"I'm just not ready to go home, but I'm happy to see you and the quiet one."

"Well, I'm happy to see you too, and so is the quiet one, but you must realize it's time to go and go we shall. Do you have everything? Did you have a chance to say goodbye to Dr. Harris?"

"Yes. We talked for a long time earlier, and we exchanged telephone numbers and will probably get together this weekend."

"Good. She's a great person to know and to stay in touch with. If she likes you then you got it made with her."

The ride to #903 was less than impressive as the three occupants of the car made small talk about the weather. The Sarge broke the ice and asked Rashida if she had a pen and a piece of paper. She responded that she did and the Sarge told her to write down his direct line at the precinct and his home number as well. This of course put a smile on Rashida's face as bright as the sun outside. During the ride to her place, she was wondering if the Sarge was truly going to continue to be her friend. Her question was answered with plenty of information necessary to reach the Sarge, day or night.

As the unmarked car pulled up to #903, people began to scurry away. The Sarge said to Smitty, "A lot of bad memories, right Smitty?"

"Too many, Sarge. Let's just hope that this goes without a hitch."

As the three entered the building, to their surprise the elevator was operational. Although it smelled of stale urine, it performed its main function of going up and down and stopping at the requested floors.

"I think that I can make it from here, Sarge."

"I think that I'll walk you to your door like any gentleman should. By the way, did your mom ever get down to see you?"

"Not at all. She didn't even call me."

"Before you put that key in the door, maybe you should knock to see if she's busy."

Knock—Knock! There was no answer so Rashida placed her key in the door and turned the top lock and then tried to put her other key in the bottom lock. The locks had apparently been tampered with and the Sarge said, "Let me try." As he looked at the lock, he noticed that glue or some other kind of substance had been placed in the bottom lock. He looked closer at the top lock and realized that the same thing had been tried but was abandoned. He said, "Smitty, look at this and tell me what you make of it." The Sarge began to look around the hallway and he found exactly what he was looking for—a tube of Superglue. "Smitty, I found what I thought was the problem. Look here— it's Superglue, but it still looks full."

"I don't like the looks of this. Call for backup."

"Sarge, what's wrong?" Rashida asked.

"I'm not sure, honey, but someone has been monkeying around with the locks. Let me see that key again." The Sarge tried heating the key with a match and finally got the key into the lock and was able to turn the cylinder. As he opened the door he was not at all surprised at the reception. Rashida's mother was lying on the floor, completely naked with a syringe in her arm. The only thing that the Sarge hadn't anticipated was that the woman was dead apparently from foul play. Rashida, accustomed to this display said, "God, I'm embarrassed." Smitty went over to feel her pulse and after doing so said to the Sarge, "We have a problem here." The Sarge grabbed Rashida and said, "Honey, your mother is dead." Rashida said, "No, she's not; she's just high, that's all. I've seen her this way a thousand times."

"Rashida, listen to me, your mother is dead honey. Smitty, call the precinct and tell them we need some detectives over here. Tell them we have a possible homicide."

Rashida went over to where her mother was lying on the floor and reached down and touched her. She jumped when she realized that her mother was cold and lifeless. Next to the death of his wife, it was the saddest moment in the Sarge's life. To see this young girl so devastated and so alone again. The sight of another victim of caine was even too much for him. He cried with Rashida and promised her that everything would be all right.

The detectives arrived and began a thorough investigation of the crime scene. One of the detectives asked the Sarge if anything had been disturbed. The Sarge replied that nothing had been touched. "Hey, Sarge, can I have a word with you?" one of the detectives inquired.

"What's up?"

"Sarge, I suspect foul play here."

"Why is that?"

"How can you give yourself a shot in the left arm when your right arm and hand are broken? Somebody pumped this bitch up."

"Watch your mouth. There's a young lady present." Rashida didn't hear the detective, but could only surmise that it wasn't positive.

"Rashida, where's your room?"

Between sniffles, she said, "It's the one on the left."

"Why don't you guys take a look in there before I let her get some of her belongings."

"Okay, Sarge, we'll do that."

"The coroner is here, Sarge," Smitty said.

"Good. Let him in so that he can get busy." The first words out of the coroners' mouth were, "It was simple. The bitch OD'd." The Sarge took him aside and said, "You had better do a thorough job and not just walk in here and say that someone

OD'd. For the record, shithead, her name is Ms. Brooks. Now get your ass busy before I report your unprofessional behavior."

"Yeah, Sarge, you're right—not very professional on my part. I'm sorry for making a judgment out of stupidity. I'll do the autopsy myself and let you know what went down. Is the kid related?"

"Yeah, that's her mother laying over there."

"God, I really feel like shit now. I'm sorry."

Everyone knew the Sarge and his reputation for being a thorn in your ass if you made the wrong remark.

"Okay, Sarge, let the little lady get her things."

"Come on, Rashida. Let's go into your room and get you some clothes to wear until we can sort this thing out. Remember, honey, I'm your friend and I gave you those telephone numbers because I care. You're going to be all right. I promise you that much."

As the two detectives were looking in and over everything, they noticed a name and number on a piece of paper on the table. It was scribbled so badly, but it looked as if it was the name of Larry the Wanderer. When he showed it to the Sarge, the Sarge knew exactly who it was: Larry Holland. The Sarge asked the Coroner if he had any idea how long she had been dead and he responded about forty-eight hours. The Sarge said to himself, Larry—you lucky sonofabitch.

Rashida gathered her things and the Sarge said to the detective as they were heading out of the door, "Keep me informed on this one, would you?"

"Okay, Sarge." The Sarge whispered to the coroner, "Give me a call as soon as you've done your work."

On the way back to the station, the Sarge kept saying to Rashida that everything was going to be all right. Smitty was quiet the entire trip, perhaps out of respect or realizing that #903 was full of death and despair.

At the station, the Sarge immediately got on the phone and called Courtney. "Courtney, I don't have a lot of time to talk right now, but I need a terribly big favor from you."

"Sarge, we've only been dating for twenty-four hours and you want a favor already?"

"When we got to Rashida's house, we found her mother dead."

"Oh, my God! I'm sorry for being so cavalier. What happened to her?"

"It looks like foul play and a drug overdose."

"Where's Rashida?"

"She's here at the station with me."

"She shouldn't be there. Do you want me to come and get her until we work out something?"

"That's why I called you. I was hoping that you could kinda keep her until I get off from work."

"I have another hour to go on my shift, but I'll see if the resident has come in yet and maybe he'll take the balance of my shift. I'll let you know in about ten minutes. Shall I call you back?"

"Yes, please. I really want to get her out of here."

"Consider it done."

"Hey, Smitty, take Rashida down to the lounge and let her rest there until I finish with Mr. Holland."

"Okay, Sarge. Come on, Rashida, you'll be all right in there. It's not at all like this."

CHAPTER EIGHT

"Hey, rookie, go down to lockup and get a Larry Holland and bring him to me."

"Yes, Sir."

"Are you being smart or you don't know my name?"

"Sir, I was just responding to your request."

"Okay, go ahead and see how well you can accomplish that task."

Ten minutes later the rookie officer was pushing Larry and saying things like, "Don't make me mad, you criminal." The Sarge, after hearing this, looked at the rookie and said, "Why do you have your hand on your gun and why are you pushing this guy? Don't you know that's bordering on brutality? Go and get your handbook and read Chapter 5, and when you've finished, get your ass back to me and tell me where you went wrong. Go on, get out of here."

"Hey, Larry, you look like shit. What happened to you?"

"Don't play me, you know what happened to me, Sarge. And as a matter of fact, I think you set me up."

"Let's get one thing straight here, asshole—I don't set people up that I'm trying to help. And as a matter of fact, I gave strict orders that you were to be protected, not hurt by the freaks that are going to be a part of your everyday life."

After staring at each other for a couple of minutes, Larry broke the ice and said, "So what's up?"

"I want to know if you are going to do that thing I asked you about?"

"Sarge, let there be no doubt left in your mind when I leave here for that other place—I'm not going to dime on anybody. Malik was just for the girl's sake."

"Larry, today detectives found a note with your name and number on it in a murder victim's apartment."

"Sarge, I told you about the person I offed. I haven't even thought of that except when it comes to myself."

"What do you mean by when it comes to yourself?"

"Listen, Sarge, I know that sooner or later, those freaks back there in the prison are going to violate me. After that, I'm going to kill them and then myself."

"You're talking suicide, Larry."

"I don't have many options left, Sarge."

"You have one, Larry, and that is to tell me the name of your supplier."

"Sarge, I'm going to die if I do that. I'm going to die in jail. In essence, Sarge, I'm going to die any fucking way. So it makes no sense for me to break the only code I know that works for me."

"Larry, the murder victim I was telling you about was Rashida's mother."

Larry flinched and said, "Sarge, all I did was do her. I didn't kill her."

"Did you leave her with drugs?"

"Not at all. I gave her a couple of hits to keep her interested in doing those freakish things to me, but I didn't have more than a dime bag when I was there."

"How many times, as you say, did you do her?"

"Sarge, I was there just once. I knew that the timing was right because I knew that Rashida always goes to the mall on Saturday around noon and I didn't want her to see me with her mother, because like I said, I like Rashida. I swear to you, I didn't kill that woman."

"I know that—because you were in jail. I just hope that the time of her death gives you a clear and unquestionable alibi. Now, Larry, I want to give you one more chance before I have you returned to prison. I want to know the name of the person that supplies you."

"Sarge, read my lips—I ain't diming on nobody. I gave you Malik because he sells drugs to the kids."

"Okay, Pontius Pilate, who do you sell your drugs to?"

"Sarge, I have never dealt to a kid. My clients are older. I don't even sell to anyone who looks like they're under 25 years old."

"That's mighty white of you, Larry. The fact is, you sell poison—doesn't matter to who. Tell me, Larry, or you're out of here to face those guys who want to do you in the butt. Who supplies you?"

"Sarge, I'm already dead. I don't fear those jerks. Yeah, they may succeed, but I'll do them permanently."

"That's mighty big talk for a guy who looks like he just had the shit beat out of him."

"Sarge, I have nothing more to say, so please let me go back to my fate. I deserve whatever happens to me. I was in the wrong business and I knew it was only a matter of time before I got caught."

"Listen you pretty, little dumb ass fool. Those guys are going to fuck you in the ass like you're a woman. You remember the things that Rashida's mom did to you? Well, buddy, the ass fucking is the first thing you'll have to do. Then you have to give guys blowjobs until they cum in your mouth. Larry, your ass will learn to like what gets put up there or you'll get a beating every day. I just want to help you. Give me the sonofabitch's name and I'll do the rest. He'll never know that you dimed on him. We'll set up a stakeout and we'll bust him on his own merits. Just help me so that I can get you out of here and out of prison. I guarantee you that I can get you off. Just help me."

"Sarge, I heard about what happens to guys in jail. What you said makes it seem easy. I'm planning on dying in jail so it won't matter, except the guy or guys that do me won't ever get a chance to do anybody else."

"What do you want to be, Larry? A martyr?"

"Hell no. I just want to get on with what I have to do. Sarge, I'm not going to dime on anybody."

93

"Okay, Larry. Sorry I couldn't help you get out of here and you couldn't help me get that guy off of the streets. Hey, Smitty, process Mr. Holland so that he can get back to his fate."

"Okay, Sarge. I told you that you can't save everybody. Some are destined to hell."

Courtney entered the busy station and asked for Sergeant Beckmire. She was bewildered by the number of people being led around in handcuffs. This was her first encounter with a police station.

"Hi, Courtney, how are things?"

"Boy, this is the arena you work in?"

"It's probably not as bad as being a doctor, I guess. This all looks out of control, but it really is manageable. Let's go and get Rashida. I think the first thing we should concentrate on is whether or not she has any family in the area."

As Courtney was about to say something, a voice said, "Hey, Sarge, thanks for the generosity. I think you understand how I feel."

"Hey, Larry, you take care now." Courtney witnessed the interaction and said, "Is he someone special to you?"

"He's like a male Rashida to me. Got in trouble selling drugs and won't dime on his supplier."

"You mean he won't squeal on him don't, you?"

"Yes, I guess. I think it's the same thing."

"I don't think so, Sarge. There's a big difference in squealing and diming on someone. As a matter of fact, you gotta kind of respect him for not doing that."

"Courtney, how right you are. I respect that young fellow a helluva lot. My problem is that within the next few days or weeks, he's going to get himself raped. He promised me, at no request of mine, that the guys who did him would not live to do anybody else and that he would commit suicide in the process. I'm real worried about him. That young guy has a polished vocabulary that blew my mind. Oh well, one case at a time, eh Doc?"

94

"God, I wouldn't want your job."

"And I wouldn't want yours, Doc. All that blood and guts everyday—no way."

As they entered the lounge of the police station, Rashida was sitting there staring into space. "Oh, baby, I'm so sorry to hear about what happened. Get your things. You're going to spend a few days with me until we can figure out what we all have to do." Rashida never said a word and continued to cry and stare into open space. So young, so fragile, and now, so alone at the tender age of fifteen. The Sarge said to Courtney, "If it's all right, I'll come by after my shift and check on you two. In the meantime, I'll see if I can find out if she has any family in the area."

CHAPTER NINE

On his return to his new home, Larry felt very stupid and confused about his false code of ethics. He wondered whether such diligence would be exercised in trying to maintain his anonymity if the circumstances were reversed. He reasoned, and correctly so, that the drug business was one of double-cross and triple-cross and that no one would be this far out on a limb for him. But nevertheless, he knew he was doing the right thing and that no one would be able to say that Larry the Wanderer gave up a name to shorten his own time. He also realized that nobody would or could give a shit about who gave up who from a drug related deal. Larry knew the Sarge's deal, if accurate, would be the best option available to him. The one thing he had learned from his father was never give up a name to save your own ass. Take the time and do it the right way. Larry was always puzzled by that statement because there is no right way of doing time.

After arriving at the prison, Larry was led away to a new cell in a different wing of the prison. After unshackling Larry, the guard said, "Your new cell mate is a trustee. You won't have any problems as long as you do what he says. Take the top bunk."

It was now time for dinner and the inmates filed out of their cells into neat rows of two's and walked orderly to the mess hall. Larry got his chow and proceeded to a table that was empty. That was a mistake because it invited anyone to join him. One of the two guys who attempted to assault Larry sat at an adjoining table and stared at him. The table where Larry was eating filled up in a hurry, and men began to talk around him as though he wasn't there. A very muscular guy at the table looked over to the table where one of the victims of Larry's beating was sitting and said, "Hey, Mop, is this the guy who beat the shit out of you and that other dummy?" All the tables in the vicinity just broke out with laughter. Larry knew it was not a good sign to embarrass a person for losing against someone half his size, but there was nowhere for him to go until dinner had concluded. The big guy once again yelled to the other table, "Did he fuck you instead?" Again, loud and boisterous laughter, but no response from Mop. The big guy looked at Larry and said, "I could save you a lot of pain and aggravation if you'll be my personal bitch." This time there was no laughter, because everyone knew he was serious as well as challenging the power base, and it was no longer a joking matter. Larry ignored the guy and chewed on his food, staring into space. "Usually when I talk to someone or ask them a question, they look at me and respond," the big guy said. Larry never took his eyes off of his plate and just kept eating. A guard came over and said, "Is there a problem here?" There was no response and he said, "Let's have quiet at this table or you'll all be put in the dark place." He walked away and the table remained as still as the night. Once the guard was on the other side of the room, the big guy said to Larry, "Watch your ass tonight. I'm going to make you my bitch and teach you all of the things that I like, baby." Larry continued to eat but was overwhelmed by that last statement, and he was visibly shakened.

Later that night, after all of the moronic activities, the prisoners were lined up in front of their cells and counted. Larry got a chance to meet his cellmate for the first time. After the cell was locked behind them, his new cellmate said, "Hi, I'm Carl. What's your name?"

"I'm Larry."

"Well, Larry, I'm happy to see that they finally put a good looking man in here for me. The last two guys were just awful— you know what I mean—all fat and out of shape and both of them smelled. What are you in for, Larry?"

"I think that's rather private, don't you?"

"Not really. Everyone will know sooner or later. I just hope that you're not in for molesting children or something weird like that, because these guys hate child molesters."

"Naw, nothing like that," Larry responded.

"When's the last time you got laid, Larry?"

"That's none of your business."

"Well, I was thinking that if it was a long time ago, you might want to sleep with me. If you don't want to do that, then if you like, I'll just suck you off."

"Hey listen, I'm not into none of that shit. Just leave me the fuck alone."

"Okay, Larry, but you'll have to do one or the other. There's always a man and a woman." After hearing that, Larry knew that he was in a cell with a nut. How correct he was, for his cellmate was a mental mess.

Prior to being sentenced for flashing children and drug possession, Carl would be a macho man one day, and the next be doing his woman thing. Carl really belonged in a mental institution, but was considered harmless by those who allegedly knew, and was deemed no threat to society. He was in his mind, whatever he wanted to be, be it man or woman. Larry the Wanderer, this night, would find out the persuasion that Carl wanted to demonstrate.

CHAPTER TEN

"Five minutes to lights out," was the command that resonated throughout the prison. Larry lay in his bunk thinking about how to handle the nut in the bunk below him. The nut below was having a soliloquy with himself trying to see who was going to come out tonight and play. There was an awful lot of fidgeting going on below Larry. He reasoned that if the guy even moved his way, he was going to knock the shit out of him.

Around midnight, the prison began to reach a point of stillness. All was quiet in the bunk below and Larry felt that maybe the nut had fallen asleep. As the night wore on, Larry began to nod. He was fighting sleep, but to no avail. Around 2:30 a.m. Larry was out like a lamp, snoring and dreaming of things that had no relevance in prison, such as girls. Without him knowing it, his cellmate was out like a light as well.

At precisely 3:00 a.m., as if possessed by the devil, the eyes of the person below opened as wide as day. Carl knew exactly who was in his body. He quietly stripped his clothes off and laid there for another thirty minutes, realizing that the guards would make their rounds at 3:30 a.m..

This night, the guard was early. He arrived at cell number C-309 at 3:20. Carl heard him coming and drew his blanket around him as though he were asleep. The guard positioned his flashlight on both men and as usual, after recognizing that they both were still there, continued on his rounds.

Like a scene from "Psycho," Carl stalked Larry while he was asleep. He looked at every inch of Larry's body, starting with his feet first, and was imagining what Larry would look like nude. Larry began to stir, and when he opened his eyes he saw Carl staring at him. Larry made the unfortunate mistake of moving too quickly. Carl hit him with a karate blow to his right temple and knocked him completely out. Carl proceeded to take Larry's clothes off. He acted as though he had all the time in the world to disrobe his victim. In essence he did, for it would be a long time before Larry regained consciousness. With catlike moves, Carl jumped up on to Larry's bunk and began to kiss his body. Carl then moved his right forearm across Larry's throat, and with his left hand inserted himself into Larry. Carl then moved his left forearm across the back of Larry's neck in a sleeper hold and began to fuck Larry as if he were a woman.

Throughout the entire episode, which lasted thirty or so minutes, Larry never knew what was happening to him. As Carl approached the zenith of this wicked and illicit action with Larry, he began to put pressure on Larry's neck to prevent him from ruining his orgasm. He pumped harder and harder until his body collapsed with pleasure. The die was cast and Larry was without input. The new whims and pleasures of the sadistic and mentally insane foodman, better known as the Chef, would create a memory for Larry for all eternity.

CHAPTER ELEVEN

As a trustee, Carl was allowed out of his cell earlier than the rest of the inmates. At 5:30 a.m. Carl was dressed and ready to make breakfast for the hungry group. As the door opened, Larry sprang from his bed in an attempt to grab Carl and was warded off by the guard's baton. "I'LL KILL YOU MOTHERFUCKER!"

"Now, Carl, what did you do to him?"

"The kid must be dreaming or something. You know I don't go that away."

Larry looked at the blood in his bed and began to vomit. The guys across the cellblock and next to Larry began to yell, "I'm next, sweetheart. See you after breakfast." The entire cellblock seemed to know exactly what had happened and they all started yelling, "He got his cherry broke."

Larry remained at the toilet, feeling terribly violated and violent. He wanted revenge in the worst possible way—murder. A guard came up to his cell and sarcastically asked, "What's wrong with you?" Larry responded, "Nothing." The guard then said, "Well buddy, you had better get used to nothing because some thing's are going to come your way all the time." The guard walked away laughing, leaving Larry further infuriated and hell-bent on revenge. Larry yelled out, "He'll be dead before midnight!"

Midnight never came that night for Carl. He was found shortly after the lunch break with three stab wounds in the back. The entire prison knew that Larry was destined for Big Jake, the guy whose jaw he broke. Big Jake had put the word out that no one but no one was to fuck with Larry. He had a score to settle and he wanted it settled in virgin territory. Carl got the word, but didn't heed the warning. Big Jake had him sacrificed as a lesson to anyone who would disobey his rule. The big muscular guy who was making fun of Mop, the other guy who Larry beat up had a choice—find a new home before he got knifed or do Carl and satisfy the embarrassing statements made in the mess hall.

It appeared as though Larry was going to get his wish—get done and get even. There were no alternatives remaining for him. He had humiliated the big man on campus and even hurt his boy. The price was going to be two-fold—mass rape and a knife in the back.

After Carl's murder, the prison was in lock-down status. All privileges were suspended and meals were served from a cart by the guards. On Larry's meal tray there was a note. The note read, "Call your lawyer and see if he can get you transferred out of here by tomorrow evening. Otherwise, you'll be gang raped and murdered!"

Everyone on the second tier of the cellblock heard Larry give the threat to Carl. Larry was first to be interrogated. It lasted for over an hour, and it was clear that Larry was in lockup status when Carl got it. Larry asked the warden if he could place a call to his lawyer. The warden said, "For what? Until your case comes up, there's no need for consultation unless he calls you." Larry then asked the Warden if he could call a Sergeant Beckmire. The Warden said, "Now that's the call you want to make." He told one of his guards to see if he could get the Sarge on the line. After a few moments the guard returned and said, "Warden, the Sarge left for the day. Is it urgent?"

"You can say that. It's a matter of life and death." The Warden reached into his open desk drawer and pulled out a card that had the Sarge's beeper number on it. He dialed the number, punched in his number and hung up the phone. In a matter of three minutes, the telephone rang. It was the Sergeant. "Hey Sarge, how's it hanging?" inquired the warden.

"For a man my age, not bad at all. I met me a girl."

"Are you shitting me?"

"Walt, I met me a doctor and so far everything is working out well. She is so fine! As a matter of fact, I'm looking at her right now. We're in the middle of another 'Save our Babies' campaign. I'd like for you to meet her soon."

"It would be my pleasure. Maybe we can get together and do our bird thing. Anyway, I don't like to beep you, but we called you at the office and they told us that you had left for the day. I have a bird here who says that it's a matter of life and death that he speaks with you. Speaking of death, Carl got it today."

"No! Who did it?"

"The person sitting across the desk from me was heard threatening him, but he was in lockup." The Sarge said, "May I speak with him?"

"Sure, hold on."

"Hey, Sarge, I need a favor from you. Now I know I upped Malik to you and that should be good for something. I need to be transferred out of here. There seems to be a death marker on me."

"Larry, what about the other thing I need to know?"

"Sarge, I gave you that scumbag Malik and that's all I'm giving you. I just want to keep the record even. You can do that by having me transferred out of here."

"Larry, did something happen to you?"

There was a pause on the line and then "Larry the Wanderer" began to sniffle.

"It's okay, son. I'll have you put in solitary for the night and then tomorrow I'll see what I can do for you. It would help if you gave me the one I need to know."

"Sarge, I'll die first."

"Okay, just hang in there until tomorrow. Let me speak to my brother."

"Your brother?"

"That's right, Larry, my baby brother." Larry thought that was just too cute. The Sarge had his hands in everything and everywhere. The warden got on the telephone and the Sarge gave him the scoop on Larry. They talked for about five minutes and the Sarge bid his brother good night.

"Okay, Mr. Holland, I'm going to work with you because my brother asked me to. Tonight you're going to sleep in a very dark place. I'll give you a couple of candles and some roach spray. You just try to sleep and tomorrow, after I hear from my brother, we'll try to get you to a place where nobody knows you, although in the prison system, word travels very fast. Before you know it, there will be a bounty on you all over the country. The guy you fucked up is really big time, but I understand you trying to protect yourself. Okay, now just keep your mouth shut and don't let anyone on to the fact that you're going to be moved."

Larry felt a little better about his chances and even better about trusting the Sarge. He realized that the Sarge was a man of many resources, and he had better try to stay on his good side. The one thing he swore he wouldn't do was dime on the guy who was supplying him the caine. Larry thought, *they'll have to kill me before I go against the only code I have and the only one I know.*

"What was that all about?" Courtney asked.
"That was about my male Rashida Brooks. The worst happened to him last night."
"Oh my God, he wasn't hurt, was he?"
"I guess in a way you can say that. The lunatic Chef raped him. The Chef was later found dead from knife wounds to his back. The entire jail heard Larry threaten the man from afar. The good thing is that Larry isn't a suspect. He was in lockup status when the Chef got it. The amazing thing is that the Chef usually goes the other way, but this time decided to exercise his rights as a man, I guess."

"Sarge, that is the most disgusting thing I have ever heard. How can grown men with normal tendencies rape and murder each other as though it were fashionable?"

"Courtney, in jail it's a different world. The normal rules of behavior and discipline are abandoned once that gate shuts behind you. You have essentially two choices: be the male and instigate conquest by any means, or be the female and be as submissive as a battered wife. You wouldn't believe the stories my brother has told me about that place."

"I take it your brother works there."

"My brother is the warden."

"Can't he do something about the attacks?"

"With the downsizing of the guard force due to budget cuts, it's a miracle he doesn't have more rapes and murder in his jail. Walt's a man's kind of man. He doesn't play that homosexual shit at all. He once caught an inmate raping another and made sure the guy got an additional ten years added to his sentence. It somewhat slowed the pace of rampant sexual molestation and abuse. The problem is more societal. You pack a bunch of horny men together like rats and the rats begin to gnaw at each other. The weak are exploited beyond their wildest imagination. It's living hell in jail and I fear each time a kid like Larry gets sent there. He hasn't a chance in hell of escaping the wrath of hardened men who see him as a virgin in need of training."

"Oh, Sarge, I feel so sad right now. How can the system be so terrible?"

"A better question is how can criminals be so intent on stealing, hurting and even killing people for the dumbest reasons?" Courtney was about to say something else when the Sarge's beeper went off again. "I'm sorry, Courtney. May I use your telephone again?"

"Of course you can."

The Sarge dialed the number on the beeper and it reached the coroner's office. The coroner indicated to the Sarge that the news was even worse than he had expected concerning Ms.

Brooks. The Sarge told the coroner to give it to him straight. The coroner indicated that Ms. Brooks had been sodomized by at least three different people. He speculated that Ms. Brooks had sex with as many as eight to ten different men. She had been given enough cheap dope to kill six 300-pound men. Whether or not Ms. Brooks consented to the sexual ordeal was insignificant. Ms. Brooks had been given lye and a fatal syringe full of air. The coroner also indicated that the syringe left in her arm had fingerprints on it, as well as the table leg she used to hold on to while they intruded her anus. The Sarge thanked the coroner and told him that he had done a good job and that if he found anything else to give him a call in the morning.

"Sarge, I hate to be inquisitive, but the look on your face while the other person was talking showed nothing but pain."

"Courtney, give me a moment. I want to say good night to Rashida before she falls asleep."

"Rashida, honey, I'll be leaving in a little bit and I just wanted to tell you that you are special to me and I don't want you to forget that. Things may be a little hard for the next few weeks or months, but I'm going to be there for you. I'm working on some things that will keep us, if not together, close enough for you to see me whenever you want to. Now I want you to be strong and remember all is not lost. Be strong and remember, I'm here for you always. Now give me a hug and a kiss." The moment was tender and emotional as Rashida continued to cry her little heart out. Courtney stood in the doorway and realized that this man was the catch of her life. She saw the kindness and the genuine caring the Sarge showed for others. She knew that she loved this man, but was afraid to tell him so.

"Listen, it's been a long and difficult day, but I do want to tell you about that last call. Can we go into the kitchen for a moment?"

"Yes, of course."

"That call was from the coroner. As many as eight to ten men had raped Rashida's mother. She had been sodomized and someone shot lye into her veins. The killer was a hypodermic full of air." Courtney grabbed the Sarge and pulled herself close to him. She said with tears in her eyes, "How could anyone be that mean?" She cried like a newborn baby and the Sarge took the opportunity to caress her, knowing that she was the woman for him, but was afraid to tell her so. As the two caressed, Rashida came into the kitchen with tears in her eyes and said, "I love you both and I appreciate all that you've done for me." They grabbed Rashida and there the three of them stood—two fully crying and the Sarge with big, red, watery eyes. The Sarge told Rashida with a cracked voice, "I don't know how it's going to happen, but somehow we're always going to be close." Courtney looked at both of them and said, "Well, what about me. Am I included?" The Sarge and Rashida looked at each other, and for the first time, they all had something to laugh about. The Sarge said, "Well, enough of this tear jerking stuff. I've got to go home and get some rest so that I can catch the bad guys in the morning. Good night, Rashida. Goodnight, Courtney."

"I'll walk you to the door," Courtney said.

After Rashida went into her room and shut the door, Courtney looked at the Sarge and said, "I need a big hug from a sensitive man." Without hesitation, the Sarge held her for what seemed like hours, but in reality was only about two minutes. After releasing her, he looked into her eyes and the magic started. They kissed once as friends would when saying good night or good bye. However, the magic was still there, and they kissed again, but this time the passion was all over them. They stopped and looked and kissed again. Courtney finally said to the Sarge, "My question still stands—what about me?" As the Sarge was about to open his mouth, she gently placed her hands over his lips and just whispered in his ear, "Don't make me empty promises that I can buy anywhere. Make me happy and be in my life forever. Think about it and let me know somewhere down the road." The Sarge looked at Courtney and kissed her gently once again and said, "Be my Valentine, for I care so very much." He turned and walked out the door.

CHAPTER TWELVE

Inmate Larry Holland was awakened from solitary confinement at 4:00 a.m. He was not allowed to shower, or anything else for that matter. Mr. Holland was whisked away under the cover of the night as though he were a major personality. In the vehicle, small talk occurred between the two guards transporting Mr. Holland. On the way into the city, the guards foiled a potential car theft by simply shining their lights on two very stupid bandits who were trying to break into the trunk of the car by beating on a side-mounted lock with a brick. Amazingly, the noise didn't awaken the owner. The guards talked about how bold criminals are these days.

At the precinct, Larry Holland was put into a holding cell to await the arrival of the Sarge. As he reclined on the less than gracious bed and visualized his less-than-gracious surroundings, Larry threw his hands into the air as if to say, *is this all I have to look forward to for the rest of my life?* The one question he did not entertain was upping the name of his supplier.

Larry the Wanderer finally drifted off to sleep and thought this might be one of the few nights that he didn't have to worry about someone trying to attack him and rape him. His dreams for the remainder of the night would surprise him, for they were about a special young lady, Rashida Brooks.

At 8 a.m. the Sarge arrived and told one of the day officers to get Larry Holland for him. When the officer opened Larry's cell door, it startled him and he jumped up into a defensive posture. The officer told him to chill out and to face the wall. Larry, half grogged, complied and said that he was dreaming and that the officer scared him. The officer apologized and told Larry to get used to having his sleep interrupted.

"Hi, Larry, how are you doing?"

"He's a little jittery this morning, Sarge. I thought he was going to attack me for a minute."

"He startled me, Sarge. I didn't know where I was and I just freaked when he appeared in my cell." The Sergeant thanked the officer and he left.

"So tell me, Larry, what's going on? I mean, what's really going on in that mind of yours after the other night?"

"Sarge, I'm fucked up."

"I know, Son, but you'll have to put that behind you now."

"No, Sarge. The dream wasn't about that. It was about Rashida Brooks."

"Rashida Brooks? Do you know why you dreamt of her?"

"I really don't, but the dream was innocent and all."

"Larry, I only agreed to help you get out of that place because you upped Malik and I owed you one. Now we're even, Larry, but I think you're going to find that you'll be calling me everywhere we send you. You see, as I said before, you're a good-looking guy, and when they barter for you on your arrival, it's hard not to fall to the victor. In other words, Larry, you had better get used to having your body violated."

"Sarge, no one can get used to being screwed in the butt. It's like a nightmare from hell, if you know what I mean. That sonofabitch had been staring over me for a while, and when I woke up, he hit me with a karate blow and that's the last thing I remember. When he left the cell to start breakfast I awakened and the humiliation became apparent when the entire cell block began saying that they were next in line for my ass."

"It's good you can talk about it, Son, because if you try to deny it, you'll end up a basket case."

"Sarge, you're the only dude I trust. Even with you, realizing how short a period of time I've known you, you seem to care and come through in the pinch."

"Larry, I'm going to ask you my favorite question, just one more time. Wait—don't interrupt me, let me finish." Larry began to squirm in the chair and knew what was next. "If you serve up the guy who supplied you, I can get you out of here right now. I mean it, Larry, I can get your ass out of here right now."

"Sarge, I got busted for selling shit. Now I've got to do the time and I've got to do it without thinking that someone was stalking me for the real rape: my life. So no, Sarge, and no and no. I will not dime on the man who supplied me the caine."

"Is that final, Larry?"

"Sarge, it's final. That's it and no more. I just appreciate the fact that you got me out of that place."

"I'm not sure that I would go and thank anybody, Larry. The place where you are destined is full of hard-timers. You'll probably have a harder time there."

"At least I won't go in with a guy all ready to kill me for beating the shit out of him and breaking his jaw."

"Larry, are you always this loyal?"

"Sarge, you used the word, not me. But if you must know, this is what separates me from them; my ability to keep my mouth shut and not cause any waves."

"Listen, Larry, I'm going to keep you here for a while, and I may have an alternative for you. But let me warn you, it's a hard alternative that has no further alternative."

"Hey, Smitty, good morning. You remember Mr. Holland, don't you?"

"Yes I do. He's the one who operates by a code of ethics right?"

"Right you are, Smitty. Take Mr. Holland back to lockup."

"Okay, Sarge. By the way, did you hear the autopsy report on that last victim of ours?"

"Just damn dirty, Smitty. Just damn dirty."

The Sarge picked up the telephone and called Courtney. He asked her how things went last night and she replied that they had a long talk. She had explained to Rashida the next steps that must be taken, from funeral arrangements to the Department of

Social Services. Courtney also said she told her not to get her hopes up too high about being able to stay with him. She told her the social worker probably would not allow that to occur. The Sarge thanked her and said he felt that the kid wanted to be with him, but it created an awkward situation. Courtney told the Sarge she had told Rashida that she could stay with her until everything could be worked out. She then said that she was running a little late and had to start getting ready for work.

After about ten minutes of paperwork and general bull, an "officer down" call came through. Everyone ran over to the dispatcher and listened to the sounds of gunfire and then silence. The location had been fixed and the Sarge told Smitty, "Let's roll."

Arriving at the scene, the Sarge found one officer dead and another critically wounded with several gunshot wounds to the head. Witnesses said the gunfight was between a guy who had just robbed and shot the storekeeper across the street and the two officers. A kid told an officer that the gunman ran behind an alleyway and jumped over a fence. The kid also told the officer that he dropped his gun when trying to get over the fence. The gun was recovered and sent to the lab for fingerprints. Everyone described the assailant and immediately an all points bulletin was sent out on him. The Sarge and Smitty began to take statements from the crowd, and someone mentioned the name Malik. The Sarge anxiously dismissed everyone else and turned to the young lady and asked, "Did I hear you mention a name?" The young lady replied, "It looked like that crazy asshole named Malik." He asked if she was sure and she reiterated the same thing. The Sarge asked her where she lived and she pointed to the front windows of a second-floor apartment, which had a strong vantage point. The Sarge went on to ask the young lady her name, and she replied that she didn't want to get caught up in all of this shit. The Sarge said that he understood, but would make contact without jeopardizing her. She agreed and in departing said, "You know where I live, but don't come dressed up like no cop and in no cop car. That fucking guy is cracked out and crazy."

Smitty queried the Sarge on what the discussion was about and he told him, "It looks as though our boy Malik has added another round to his golf game." Smitty retorted, "He's definitely making a name for himself. It will be a shame to waste good taxpayer money on this guy. We need an edge." Around and around in the Sarge's head those words spun. He too realized that they needed an edge, but it wasn't good police ethics to think in those terms.

Back at the station, everyone was talking about how easy it was to get shot while doing police work. They all concurred that the bad guys don't give a shit about their lives.

The Sarge received a call and never said a word. It was from someone upstairs, and the news was good, because he was smiling. "Hey, Clyde, how 'bout a word with you?"

"What's up, Sarge?"

"How's your partner?"

"He's resting at home now and will probably be out for a month or so."

"You call him and tell him that I said, get better and forget that other thing because it's going to be shelved for good." Clyde looked at the Sarge with tears in his eyes. He started to say something when the Sarge interrupted him and said, "I know how you feel. Just keep your shit clean and above board." Clyde thanked him and walked away. He went over to the lieutenant's desk and asked him if he could have the balance of the day off. The lieutenant asked why, and Clyde told him that he needed to go to church and pray for a while.

At lunchtime, the Sarge told Smitty to go out and get them a couple of cheesesteaks. He then changed his mind about the number and told him to pick up three.

Later on after Smitty returned, the Sarge put his pistol in lockup and entered the cell area where Larry was being held. He gave Larry the cheesesteak and said, "Try this out, the best in town." Needless to say, Larry was overwhelmed by his generosity, since he loved those greasy sandwiches. The two sat there talking about little things and where to get the best steak sandwiches in the city. With a mouth full of food, the Sarge mumbled something unintelligible to Larry and he said, "I didn't understand one word of what you just said. Didn't your parents tell you never to talk with food in your mouth?" The Sarge just kept on eating.

After finishing the sandwich, the Sarge stated, "Now that was a great grease sandwich. I could probably eat another, but I have plans for tonight."

"Going out on the big date, eh Sarge?"

"Maybe, Larry. When this is finally over and the judge has sentenced you, what do you think you'll do next, or better stated, what will you do when you get out of the joint?"

"You can bet your sweet ass, Sarge, that I won't be selling that shit any more."

"Why not, Larry? Wasn't it profitable?"

"You could say that, but the problem was that you were always looking over your shoulder for either the bad guys or policemen."

"I guess you got a point there. But tell me, what would you do if you got out of here in a couple of months?"

"I would take my butt down to Community College and enroll. I have the grades."

"Where would you get the funds to go there?"

"Sarge, other than incidentals—never mind, I think I'm getting too personal."

"What do you want me to say, Larry, that the conversation is off the record?"

"Boy, Sarge, you really are a genius. How did you know I was thinking that very same thing?"

"Okay, smartass, the conversation is off the record."

"Well, as I was about to say, I probably saved up about 85% of what I made. I must have about $45,000 stashed here and there."

"You lie."

"I kid you not, Sarge. There are big bucks in selling caine, as long as you don't overdo yourself with the ladies and their habits."

"You mean like Ms. Brooks?"

"That was a fluke. I was sent to give her the stuff, but I made her do me for it instead. Apparently she was doing the Man, as well as anybody else for that matter."

"They did her bad, Larry. They pumped her veins full of air after eight or nine of them screwed her every which way but loose."

"Sarge, it doesn't surprise me. The woman had a caine habit and would do anything, and I mean anything for it. I remember once the Man had said that she offered her daughter when she was on the rag, but he said no."

"You mean the woman tried to give Rashida to a dealer for some drugs?"

"I mean exactly that. I think that if the child had been there, she too would probably be full of drugs and air as well. That woman was a shonuff freak. She did things to me that I had heard about but didn't believe people did. Don't ask me what. I see that cop look in your eyes." There was a long pause and the Sarge drifted off to the point in time when he took the oath to be a policeman. He stood there as if he were half-in and half-out of the cell. To the Sarge, this state represented a diabolical metamorphosis between good and evil. Larry watched this intense state and decided to interrupt it by saying, "Earth to Sarge, Earth to Sarge, come in Sarge." The Sarge said, "I guess I was hanging out there on the fringes of reality."

"Larry, how did you feel after you knocked that guy off?"

"What brought that on, Sarge?"

"I guess I'm looking for salvation right now, and you seem like the likely person to offer it to me."

"Damn, you really were out there for a minute. Do you often get like that? Anyway, don't answer. At first I felt rather bad, but then I realized that he was trying to do me and therefore it was either him or me. After it was over, I realized that I had saved the system a lot of money by just taking him out."

"Could you do it again?"

"I almost did it again, Sarge. I promised myself that the dude that hurt me in jail was going to die before midnight. I failed in my plan because someone else did him before I could."

"Suppose I said to you, Larry, I want you to rid the world of a scumbag. Would you do it?"

"Sarge, it takes a little more than just your holiness saying knock someone off. It would have to be a part of a greater picture, or the big picture, if you know what I mean."

"I think I do know what you mean. I have another question, and this is the last time that I will ask you for the name."

"Sarge, you always spoil our little meetings by trying to get me to give up the Man. I have nothing to say about him and I will not, for the last time, give you his name."

"Would you be that loyal to me if I got you out of jail?" Larry looked at the Sarge and saw that the man was as serious as a heart attack. "If you got me out of jail and asked me to do something for you and in the process I got caught, the answer is the same as it has been about the Man, even after being raped by a crazy person. The question is what do you want me to do and are you for real about getting me out of here?"

"No, Larry, the question is about your loyalty and your ability to keep your mouth shut, not that I want you to do anything."

"Sarge, this is serious, isn't it?"

"Larry, I'm trying to figure out a way to save your ass. Now you tell me if that's serious or not."

"I don't remember what happened, but I do know that I was violated and there are a lot of guys who know it. That doesn't make me feel very good, and you're the only person that I can even pull my lips apart to mention it to."

"Well, you treat this conversation like you treat your rape, and that's between you and I. Don't open your mouth to anyone. If I pull this thing off, you're going to go to school full-time and do some work for me part-time. Oh, by the way, your friend Malik, shot two cops today. We want him, but we want an *edge*. We don't want to waste money in court. Now you think about how you can help me and I'll think about how I can help you. Watch your mouth. I have no intermediaries, just you and me. Got that?"

"It's the best deal I've heard in my entire life. Oh and, Sarge, I'm loyal no matter what I do. I do it, and nobody else."

"See you around, Son."

CHAPTER THIRTEEN

The Sarge called Courtney's house and talked to Rashida for a few minutes. He inquired about any insurance that her mother may have had. Rashida told him that she was not aware of any insurance. The Sarge told Rashida that they would have to go and see the social worker tomorrow to see what the next steps were. Rashida told the Sarge that she would like to bury her mother in a few days. The Sarge asked her about relatives, and Rashida could only tell him about an uncle and a cousin. The Sarge told her they would have to go back to the apartment to look through things and see if they could come up with addresses of relatives. Rashida agreed, but indicated to the Sarge that the uncle was a crack head as well. The Sarge thought to himself, *some family.*

The two talked for a little while and the Sarge promised her that he would see her later. Before ending the conversation, the Sarge told her that the next few days would be difficult and probably without meaning to her, but there were laws that had to be obeyed. He explained to Rashida that when young people become a ward of the state as a result of the death of parents, it's up to the system to find suitable housing and care for the children. To make sure that Rashida didn't think that once again in life she was being abandoned, he told her that he would do whatever he could to see that she was placed in his custody, a conclusion that would bring happiness even for the Sarge. He jokingly told her that he needed someone to do the housework for him. Rashida responded by saying he was really going out on a limb and he should consider what he was saying to her. The Sarge told her in no uncertain terms that if it could be worked out and she would agree to obey him and do all of the right things, then he would make every effort to obtain custody. He reiterated the term "custody" to make sure she understood he would consider it a privilege to become her new guardian. He could hear the child on the other end of the telephone crying her heart out. The Sarge said, "It's time to bury the dead and the past. We must look forward to tomorrow and see what blessings are in store for us." He also told her she would have to be strong and understand that things just don't happen at the drop of a dime. He indicated to Rashida that it could be months or years before they would rule on a custody case, but for her not to get weary because he wanted her to be a member of his family.

After talking to Rashida, the Sarge decided to call Courtney and see if they could have an early dinner. She agreed to meet the Sarge at a restaurant in the city.

Feeling that he had accomplished a few things already, the Sarge called out to Smitty. "Hey, Smitty, do we have a picture of Malik yet?"

"Not at all. The pictures or composites are different based upon who saw him."

"I know someone who knows him, but I'll save him for last." The Sarge thought for a minute and called Smitty again. He asked Smitty to get him the number for the FBI agent in charge of the Holland case. He then asked Smitty to get him the number to Judge Lassiter's office. The Sarge then went to the men's room and looked in the mirror and asked himself if he was sure of what he was about to do. The answer was an unqualified maybe!

Sergeant Beckmire talked to the FBI agent in charge of Larry's case and told him that he was interested in making Mr. Holland a ward of his. He told the agent that he wanted the agency to be lenient in this case because he thought that he had the chance of turning this kid around. The agent told the Sarge that the conversation never happened and that he would see him in court. The Sarge heard exactly what he wanted to hear from the agent and then decided to go for two out of two. He called the judge's chambers and was surprised to get hooked right to him. They made small talk and the Sarge told him that he was about to try to save another soul and that he needed the judge's help. The Sarge told the Judge he was prepared to go all out for this kid, even to the point of making him a resident in his home. The judge said to the Sarge, "This conversation never happened."

The Sarge, now feeling good about his day, said to himself, *what else do I need to get done? I'm having a helluva good day—can't waste any points.*

"You look like you just won big money, Sarge."

"Smitty, I think I just hit the lottery. Find my favorite charities so that they can line up for the reward. I think I'll go and pay Mr. Holland another visit and see if he has changed his mind."

"Sarge, the guy is not going to give up any names. It's not his character, and frankly, I rather admire that trait in him. He's strong and realizes that he is in jail, and ain't no sense in dragging no one else in for his stupidity."

"Well put Smitty, but I have to try, don't I?"

For a moment on his way to lockup, the Sarge remembered the twins that died in their mother. He paused and said to himself, they may not be mine, but I think I can help them and they me.

"Mr. Holland, what are you doing sleeping during the middle of the day?"

"I guess that's all I have to do, Sarge. Would it be too much to ask for a newspaper or something to increase my intellect?"

"I'll see what I can do. Get in touch with that fifteen-cent lawyer of yours and tell him that the docket has you on it for 10:30 on Friday. Tell him that you're going to plead guilty as charged for a lesser sentence. I'm sure he'll go along with that because then he'll have you out of his hair."

"Sarge, does that make sense for me to plead guilty without having a fight or looking for a technicality?"

"Never use that word with me, Larry. A technicality is when you get shot accidentally. If you want to get out of this place

123

with the minimum amount of time, then I would suggest that you do as I say. Now, if you don't think that you can trust me, then you plead not guilty and see how much time you get."

"I trust you, Sarge, and I'll do as you ask."

"Good. After the trial is over, you won't and cannot make a move without me directing your every step. Is that a deal?"

"Sarge, you get me out of here or short time and I'll cling to you like a pair of underwear."

"Not that close, Son, but close. Okay? I can pull your chain any time I want to Larry, so when you walk from this place or wherever they send you, remember who's the boss or I'll have you do your complete trip."

"Sarge, what about the Feds?"

"Let me handle the Feds. You just remember who you belong to. And by the way, who do you belong to?"

"I owe my ass to Sergeant Beckmire!"

"Good man, but I don't do asses. So you'll kinda be my cleanup man as well as my *edge* against slime."

"Sarge, when I do work, I do good work."

"I hope so, Larry, for your sake. Then enough said. Do we have a deal.?"

"Yes, Sir, we have a deal."

"And Larry, remember I have no intermediaries."

Back at his desk, the Sarge was listening to a conversation that had everyone's ears. He inquired as to what all of the gabbing was about and was told that they almost had the suspect who shot the two officers. The Sarge asked how the suspect got away and was told the guy was like a rat—he can smell a hole and disappear into it.

The Sarge thought about Malik and decided he would get him sooner than later. He called Courtney and chatted for a while, mostly about nothing. He asked her if she had checked on Rashida and she replied that she had, and as a matter of fact, five minutes before he had called. Courtney told the Sarge that she wanted to do the right thing by her, but was not sure exactly what that meant. The Sarge commiserated with her and said that he too felt helpless insofar as she was concerned. He asked if it would be all right if the three of them went to dinner instead of just she and him and Courtney thought it was a great idea. They hung up and each in their own way smiled about their newfound friendship that was heading for the stars.

CHAPTER FOURTEEN

A call came into the dispatcher stating that a bank robbery and hostage situation were in progress. The Sarge called out to Smitty and told him to get a move on it. The two men raced from the station and entered the squad car with the Sarge driving. He put the car in gear and started out of the driveway, almost hitting another car. He looked a little pink and Smitty asked if he was all right. The Sarge told Smitty that he felt a little lightheaded and that he had better drive. The two men changed positions and Smitty watched as the Sarge began to sweat like an athlete during training. Without asking any questions, Smitty took off with sirens wailing and lights flashing, but in the opposite direction of the bank robbery. The Sarge said, "Smitty, you dummy, the bank's the other way." Smitty replied, "I know that, Sarge. That's where I keep my pennies. I'm heading for the hospital; you don't look too good to me." There were no macho sayings like, "Oh, I'm okay," just silence as the Sarge slouched down in the seat and Smitty drove like a racecar driver to the hospital.

By the time they reached the hospital, the Sarge was all but out in the seat. Smitty got out of the car and ran inside and told the receptionist that he needed a doctor because his partner looked as if he was having a heart attack. Two orderlies ran outside with a stretcher and helped the Sarge out of the car. He was immediately taken into the emergency examining room, where an IV was hooked to his arm and his blood pressure was taken. Smitty went in and took the Sarge's weapon off of him and the doctor took his shirt and vest off and hooked up the electrocardiogram machine. The results looked fine. Then the doctor took blood from the Sarge and made him give them a sample of his urine. After resting for a while the doctor came back and said, "Your sugar is way too high and your cholesterol count is over 220." The doctor then asked Smitty to step outside while they conducted further tests.

Smitty went to the pay phone to call the station and report in. As he was about to hang up the telephone, Dr. Harris came by and said, "Hi, Smitty, what brings you down here?" Smitty looked at her and said, "The Sarge isn't feeling too good." Courtney asked Smitty where was the Sarge and ran down the hall to his room. After seeing the Sarge almost unconscious, she became flustered and started asking questions. She was briefed on the situation, and then said to the Sarge with tears in her eyes, "Don't you ever scare me like that again. Don't you know by now that I need you?" She held the Sarge's hand and said, "I had better pay closer attention to you or you'll make me very sad one day." The Sarge looked up at her, smiled and put a little pressure on her hand, indicating that he was happy that she was near.

Three hours later, after stabilizing the Sarge's sugar count and blood pressure, he was allowed to go home. Once checked out of the hospital, he asked Courtney if she would come by that evening and check on him. She stated it might be best if he stayed at her house for a few days. That way she could keep a closer eye on him. The Sarge dismissed the idea and insisted that Smitty take him home. He obviously didn't realize what a strong and stubborn woman he had met, and was about to fall in love with. Courtney told Smitty to disappear, because this man was not going anywhere other than to her place, where there were two women to nurse him back to health. Smitty kind of liked the idea and said to the Sarge, "You know, it's about time someone had the ability to tell you what to do and not face your foul temper. Doc, make him not only healthier, but see what you can do with that attitude of his while you have him."

"When you next see him, Smitty, you won't even recognize the man." The Sarge just looked like a whipped dog and tried hard to keep a straight face.

As the trio was leaving the hospital, the Sarge recalled that Larry was still in lockup. He told Smitty to make sure that Larry remained at the station as well as isolated. He also told Smitty to tell Mr. Holland that he was a little ill, but would be in touch real soon and for him not to worry. As they walked a little further, he told Smitty to spring for a cheese steak for Mr. Holland and that he would reimburse him later.

Upon arriving at Courtney's house, the two were met at the door by Rashida. She said, "What's up, people? I didn't expect you for another two hours at least."

"Your favorite friend and mine has been neglecting his body and had to be rushed to hospital for treatment."

"Oh, no! Are you all right, Sarge?"

"Sure, honey, I'm just fine and in need of a little sympathy, that's all."

"You don't need to come to my hospital half in and half out for sympathy. You can get that from me anytime and any place you would like." Courtney said.

"Courtney, if you're not careful, you may just find it hard to rid yourself of me."

"Sarge, I looked into my crystal ball the other night, and you know what it told me?"

"No, but I'm sure you're going to tell us."

"That old ball of mine told me that a knight, not necessarily in shining armor, would show up in my life and it wouldn't be the same from that point on. So far, that old ball of mine has been right on the money. Now let's get ready to relax you and fix you a home-cooked meal. Rashida, come on in the kitchen so that you can help me fix my, or rather our, favorite friend something to eat other than cheesesteaks."

The Sarge rested on the sofa, scanned the cable stations and decided that as usual there was nothing intelligent to watch. He called out for Rashida and she responded by saying, "What can I get for you, Sarge?"

Rashida entered the room and the Sarge said, "Nothing, honey, but I would like to talk to you a few minutes about our last conversation. Rashida, did the social worker call you today?"

"Yes she did, and we talked for about an hour."

"What did she have to say?"

"Well, she just talked about the fact that she was looking for a foster home that had children about my age. She told me that according to the law, the state had to settle me in a foster home until I turn eighteen years old. I just said to her that I hoped that I didn't have to leave town because I had two new friends here."

"Did she tell you when all this would be done?"

"She is trying to keep things as they are until after my mother's funeral."

"When is the funeral scheduled?"

"The city is paying for everything and she said it could happen on next Tuesday."

"Okay, I'll be sure to schedule the time off so that I can be with you. I'll talk to Courtney and see if she can come with us as well. Okay, honey?"

"Sarge, I don't know what I would have done without you two. I've learned the hardest lesson in life and I don't ever plan on going that way again."

"You don't have to worry, because I'm going to be somewhere around looking over your shoulder to make sure you realize that there are positive things and role models for you to pay attention to. I'm just happy that we're friends. As a matter of fact. Courtney, come in here a minute."

"Yes, what are you two scheming about?"

"Nothing, sweetheart. Give me your hand and catch hold of Rashida's hand. We are going to have a silent prayer and thank God for letting us touch each other's life, no matter how short or how long."

It was at least two strong and emotional minutes before they released each other's hands. The Sarge embraced Rashida and kissed her on the cheek and then embraced Courtney and kissed her on the lips. Courtney said, "My God, what was that all about?"

"It was about love and friendship," the Sarge said. "One Sunday, we are all going to have a date with the Lord. I'm going to take you sinners to the House of the Lord for some soul searching and inspiring good old Negro hymns."

"Sarge, can you ask Smitty to take me home so that I can get some of my things out of there?"

"What's wrong with all of us going over after dinner?"

"Sounds like a good idea to me," Courtney said.

Dinner, to the Sarge's surprise, lacked all of the things that he enjoyed most. There was no cheese dripping all over the place, no capellini done up with garlic and a heavy cream sauce. No, it was broiled, skinless chicken breast, cooked in white wine with a little garlic and plenty of lemon juice. There was a bowl of steamed vegetables and wild rice. The Sarge's immediate reaction was that he needed some cheese on this stuff to make it look edible. Courtney's response was less than tactful. She indicated that with a cholesterol count as high as his currently was the last thing that he needed, unless he was suicidal, was cheese. He pouted like a child for a minute and then retreated into himself by remembering the dinners he had with his wife. Courtney asked, "Sarge, is there anything wrong?" He responded by saying, "It has been a long time since I felt at home."

CHAPTER FIFTEEN

It is said that in New York one can get lost in the crowds. Those were Malik's sentiments exactly. For he would be safe from harm and the long arm of the law as long as he maintained an extremely low profile—a bit of a challenge for a guy like Malik.

On the bus ride to New York, Malik met a woman who was old enough to be his mother, but young enough in stature to be his lover. The woman sat across the aisle from Malik and he couldn't take his eyes off of her. He finally made a lame statement to her concerning the weather. He introduced himself with all of the finesse that he could muster. The woman told Malik that her name was Monica and that New York was her final destination. She asked Malik where he was heading and he indicated that New York was his final destination as well.

As customary, when people don't want anyone to sit next to them on a bus or a train, they occupy the outside seat and place a bag on the inside one, which is exactly what Malik and Monica had done. The only thing that separated Malik and Monica was the aisle. Malik asked the normal questions, such as did she live there? Where in the city did she live? Was she married? Did she have children? A continuous line of insignificant chatter and questions were followed up by complimentary statements.

Halfway up the turnpike, Monica reached into her carry-on bag and pulled out a ham, turkey and cheese sandwich with lettuce and tomato. It was a huge sandwich and with her good manners and grace, she offered Malik half. He initially declined, but she told him that it was a long trip and he might as well share the sandwich with her. Realizing that Monica was being friendly, Malik thought to himself, *if she offers me a sandwich, no telling what else she might offer me*. He accepted the half of sandwich and the two talked about how good it was. While they were eating, Monica asked Malik why was he going to New York. Malik told her a sad story about how he needed to get away from a girlfriend who was unbeknownst to him everyone else's girl as well. He told her that he really liked her, but that she had no respect for their relationship or even herself. Monica told him that she too had problems with her friend. She indicated that she had met her friend about three months ago and thought that he was a good person. She told Malik that she had to get a hotel room because he failed to meet her at the bus station. When she finally reached him, he told her that he would be over later to spend the night. Monica explained to Malik that her friend did not want her to come to his place because he had his parents there. She indicated to Malik that she smelled a rat somewhere and didn't bother to stay around to find out all of the details. The two talked for a while about the unreliability of relationships and people in general. Monica started opening up to Malik and was reassured by his "knowledge of commitment."

As the outline of the Twin Towers became evident from a distance, Malik told Monica that he wanted to take her to dinner when they arrived in New York. He knew if he had dinner with her, that he would probably wind up with a place to stay. She accepted the invitation, but told him that she wanted to go to her place first. She asked him where was he staying and Malik told her that he had to get a hotel room. Monica then told him that he might as well come to her place with her and from there they could go over to 8th Avenue to a restaurant. He agreed and felt confident that it was all going to happen in one day.

At dinner, Malik said to Monica, "You have a lovely place. What do you do for a living?"

"I work for BT&T."

"It must costs you a fortune to live in that building with the doorman and all."

"It cost a fortune to live anywhere in New York, even if it's on the streets."

134

"You know, Monica, I really have a good feeling about being with you."

"Malik, you can't be over 25 years old." That comment caught Malik off guard and for a minute, he was speechless. He retorted, "Does it matter how old I am, or does it matter that I'm having a helluva rush just being here with you?"

"I guess it all matters, but you are probably the first guy that I've met who didn't have a lot to hide or baggage to carry."

"How do you know I don't have a lot to hide?"

"You seem to be at peace with yourself, and besides, I can tell when there's a rat around."

"Monica, you're right, I'm 25, but I know what I like. How old are you?"

"First lesson, Malik, never ask a lady her age."

"Well, you were quick to comment on my age and I just thought that you could give me a range."

"Let's put it this way. I'm old enough not to be fooled by foolish men, and I'm young enough to want to have dinner with you."

"That didn't tell me a thing."

"Malik, I'm almost fifteen years older than you are."

"Great! Now that we're past that milestone, how about after dinner going to the movies with me, and after that having a drink or two with me?"

"After sitting on that bus, I really don't want to go to a movie, but the idea of having a drink sounds real good to me." The dining affair continued and Malik knew that he had it made in the shade.

After dinner the two held hands and went to the bar in the Mphony House. They had two drinks each before Malik told Monica that he was getting tired and wanted to get his bag and check into a hotel. Monica suggested that they have one more drink and then they would go to her place so that he could get his things.

The short ride back to her place in the cab confirmed Malik's belief that he would be staying over with her. Monica placed her hand on his knee and said, "I hope I didn't offend you about your age." Malik just tried to look cool and confident. He said, "I hope something as artificial as age doesn't get in the way of what I consider the beginnings of a true friendship."

Monica insisted on paying the cab fare. Once in her place, she told Malik that she had to go to the loo. Malik inquired, "You have to go where?"

"To the loo."

"What is a loo?"

"It's several things. The bathroom, the John, the toilet and a few other names that I don't think I need to say."

When Monica returned, she said, "How about one more drink before you go?"

"Sure, why not."

As they toasted their new friendship, Malik swallowed and then stared directly at Monica's lips. As though acting out a part in a movie, Malik slowly placed his lips on hers and began to kiss her gently. They stopped momentarily and Monica sat her glass down. Malik, with his glass still in hand, reached for Monica with his free hand and kissed her again. This time he searched the depths of her mouth with his tongue. Monica responded with tremendous passion and accidentally knocked the glass out of Malik's hand, spilling the drink onto the carpet. He immediately reached for a napkin and began to soak up the drink when Monica said, "Leave it! That's not what I'm worried about at this time." Their lips met once again and the fire began.

After thirty minutes of the best kissing that Monica had ever experienced, she stopped and said, "I want you to stay here with me tonight." Malik responded by saying, "I was hoping you felt the same way I did and that you would ask me to stay."

"Well, now that you have that piece of information, where do we go from here?"

"Monica, I suggest we take a long hot bath together and have another drink. I wasted most of mine, or should I say you made me waste it."

"Say what you like. I'm glad it happened. It created a pretty good feeling for me to see you act so responsibly in trying to get it up. I like the little things that show responsibility because the big ones don't always tell the true story. I'll be right back. I want to draw us a bath."

"How do you draw a bath?"

"It's quite simple. You plug the drain and run the water. It's very European to use terms like drawing a bath and going to the loo. Have you ever been to Europe?"

"I haven't really been out of Philly much. I hope you won't laugh at me when I tell you that this is my first time to New York."

"Why would I laugh, Malik?"

"Well, it seems as though you've been quite a few places, and I would hate to feel as if I had nothing to offer you. You know what I mean?"

"Yes, I do, but I accept you for who you are and not where you've been. At the rate we're going, you might get to Europe and a few other places real soon."

"Oh, really?"

"Oh, really. After the bath, we'll do Paris and then London and maybe even a little of Australia."

"And how do you suppose we do that?"

"I have some videos of my trips, and I can tell you all about those places unless it bores you."

"Monica, I'm from the projects. I haven't been anywhere, and lately, I've just been doing absolutely nothing at all."

"Okay, we'll talk about all of that and other things soon, but for now, give me a kiss."

They kissed for a few minutes and Malik could feel her body gyrating against his. Monica could certainly feel the stiff member of this young man's body. In the middle of her living room, Monica unfastened her blouse then her skirt and slid most

137

sensuously out of each. There she stood in matching bra and panties, but panties that were so skimpy that they almost represented nothing. "Thongs" were her favorite because they showed off her most voluptuous ass. Legs as slender and shapely as possible rounded off by breasts with nipples that any man would love to suckle for a lifetime.

"Shall we enjoy the bath?" Monica inquired. Malik nodded his head and her words were the last audible words that would be spoken for over an hour.

In the bath, the two looked and admired each other's bodies, but never spoke a word. Malik instinctively washed her back and gave Monica the subtle rewards of lust and then pleasure. She complimented him by standing up and moving in back of him. There she began to wash his back from a closer angle than he had. Her legs were stretched out and her body touched his quite firmly. After soaping and then rinsing his back, she reached around and gently stroked his penis while kissing his back and the nape of his neck, all while she moaned and gyrated against his body. She then stood up in the tub and moved around in front of Malik, exposing her wonderfully sculptured love zone. Never before had Malik been confronted with sex in this manner, but he realized that this could be where he wanted to be. He cautiously looked at Monica's love zone, then back at her, and then he gently placed his lips on her as though he was kissing her mouth. Monica moaned for a few moments, then backed away smiling and stepped out of the tub. She grabbed a towel for herself and threw one to Malik. After drying off, the two entered the bedroom and the bliss began.

Orgasm after orgasm left Monica shaking like a leaf on a tree in the middle of a storm. Malik, now playing in the big leagues, figured this was the way to do things. Monica, on the other hand, had been very generous in her lovemaking to Malik. He learned new and illicit ways to use his tongue, and with each new experience, his walls of inhibition came tumbling down.

Now at his threshold of endurance, and as a matter of fact, the first time in his sexual career to reach this point, Malik began to have a thunderous ejaculation. Never before in his quest for sexual fulfillment had Malik enjoyed the full fruits of lovemaking. Most of his acts had been hit-and-miss fuck sessions. But with Monica, for the first time, Malik realized that real lovemaking required giving and consideration for your mate. It had been nearly two hours before any real words were spoken. "Monica, I've just learned the true meaning of being satisfied and how to really satisfy someone else."

"I have never made love this long, Malik, in all my years. Nor have I ever wanted to do things that I have seen done before, but did not have the nerve to try them. I enjoyed every move, moment and kiss we shared. I hope we can do this again, soon."

"Monica, I have to tell you the truth. I've never made oral love to a woman before. I've certainly never reached the dark parts of woman's body with my tongue and enjoyed it. I thought that all that shit was for freaks, but now I know that when you feel that special feeling for someone, you just got to let it go and do what comes to your mind."

"Would you like a Coors Light?"

"I really can't drink a whole beer, but I could share one with you if you don't mind."

"That sounds good to me. I never drink as much as I drank today. It must be the company that I'm keeping, turning me into an alcoholic."

After finishing the beer, Monica started drifting off to sleep. It was now around midnight and she usually cashed it in around eleven. Malik, on the other hand, got out of bed and watched a little television.

Around 1:30, Monica got out of bed and came in to see what Malik was watching. She sat next to him and placed her head in his lap. The next thing he knew, Malik was being stimulated again by her hands and tongue. She made oral love to Malik for about twenty minutes and the two turned the sofa into their new lust nest. Malik stopped in the middle of the action and stated that he wanted to continue in the bedroom. Monica started leading him to the bedroom, but made a quick turn into the kitchen. There she slid along the wall, and once near the counter, Malik, racked with passion, began to sex her once again up against the wall. He picked her up and held her gently against the kitchen counter and stroked her like a wild dog. Monica, on the other hand, reached two quick orgasms, something that she was not used to accomplishing with previous lovers. It was always once and then either good night or sound asleep for those guys, she thought. With Malik, this buck was full of strength and a passion to experience new and wonderful feelings. As Malik was about to have another orgasm, Monica slowed the pace and slid off of him and down to her knees, where she proceeded to give him the best head that he had ever had. She pumped his penis until it spewed every last drop of semen that it could muster. Malik's body went into convulsions and he enjoyed the mother of orgasms.

CHAPTER SIXTEEN

"Hi, Sarge. How you feeling?"

"I feel like new money—crisp and sharp and ready to be spent all over again. What's been happening, Smitty?"

"The regular bullshit. Your boy Mr. Holland was visited earlier by his lawyer."

"Oh, really? Have you talked to Mr. Holland at all?"

"Yeah, I talked to him for about an hour yesterday. He's a funny guy, but I find it hard to see him selling the caine."

"I know, Smitty. He's just a victim and I'm going to try to give him that second chance that we all need occasionally."

"By the way, Sarge, did you do her yet?"

"I think that's personal, Smitty."

"Right, Sarge. Was it personal when you bugged the shit out of me about whether or not I did Mildred?"

"Okay, Smitty, just forget it. But to satisfy your curiosity, the answer is no, not yet."

"Now that's my boy—always making the future another possibility. I know that if you don't hurry up and do her, Sarge, someone else might slip in there and take care of her womanly needs. So you had better get busy, guy."

"Thanks for the lessons."

"I think you need to go in and see the Captain. He's been looking for you every day since you left."

"I've talked to him twice, Smitty. Is the man going lame brain?"

"No, not really. I just think that he and you have a special relationship and he's been obviously worried. The other day he came out and stood by your desk and said aloud, 'You got shot and now you may have a heart problem, and I'm worried.'"

"Are you serious, Smitty?"

"Those were his exact words, Sarge. I heard them."

141

After about twenty minutes of going through the paperwork on his desk, the Sarge got up and went to the Captain's office and knocked on the door.

"Come on in, you sneaky sonofabitch. Why didn't you come in here first and speak to me?"

"Captain, I know how busy you've been lately. Come over here and give me a hug, man. You really are beginning to worry the shit out of me."

The two men embraced and made small talk about the Sarge's health. As the Sarge was leaving the Captain's office, people started yelling, "Which one is the fag?" The Sarge retorted, "It's not me so it must be the Captain." The Captain hearing this came out and said, "I know I'm not gay, but I have been worrying about the Sarge. It must be him." The place went into an uproar, demonstrating the closeness of this group of police officers.

In the lockup area, the Sarge was greeted by an anxious Larry Holland. "Hey, Sarge, what happened to you, man? You had the shit worried out of me."

"I love you too, Larry. I just felt bad from eating all that shit. No more cheesesteaks for me, son."

"Well if that's what it takes, then I don't blame you."

"Larry, were you worried because I have the key to your cage or what?"

"I was worried because you've not only the key to my cage, but the key to my friendship. I only got one and I sometimes wonder if you're really a friend."

"Boy, I like your honesty. Anyway, I'm okay and as I said, too much junk food and not enough rest. I am your friend and salvation, Larry, and never forget it. Had something happened to me, Smitty would have taken care of the situation. If by chance something does happen to me, Larry, you'll know what I want you to do. As a matter of fact, this afternoon I'm going to test the waters with a few hypothetical situations. Do you want anything special for lunch today?"

142

"Damn, Sarge, you're reading my mind. If it's not a bother, I would like some Chinese food, but with no MSG."

"Anything in particular?"

"You like Chinese food, Sarge, so Smitty says."

"Smitty says too much sometimes, but he's right. I do like the shit. I'll surprise you. Talk to you later." As the Sarge turned to walk away, Larry yelled, "Damn glad to see you back, brother." The Sarge never turned around, but a great smile appeared on his face. The Sarge liked that Larry Holland.

Just prior to midday, the Sarge called Courtney just to see how things were going. He reminded her that the funeral for Rashida's mother was on Tuesday. Courtney indicated that she had made arrangements for someone to cover her shift and that she would be there. On a lighter note, the Sarge said, "I would like to spend some quality time with you at my place this evening. Do you think you can manage to get away and come over? I'll cook!" On the other end of the telephone one could feel the quiet. Courtney said, "I've been waiting to hear those words from you. I'll be over after I finish work. In the meantime, I'll call Rashida and tell her that I'll be late." The Sarge exclaimed, "Wonderful! Talk to you later."

"Hey, Smitty, I need you to make a run for me."

"What do you want for lunch, Sarge?"

"You know, Smitty, you're such a smartass. I need for you to go over to Chung Hey's place and get me two orders of my favorite. You can order something for yourself if you like."

"Your timing is perfect, Sarge, because I'm broke as shit."

"Here's twenty; that should do it."

"Sarge, give me thirty just in case."

"You got it."

After ordering lunch, the Sarge made a few calls and then settled back to wait on Smitty. He called the courtroom and made sure that Larry Holland's case was scheduled for a hearing.

To his surprise, the case was listed for Tuesday morning instead of Friday. It caused the Sarge a little anxiety because it was the same day as Rashida's mother's funeral. He tried to prioritize the situation, but decided it didn't really matter because he was going to be at both places somehow. He realized he would have to check with the Clerk of the Court and see if he could work his magic.

Having placed the call to the Clerk of the Court and realizing his goal, the Sarge thought to himself, *how long can this string of luck run?* In any event, he thought, he had to run with this course until it got sloppy.

When Smitty returned, the Sarge gathered the food and headed towards lockup. After entering Larry's cell, he immediately said, "If I get you out of here, you're going to be the *edge*." Larry responded by saying, "What do you mean by edge? You keep mentioning that word."

"I simply mean that whatever I need done on the outside, you're going to do it or all bets are off."

"You said that you and I were going to talk hypothetically. Let's talk."

"I'm going to cut through the bullshit and get right to the point." The Sarge looked around to make sure that no one was near and told Larry to assume the position. Larry looked at the Sarge and asked what was up. The Sarge told him again, but this time with a hostile look, to assume the position. The Sarge then frisked Larry to make sure that he wasn't wearing a wire. He then said, "Larry, I had to do that. A lot is at stake here and I can't afford any slip-ups."

"Sarge, aren't you being a little dramatic?"

"No, Larry, I'm being cautious." Without any further ado, the Sarge said, "If I ask you to off someone, what would you do?"

"I would do as you asked as long as I knew that you were on my side."

144

"Suppose I target the person and then said to you that you were on your own?"

"That makes sense to me. It's like selling caine. If you get caught, you do the time and keep your mouth shut."

"Then you now understand why I'm going to save your ass. I want to clean up certain parts of the city, and I need a smart, calculating, opportunistic and cautious individual to do the work."

"Sarge, I told you once, if you get me out of here, my ass is yours to command."

"Larry, tell that fucking lawyer of yours to do as you instruct. Plead guilty and you walk. Plead innocent and you do the maximum time. After you walk, you get all that you have and place it in a storage locker. Then, you get on a plane to the west coast for a few days. Next thing we do is we change your looks. No more close crop haircuts and we start you with make-up lessons. Your success and survival depends on your ability to look different each time."

"Sarge, how do I live in the meantime?"

"I have a plan for that as well. You'll live modest, drive a wreck of a car and wear clothes that I'll pick out for you. You're going to be the ultimate system for those who escape judgment through technicalities and walk free for their crimes. You'll only do those who I instruct you to do. First we go to Mankos, late at night and make signs giving them fair warning to stop or pay the ultimate price. Every time you do someone, it will be a clean shot to the head, and then you spread the trash over their bodies where possible. Each piece will be different and untraceable. Do you have any questions or reservations?"

"Why are you playing judge and executioner, and do I have a say in how it's done?"

"As a matter of fact you do. We'll discuss the warnings to the slime and then how and when it will be done. You are never to act on your own. I'll draw up your list and make sure that you have the perfect alibi. Nothing will be done if it doesn't feel safe, clean and without harm to any innocent bystanders or yourself. The question is very simple Larry—do you have the stomach to kill another human being?"

"I don't know, but I'm willing to go on this trip with you because I think that for once I'll be doing the right thing."

"The roadsters we're not interested in. We're going to hit those people who have the bodyguards and who think that they are invincible. We'll do a few at a time and then slack off. But the message will be real and final—get out of town or get buried. Hey, and Larry, if you fuck up, you're on your own. I hope that you'll be as faithful to me as you were to your supplier."

"Sarge, give me a break. He's shit. You're quality, but a little crazy. Don't worry. I'll do the time by myself. I won't need your company if I get caught."

"Then I guess we have a deal, Larry. It's you and me against a whole world of slime. I'll be in and out of your trial. Just make sure that your lawyer doesn't try to show how smart he is. Talk to you later."

The rest of the day went pretty smoothly for the Sarge and he lingered around making jokes and being his jovial self. At shift change, he told Smitty that he was going to make the record books tonight. Smitty inquired how and the Sarge told him that he had invited the Doc over for a dinner that he was going to prepare. Smitty held his head and told the Sarge that he might do better if he bought it from a store and then reheated the food in pots. The Sarge gave him the bird and packed up his things for the ride home.

As the Sarge was heading home, he saw caine deals being done right in the open by slime with no fear of being arrested. He thought to himself, how insolent these jerks are. In the middle of a busy intersection, these guys are openly selling trash. After turning another corner, he pulled into the parking lot of the local supermarket. He went into the store and picked up some vegetables, skinless chicken breasts, cream of mushroom soup, mushrooms and hearts of palm. As the items were being tallied, he realized that he needed a few lemons. He told the clerk that he had to pick up a few lemons. The clerk sighed and said, "You'll just have to get back in line again." The Sarge retorted, "No, I won't. The lemons are right over there. Now you can't wait less than a minute?"

"Frankly, Sir, you're wasting everyone's time in this line."

"Listen, jerk, you hold this order a minute or I'll give you something to think about."

The Sarge proceeded by the other people in line and went to the fruit section, picking up two lemons and returning to the express lane. The clerk in the meantime had voided out his purchases and was waiting on another customer. The Sarge said, "All of the shit I have to deal with in the course of a day, and I have to come to a store with a jerk behind the counter who aggravates the hell out of me." While waiting in line again, the manager came over and asked the Sarge if he had a problem. The Sarge said, "Pete, where do you get these insensitive jerks from?" Pete asked the Sarge what had happened and the Sarge told him. Pete told the clerk to finish up the current customer and meet him back in the office. After getting the assistant manager to finish checking out the customers, he told the clerk on the way to the back, "You're fired. Pick up your check tomorrow. The cop you just finished messing with put his life on the line to save two clerks and customers from a robber. Seems to me he deserves a little better treatment than what you gave him."

The Sarge never considered the altercation any further. Instead, as he pulled up in his driveway, he was wondering how he was going to pull this meal off. He remembered that his old buddy Billy had told him how to prepare a killer meal with chicken and mushroom soup.

Once in the house the Sarge began to look through the cookbooks for recipes that seemed simple, but yet provided a flair for both creativeness and taste. The books seemed a bit cumbersome to the Sarge, and he cursed the notion of measurements. He returned the books to their resting place and decided to use Billy's recipe for the chicken. He washed the chicken and placed the four pieces in a skillet. He then added seasoning salt, pepper, squeezed lemon juice from the controversial lemons and a tablespoon of crushed garlic. The Sarge, in his own infinite wisdom, added about two shot glasses of white wine and covered the skillet.

After the chicken looked as though it was done on the one side, the Sarge turned the pieces over and re-covered the skillet. He then realized that he had to fix rice or pasta or something to go with the meal. DING DONG! "Oh shit, is she here already?" He opened the door and found the person he was trying to fix a good meal for. "Hi, Courtney, how are you?"

"I'm fine, Sarge. Something smells wonderful."

"I hope it's as good as it smells. Now hang your coat up and turn on the television and promise me that you won't come into the kitchen."

"I promise. But what's going on in there? Is there another woman in there?"

"I wish there was, but no such luck. I mean, I wish there was someone in the kitchen cooking for me."

"Sure, Sarge, go and do what you have to do. I'm getting hungry."

With the pressure now on, the Sarge went back into the kitchen and checked his concoction. He asked Courtney if she would care for a glass of wine or something and she said yes. He poured two glasses, handed her one and said, "Let's make a toast."

"To what shall we toast?"

"Courtney, I would like to make a toast to you for being a part of my life."

"Then I would like to toast you on the same issue."

After toasting and retoasting, he put his glass down and did a mad dash for the kitchen. He then quickly cut up the mushrooms, placed them in the skillet and added a touch of

148

tarragon to the stewing liquid that flavored the chicken. The Sarge opened the can of mushroom soup and added the contents in the skillet and said, "Billy Montagan, if this shit blows up, I'm going to kick your ass." Courtney asked if he was talking to her and he just yelled that he was talking to himself. He picked the two best potatoes and washed them, scraped them with a fork and placed a wet paper towel around them. He set the timer on the microwave oven for ten minutes and then watched. The Sarge then opened the hearts of palm and a can of asparagus and placed the contents in a saucepan. He instinctively stirred the soup and juices around in the skillet and decided that this was going to be a killer meal.

"Are you about ready to eat?"

"I'm starving. I've been ready to eat."

"Ten more minutes and we shall dine. Can you come and get some things and set the table for me?"

"You made me promise not to come into the kitchen. So I'm going to keep my promise as a loyal faithful servant always does." The Sarge said nothing and came out of the kitchen with plates and silverware. He set the table and placed cloth napkins in two spiral napkin holders. Courtney was impressed at what was happening and further committed herself to making this man her very own.

The Sarge placed the food on the table. Everything looked as though a master chef prepared it. The two sat down to eat and the Sarge blessed the food and ended his blessing by saying, "I hope no one gets sick from this meal." Courtney sliced a piece of the chicken, placed a piece of mushroom on her fork and then forked the chicken. As she chewed on the meat, her surprise was evident. "This is great. Where on earth did you learn to cook and season food like this?"

"A friend of mine named Billy Montagan told me about this recipe."

"My goodness, this is the best chicken I've ever eaten. It's flavored so masterfully. You have to give me the recipe for this

149

meal. Sarge, I need to marry you just so that you can cook for me."

"Marry me, did you say?" There was a pause because Courtney could see the serious look on the Sarge's face.

"That's right, marry you. But right now, I just want to enjoy this meal and savor each bite."

They finished all four pieces of chicken and moved to enjoy the wine in the living room. The Sarge then lit the fireplace, and it was obvious that a romantic mood had just been established. He looked Courtney straight in the eyes and slowly, but methodically, kissed her lips. They embraced for a few minutes and then just held hands and watched the fire grow and grow. The Sarge tapped Courtney on the shoulder and said, "Don't play talk about such things as marriage. It's an important institution in my life." Without any sign of consternation, Courtney retorted, "I don't play talk about things as important as marriage. Now if you really want to have a conversation, then let's have one. Let's talk about the kinds of feelings that I have and maybe, just maybe, I'll get an opportunity to look deep within your soul and see who's play talking." The room grew silent except for the sounds of the music being played.

After about three minutes of wondering who was going to take the first step, the Sarge suggested that they just have a good evening together and avoid any taxing conversations. Courtney, on the other hand, told the Sarge that it would not be relaxing now that an important issue had been brought to the front. She shifted her position on the sofa and said, "Do you really want to know how I feel, Sarge?"

"I guess I do, Courtney."

"Well, let me tell you that from the first day I laid eyes on you, and the way you dealt with Rashida, I thought about how it might feel being close to someone as sensitive as you are. You know what I mean—none of that macho shit. Anyway, as time went by and as we became closer, I said to myself, I want this man in my life for a long time. So you see, I'm not play talking.

150

I'm talking about trying to develop a relationship that would indeed get me to the point of wanting to marry you as opposed to fantasizing about how marriage between us would work out."

"That's a mouthful, Courtney."

"You haven't heard anything yet, Sarge. If you want a passing fancy or an affair, I'm not your girl. If you want illicit sex and friendship, I'm still not your girl. If you want a friend, then I could settle for that. But let me make sure that you understand where I'm coming from, Sarge. If you want me, then damnit, you had better make some strong indications that you do. I have had enough weak relationships, and I don't plan on entering anymore. So you see, if you want to play, then I'm not your girl. If you want to love me and be loved by me, then I'm your girl. Other than that, I'm wasting your time and you're definitely wasting mine."

"Courtney, that was another mouthful. I just got one damn thing to say to you. Woman, I love you and I would marry you tomorrow if you agreed. I'm not much on words like you, but I can tell you one thing, my heart cries out for understanding from you. I'm a cop and that's all I know how to do. You're a doctor and apparently a good one. We match like fire and gasoline. You have to understand where I'm coming from. I need you, I want you and I'll always want you. Sure, I've had a few relationships and affairs since my wife was killed, but I have never felt this way about another women since she died. I have a problem relating to your profession versus mine. If you can get beyond what I do for a living and truly deal with me for who I am then, I'm your man. If you want to make me into something I'm not, then—I'm not your man. As that fire burns high and glows so beautifully, all I want to do is to hold you and make passionate love to you, something I haven't done in a while. So you see, if you want bullshit, then I can't help you. If you want me for who I'm not, then I'm not your man. However, if you want a man who flusters when he thinks of you, then I'm not only your man, but I'm the spirit that will make you happy with what I have." Again, a pause for great concentration and anxiety occurred. They both sipped on their wine and stared aimlessly at the burning fire. The Sarge placed his hand on Courtney's thigh and began to stroke it with great intensity. Courtney shifted her position on the sofa until she was slouching. Her legs began to part slowly, counterfactual to what her body and heart were feeling. She began to circumduct her body as well as relax to the point of acquiescence. The Sarge kissed her lips ever so gently, but with the passion of one in love. The two played the game and both of them won. Being a doctor, Courtney knew that one essential ingredient was missing. She reached into her purse and gave the Sarge one of those things—a condom.

The lovemaking between the two new lovers was ineluctable. The duality of fulfillment was beyond expression. Courtney and the Sarge felt that it was inevitable that the results of their lovemaking would be a bond beyond defilement. At the point of joining, it was clear that she would belong to him and he to her. The bliss continued and the enjoyment never ended. There was no fanfare or great debate when the Sarge asked Courtney to marry him. She simply agreed by telling him that she loved him and always wanted to be with him.

CHAPTER SEVENTEEN

In court, Larry's court-appointed lawyer was about to enter a plea of not guilty, even though he and Larry had discussed the issues facing him. Larry was smart enough not to tell the lawyer why he wanted to plead guilty. The lawyer, on the other hand, insisted that he could not represent him if he continued on this course of self-destruction. Larry, in no uncertain terms, told the lawyer, "You will do as I instruct you. I am pleading guilty and will place my sentence on the benevolence of the court."

"All rise. The Honorable Walthro M. Lassiter presiding." The judge was a man of enormous stature and demeanor. He entered the court and assumed his rightful place at the throne of justice. The bailiff read the docket and the judge asked Larry's attorney if he was ready, and he then asked the prosecutor if he was ready. The prosecutor looked a little bewildered because he had assumed that the judge got the same call that he did. All of a sudden the doors to the courtroom burst open and in walked Sergeant Beckmire. Larry turned around to see who it was and was delighted and thankful that it was the Sarge.

The Sarge walked to the front of the courtroom and took a seat. The judge acknowledged his presence by saying, "We have the law in our courtroom this morning; all should feel safe." The Sarge smiled and winked at Larry.

Four years ago, Judge Lassiter's teenage daughter, Luana, had picked up a bad habit—caine. The child was stealing her mother's jewelry and her father's money. The judge called the Sarge and broke down and told him he suspected that Luana was an addict. The Sarge went undercover and followed her for a few days watching who she hung out with. Needless to say, the child was using every part of her body to obtain the caine. She was being prostituted and used in orgies for caine. After watching Luana for three days, the Sarge told the local dealer to stop feeding her or he would bury his ass. The Sarge then went into the hole in the wall where she hung out and carried her out of there screaming. For the next five days, Luana spent her time trying to beat the worst enemy a person could have: caine.

After spending time in a sanitarium as a Jane Doe, Luana began to show signs of recovery. The Sarge picked her up and took her to his house, where he kept her for the next five days. Making sure she was bored out of her mind, but not enough to return to the artificial euphoria of caine, Luana completely beat the habit. The Sarge took her home, where her parents welcomed her back to life. The judge never forgot that favor and probably never would.

Meanwhile, back in the courtroom, the judge asked for Larry's plea. His lawyer said that he was pleading not guilty. The Sarge almost jumped out of his seat. Larry shouted, "I told you that I was pleading guilty. I know what I've done and there is no excuse." He then turned his attention to the judge and said, "Your Honor, I am pleading guilty and if this goes any further, I will need a lawyer who will do as I ask." The judge called for a sidebar and asked the prosecutor how he wanted to proceed. The prosecutor turned and looked at Larry and then said to the judge, "I don't think time will do him any good. I basically believe he's a good kid. I recommend that we place him in someone's custody that we both know." The judge looked at the court-appointed lawyer and said, "Do you have a problem with that?" The attorney said, "Not at all, your Honor." The judge said, "Okay, then let's get on with it." He motioned for Beckmire to come to the bench. The judge said to the Sarge, "We have decided to give him to you. Can you handle him?"

"Absolutely, your Honor. It would be my pleasure."

Larry was remanded to the Sarge and was a free man. The Sarge told Larry to wait for him outside of the courtroom. After speaking with the lawyer about his decision to plead not guilty, the Sarge winked at the judge and then the prosecutor and left the courtroom. A very happy and excited Larry Holland was waiting to grab and hug the Sarge. The Sarge comforted his new ward and the two men left the court building.

On the way to Sarge's house, he told Larry that he knew the deal and gave Larry a key. He told Larry when they got there to go in and get his car keys and then to go and get his things. He also told Larry to have as little conversation as possible with his former associates. Larry thanked him and told him that he was on the straight and narrow from this moment forward. When he arrived at his house, he told Larry that the alarm was right next to the door and the code was 1119. He then said, "Larry, this is your new home. Respect it and it will be there for you. I don't have to tell you what would happen if you do anything dumb."

"Sarge, you can count on me." The Sarge then told Larry that he wanted him to hang around the house for a few days and then he would be off to the west coast, where he would meet a guy who would show him everything he needed to know about make-up and disguises. He then told Larry that he had to go to a funeral and that he would see him later.

At Courtney's house, the two women were just about ready when the Sarge arrived. Courtney opened the door and they hugged and kissed. The Sarge asked how Rashida was. Courtney indicated to him that she was very quiet, but otherwise all right. Rashida called down to Courtney and asked if that was the Sarge. She told her yes and the little lady said to tell him that she would be right down.

It was obvious that Rashida had been crying. "Come here, sweetheart, and give me a hug," the Sarge said. She came over and melted in his arms as though she was his only daughter. Rashida just held on to the Sarge, never saying a word. The Sarge finally said, "Sweetheart, we have to go now. The services are scheduled to start in a little while. Now you go up stairs and dry your eyes. Do you have a hankie?"

"No."

"Courtney, do you have an extra one?"

"Sure, I'll get her one." As Courtney was ascending the steps, the Sarge said, "Rashida, Courtney has been very good to you. When she comes back, I want you to give her a big hug and kiss and tell her how much you appreciate all that she has done for you."

"Okay."

As Courtney came down the steps, Rashida ran over to her and said, "I feel terrible."

"I would feel terrible too if I was about to go through with what you have to do."

"No, I don't mean that, Courtney. I feel terrible because I've never thanked you for all you've done. The Sarge had to remind me to thank you. Courtney, please believe me when I say that I just forgot. You are so important to me and I love you."

"That's okay, baby. I understand and I want you to understand that we will always be here for you."

"We had better go," the Sarge said.

As expected, the service was sad and lonely. No one from Rashida's family was in attendance. As a matter of fact, there was only the social worker and the hired attendants, who didn't represent the family or know the deceased. The Sarge told the social worker that things were all right for the moment and that he would have some ideas for her later in the week. He also told her that it would be the worst thing possible for Rashida if she were moved right away. The social worker agreed and told the Sarge that she looked forward to hearing his ideas.

Later at the burial site and after the graveside service, Rashida told the Sarge and Courtney that she would like a moment alone with her mother. They told her they would be in the car. Rashida sat down on the cold ground next to her mother's grave and cried for ten minutes. The Sarge thought that he had better go and get her but was stopped by Courtney, who said, "She needs this time. Let her be."

Rashida got up from the gravesite and returned to the car. She got in the car and the trio left. Rashida surprised everyone by saying, "I'm hungry. Can we go somewhere to eat?"

"Anywhere you'd like," the Sarge said.

They went to an Italian restaurant and enjoyed their meal. The Sarge asked Courtney if she had to go to the hospital today and she replied yes. Rashida told them she was all right and that they could just drop her off and go about their normal day. The Sarge and Courtney were both amazed at what they were hearing, but were happy to see that she was attempting to normalize her life, especially on this day.

After lunch, they dropped Rashida off. The Sarge then dropped Courtney off and told her to call him when she wanted him to pick her up. He also told her that last night was the best night that he had experienced in a very long time. She agreed and told him that they must try it again sometime.

BOOK THREE

CHAPTER ONE

All of the preparations had been made and Larry the Wanderer was about to get real serious with his new calling. He and the Sarge had many conversations about the need for an *edge*. The one thing that Larry liked about his relationship with the Sarge was that the Sarge always put him first. The Sarge would say constantly, "Never do a thing if it doesn't feel right." They altered their notions of killing people to one of making sure that they got the message. If in fact that didn't work then they would do them, permanently.

Signs began to appear everywhere warning drug dealers to leave town, get a new job, go back to school or die. The very corner where the dealers made their deals leaflets and signs could be found saying such things as, "DRUG DEALING IS DEADLY TO YOUR HEALTH." The dealers would tear them down and brag about their firepower. In the projects, the mailboxes were filled with information to the tenants telling them that it was time to stop living in fear and to rise up against the parasites who poison the community with caine. The leaflets would tell the tenants about the rape of their community, as well as the economics of caine. It asked the question, "When is the last time you saw your neighbor?" It was propaganda, but those tenants who could read or had someone to read for them slowly began to get the message. The message was clear, "Together, we must retake our neighborhoods and our streets."

CHAPTER TWO

While on the west coast, Larry purchased almost every kind of outfit that could get him into a building without drawing suspicion. The Sarge's friend, Bob Taegert, gave Larry a crash course in applying make-up and creating images. He showed Larry how to apply the right amount of powder and other substances to give him the white look or a definite African American persuasion. Bob was an expert in creating scars and had won awards for his efforts. The scar tissue creation was to become Larry's most famous guise, but he would never use it in his work. Larry spent almost a week working with Bob and learned a lot in the short amount of time. Bob called the Sarge and said, "This guy is as good as I am, and I'm not kidding you. He can create totally new images in a matter of minutes." The Sarge thanked Bob and said, "You know that thing that you owe me, just forget about it. Maybe one day you can help me out again."

"Sarge, you knew when you leant me that money that it would be hard as hell for me to pay you back, didn't you?"

"I figured you would help me out some way, and the money really didn't matter. I just didn't want to come to your funeral because you made bad investments on the horses."

"Thanks, Sarge, and as usual, no questions. By the way, he is a helluva nice kid. Where did he learn all of those words from?"

"I'll remind myself to ask him when he gets here in a few days."

CHAPTER THREE

On the day before "DD DAY" (DEATH TO DEALERS DAY), Larry dressed as a boiler inspector. Once in the basement of the project building, he attached wires to the telephones of suspected house dealers. Once he had copied the dialing sounds onto a recorder, he then knew how to reach them directly. The Sarge, in his infinite wisdom, had made phone numbers and beeper numbers available to Larry for harassment purposes.

During the wee hours of the morning, the Sarge and his new ward would write and put together their newsletter to the community. They called it, "From The Bottom To The Top." Somehow every Monday, the paper would mysteriously appear at the front of the project buildings. There was no formal means of distribution, but somehow the papers got to everyone, including the dealers. The dealers simply would throw them away and laugh at what the ghostwriter was trying to accomplish. On "DD DAY," there would be no more laughing at the newsletter.

CHAPTER FOUR

The Sarge told Larry to always be sure of who it is you're going to do. He gave Larry his first assignment at exactly midnight. He told Larry to study the picture and read the briefing paper he had developed on a mid-range supplier. The briefing paper gave Larry all the details about the subject. The Sarge told him that he was picking up caine at 3 a.m. He also told Larry that he was leaving the action totally up to him. In other words, he was telling Larry to make the call himself based upon the information he provided him.

Larry would have to walk to where they kept the wreck that would sometimes be used for the work. As he was getting ready to leave, the Sarge said, "Let's have a moment of prayer." Both men got down on their knees and the Sarge asked the Lord for forgiveness and protection for Larry. The prayer concluded with the men saying, "Amen." At the door, Larry had his outfit, the weapon and rubber gloves in his bag. The piece was a 38-caliber Smith and Wesson. The Sarge held out his hand and Larry shook it. The two men embraced. The Sarge said, "Remember, if it's not clean then walk away. No chances, Larry, or we'll both be protecting our asses in jail." Larry smiled and left.

THE SUBJECT

Fishbone, as he was known, had been dealing caine for over six years. He had a record as long as a country mile ranging from possession with intent to sell, to murder. It was well known on the streets that Fishbone had killed at least four other dealers who had tried to either enter his territory or to rob him of drugs. He was a vicious sonofabitch who gave no mercy if anyone crossed him.

Larry wondered if just a shot in the butt would give this guy a message. He reasoned that most likely it wouldn't. He burned the papers the Sarge had given him and changed into his outfit. He then put on his surgical gloves and another pair over them.

The car, also known as the wreck, started right up and Larry was on his way. He knew the area well and figured out the best place to leave the wreck. He drove past the place where Fishbone would be leaving and surveyed the traffic as well as the people looking for the caine. He parked the wreck and then proceeded on foot. About 3:15 the subject came out of the building. He looked both ways as if he were crossing the street. Larry positioned himself about 25 yards from the subject's car. Fortunately for Larry, the subject's car was tightly parked between two other cars. As the subject got into his car, Larry seized the opportunity. From out of the darkness, Larry, looking like a homeless person, fired two shots into the car hitting the subject in the head. Larry then reached into the shattered window and grabbed the bag of caine. He tore it open and threw its contents all over the body and car. Larry also left a note that read, "SELL DRUGS AND YOU DIE." He walked away as though nothing had happened.

Back at the wreck, he changed his outfit and drove off. Heading across the nearest bridge, Larry engaged the flashers on the wreck and got out of the car. He acted as though something was wrong with the wreck, but after seeing that no other vehicle was approaching, he took the pistol out of his pocket and threw it as far as he could into the river below. He then kicked the tires and drove off.

At the base of the bridge there was an all-night diner. Larry parked the wreck and went inside to have a cup of coffee. After ordering the coffee, a hand on Larry's shoulder scared the shit out of him. "Damn, Sarge, are you trying to give me a heart attack?"

"No, Larry, just trying to reassure you."

168

"Try another way."

"How did things go?"

"You must know how they went. Otherwise what would you be doing here?"

"You did fine. I'm proud of you. My real question is, how is your head?"

"I'm not sure yet, Sarge. I think that everything is going to be all right and it's going to be hell on those dudes."

"You feel like some breakfast?"

"Sure, why not? Let's move over to that table in the corner."

"We made one mistake tonight, Larry."

"What was that?"

"The subject had a man watching out for him."

"What happened to him?"

"I helped him to have a good night's rest. In other words, I cold cocked his ass. We can't be too careful, Larry. So if you find a flaw in our planning process, then we have to talk about it. Next time we'll do more planning and surveying to make sure that we don't have any loose ends. You know what I mean?"

"Hell, Sarge, I'm just glad to know that you were out there to protect me from someone I didn't even see. I thought I surveyed the place pretty good, but apparently not."

"I guess from now on I should operate in a backup mode. When I saw that dude watching you, it really worried me. I can't have anything happen to you. By the way, did you get rid of the gloves and the rest of the trash?"

"Everything is gone. I sprinkled the trash all over his body and left him our note. Everything was done with an antiseptic atmosphere in mind."

"Good. By the way, I have a guy I want you to meet tomorrow. He's the President of Cruza University. You're only one week late, but he said that he could get you in for me if you wanted to. I took the liberty of telling him that you were dying to get into college. Did I do the right thing, Larry?"

"Sarge, you always do the right thing and, I thank you. I was going to talk about that with you, but I guess I was waiting for the right moment."

"Larry, don't wait for moments with me. Just do and say what you have to. That way we'll always have two way communications."

"Where's the waiter?"

"We need to hurry so that you can get a few hours of sleep. Your appointment is for 9:00 am."

"Damn, Sarge, why so early?"

"I want to get you into some good character-building habits."

They both laughed and ordered bagels and cream cheese. As the Sarge was about to bite into his bagel, Larry grabbed it and said, "You had better order something a little less life-threatening."

"Larry, give me my bagel."

"Sarge, if you eat this thing, then I'm not going anywhere in the morning. I have to look out for you and you have to look out for me and that's the only way we're going to be able to survive."

"Okay, you're right. How about one bite?"

"Just one, Sarge. Don't piss me off." The Sarge positioned his mouth as though he was going to try to eat the whole thing in one bite, but threw it down and said, "You're right, son. I don't need this shit, but I do need something. Any suggestions?"

"How about some granola and light milk. I hear that's good for what ails you."

"You know, Larry, you're becoming too smart for your own sake."

"I have to, Sarge, if you're going to do dumb things that affect the both of us."

"Boy, I like you. I'm going to keep you around for a long time Larry, at least until I see you through college and married."

"College yes. Marriage, I don't know about that."

"Finish up so that we can get out of this dive."

Later that morning the Sarge considered all that had happened. He realized that he had to find a better way to protect Larry. *The mistake I made earlier could have cost Larry his life*, he thought to himself. He knew that he couldn't involve anyone else because the more people involved, the easier it was to have a weak link. The Sarge knew that he had to do a better job of planning.

He knocked on Larry's bedroom door and said, "Son, it's time to get ready." Larry opened the door and said, "I want to sleep some more."

"Larry, get your butt in gear. Today is a very important one for you." Larry wandered into the bathroom and started the shower. He took a long, hot shower and felt good when he came out. He started to sing a cowboy song suggesting that Larry might have enjoyed what had happened. The Sarge fixed a pot of coffee and asked Larry if he wanted anything to eat. Larry told him just a cup of coffee. While having coffee, the Sarge said to Larry, "I noticed the song that you were singing in the shower. It was about a gunfighter who thought that he was invincible, wasn't it?"

"That's true, Sarge. Why?"

"Is that the way you feel this morning?"

"Sarge, be for real. I've been singing that song for over 10 years. There's nothing to it."

"Good. I would hate to think that you felt that way."

"Naw, Sarge. You get cocky and you get caught. I don't plan on doing anything stupid like getting a big head and causing trouble for us."

"Good, Larry. To change the conversation, we need to go out and buy you a car when you get back. Got one on your mind that you would like?"

"Sure as hell do. How about a Porsche?"

"How about a Hyundai?"

"Nothing Japanese. They think that all black people are stupid and inferior to them."

171

"Good social conscience, Larry. Now let's be practical. What do you like?"

"Sarge, all I need is transportation. Nothing fancy that will catch the wrong eyes, just something simple and powerful."

"Well, for now you take my car, and when you get back maybe you'll have some ideas about what we can buy. Now the President's office is on Broad Street. Here's his card and he'll work out all of the details with you. You will probably be starting school on Monday, so don't make a lot of plans for the weekend."

"On Monday? Why so soon, Sarge? You know I haven't acclimated myself to this freedom yet and here you go, getting me in school on Monday. Nevertheless, I thank you for all you've done for me and no, my profile is going to be as low key as possible. I'm thinking about even buying some nerd clothes to escape notice."

"Good thinking. I think you'll wear them naturally."

"You know, Sarge, sometimes I don't like you very much. See you later."

The Sarge decided to work on the newsletter for a little while. He wanted to get a stronger message to the community. He wanted them to call the police and give them tag numbers of suspected dealers, pushers and buyers. He urged the community to fight back now, or forever endure living in hell. He cautioned them about taking any actions on their own at this time, but promised them that there would be a day when they could come out of their apartments without fear of terrorism. He explained why there were those who would take advantage of others. His satire on illiteracy was the best. He spoke of the known fear of illiteracy and why most of those involved on the local level were just pawns in a bigger scheme leading to the boardrooms of the largest corporations and banks, to those who manufacture the poison in foreign lands.

His little newsletter became a shining star in the midst of so much poverty and ignorance. He listed the murder statistics

172

from around the country that were directly related to caine. The Sarge felt that he had accomplished a lot this morning and his new ward was indeed the perfect choice for the *edge*.

The telephone rang and it was Courtney. He asked how she and Rashida were doing. He told Courtney that he had a meeting with the social worker next week and he needed to come up with some unique strategies in order to keep her out of an orphanage. Courtney indicated that the best solution was adoption. The Sarge asked her what she meant, and she told him once again, adoption. The Sarge asked if she would like to have lunch later. She said that she wanted to have more than lunch. She indicated to the Sarge that it was her day off and she wanted to do something with him. He asked her what about Rashida and she told him that she planned on bringing her so that they could go shopping. The Sarge growled and told her that maybe he should catch them later. Courtney told him in no uncertain terms to be there in an hour. She hung up the telephone and called upstairs for Rashida. "Get dressed; the Sarge is taking us out today." Rashida responded, "You two go and spend some time together. I'll be all right."

"Rashida, if I wanted to spend time alone with the Sarge, then that's what I would do. Now get up and get dressed. He's going to be here in an hour."

"Where are we going?"

"Girlfriend, we are going where every woman loves to be— the mall."

"In that case I'll be ready in five minutes."

"I thought so."

After Rashida dressed, Courtney put her arms around her and said, "I appreciate you trying to get me time with the Sarge, but we want you to come as well."

"I just don't want to be in your way, that's all. I know you like him and you guys get very little private time together because I'm always around like a third shoe."

"Oh, nonsense. You have to learn to keep a positive feeling about yourself and us. If we can work it out, you'll be with one of us for the rest of your life. If we can't, it won't be because we didn't try. It's important that you understand that."

"Oh, Courtney, I love you. I'm big enough to understand that things don't always work out the way you want them to. I had a long talk with the social worker and she told me I would probably have to be placed in a home. If that happens and you promise to visit me and stay my friend, then it won't matter where I'm living."

"Is that what she said?"

"Yes."

"Rashida, that doesn't mean she knows what she's talking about. The battle hasn't begun yet. She needs to keep her mouth shut until the last card has been played. Wait until I tell the Sarge."

"Courtney, please don't tell him. He might feel obligated."

"He's already obligated young lady. That man really cares about you and what happens to you. Do you know why the Sarge isn't married?"

"Not really. I just thought he never wanted to be married."

"He was married once and his wife was expecting twins. She was in a car accident and his entire family and dreams for the future were wiped out in a matter of seconds. So you see, you're like the child he never had, and I would suggest that you never forget that. He is your friend."

"Now I really feel like shit. Oh, I'm sorry."

"That's okay. A slip now and then won't kill anyone. Just don't ever let the Sarge hear you slip, okay?"

"Don't worry, I only make that mistake once a year."

"Good. I'm glad we had this talk."

"So am I. If I've been a jerk, please forgive me."

"You've had a lot on your mind lately. The one thing that you need to start preparing for is school on Monday, young lady."

"Oh, Courtney, I need at least another week."

174

"Then tonight when we get home, you go to sleep and dream that you had another week out of school. Then on Monday, it won't matter will it?"

"I get your drift."

"Good. And guess who's getting out of a cab?"

"Who?"

"The Sarge. He must have had a problem with his car."

"What happened to your car?"

"Nothing. Larry has it."

"You mean the kid that you told me about?"

"That's the one. He had an interview at Cruza this morning."

"Oh, good."

"Do you mind if we drive your car?"

"Not at all. Are we ready?"

"I'm ready," Rashida said.

"I guess I'm not loved today. No kisses, no hugs, no nice to see you. Boy!"

The response was overwhelming.

CHAPTER FIVE

Since Larry had to wait an additional hour to see the President of the University, he found time to browse through the Sports Illustrated magazines in the office. The issue that had the swimsuit competition in it was the one he paid the most attention to.

The receptionist finally showed Larry into the office and the two men began to chat. The President told Larry about the tremendous amount of respect and adulation he held for Sergeant Beckmire. He told Larry how the Sarge was always trying to help people. The conversation then turned to Larry and his aspirations. Larry told the President that he wouldn't mind pursuing a course of study in law. The two men talked for the better part of an hour and concluded with the President telling Larry that he would be enrolled in four courses on Monday. Larry thanked him and left his office.

As Larry was driving up Broad Street, he picked up the cellular phone and called the Sarge, but got only the recording. He decided to go to the mall and shop for a while. After spending 45 minutes in Bloomingdale's he had acquired some nice pieces. Leaving the store, he was surprised to see the Sarge, Rashida and another lady. Larry, not knowing the situation, decided to keep moving. As he passed the Sarge on the other side of the mall, the Sarge turned around and gave him the peace sign. Larry realized that he had done the right thing—a thing that would surely get him rewarded with his own set of wheels. As Rashida and Courtney entered a store, the Sarge told them that he would be back in a minute. He caught up with Larry and said, "You did the right thing back there. I'm not ready for you to go social with the ladies yet. I see you got some things. Do you need any money?"

"I've got about two hundred left. I didn't see anything else that I wanted."

"How did it go at Cruza?"

"I start Monday."

"Good. I called this car dealer friend of mine. Later tonight when I get a break from these hens, we'll take a ride over and see what he has to offer."

"Sarge, I hadn't planned on going back yet. As a matter of fact, I was thinking about having some lunch and then going up on 309 to one of the movie houses. Do you need the wheels?"

"No, son, you got them. But try to be back before seven so that we can take that ride and rid ourselves of this car sharing shit. Deal?"

"No sweat, bro. See you later."

"I may have a situation that needs taking care of later. You think about it and we'll discuss it when I see you."

"You mean a situation like last night?"

"Precisely. A bad guy is coming to town to spread his filth, and I've been wanting to lay him aside for some time now. If you don't feel up to it later, then we'll wait for another opportunity."

"Sarge, if you want it done then give me the briefing papers and the route. Will you be my hidden backup again?"

"Without a doubt. I'll be placed strategically to make sure that there are no glitches."

"Then the die is cast."

"Only if you say so."

"I say we do a bunch, send a message and let me become a student without employment for a while."

"Let me think about that. I kind of like that idea. You may be on to something, Larry. Do me a favor. Never stop thinking."

"That's a bet."

The Sarge waltzed back to the store where the two ladies were doing their thing trying on outfit after outfit. The Sarge told Rashida that she had a $250 limit and not to be foolish. She gave him a bear hug and then proceeded to count the numbers on the outfits. The outfits came to $379. He told Rashida to choose the one she had to have least. Rashida picked up a two-piece and put it back on the rack. She was happy to get what she got. On the way out of the store, Courtney said to her, "Since you were such an adult about the cost, I'm going to treat you to that outfit." She smiled and kissed Courtney and told her that she was spoiling her. They all laughed and decided to get something to eat. While standing in line Rashida said, "Everyone got something except you, Sarge. We have to go and get something for you or I won't feel right." The Sarge said, "I have everything that I need in you two." The man got two big, wet, juicy kisses and that's all he wanted.

Courtney told the Sarge she wanted to go to Sraes Department Store to see if they had hooks for hanging pictures. As they entered Sraes, people were gathered around the television watching the news. There was a graphic picture of a man who had been shot and was covered with a white substance. The reporter said, "It appears as though someone had taken the law into his own hands and dealt this known caine pusher the ultimate high." People standing around the television made comments like, "It serves him right" or "One for the People," and, "Maybe if more of them showed up this way, the problem may go away." The Sarge urged his group on to the appointed area for hooks. Unbeknownst to Rashida, it would later be found out that Fishbone was in with the group that murdered her mother.

CHAPTER SIX

"How was your day, Sarge?"

"It was good. Have you seen the news?"

"I try not to watch that stuff. It's only full of murder and drug deals gone bad."

"Yeah, I know what you mean. Just so you'll know, the subject was shown in full dress on television."

"That's too bad. I hate to think that a lot of little ones saw him like that. Anyway, I've been thinking about our conversation, and I think that if we do a few here and there, that ought to get their attention."

"I think that we do two key ones and a lesser one, then we call it quits for a while. By the way, did you end up owing that supplier of yours money?"

"I owe him a lot, Sarge. The deal that went sour at Thurday's was well over five grand, and I know I owed him another $8,500."

"In that case, I think I should have the honor of liquidating your debt."

"You can't do that, Sarge. You're the buffer zone. When he finds out that I'm out, he's going to come looking for me and his money."

"Larry, I don't want you to have to deal with him. I'll take care of him. You do the other two. I appreciate the fact that you tried to keep me out of the action, but if you go down I go down. I've decided that we're a team instead of a coach and a player."

"If you insist on this course of action, you'll spell ruin for both of us. Let's keep the original deal. I do the work, and you make sure that I stay free and out of trouble. If we both start doing, then the alibi gets out of shape. Trust me. I know what you feel and I know that this is the only way for it to work."

"Larry, I'm going to do your guy and that's it. Now get your coat on—we have to go and look for a car. By the way, any problems with the wreck?"

"None whatsoever. It ran perfectly, but a bit loud. Maybe tomorrow I'll go over and see if I can patch the pipes."

"Not a wise idea, Larry. I have someone watching that car at all times. I don't need for them to know and get a picture of you. Just leave it be. I'll have one of my friends take a look at it."

"For a cop, you sure have a lot of friends in high and low places."

"Better to protect us. When you get back from school on Monday, remind me to see a lawyer. I need to have a will constructed for you and Rashida."

"You need to do what?"

"What part didn't you understand? I wasn't speaking French, was I?"

"Okay, Sarge, it's time for us to have a heart-to-heart talk."

"Later, Larry. Right now we've got to see the car dealer before he closes. So again, get your coat so that we can leave."

"Look at that jerk. Can't he see the light has been green for a minute? I hate blowing my horn because you never know if that's the sound that sends a crazy man over the top."

"Sarge, if you wait any longer, we might as well get a room for the night." The Sarge tapped the horn a little and the guy gave him the bird in the mirror. "You see what I mean, Larry. I didn't lean on the horn; I just tapped it once and the results were the same—the bird." They both just laughed. Pulling into the car dealer's lot, Larry said, "How much are we talking about here?"

"Maybe fifteen to twenty."

"Sarge, are you serious?"

"I haven't lied to you yet, have I?"

"Sarge, I can't let you spend that much money on a car for me."

"Who said it was for you. It will be mine for you to use."

"Then if that's the case, I'd like to be a partner in this action. I'd like to give you ten towards the purchase price of a four-wheel drive." The Sarge paused for a minute and then said, "Where are you going to get ten from?"

"I told you long ago that I had quite a bit saved up from dealing that shit. I'd like to do that. It would make me feel like I'm not just living off of you and that I'm kinda contributing."

"Where do you keep your money?"

"I keep it in a safety deposit box at the bank where I have a little savings account."

"You don't have a checking account?"

"Sarge, in my former business, you didn't write checks unless you wanted to admit guilt. Everything was done on a cash-and-carry basis."

"Okay, on Monday when you have a break, give me a call at the station. We are going to open you up a checking account, and then you are going to learn how to invest money. I have a few good stock picks that I feel are just right."

"Yeah, I'm sure. You probably own a couple of gold mines too, don't you?"

"Nothing that risky, son. Let me tell you something about me. When my wife died we had a million-dollar policy on us and plus I had other money I earned through an illicit venture in Vietnam. Don't ask, Larry. The house I live in was paid for almost ten years ago. I subscribed to Barron's and would basically go with their analysis. Even prior to that, I bought gold at $37.50 and sold it at $845. I had fifty thousand tied up in gold. I brought some pharmaceuticals at a rock-bottom price and sold them at an astronomically high price. I currently have a portfolio valued in excess of $4 million dollars. In other words, you snotty-nose little bastard, I'm RICH! So you see, we'll take twenty of yours and twenty of mine and we'll see who can make the most money in two months. The winner takes the loser to dinner. Is that a bet?"

"You're on. But I think I should be given a spread or something. You know what you're doing. This will be my first time trying the stock market."

"Okay, later we'll figure it out. But now I think we need to consummate this car thing. Now I'll get the four-wheel drive if you promise that I can drive it when I want to. Oh shit! Look, Larry! Now that's a truck." A black Range Rover pulled into the lot and caught the Sarge's attention.

"Yeah that thing is a bus, but I like it. Anyway, I promise you I'll let you drive it if you allow me to put in the ten."

"Deal! Now let's go in here and take advantage of this guy."

"Hello, Walter. How the hell are you?"

"I was doing good until you showed up, Sarge. I know that you're going to want everything in here and not want to pay a dime."

"Larry, meet Walter. He's the funniest guy on earth and I love him so. Anyway, we want a four-wheel drive and you're right—we're not going to pay a lot for it."

"What are you going to do with a four wheel drive?"

"See what I mean Larry. That's so original. Anyway, I just want to park it outside of my house."

"Any particular color in mind?"

The Sarge looked at Larry and said, "Well?"

"Ah, ah—that new green they have out."

"I only have the new green in an 8-cylinder. It cost a thousand or so more."

"Where is it?"

"It was being prepared for a customer, but he had to renege on the deal. Do you want to see it?"

"No, Walt, we just came here to see you."

"In that case, I'm leaving."

"See what I mean, Larry. He's so funny. Take us to the truck, man."

After walking through the showroom and into the back, there it was, a green Grand Cherokee four-wheel drive truck. Larry got in and said, "Sarge, this is it."

184

"How much do you want for that thing?"

"I want what's on the sticker."

"Now that we know you're not going to get that, what do you want?"

"Come on in and let's sit down and talk numbers." He offered the Sarge a number and the Sarge balked. Larry came in and said, "What's the number on the truck?" Walt showed him the figure and Larry asked if he could borrow his calculator. Larry put a series of numbers in and told the Sarge that he was asking too much for the vehicle. With amazement, the Sarge looked at Larry, then at Walt, and said to him, "You heard the man, you want too much for it." Walt asked, "Who is this, your second coming?"

"Larry, isn't this guy hilarious?"

"He's funny like a fox, Sarge, and so are his prices. Tell you what Walt, we'll go down the road a piece—you know where I mean—and see what that dude wants for the same product."

"Wait, Larry. Walt and I always go through this. Now, Walt, give me your best deal or I'm going to spread the word over at the station that you sell a shitty product."

"That's blackmail."

"No it's not. It's fact."

"And you call yourself a cop, huh? Thank God no bad guys are in here. Just wait here till I see the man."

"Larry, he's taking 10% off."

"No, Sarge, he's taking 6% of the Manufacture's Suggested Retail price. In essence, we should be able to get this truck for 16% off, plus the dealer's rebate of $1,000."

"You might win that investment bet after all."

Walt returned and said, "Sarge, the man said that he would give you 12% off plus the dealer's rebate."

"You tell the man that I said I want 16% off plus the dealer rebate and the truck goes out of here tonight."

"Be right back."

"Larry, how do you know so much about rebates and MSR's?"

"I've always studied these things so that when I finally went to buy something, I would get the best possible price."

"Smart thinking, Larry."

"Okay you guys, this is the best and final offer. I'll give you 15.5% off of sticker and the rebate."

"Come on, Sarge, let's go. This guy is playing for pennies."

"You heard the man, Walt. I take my cues from my second coming."

As they got up to leave, the so-called "man" came out and said, "Do we have a deal?" Larry retorted, "Only if you give up the right numbers."

"I can't believe that you guys would walk on a half of a percent." Larry said, "It's the principle, not the price. Now if you really want to deal, throw in an alarm system and we're out of here."

"Now that I can do at relatively no additional cost. You got yourself a deal."

"Pay the man, Sarge. I have to go and give our new vehicle a once over to make sure there are no visible problems."

"Sarge, who is that guy?"

"Family, Walt. Just good old-fashioned family. Kind of sharp too, isn't he?"

"I'm glad I only have to sell him one vehicle." Larry returned and said, "There's a little scratch by the left rear parking light. I'll drop it off next week for the alarm and the scratch. Will Tuesday be okay?"

"Even if it wasn't you probably wouldn't buy the car if I told you no."

"Walt, you act as though you've known me all your life."

"No, Larry, just your finicky type."

"See, Larry, I told you he was a funny guy."

The Sarge finished all of the paperwork, wrote the check and thanked Walt. He told him that, as usual, it wasn't good doing business with him, but that he would see him in two weeks for their meeting. Walt inquired as to where the meeting was being held and the Sarge told him at his place. Once a month a group of guys got together to lose a few dollars to each other by playing cards and talking shit.

Larry started the truck and told the Sarge he would see him at home. He told the Sarge to come straight home because he wanted to take him for a ride. The Sarge told Larry that he would see him in twenty minutes.

When the Sarge got home, he found Larry sitting in the truck. He knocked on the window and asked Larry what was he doing. When Larry turned around the Sarge could see that he was crying. He told him to take the keys out and come in the house. Once in the house the Sarge went to the refrigerator and got two beers. "Okay, sit down and have a beer with me. Tell me why you were crying out there. Was it because of what we did the other night? Or is it something I said?"

"Listen, Sarge, I was crying for one reason and one reason only. I mean, here I am in jail for selling caine and you befriend me. You take me into your home, give me my first beer here, and you buy me a brand new $30,000 vehicle. I mean, I have never, ever, even been talked to the way that you talk to me. You treat me with respect and respect my decisions and my input into things, and it's all very new to me. Damn, man, my heart is heavy because I don't know how in the hell I'm ever going to repay you. You get me out of jail, you get me in college and you feed me. Shit, I've never known this kind of treatment and I don't know how to take it. I mean, how would you feel if I did all of these things for you out of the goodness of my heart? You tell me that you need to see a lawyer to get a will drawn up for Rashida Brooks and me, and what am I to think? I mean, I feel bad because even when it comes to Rashida, I did her Mom and she did some pretty wicked things to me. I'm sorry, Sarge, it's just too much too fast, and I guess I just didn't know how to thank you for it. I'm not going to say some lame shit, like I love you and all, but you know that I would do anything on this earth for you. At least I hope you know that."

"Come here, Larry. Sit right down here. Let me tell you something, I love trying to redirect and save lives. You went through hell in jail and you got hurt, but you don't dwell on it. You could have avoided all of that by giving up the supplier. You have a deep sense of loyalty and honor. I haven't seen that kind of loyalty in a long time. I knew that if you gave up the man to save your own ass that you were probably weak. You held fast and I respected that. All of our sessions in lockup taught me a lot about you. I knew that you believed in a more perfect union and a higher spiritual being. Look, I'm getting old and have no family. You and Rashida and one other kid that I know are all the family I have and need. I mean with you guys, if you get on my nerves, I can send you away. So, Larry, don't get on my nerves and—it's okay to cry. It doesn't show weakness to me, it shows character and strength. This is your home, son, and it is here for you as long as you like. No strings attached and no morality inflicted. Just treat it as your home and me as someone you care about and that's all I ask. The car thing is nothing but a piece of metal; no soul and no mind. Last year, I purchased some stock in a little company, and guess what, look at this check." The Sarge showed Larry a check for $45,000. "So you see, Larry, it's not the money that matters to me—it's trying to make a change in young people like yourself and that is exactly what I expect you to do. I expect you to get involved with organizations that try to help people, like OIC. If something ever happened to me, I now know after that show at the car dealer, you would follow my lead and help people with whatever I leave you and Rashida. Son, you are my protégé and my family. All I ask is that you remember the little guy, the homeless person and the addict, and you try with all your might to help them." Larry hugged the Sarge and said, "I will be a shining star in your eyes. I won't let you down."

CHAPTER SEVEN

The dealer from out of town was met with a rousing reception. When he and his cronies went to do the deal there was a shootout. Two men were wounded and an eleven-year-old boy watching television in the safety of his home was felled by a single bullet to his head.

The policemen were everywhere looking for the perpetrators of this drug deal gone bad. The two men taken to the hospital were in critical condition and were not expected to survive. According to witnesses, three other men fled in a black sedan that was either a new Chrysler product or a Japanese automobile. These guys were long out of sight and had ditched the stolen car and were about to board the train for their ride back to Baltimore. As Larry and the Sarge watched the special bulletin on Channel 6, the commentator, Lisa Thomas Tora said, "Our children aren't safe anywhere as long as there are those who deal in the cocaine business."

"Tomorrow, Larry, we're going to buy a computer and printer and do our own stuff. Can't take any chances on printing outside any more. We have to make an example of that child. Are you up to a little garbage work tonight?"

"I'm ready more than ever now."

"Then good. I'm going to make a run in your new truck and scout the area where I know a scumbag who has laughed at the law for a long time."

The Sarge left and Larry went into the basement to try to decide what his disguise would be for the evening. He concluded that the homeless look gave him a certain freedom. It allowed people to shun him and for him to wander near places where his kind are supposed to be. Homeless it was, he concluded. He methodically applied the make-up to give him that rough, dirty and diseased look that people tried to avoid. He started to spray his outfit with skunk perfume, but realized that it would remain in the house for a while. Under each outfit, Larry would dress in biker clothes that could double for a running outfit. He was ready and unrecognizable. As he looked in the mirror, for a moment he wondered to himself whether or not he and the Sarge were doing the right thing. The question didn't linger, because he had seen what caine could do to anyone foolish enough to get hooked on it. He recalled the days that he dabbled in the stuff, but realized that with all of the people strung out on caine, it was a high that he didn't need. He didn't fault addicts in general, he faulted the fact that they didn't try to get help. He remembered his dealing days of not long ago and prided himself on the fact that he only sold to blue bloods. They always said that they weren't strung out and that they just liked it for recreational purposes. He rationalized that there is no recreation in caine, just disaster and ruin.

When the Sarge returned home, he reached for his weapon and Larry said, "It's me. What are you about to do, shoot me?"

"Jesus, Larry, I left you in one outfit and when I come back you look like a homeless person who has found a home. Sorry, kid, you scared the shit out of me. I think in the future you should dress away from the house. We don't want any suspicious neighbors trying to figure out what's going on."

"You're right, Sarge. A small detail, but a very important one. Now that you mention it, I think that we should try to get a place. You know, somewhere that we can make the changes. Oh, and one other thing. I think that we need to use quieter weapons. That 38 made a helluva bang. Any chance we can get some silencers to muffle the sound?"

"Son, now that you're in, I'm going to show you something. Come on downstairs."

The two men descended the steps and the Sarge took Larry to the back of the basement and said, "What do you see?"

"Damn, Sarge, don't go crazy on me now. It's a wall."

"Wrong! It's a closet that I built myself."

"Okay, how do you open the closet?"

"Hand me that old greasy garage door opener." Larry handed him the thing and the Sarge flipped it apart. He got a small screwdriver and punched in four numbers. The wall slid forward and then sideways, and there was his real cache. The Sarge over the years had amassed a number of pistols that had never been fired.

"Where did you get all these things from?"

"I used to go down to Virginia and hunt all the time. Every time I was there, I would purchase a pistol. That state has basically no gun laws. You can buy a pistol a month without any problems. Here are your silencers. I also brought a few barrels from a guy who died about three years ago. With these 9 mm pistols, all we have to do is break the weapon down and just get rid of the barrel. It's untraceable this way. What do you think?"

"Sarge, I think you are crazy as all hell. But for what we got to do, you're crazy like a fox. Don't ever stop thinking or we'll be in a world of trouble."

The Sarge had a serious look on his face. He said to Larry, "Do you really think that I'm crazy?"

"Hit a nerve, did I? Anyway, we are all just a little crazy. In your case, you are crazier than me and I am crazier than most. So as you can see, we are two crazy sonsabitches trying to give the *EDGE*."

"Okay, first question I have is do you know how to break one of these things down?"

"I really don't."

"Okay, it's real simple. Even a crazy person like you can do this. Now watch carefully." The Sarge showed Larry how to dismantle the barrel and how to put the few key pieces back together. After three attempts, Larry mastered the process and was able to do it in a matter of seconds. The Sarge smiled and mumbled, "Not too crazy."

"What did you say?"

"Oh, nothing."

"Come on, Sarge. What did you say?"

"I said, not too crazy." They laughed and loaded the weapon. The Sarge said, "There are fifteen shots in this one. Do you want them all?"

"I don't know. Are we doing fifteen people tonight?"

"Funny. No, we're doing three. You two and me one."

"Sarge, I'm going to try this one more time. I need you as the buffer, not as the doer."

"Larry, have you ever been around people you like and they decide to do reefer because they think you're cool? When you back out they all get panicky. So what do you do? You take a hit on that shit and they all feel safe again. I say that to say this. I don't want you doing your man because he's all mine."

"You don't even know who my man is, Sarge."

"Your man goes by the name of Sleeper." Larry looked at the Sarge and said, "How did you know that?"

"I knew that from day one, son."

"Anything else you want to tell me?"

"As a matter of fact, there is. He did a cop in the head and nobody would testify against him. I never talked to the Man, but me and a bunch of other cops gave him the look of death. This was four years ago and all we could do is arrest him on possession. So you see, in this case it's personal, and therefore I'm going to do him."

"Sarge, you're too obvious. You look like a cop when you aren't playing one. Now don't mess this thing up by trying to avenge history. I know this guy and he's a rotten bastard. He may have been involved in the doing of Rashida's mother. Just let me work the angle that we've designed and do the work. If you refuse to be my buffer and you get in on the actual act, then we're going to have trouble. If I need you to do someone because the heat is on a homeless man and suddenly we need to make him a big homeless man, then you do it. But right now, you're only going to fuck things up. Oh shit, I'm sorry, I didn't mean to use the "F" word."

"I occasionally use it myself, and I thank you for respecting me enough to apologize."

"This is my home Sarge. I don't have another. Let me do the work and you be the buffer and the brains. You tell me the conditions and the best way in and out. You tell me how many to expect and if it feels good. Don't do the work and try to help me because you'll only screw me up. Now I want you to promise me like a father to son that you'll make sure that I'm safe, and I'll do the work."

"Are you sure that I'm not your father? Boy, you sound so much like me. I don't know how I can stand you. Let's get busy. Oh, by the way, the number for this thing is 2124. To close it, you have to cover the garage door opener and hit this camouflage bottom that looks like a nail head."

"Can't be too careful, can we, Sarge?"

"You know, Larry, you're really a nice kid. Your problem is that you're a smartass."

After going over the layout of the area, the two men talked about where the wreck should be left and other details. As if they were airline pilots going through their preflight take-off routine, the two checked and double-checked. There was only one item that was missing in the check off—the surgical gloves that were very important. Larry's explanation was that when the Sarge came in and reached for his weapon, Larry forgot about them and focused on the issue at hand, mistakenly getting shot.

"Listen, I have to call Courtney and Rashida and tell them that I won't be over until later. In the meantime, put that plastic raincoat on over your things and pull the hood up so that no one will see your face. Once you get to the wreck, I'll drive by and you follow me to where you should leave it. Then on foot you'll walk about three blocks and you'll see these guys in the picture. Your man won't be there. He'll be in his car about a mile from there. There will be two guys, one outside and a guy in the hallway looking out. You'll see a liquor store on your right. Go in there and pick up two bottles of cheap wine—Ripple or

Thunderbird. Put one in your free pocket and keep the other one in your left hand. Rinse your mouth out with the shit and pour a little on your clothes so that they can smell you before they see you. Any questions?"

"No, everything is pretty clear."

"Once you've done the work, keep heading north on that street. Don't run, just walk naturally, drinking your wine and cursing like a sailor. Turn the corner and walk up into the alley and you'll see some winos drinking and trying to stay warm by a can fire. Act like you're at home with them and give them the wine. Stay there for five minutes and then walk back to the wreck. At exactly 10:30 your man will be there on the corner of 46th and Girard. At 10:45 he'll be expecting his dope. The guy in the hallway will have the dope. Spread one bag on them and save the other for the Sleeper."

"We had better get a move on it. Time is running out."

"Okay, you go ahead. I'm going to make my call." The Sarge called Courtney and had small talk about little things and told her that maybe he would see her about 11:00. He asked her if he should bring a pizza. She told him they had eaten a snack and that pizza was not in the cards for him.

Larry the Wanderer should have been an actor. After rinsing his mouth with the cheap wine, he strolled down the street at a snails pace, yelling obscenities at cars and passersby. A woman passed him with a pizza in her hands and he said, "You need another slice of pizza like I need another drink." She was polite and said, "Go fuck yourself, drunk." There were a few young people hanging out on the corner, and he knew they were dealing the caine. As he walked by, one of the dudes said, "Hey you drunken motherfucker, put that shit down and get with the caine." Larry just staggered on by and said, "I hope I don't see you in church, son." In other words, Larry was hoping that one day he didn't have to do him.

One block away from the subject, Larry began to survey everything. He crossed the street to see what windows were

194

available for someone to see him, and then he crossed back to the side he was originally on. He staggered and bumped into cars and even took his penis out and took a piss. He watched every movement in the entire block. Someone yelled out of a passing car, "Hey you fucking drunk, stop pissing in public." Larry yelled back, "Fuck you, asshole." He knew that the guy outside of the building heard him and this was the perfect opportunity to have the guy just ignore him. As he walked the block, he yelled at every passing car. He stopped on the corner and took a real drink of the cheap wine. He sat on the curb for about five minutes surveying the action. He saw the Sarge drive by and knew that everything was reasonably ready.

A bottle of wine in his left pocket, a bottle in his left hand and the safety off of the 9 millimeter in his right pocket; he knew that he had chambered a round prior to leaving the house and he knew the weapon was ready. The only question he had was whether or not he was ready.

Fifty feet away from the subject, Larry's brain raced and he scanned the area. When Larry got within ten feet of Subject #1, he wrestled with the bottle in his left hand. The subject said, "Get the fuck away from here, you drunken motherfucker." In his right hand, Larry had complete control over the weapon. As he was about to do Subject #1, the door opened and a woman and her child came through it. Subject #1 said to the woman, "What the fuck are you looking at?" She commented, "Nothing" He said, "You'd better not be looking at me if you know what's good for your ugly ass." Larry kept walking and Subject #1 said, "Look at you, you pathetic motherfucker. Go on, get the fuck away from here." Larry just kept walking, saying to himself, it's not right. I'll catch him later.

Two blocks away, Larry was standing on the corner with his hand out like he was begging for money. The Sarge drove up and said, "What happened?"

195

"Just as I was about to do that bastard, a woman and her kid came through the door. It wasn't right. Give me some change in case someone is looking. I'm going to the other spot."

"No, let's just forget about tonight."

"I'm going to the other spot. When they all show up, I'll do them all at the same time if the timing is right."

"I'll be near. Just be careful." Larry then yelled, "I ask you for a dollar and you give me fifteen cents. How cheap can you be?"

Larry ran to the wreck, got in and drove like he was in a hurry. It was 10:25 and he knew that the Man had a thing about punctuality. At 10:28 he was about 3 blocks away and saw a parking space, but decided that it was too direct. He drove around the block and parked in a vacant church lot. He got out of the car and started running. He knew that 10:30 was just the location time and that 10:45 was the actual drop time. He walked up to a wall like he was about to take a piss and made sure that the weapon had a round chambered in it.

The Sarge drove by and spotted Larry. "I made a definite on him. He is in the first car on the corner, a brown Beemer. He's alone, and at the right time he will have the other two with him. Do you have a plan?"

"I'm going to crawl like a baby within about fifty feet from there."

"Larry, I don't like it. It seems to be getting out of our control."

"One of those jerks insulted a woman in front of her kid and all but hit me. If it doesn't feel right then it won't happen tonight. Just get out of here before someone sees you talking to me."

Larry had rid himself of the plastic raincoat and was now in his infamous homeless clothes. He ducked behind a car and got on all fours and stayed there for five minutes. He prayed that no one would come out to move their cars. Five minutes before the

196

reunion, Larry began his dirty mission.   He crawled like a Marine in bootcamp.

Two minutes to go and he could hear a car running. On the other side of the street was a space big enough for a car, but near a fire hydrant. As luck would have it, the passenger got out of the car, went across the street and got in the Beemer. Larry said to himself, now or never. As he was about to roll from under the car, he saw headlights shining from behind him. He realized that there was nothing he could do at this point. As the vehicle got closer, Larry realized that it was a bus, the perfect cover. When the bus came to a stop, Larry rolled from under the car and put six quick shots into the Beemer. As the bus passed, he ran behind it and placed two shots in the head of the driver of the other car. Larry then ran back to the B'Mer and grabbed the dope and poured it all over the passenger and the Man, his ex-supplier, and then saved some for the corpse across the street. He then coolly walked around the corner and down the street as though nothing had happened. He dismantled the gun while he was walking. He turned another corner, slid into an alleyway, snatched his button-up outfit off and placed it under his arm as though he was a jogger.

Back at the wreck, he placed everything in a bag and drove back to where the winos were. He gave them the unopened bottle, took a swig out of the open bottle and gave it to them. He then took the bag of clothes and placed it in their fire and told them that he was done with wine and was about to start a Christian life. He walked away, but turned to make sure that the fire had consumed the bag. Satisfied, he walked past where the work was supposed to be done and ironically ran into the woman and child who the ex-caine dealer had insulted. He smiled at the child and kept walking.

Larry drove the wreck to the bridge and again put his flashers on and acted as though something was wrong with the front end. He cut the lights out and pretended to open the hood.

He went into the car and got the barrel out and slyly threw it into the river. He drove to the all-night diner where the anxious Sarge was waiting. Larry saw his car and decided to park on the other side. He went in and the Sarge was at the back table having a cup of coffee and apple pie. He smiled at Larry and asked, "Are you all right?"

"I'm fine, Sarge, but there was no need for you to show up here."

"I know. I saw you at work and I was kinda proud of the way you handled the job."

"What do you mean, kinda proud?"

"Kinda, because what we're doing isn't right, no matter how we try to justify it."

"You have a point there. We'll do the newsletter and then we'll slow down a bit. I need to get home and scrub. I crawled in all kinds of shit tonight. I used the wine and boric acid to wash any possible traces of that shit off of me. That's the one thing that we're going to have to improve on. It usually flies all over me."

"You go home and rest. I'm going to see my friend for a few minutes. Are you going out?"

"I think so. I'm going to go to the late show at the movies. Plus I want to ride around in my new truck—well, our new truck—and see how she handles. Don't wait up for me."

"Be careful. I'll see you later. Oh, and Larry, that was the best work I have ever seen. I'm going to get the piece from under the seat and save you some problems."

"Thanks, Sarge. Be careful."

CHAPTER EIGHT

The past week or so has found Boyfriend at museums, symphonies, operas and two plays. He enjoyed the Phantom of the Opera the most and thought that Les Miserables was excellent. He enjoyed dining on the East side and drinking over on the West side. His favorite club in New York was Chelsea Place, down on 8th Avenue around 15th. Monica had made a true gentleman out of Malik. While she was at work, he cleaned, cooked and did the shopping.

As their experimentation with sex reached higher and higher degrees, Malik began to show signs of his old self. He became abusive and then apologetic, mean and then sweet, and finally aggressive and sadistic. Monica, being ever so sagacious, knew these behaviors would only increase as opposed to diminish. What really bothered Monica was Malik's obsession with and preoccupation with having her try caine. This woman had been around for a few years and had witnessed the results of casual use of the less-than-understood drug. During their sexual sessions he would often tell her how wonderful she would feel if she just had a little hit of caine. On one rare occasion, when she experimented with anal intercourse, Malik was as vicious as he could possibly be. He attempted to hurt her, and by doing so, he thought she would commiserate with him about the caine. The next morning, Monica was almost unable to walk. She cried in the bathroom at the thought that she had let a monster in her home as her lover. She knew that she had to get rid of him at any cost.

Two days later, Monica told Malik before she left for work that she was going to leave him two hundred dollars for food. She told him that if he wanted to buy a surprise for her she wouldn't mind. He asked her what she had in mind. Monica told him that if she had to tell him, it wouldn't be a surprise. Malik, still puzzled by the notion asked, "Is it something that I have been trying to get you to do for a long time?"

"Bingo."

"Oh, baby, come and give me a big kiss before you leave." He kissed her and she knew that he was going to try to have sex with her, something that she was in need of. She told him that she wanted to have sex before she left for work, and he got right on the job. He started with his mouth all over her body and then ended up giving her great pleasure before work.

After the act, Malik said, "Baby, that was wonderful. As soon as you try the caine, it will be even better, I promise you. Don't worry about getting hooked. We'll only experiment with the stuff and use it in our love-making."

"Malik, I'm putting everything in your hands. Please don't hurt me anymore. Love me, don't hurt me like you did two nights ago."

"Baby, I'm sorry, but you'll see, everything will be better for us starting tonight. I'm going to go and get something special for dinner and then I'm going to go and negotiate some caine for us." She kissed him goodbye and told him that she loved him.

On the way out of her building, she told the concierge, "As soon as my guest leaves, have the locksmith change the locks. Give him this envelope and tell him that he can pick-up his things later. The note is self explanatory, but just in case he has a problem reading it, tell him that he is not to ever come back here again. Tell him that the police have been notified and are on their way here. Mel, I'm sorry to ask you to do this, but things didn't work out and the guy was trying to get me to use caine."

"Monica, we all make poor choices sometimes. But I assure you, you're doing the right thing this time. He won't cause any trouble. Bubba is working downstairs, and I'll tell him that you have a little problem that you want us to take care of."

"Thanks, Mel. I'll see you later. I probably won't come home tonight. We have a training session over in New Jersey and I'm sure I'll be safe over there."

"Okay, Monica. You take care now. Don't worry about the problem. We'll handle it."

"Oh, and Mel, could you go up and get his things? There is no need for him to go back here. They're all neatly tucked in the big chest of drawers. He has three pair of pants in the closet and that's all. He never takes his gaudy jewelry off so that's all he has. Be careful with that envelope. I put $800 in it for him to get wherever in the hell he needs to go. Thanks again, Mel. I really appreciate your help. I just don't want him around here."

Two and one half hours later, Malik came strolling out of the elevator with a shit-eating grin on his face that no one could erase. He realized that he had accomplished his every goal: a place to live, a good-looking woman, plenty of clean sex and now the after hour powder, caine. Mel greeted him as usual and told him to have a nice day. After Malik was out of sight, Mel called down to Bubba and told him to go up and change the locks in Monica's place. Mel was not concerned whether Malik was gone for ten minutes or ten years, because as big as Bubba was, no one in their right mind would fuck with him.

Two hours later, the locks changed and Malik's things out of the apartment, Mel awaited the arrival of the outcast. Malik apparently couldn't wait to get back to Monica's place before he tried the caine. He was high when he arrived and it was noticeable.

"Sir, may I have a word in private with you?"

"Sure, Mel. What's up?"

"Sir, I have some rather depressing news for you. Your friend, Monica, has had the locks changed on the door and I have your things all packed for you. She also left this message for you, Sir. I'm sorry, Sir, but I cannot allow you to enter the premises. I would expect that you will handle this like the gentleman that you are and not create a scene for yourself."

"What the fuck are you talking about, Mel?"

"Sir, please refrain from using that vulgar language. I will try to explain it in another way." As Bubba rounded the hallway, Mel became more assertive. "I tried to use the Queen's English and explain to you that you have been evicted by your friend. Apparently, you did not understand that message. So, now I will try it another way—get your greasy bag and take your black ass out of here before I have you arrested, or even worse, before Bubba gets a hold of you. I hate to tell you, but for eight years now, Bubba has been in love with Monica, and he would probably love beating the shit out of you. So, Sir, please take your bag and this money and be gone. I would not try to see her again or come near this place if I were you. As you can see, you are on camera. A copy of a headshot of you has been forwarded to the police department. If by chance you have any outstanding warrants or traffic violations, they will be here shortly. So Sir, if I may be so bold, I suggest that you leave. NOW!" Malik started to say something and Bubba said, "Don't talk, just walk. If you say one word, I'll put this size 17 shoe up your ass." Malik looked at the opposition and realized that there was no winning here. He grabbed his bag and threw it over his shoulder. Upon reaching the door, he turned to Mel and said, "Fuck you, faggot." He looked at Bubba and said, "I would hate to put a hole in that big fat black belly of yours, motherfucker." He then pimped out of the door and never looked back.

He opened the envelope and thought to himself, *at least the stanky, scant bitch, paid her dues. I was about to ask her for rent money for using my dick.* Malik walked over to 5th Avenue and caught a cab to the rail station. He reasoned that if those guys sent his picture to the cops, they were for sure going to want to talk to him. He said to himself, *I'm going to hang out in Philly for a while and then head for DC.*

Arriving at the train station, Malik purchased a ticket on the Metro liner and awaited the announcement of the track number. He went into the only bar in the station and ordered himself a Coors Light. He guzzled the beer down and said aloud, "That bitch ought to be glad that I taught her how to fuck. A sorry motherfucker, don't do caine. You know I don't need to be with a bitch that don't do the Master."

The stairway to the train was announced and he descended the auto steps and got on the train. As he sat there looking at the Amtrak publication, a young woman got on and needed help with her luggage. Malik picked her bag up and placed it in the overhead bin. The woman thanked him. He knew that he had caught her attention, but decided to see where she was going before he made a play. The train started moving and the woman got up to go to the snack bar. She asked Malik if she could bring him something back. Malik told her that he would have whatever she was having. The woman said, "By the way, my name is Gina. What's yours?"

"My name is Malik and I'm pleased to meet you." As Gina walked away, Malik watched her curvaceous body disappear into the next car. He said to himself, *damn she got a bad body!*

When Gina returned she had two grilled chicken sandwiches, four bottles of Vodka and two bottles of Cranberry Juice. Malik looked at her and smiled. He said, "I was only kidding."

"You shouldn't kid with me, buster. I take everything at face value." She handed Malik his portion and returned to her seat. She said to Malik, "Do you mind if I sit next to you?"

"Of course not. It would be my pleasure if you did," he said.

Malik found out that Gina was on her way to Philadelphia and lived in Fort Washington. He asked her what she did for a living, only to find out that she was an investment broker for Merrill Lynch. Malik told her, when responding to the same question, that he was in his fourth year at the University of Pennsylvania. He immediately told her he didn't want to talk about careers or school because he had just had a whole week of that discussion with his mother and father in New York. To keep the conversation out of areas he felt uncomfortable, Malik spent his time talking about the two plays that he had seen. Gina had also seen them and was as impressed with them as he was.

The conductor came through the car collecting tickets. He told them that it would be an hour and fifteen minutes to Philadelphia. Malik realized that he had to work fast if he was going to take advantage of her. He took the opportunity to get right to the point. He asked if she lived at home and was happy about the response. She asked him where he lived and he told her with an aunt while he was in school. He talked about life and feelings for thirty minutes and completely captured her attention. All she could think of was that he was a sensitive man. A breed that's hard to find these days.

Fifteen minutes from the station, Malik asked her if she would like to have dinner with him that night. She agreed and he proceeded with the line that worked the best for him. "Can you meet me in town later?"

"I guess so, but it might be better if you just came to my place and we ate in the burbs."

"That sounds great, but I don't have a car at this time."

"You know, I would much rather have dinner tomorrow. I really have to prepare for work. All you have to do is catch the train out there and I'll pick you up. Maybe, if I'm not to tired, I'll cook for you."

"That sounds like a better deal to me," Malik responded. "Why don't you give me your number and I'll call you later?" Gina wrote her number down on a piece of paper and gave it to him. He helped her with her baggage and told her that he would carry it to her car if she wanted him to. She told him that she caught the train down because it was easier to leave her car in Fort Washington than it was to drive to the station. They shook hands and went their separate ways.

Malik went to the telephone and called one of his sleaze bags. She told him that there were guys around asking questions about him. Malik asked her what she said and she told him that she said she had only seen him twice. He asked her if she still had the credit card he gave her and she said yes. He told her to meet him over at the spot so that they could spend some time together and enjoy some good shit. Her response was, "What time?" He told her he would call her.

Malik really didn't trust Gail and decided that he would go to one of the motels on the strip and just hang out there. He caught a cab and told the driver where to take him. When he arrived, he checked in and gave the man a hundred and told him that he would be staying there for a few days. He entered his room, called Gina and started telling her how good it has been to meet her.

The conversation lasted for over two hours, and Malik knew that he had this one in the bag. He told her where he was staying if she got lonely. He told her he checked into the motel to escape the lip that his aunt was going to give him for getting two D's. Gina believed everything he said and told him that if she got lonely in the next hour or so, not to be surprised if someone knocked on his door. He hung up the phone and started watching television. The news was depressing for Malik. It started off with a caption that read, "IS THERE A VIGILANTE OUT THERE KILLING DRUG DEALERS?" Midway into the programming, the story was told. He knew every one of the dead caine dealers. He concluded with the idea that he had better get his ass out of town as soon as possible. He thought, *all I need now is a vigilante looking for me along with the cops for those two that I did.*

Malik started to watch HBO, but fell asleep. He had been asleep for over an hour when there was a banging on the door. It was Gina, looking for the ride of her life. Little did she know, she was with the right charlatan.

He started the conversation off by saying, "This must be my lucky day. I really didn't think that you were going to come all the way over here."

"I told you on the train, I take people at face value, and your values were something that I wanted to find out more about. Do you have anything to drink?"

"No, not really. Would you like to go out and have a drink?"

"I don't think so. Do you mind if I smoke a joint?"

"Not really, but I suspect we had better do it in the car or outside. I would hate for someone next door to call the manager and tell him we're smoking dope."

"Good thinking. Come on, let's go out and smoke this shit," Gina replied.

In the car, Malik asked her if that was all she did. She responded by saying, "I sometimes do a little caine."

"When we finish this shit, let's go back in. I think I have something that will make you real happy."

"Well, let's not waste time on this weak shit. Let's go and do a little caine." She put the reefer out and hid it beneath the carpet on her car floor. They entered his room and Malik pulled out his stash. They began to do the caine and it was obvious that Gina was already high from the reefer. He started kissing on her and she responded by taking off her sweater and blouse. The party was about to begin.

After much kissing and feeling, they started to have sex. Malik as his wicked self, jammed her legs behind her head and started pumping her as hard as he could. It was obvious that he was hurting her, but it didn't matter to him. She pleaded with him not to be so rough. He momentarily felt bad and slowed down his pace and the hard pumping. He pulled himself out of her and told her to take another hit on the caine. She jumped to the caine and took a big hit. Malik in the meantime remembered that wonderful ass he had seen on the train and decided that he was going to do her there. She resisted and told him that she had

206

to go, but he told her that after she sucked up all of his caine, she was going to earn it. At this point, the noise level was high. She was pleading and screaming and he was manhandling her and trying to negotiate her body into a no-denial position. She told him that he was raping her and he said, "Fuck you. You just did all of my caine. They don't call that rape; they call it payback." She tried to get up and Malik punched her in the back of her head. As she lay there motionless, Malik inserted himself into her anus and her entire body responded with a violent convulsion. Malik thought she was now beginning to enjoy herself. She tried to get him off of her, and again he punched her in the back of the head, but with much more authority. As he started his climb for the mother of orgasms, he grabbed her by the neck to make sure that she couldn't get away. He steadily pumped her harder and harder. When it came time for his orgasm, he grabbed her by the neck as tight as possible and shot his load into her anus. As he lay there, he mumbled to her, "Baby, I'm sorry. But it was wonderful." She didn't say anything because he had punched the base of her skull into her brain. The poor child, looking for face value, was now dead. Malik, feeling spent, fell asleep on Gina, not knowing that he had just committed another murder. It would be morning before Malik realized what had happened.

BOOK FOUR

CHAPTER ONE

FIVE MONTHS LATER

For the few minutes she spent sexually with Malik, Rashida had no idea she was carrying his child. She had no idea that she was pregnant and neither did anyone else. The Sarge, Courtney and Rashida talked about the issue at great lengths. There was only one feasible course of action, and that was for her to stay in school and have the child. Since Rashida was in the temporary custody of Courtney, a bad situation was made good. The one thing Rashida had that a lot of poor African American kids did not was a strong support system from Courtney and the Sarge. Each message was strong and supportive.

Five months later also found the Sarge and Courtney making plans for their wedding and the adoption of Rashida. Larry, on the other hand, was busy being a full-time student, and a good one at that. His first semester grades netted him a 3.67 grade point average. Larry and the Sarge had performed surgery only twice in the last five months.

Somewhere between Philadelphia and Miami, Malik was still doing his thing. The problem with catching Malik was that there were no pictures of him, and the composites only favored him by about forty percent. Besides being wanted for the deaths of the two police officers and the murder of Gina, Malik had several other charges lodged against him from DC to Miami. He hadn't changed a bit and would probably never change until he was dead.

CHAPTER TWO

Things in the community were beginning to show positive signs of reform. Neighbors were more likely to report dealers hanging around and selling caine. This was the beginning of an all-out crusade against the drug problem in the community. The newsletters kept coming from suspicious sources, giving the residents hope and determination.

There were territory feuds that left a few dealers dead on a corner that they did not own. The infamous SELL DRUGS AND DIE signs were being mailed to known and suspected dealers' places of residence. The police halfheartedly looked for the killer of the dealers and often spoke of how nice it was to have an unknown *edge*. The Sarge and Larry continued their program of harassing the dealers. Many had been evicted from their apartments in the projects and were basically shit out of luck. The one thing that the dealers realized was that they couldn't go just anywhere and sell caine because that was a sure way to get themselves killed. The slime from Baltimore had other plans. He saw a wide-open territory and often jokingly thanked the vigilantes for helping his business to grow. He had told his cronies that he wanted to have a meeting with them to work out the details of a new protection scheme. He set up a meeting for Thursday night.

During his normal workday, the Sarge often heard the undercover cops talking about something major about to happen in the community. He asked one of the officers what was happening. He told the Sarge that one of his stoolies had told him something big was about to happen and that a guy from Baltimore was spearheading the action. The Sarge asked what their plans were and was told that they were just going to watch and take pictures. He also told the Sarge the dealers were concerned about the many hits that had taken place against their brethren. He told the Sarge, in case of problems, they wanted at least four black & whites on standby. The Sarge told him that it would be done.

Later that night, the Sarge and Larry were sitting around talking about what was expected of Larry as one of the groomsmen for the Sarge's wedding. As the news came on, the same old grim headlines caught their eyes: MAJOR DRUG WAR GEARING UP IN SOUTH PHILLY. They listened intently as Lisa Thomas Tora began her breaking news story by saying, "It looks as though the vacancies for drug dealers in South Philly are drawing scum from near and far." The two men listened to her story and agreed that this was the one that would probably keep the dealers away for a long time. Larry asked the Sarge if he could get any preemptive information. The Sarge told him that he was working on it. Larry excused himself and told the Sarge that he had to study for two exams tomorrow and that he wanted to ace them. Larry then told the Sarge he would rather get them going than coming. The Sarge looked at him and shook his head.

On Thursday, the so-called day of the pow-wow, nothing happened. All of the information provided by the stoolies was designed to cover-up the real day of the meeting. The Sarge felt this was too well publicized for anything to come of it. As he and Smitty talked about the situation, the dispatcher received a call that there was a gun battle in progress at Building #903 on South 2nd street. The Sarge reminded Smitty that it was that building where they both got shot. He asked Smitty if he wanted to go and Smitty told him, "Stop talking and let's get over there."

There must have been fifteen black & whites on the scene when the Sarge and Smitty arrived. The Sarge asked the first officer he ran into what was going on. He was told that it seemed as though two dealers shot three people because they believed they were the leaders of the group trying to put them out of business. He was also told that there was a message on the walls for all of the residents of the building. The Sarge and Smitty walked into the hallway and saw the sign in big red letters—FUCK WITH OUR BUSINESS AND YOU WILL BE NEXT! The sign infuriated the Sarge and he cursed like a sailor at the wall. Smitty tried to calm him down, but to no avail. The Sarge asked the detective in charge, "Do we have any descriptions of the punks?" The detective said, "What do you think? You have three people shot for trying to get rid of those motherfuckers, Sarge. Don't ask me a dumb question like do we have a description. No one is talking." The Sarge stared at the detective and never said a word. As he was walking away, the guy said, "Hey, Sarge, I'm sorry man. I just thought that we had made some inroads here and I hate to see those little fuckers hold these people hostage. I didn't mean to sound off on you like that."

"It's okay. I think that we have the same interest and I was just a little irrational when I saw that sign. No harm, no foul. We'll find those little bastards." On the ride back to the station, not a word was said and Smitty knew that the Sarge was pissed. He had never seen the Sarge blow his cool like that.

As the shift was about to end, Smitty saw that the Sarge's demeanor hadn't changed a bit. He put his hand on his shoulder and told him, "Relax this evening and don't think about this shit." The Sarge told Smitty that he would see him tomorrow.

At home, a pensive Larry was walking back and forth with no destination in mind. When the Sarge opened the door, Larry told him that his antics had been captured on television. Larry then said, "We have to do it big time this time." He told the Sarge to sit down because he was going to get them both a Coors Light.

"Take a big hit of this, Sarge. Do you have any idea who had this done?"

"I think I do, Larry. I think I do."

"Well, are you going to enlighten me or keep me in suspense?"

"I think that dude from Baltimore had something to do with it. I just feel it. It looks like his style of terrorism."

"Do you know when he's coming to town?"

"I think he's already here. I think I know how to find out, but it may tip our hand."

"Then leave it be. Get me a picture of him and I think that I can find him. I'm sure he's not going to hang around town much longer knowing that he may have caused the execution of three people. If you get his picture, I'll just hang around the station for a day or so."

"I know a better way. Two of the people he'll most likely meet with are egomaniacs. If we do them, then the man is going to get the hell out of town in a hurry. I think that we can get them tonight if you want to."

"Oh, I want to, Sarge. I know old man Wilson and he never bothered anyone."

"Okay, it's five o'clock now. I'm going to change and go to a few bars that I know these dudes frequent. I'll call you about ten or so. They're night owls and I know where they'll most likely be after their meeting with that jerk from Baltimore. You may only have an hour or so to get the work done. But if I call you, you only do the work if it's safe and you can get away without running."

"Don't worry, Sarge. My goal is to finish college on campus and not by correspondence."

"You're such a nut, Larry. I don't know why I like you."

"Because I'm a carbon copy of your ass, Sarge. I love you too."

Calmly and attentively, Larry went back to studying. The Sarge reminded him of the number to the equipment room and Larry said to himself, *he really must think I'm daft.*

After about an hour and a half of studying, Larry decided to install the barrel in what was to become his favorite piece. He

216

went to the basement and checked the weapon and realized that there was something loose. He donned a pair of surgical gloves and picked another 9 millimeter and a fully loaded clip. He looked at it and decided he had better take two clips just in case. He was aware that there would be plenty of targets tonight and felt that the additional clip may come in handy. He went over to his stash of disguises and decided that homeless was indeed the thing he didn't want to be, therefore, looking this way would certainly keep his goals in front of him. Everything now ready, he went over his make-believe checklist and again noticed that he had left out surgical gloves. Now all he could do was wait for the Sarge to tell him what was up. He picked up one of his books and began to read.

At 9:45 the telephone rang, and to his surprise it was Courtney. They talked for a few minutes and he told her that he would give Sarge the message. He asked her how Rashida was doing and promised to get over soon to see the both of them, or as he put it all three of them. Courtney reminded Larry that Rashida was in need of all of the friends she could come up with. Larry told Courtney he would be over tomorrow.

At ten o'clock, Larry began to get comfortable. At 10:05 the telephone rang and it was the Sarge. He told Larry that he would not believe who was in the bar with him at 8th & Race. Larry asked the Sarge who and Sarge said, "Lord Baltimore" and that he should come over and kiss his ring. Larry told the Sarge that he was out the door.

Exactly 30 minutes later, looking like a bum, Larry drove by the bar and then two blocks east and parked the wreck. He hurriedly walked towards the bar. He went in and asked the tender for a glass of wine. The tender told him, "Get the hell out of here and don't come back." The Sarge was not sure it was Larry, but somehow suspected that it was him. Larry pulled out a crumpled five spot and told the man that he had money and wanted a glass of wine. The tender told him that if he didn't get his raggedy ass out of there now, he was going to beat the shit out of him. The man from Baltimore whispered to one of his cronies to buy the bum a glass of wine, but to throw it in his face. The tender poured the wine and the guy picked it up and threw it in Larry's face. He then grabbed Larry by the collar and threw him out the door. The Sarge saw this action and decided that he had better get out of there in a hurry. As Larry staggered up the street, the Sarge got in his car and drove around the block. Larry turned the corner and the Sarge caught up with him and asked him if he was all right. Larry told him that he was fine and that everything would happen without a hitch. He told the Sarge to go home and not to the diner, he wouldn't be going there tonight. He had to study. The Sarge told him to be careful and drove off.

As he walked back towards the bar, Larry saw one of the guys on the work order looking around and then proceeding up the block. Larry put a hustle in his step and saw that the guy was getting the car for the subject from Baltimore. As the guy hit the remote alarm to the car, Larry put a round right in the back of his head. He fell down between two cars and Larry ran up on him and took his hat, coat and car keys. Larry was hoping that he was supposed to get the car for the others. He then drove the car around the block and parked it right in front of the bar. First out of the door was the ruffian who threw the wine in Larry's face. After scanning the mirrors to see if there was traffic, Larry knew that it was now or never. As the hooligan opened the door for the subject from Baltimore, and as he bent down to enter the car, Larry put a round right in the Man from Baltimore's mouth, blowing the back of his head completely off. He shot the doorman in the belly first so that he had to bend over, and after bending over the hood caught a round in the forehead. Larry got out of the car and walked up the block as though nothing had happened.

Once in the wreck, he drove down to South 2nd street. Right in front of the building numbered 903, three guys were selling

218

caine. Larry knew one of them and realized that they were just roadsters. He walked through the breezeway and one of the punks said, "Who the fuck are you?" Larry, still acting as though he was drunk, said, "Fuck you and leave me alone." The guy ran up behind Larry and kicked him in the ass, at this point a sore spot in his psyche from the prison rape. Larry pulled the 9 mm and blew his head off. The other two tried to run and Larry capped them both. One was still alive and Larry asked him in no uncertain terms, "Who shot those people here the other day? If you don't tell me, I going to put a bullet in your dick and then one in your mouth." The wounded guy said, "Harvey D and Jake Smith did them." Larry started walking away and heard the sound of a weapon being cocked. He turned and put the ending round in the guy's head. He took their drugs, spread them over their bodies and then put the sign on them, "DEAL DRUGS AND DIE!" Larry never missed a step and never panicked.

Upon reaching the wreck, he started it and drove off. He pulled onto 95 South, pulled over with the flashers on and got out of the disguise. He knew the wreck was becoming too visible and decided that everything had to go. He got back in the wreck, pulled off of 95 South at Broad Street and made a U-turn around the sports complex and then on to 95 North. He drove up to Croydon near the water. There he started a fire and burned the clothes and took the battery out of the wreck and threw it into a stagnant pool of water. He walked for a while and threw pieces of the disassembled weapon into various parts of the river. Larry found his way to the rail line and caught the train into the city. He caught a cab from the train station to home, where an anxious Sarge was awaiting his arrival.

"What the hell happened tonight?" the Sarge asked.

"I just figured I would do a little housecleaning and send a stronger message, that's all."

"Jesus, Larry, you left six people dead tonight."

"I know, Sarge, and I feel like shit. I hope you're not going to make me feel any worse."

219

"No I'm not, but I thought I was the buffer and you were the workman?"

"You are, Sarge, but after I did the work at the bar, I drove down to the community and took a walk. A roadster kicked me in the ass and I did him and his caine-selling buddies. It was clean. I placed the shit on them and then the sign and walked away."

"What did you do with the equipment?"

"I got rid of everything, including the wreck."

"Oh no, not my baby?"

"If that was your baby, then I don't want to see your lover."

"I'm just kidding about that, but I'm not kidding about the fact you acted on your own. Don't ever do that again. Is that a deal?"

"I promise you, Sarge, I will never act alone. I told you that they knew who did old man Wilson and you should have known that I was going to go for them. I got the name of those guys who did those people in the community."

"Who are they?"

"A Harvey D. and Jake Smith. I know them both, and it will be easy to do the work on them if you'd like for me to. But right now I have to go and study. We'll talk about what's bothering you tomorrow. Oh and by the way, I told Courtney that I would visit Rashida tomorrow after school, and she told me to tell you to call her."

"You know what's bothering me, Larry?"

"Sarge, you're wondering how I can do the work on six guys and tell you that I have to study. Am I right?"

"On the money."

"It's simple, Sarge—because I have to study. Okay, all jokes aside, I don't like those guys, Sarge. They're the scum and if it wasn't for you, someone might be out there doing the work on me. I hate to see what it has done to an entire community. I want to help in cleaning it up. My mind has mixed feelings at times, but when they do people like old man Wilson, I know that what we're doing is right because we have what the police don't."

"What's that, Larry?"

"*The EDGE*, Sarge. We have *The EDGE*."

"Larry, on Sunday, we're going to church. So don't make any plans. We need divine guidance."

"A splendid idea, Sarge. I feel strongly that I need to be purged and forgiven for what I've done, no matter how right or wrong. I look forward to Sunday. Sarge one more thing. You're the man and I am your subject. I respect you and love you and I am eternally grateful for what you have done for Rashida and I. I will never do what I did tonight under any circumstances, I promise you. See you later, Pop."

The news stations were covering the story with wild enthusiasm. All kinds of headlines suggested that caine dealers were a dying breed. Other headlines stated, "LIKE THE SPOTTED OWL, GRIZZLY AND BROWN BEAR, COCAINE DEALERS ARE IN NEED OF PROTECTION OR THEY WILL SOON BECOME EXTINCT." The good news out of all of this was that the police were without a clue and could get no information on the Shooter. There was no information about his motives or anything else, and this left the police in a quandary. In the newspapers, including business papers like the *Bald Street Journal*, the Shooter was being heralded as a prelude to justice for caine pushers. One Midwest paper called the Shooter, "The Second Coming of Christ." Talk shows were hosting people of character and position and asking them about the good and the bad of the Shooter. Reggie Bilkes of the *Today and Last Night Show,* programmed a solid hour of interviews with experts and average people to solicit their feelings on the good or bad of the Shooter's activities. All in all, the consensus was unanimous. "Good work, Shooter! Keep it up!" The experts, concerned that these comments had the notions of anarchy, continued to express the tenants of the Constitution and the laws that govern a democracy. Their contention was that the Shooter was a lawless judge and jury and a criminal himself or herself. But the average citizen responded by saying, "The Shooter is keeping the streets clean of filth and he should be applauded and paid."

Also in the news that night, "Woman's Body Discovered in Motel Room." The story of Gina and her unfortunate night of looking for face value was starting to unfold. The fingerprints and the description of the suspect pointed to the elusive and well sought after Malik. Malik was beginning to make the situation a bit easier for the police. He was seen getting out of the victim's car at the train station. The law now knew which direction to look for this elusive and unidentifiable character that was also wanted for the shooting deaths of two police officers.

CHAPTER THREE

The next morning prior to leaving for school, Larry and the Sarge met in the kitchen and Larry said to the Sarge, "You owe me dinner, big time, Sarge."

"What for, Larry?"

"Although it has been longer than two months, I think that my return on investment beats yours by $1,800."

"No way, Larry. You couldn't have made $1,800 in this amount of time."

"Sarge, you lost the bet. I made investments in TEP and CML. I brought CML at $14.25 and it's now selling for $36.75. I got TEP at $1.12 and it's selling now at $3.75. The overall increase in my portfolio is $1,800."

"You think you're smart, don't you?"

"No, I don't. I think you owe me dinner, that's all."

"Good work, Larry. However, let me tell you what I've been able to do. I brought IBM at $46.25; it's now trading at $55.75. I've also brought Intel at $53.50, and its now trading at $119.75. I increased my portfolio by $15,500. I guess that you need to reconsider who owes whom dinner. I like when a novice tries to show off for me. But I will say one thing—you have learned to work that system. Now keep it up and you'll have financial independence well before I drop dead."

"Sarge, don't talk like that. I mean it. Don't talk like that." Larry rushed out of the kitchen and went upstairs into his room. The Sarge came behind him and found his young protégé crying on his bed. "Son, what's wrong?" Larry told the Sarge that he was all he had and didn't want to think of him just dropping off like that. He also told the Sarge that it wasn't a joking matter or a conversation that he held lightly. The two men embraced and went back downstairs to finish their coffee. The Sarge told Larry that he had to go and wanted to know what night dinner was. Larry told him to pick any McDonalds and he would meet him there. The Sarge told him that he had better save at least $300 because dinner at LeBec Fin was an extravagant and costly experience. The two men went their separate ways—the Sarge to work and Larry to school.

CHAPTER FOUR

The metamorphosis occurring in the community was unbelievable. Residents in each of the buildings were coming and going with a newfound sense of freedom and immunity from fear. They began to hold social events once again and organized a group called "TAD" (Tenants Against Drugs). TAD was designed to provide the tenants with a comprehensive strategy and action plan against being terrorized by pushers and dealers. They developed a forum that warned, "If you hurt one of us, we'll hurt five of you." The tenants were doing exactly what the Sarge had hoped, organizing their community against those who would deal in caine. Old man Wilson was the cornerstone of the organization, and all of the members were determined to never allow the kind of terrorism that existed for eight years to ever threaten them again.

The dealers and pushers, on the other hand, recognized that there was a villain out there decreasing the size and scope of their network and workforce. The temporarily abandoned neighborhood was also the topic of high-level discussions among those who would finance the activity on a large scale. A group called the "Association of Bankers" met monthly to discuss profits and losses in their illicit underground financial business. It had been reported that profits had decreased by over 2 million dollars in the last 9 months. The key reason was that the Shooter had been spreading the product over his victims. Mr. Joshua Bunbury, the chairman of the group, had one message for the organization to give to its dealers: "Make an example of those niggers and get our money back." This statement was tantamount to all-out war with the community. The group decided that it needed a new enforcer and suggested that Ray Z. be made the new team leader. This, of course, would require the elimination of the current enforcer. They all agreed and Mr. Bunbury said, "We'll kill a few niggers and spics and make it look like the Shooter did it. They're not a part of our world and that's why it's good business for us to keep them in their place, but using our product." The meeting ended with Mr. Bunbury indicating that he would take care of all of the necessary arrangements.

For almost seven years, the Sarge and nearly every policeman on the force had tried to find a way to nail Mr. Ray Z. It had been alleged that he was the mastermind behind the fire bombing of a policeman's house that killed the officer, his wife and three children. The case was never brought to court because there was no real evidence linking Mr. Ray Z to the crime. His alibi was impeccable and it never once deviated. He was known for his ruthlessness. It was once alleged by an associate of Mr. Z that he filled a hypodermic full of heroin and shot it into the neck of a guy who stole five dollars worth of drugs from him. There were other stories including one about the murder of a child because the child's father wouldn't tell him where he hid his drugs. Yes, Mr. Z was definitely a bad one.

About an hour after his meeting with the Association, Mr. Bunbury made a call to Mr. Z. He told him he wanted to place him in charge of the distribution centers and for him to take care of all of the loose ends. He suggested to Mr. Z that he make it look like the work of the Shooter. He also stated he would set the stage by telling the people he would be there for a meeting.

Later that night, Mr. Z and three of his thugs went to the distribution center to have the so-called meeting. He said to the man answering the door, "My name is Mr. Z. I have a meeting with the Man. Is he here yet?"

"No, he's not, but come on in. He called ahead for you."

Mr. Z and his crew went in and surveyed the place. He asked, "Where's Charlie?"

"He's in the back. Come on, I'll show you." Mr. Z motioned to two of his men to hang back and take care of the three guys packaging the product. He spoke to Charlie and told him the Man wanted him to handle that problem in the projects. Charlie said, "I think we're making a big mistake. We should just stay the hell out of there for a while." On that note, Mr. Z pulled his weapon, equipped with a silencer, and shot Charlie in the head. Mr. Z also fired a single round into the head of the woman who was keeping the books. He went over to the safe, opened it and placed all of the money and caine into a briefcase. He then went outside of the office and gave the signal for his men to shoot the others. BANG! BANG! BANG! BANG! Mr. Z told his men to drag the bodies out of the office and put them all together. He took the remaining product off the counters and placed it into the briefcase. He saved a little and threw it on the bodies. They neglected a telltale sign—the shooter always left the bags.

After making sure the scene looked like what he thought the Shooter would do, Mr. Z took one last look around the place to make certain everything was in order. He then went back into the office and picked up the books, which had blood all over them. The four thugs left the premises. Once in the car and underway, Mr. Z picked up the cellular phone and called the police. He said to the person answering the call, "This is the Shooter. You can find more slime at 1231 North Broad Street." He laughed when he hung up the phone. He told his men he needed a new place to set up distribution and he needed it by the weekend.

Two squad cars were sent to the address to check out the call. Arriving at the scene, the officers entered the premises and found the remains of five people, some with a single bullet to the head and others with various wounds. They reported the crime scene to the station, and the coroner and others were dispatched to the scene. One of the officers on the scene told the watch Lieutenant that it looked like the work of the Shooter. The Lieutenant agreed, but remarked that it was the first time the Shooter had ever called in his work. He also noticed that the bodies were neatly arranged, something that the Shooter never took the time to do. He finally admitted that there were too many similarities as well as inconsistencies and ruled that it wasn't the Shooter. He said, "This scene was created to make it look like the work of the Shooter from where I sit. I'll know more after the boys do some work on the bullets and dust for fingerprints. The Shooter never would have wasted time touching a victim after the fact unless he too has no consistent pattern of committing murder." The investigators continued their work into the early part of the morning.

CHAPTER FIVE

It seemed like deja vu as the Sarge and Larry met in the kitchen once again to have a cup of coffee. Larry said to the Sarge, "I didn't hear you come in last night."

"I guess you were studying too hard. I came in your room and turned the light out and you never moved, turkey."

"I guess I was a little tired. Is everything all right with you?"

"I'm fine, Larry. How about you? Is everything going along as usual?"

"I guess so. You know, Sarge, school is hard—okay, Sarge, don't give me that look. All I'm saying is that school is hard and takes its toll on you. You can bet your last dollar I'm not going to quit, but it's hard to try to pull a high average each time. I would like to graduate from college on the dean's list for all four years. As a matter of fact, I've been thinking about loading up on my courses and finishing early. The only problem with that is I think I need a job to contribute to you and the house."

"There's only one contribution that I want you to consider, Larry. The way you're investing your money should net you a pretty penny. I want you to take the dirty money and give it to a charity or start a scholarship fund with it."

"I swear you must be clairvoyant. I was thinking last night before I fell asleep that I should get rid of that money. I think it's dirty and every time I think about the shit, it reminds me of how I got it. I don't need that head job each time I spend a dollar."

"Then, son, do us both a favor and get rid of it. I think about it and I feel compromised. I say to myself, I can't force this issue on him considering the other things we're about, but it's important that we both have good mental feelings about that money."

"Sarge, I think I have the perfect solution."

"Well, don't stand there like a clown. Tell me what the solution is."

229

"I think I'm going to give half to a rehab center for drug and alcohol abuse, a quarter to OIC and a quarter to the United Negro College Fund. I like what Bill Wray is doing with that organization."

"Good man. I like you even more now than I did two minutes ago."

"Okay, I've got to get going. Tomorrow I'll drive over and get the money. We'll just make cash contributions and forget about it."

"Cash has the ability to compromise people, Larry. I suggest you get the money and bring it here. Then we'll make contacts with the organizations, write them a check and deposit the money to cover it. Each transaction should be about $10,000 and that way no one should get suspicious. If we're ever asked, we say that we hit the number and made some of it in Atlantic City. As a matter of fact, I would like to take a run down there and see if my luck is any good."

"That place is a sucker's bet, Sarge. You can't win down there. But if it makes you feel any better, I'd like to see if my luck has changed any. It can't be any better than it is now that I'm with you."

"You know, I don't know if you're hustling me or you're for real sometimes."

"Trust me, Sarge, I don't kid around with how I feel about what you've done for me. It's a real feeling."

"Get going before you're late for school, turkey. I'll see you later. Did you stop by and see Rashida yesterday?"

"No, I didn't have time, but I called her and told her that I would pick her up from school and take her for something to eat."

"Good man. Treat her like your sister and make sure that she doesn't need anything. If she does, take care of it and I'll take care of you."

"Give me a break, Sarge. If Rashida needs anything while she's with me then I'm going to take care of it, and I don't expect you to take care of me for doing it either. I would do it because I want to."

"Good man. Don't forget to tell her about church on Sunday."

"Don't worry. I think after we eat, I may take her shopping for a few of those maternity outfits. I'm sure she could use a few things."

"How much money do you have with you?"

"I have $350. That should be enough if she needs anything. Okay, Pops, I've got to go. I'll see you later." As Larry was about to leave he grabbed the Sarge by the shoulder and froze. He said, "Sarge, did you forget something?"

"No, Larry, why?"

"Where's your vest?"

"Oh shit, how could I forget that thing? Thanks, kid, talk to you later."

At the station, everyone was talking about the latest work of the Shooter. The Sarge joined in to hear the latest and was terrified at the thought that Larry had developed his own list. As the officers continued to say how the Shooter had changed his M.O., the Sarge felt a little better thinking that it was a would-be clone trying to lay the blame, but nevertheless, he was going to try to reach Larry to see if he was responsible. He realized the one thing Larry had never done before was lie to him, and he felt confident that if Larry had done the work, he would tell him.

"Hey, Sarge, what's happening?" a joyful Smitty rang out.

"Nothing much. What has your belt so tight today?"

"I met her last night."

"You met who, Smitty?"

"I met the woman who I'm going to marry. She's incredibly beautiful and as smart as can be."

"Well, I wouldn't marry her if I were you."

"Why not?"

"Well, if she's as smart as you say she is, then it won't take her long to figure out that you're not a rocket scientist or even a smart cop."

"Nasty, Sarge, nasty."

"Come on, Smitty, you know that I'm only picking you. Where did you meet her and when will I meet her?"

"We met at the bowling alley last night, and don't worry, you'll never meet her."

"Smitty, I was only kidding. Now lighten up."

"Got you! I know that man, stop being so sensitive. Your big day is in three weeks. Are you ready?"

"I didn't know that I had to do so much to get ready. All I have to do is show up, right?"

"That's a lot for the average man, Sarge. To show up is to complete your fate. Did you hear that the Shooter has changed his M.O.?"

"I heard them talking, but I didn't get the details. What did you hear?"

"The Shooter called after the hit to tell us where to find the bodies. This time our boy made a few mistakes. There were fingerprints all over the place, and a witness saw a car leaving the scene at about the right time. The boys downstairs are running a make on it now."

"Why would he suddenly get careless like that, Smitty? It doesn't make sense to me. Do you think he wants to get caught or something?"

"You know, Sarge, you're right. That doesn't make sense at all. Why would a guy who we don't even have the smallest clue as to who he is, suddenly start leaving fingerprints, making telephone calls and allowing himself to be seen leaving the scene? I think we have a copycat out there who may be a little more dangerous than the Shooter. The Shooter is an expert; this clown is scary."

"That was a good piece of police work, Smitty. You analyzed that scene perfectly. Now that you've said it, I really don't believe it was our boy, if he did all of those dumb things. Good police work, Smitty. Tell the Lieutenant before he goes home."

As usual, the Sarge called his bride-to-be and told her how much he loved her. She in turn asked him when was he going to get over to show it so that she could feel it. He asked her to think about what they were going to do with two houses and that he would ask her again later. They hung up and Courtney became ecstatic. She went down the hall saying out loud, "He wants to know what we're going to do with two houses. We're going to sell them and buy one big one." Of course people looked at her as if she had just lost her mind, but it didn't matter to Courtney because she was in seventh heaven.

Everybody's day had gone well except for Rashida, and Larry was about to fix her problems. At three o'clock, he waited outside the school for Rashida. Rashida came out the door with tears in her eyes and was followed by two rough looking girls and two thugs. One of the girls ran up behind Rashida and hit her in the back of the head, knocking her to the ground. The others just stood there laughing and yelling, "Get up, slut! Because you're pregnant ain't going to keep us from kicking your ass." Larry jumped out of the car and ran toward the crew. He punched one of the guys in the mouth and neutralized the other with a swift kick to the groin. He grabbed the girl who slapped Rashida and slapped her into next week. The other girl reached in her bag and pulled out a butcher's knife. She swung it at Larry, catching just a small part of his left arm. Larry anticipated her next swing. When he jumped back she missed, and Larry caught her with a left hook to the jaw, breaking it on contact. By this time a crowd had gathered and the policeman on duty interceded. The two guys were still trying to get to Larry when the cop pulled his nightstick and hit one of them across the arm and told him the next blow would be up side his head. The officer radioed for assistance, and within minutes two cars were upon the scene. As they dispersed the crowd, the officer began trying to sort out the details of this altercation. One of the guys told Larry that he was a dead man. Larry, with the coldest possible stare, said, "You would rather commit suicide than to fuck with me or my sister again." Those words would ring in the ears and heart of Rashida for a long time, because it only solidified the fact that she wasn't alone in this world.

As the officers attempted to sort through the circumstances of the event, it was decided that they all would be taken to the police station. Larry asked if he could drive the car and follow them. One of the officers told him to place his hands behind his back. Larry asked, "For what?" The officer instructed him to do so or face the consequences. Larry told the officer that the car belonged to Sergeant Beckmire and that he would at least like to lock it up. The cop told Larry to shut up or he would shut him up. Rashida and Larry were placed in one car and the others in another car.

At the station, a surprised Sergeant Beckmire witnessed Larry being brought in. He ran over and said, "What the hell is going on?" The smartass cop said, "This jerk beat up four kids at the school."

"Is that true, Larry?"

"Sarge, that chick hit Rashida in the back of her head and knocked her down to the ground. Now, was I supposed to sit there and watch them hurt her and maybe even the baby?"

"No, son, you did the right thing. Where is Rashida now?"

"I think she went to the bathroom."

"I'll be right back. I'm going to check on her. In the meantime, get those damn cuffs off of my son."

Smitty turned a corner and said to Larry, "What's going on?" Larry told Smitty that he now understood why so many people disliked and distrusted policemen. The rookie cop knew that his ass was in a sling, but stood there as though he was correct in his handling of the situation.

Returning from having a female officer check on Rashida, the Sarge asked Larry, "Where is my car?"

"That overzealous officer wouldn't let me drive it or lock it up. I told him that it was your car, but it didn't seem to matter to him."

"Is that true, officer?"

"How was I to know that it was your car?"

"Did my son tell you it was?"

"I don't remember."

"MacMillan, did you hear him tell you guys that it was my car?"

"Sarge, I did, but I was busy trying to make sure that blade was recovered."

"Looks like you got scratched, Larry."

"Yeah, that rough looking one tried to cut me to pieces."

"Okay, son, just watch out for Rashida when she comes out. I'll be right back. What's wrong with that girl over there?"

"I don't know, Sarge, but her friends said that Larry hit her in the mouth."

"Is that true, Larry?"

"Yes, Sarge. She tried to cut me with that knife."

"Good man. You should have broken her damn jaw."

Rashida came out of the bathroom and was greeted by a big hug from the Sarge. He told Smitty to take her in the Captain's office for a few minutes until he finished up. The Sarge then told the three officers who were at the scene to come into the interrogation room. In the room, everyone heard the Sarge through the sound retarding windows, (kicking their asses). He told the smartass cop that he was going to recommend that he be suspended for improper behavior inconsistent of a police officer. The Sarge continued to kick their asses. The sweat running down their faces as the Sarge charged over and over again, into their asses. The Captain came back and saw what was happening and said, "Oh shit, I see some people getting time off for bad behavior." The precinct was as quiet as possible. Everyone knew that the Sarge ran the whole show from the cells to the court.

After leaving the room, the Sarge went into the Captain's office and introduced Rashida as his daughter to the Captain. She had already explained to the Captain what had happened, and he wanted to lock those little bastards up. The Sarge assured him that he would take care of the problem and requested that the Captain entertain his child for a few minutes.

The four young thugs had witnessed the Sarge go off on the cops. The Sarge told them to get up and get their asses in the room. Once inside, he realized that the girl's jaw was broken. He called for a female officer to take her to the hospital and to contact her parents and to tell them that she would be arrested for assault and battery and for carrying a concealed weapon. The others, hearing this, knew that their shit was downhill as well. The looks on their faces were no longer the looks of tough kids. The Sarge lit into them like new money. He ranted and raved for over an hour, stopping just long enough to have someone come in and get their telephone numbers, so that their parents could be told where they were and where they would be for a long time. He asked each of them, "How on earth could you hit a pregnant lady?" Every time they started to answer, he would light into them again. He called Smitty in and told him to "book these thugs." The kids broke out crying and the Sarge told them to shut the hell up or he'd lock them up in the dungeon with all of the killers, rapists and real bad people. When he came out of the room he was still mad as all hell, and everyone knew to keep their distance. He told the smartass cop, "You had better get my car back here in a matter of minutes." He also told him that he hoped it had been vandalized so he could make sure that he got rid of his sorry ass. He told the cop this in front of all of his peers, a punishment that was worse than suspension without pay.

After doing a little paperwork, the Sarge told Smitty to transfer the punks to juvenile and make sure that they were kept overnight. He also told Smitty to make sure nothing happened to them, meaning to keep them isolated from the real bad kids. He asked Larry if he needed to have his arm checked and Larry told him that it would be all right. The Sarge told him just the same, they were going to go over to the hospital to get him a tetanus shot. On his desk, the Sarge had the latest composite of Malik. Larry told him to add a mustache and shorten the sideburns. The Sarge whispered, "Thanks, Son."

As the Sarge was preparing to leave the station, he turned to Smitty and said, "I'm going to take care of my family. Tell the Captain that I left a little early. I'll see you tomorrow."

"Sarge, before you go, I want you to know that while you were in there with those officers, the whole precinct was on your side. They felt real bad for Larry and Rashida. I just wanted you to know that, Sarge."

"Thanks, Smitty." The Sarge got to the door and decided to turn around and thank the men. "Hey guys, hang in there. If we don't look out for our own, who will?"

The men felt those words and knew that he meant them. The Sarge was a man who would do anything for a fellow police officer and had often supported the wives of fallen victims with scholarship monies for the kids. They all knew that he was a helluva guy, and they hated to see those cops shit on him and his adopted family in public.

The Sarge and Rashida got into the car and Larry followed him in the truck to the hospital. Once at the hospital, he pulled them aside and said, "You've got to look out for each other." He looked at Larry and said, "No one puts a hand on your sister, ever!" He looked at Rashida and said, "I love you, little lady, or should I say I love both you and the baby. Since Larry has to get

237

looked at, I'll have the doc look at you too, Rashida. Can't have anything happening to you two from some B.S. now can I? This will give me an opportunity to see my bride-to-be."

"That's probably the only reason you insisted that we come to the hospital in the first place," Larry responded.

"So what if it is. Do you have a problem with that?"

"Not at all, Casanova. I like watching you meet your match. It gives me a good feeling."

The Sarge looked at Larry and Larry knew that a question from left-field was on its way. The Sarge pulled Larry aside and said, "Speaking of Casanova, Larry, did you do five people in a warehouse last night?"

"Hell no, Sarge. I didn't do anybody last night."

"I figured you didn't. We may have a problem. It seems as though someone tried to imitate your style last night, but made some critical mistakes. He left his fingerprints, arranged the bodies and spread only a little bit of the product on the bodies."

"That's not how I do it. You know how I do it."

"I know, but for a minute, when I heard about the work, I immediately thought about you."

"Trust me, Sarge, it wasn't me."

"I know that, but I thought you might be able to appreciate the fact that you have a poor excuse for a clone out there."

At the hospital, everyone was okay and the Sarge got to see Courtney. He told Larry that he would see him later and got into the car to drop Rashida off at Courtney's.

CHAPTER SIX

The morning following the unfortunate incident, the police determined that it was not the work of the Shooter and had secured positive identification of the suspects. The suspects in question were known drug dealers and considered dangerous. This information was passed on to each officer during roll call. The identification and mug shots of two of the perpetrators were given to each squad. The Sarge looked at the shots and said, "Ladies and gentlemen, be careful. These two are known henchmen for the one and only Mr. Z. Most of you know what we'd like to do to that vermin, so be careful. They would rather kill us than pay a parking ticket. Also, this situation looks like a reorganization to me, so don't be surprised if you find more members of this group dead." This sobering information sent an uneasy and visible chill up the officer's spines.

Meanwhile, on the dark side of town, Mr. Z was setting up his operation. He had talked twice to Mr. Bunbury and assured him that they would be back in the community before the weekend was over. The community was a strong source of revenue because the drugs were rationalized as an escape from the horrors of poverty. The community members, on the other hand, had set up a neighborhood watch. They recorded tag numbers and gave general descriptions of people hanging around like the caine dealers of the past used to do.

Mr. Z instructed one of his men to find a dealer by the name of Frisco. Frisco had no heart and was considered soft in the world of dealing. However, he was the best marketer of products and generally had the best dollar return on investments. Mr. Z's idea was to fuse Frisco and some hard-liners in the community, thus creating a balance between sales and terrorism. His idea for a terrorist was a guy named MacKiller, so titled because he loved to use a machine pistol on people. MacKiller had another trait that few people knew about; he was an expert with explosives, which he learned during the Vietnam police action. The brains behind the killing of the police officer and his family may have been Mr. Z's, but the handiwork was that of Mackiller.

With the scene now set for a new market strategy, Mr. Z had the best of both worlds—the best salesman and the best enforcer. He told his people to have everyone in the community by five o'clock. He wanted to have a test run that evening to see how things worked out. Mr. Z realized that there may be some shooting, but was not bothered by that fact. In essence, he was looking forward to the work of MacKiller.

Later that evening, everything that could go bad went bad for Mr. Z. His two henchmen were involved in a gun battle with the police. One was shot dead and the other wasn't expected to survive. Three officers received minor wounds, the most serious being in the arm. A female officer received a wound to her wrist, but was able to fell the assailant with a bull's-eye through the heart.

At the hospital there was a beehive of activity in progress. Doctors were gallantly trying to save the life of the wounded suspect and had completed all they could possibly do for him. Detectives waited anxiously to interrogate him. The Sarge showed up at the hospital to check on the status of his personnel and was happy to discover they would all be okay. As he talked to the female officer, she told him that his words were as true as all hell. She indicated they stopped the guy for not having a tag on his car, and when they pulled him over, he started shooting.

Unbeknownst to anyone save Smitty, the Sarge knew the wounded victim. About ten years ago, the Sarge had tried to save him from the hangman, but the guy cursed the Judge into the middle of next month. There was nothing the Sarge could do for him. The Sarge entered his room and looked at all of the equipment hooked up to save his life. He leaned over the bed and said, "Hey Gus, anything I can do for you?" There was no answer and the Sarge asked him, "What is Mr. Z planning to do, Gus? I know you guys whacked those people at the distribution center. So why don't you do me a favor, like I once tried to do for you, and tell me what Mr. Z is planning?" Gus stirred a little and motioned for something to write with. The Sarge gave him a pen and a piece of paper and Gus wrote, "Fuck you." He then wrote, "Kill him and the banker Bunbury." He then died. The Sarge took the note and walked out of the room. The beepers came on indicating a cardiac arrest. The Sarge held the door open as doctors and nurses entered to perform their functions.

The Sarge went to a telephone, called Larry and told him to hang around—there was some business that needed taking care of. The Sarge knew he had to destroy the note, for any action against any of the parties would lead back to him and Larry. By the time the Sarge got home, Larry had packed his bag and selected a weapon and clips. "What's up, Sarge?"

"I think we can make a real difference tonight, Larry. There is a man whose name is Mr. Bunbury, who may be high up on the wheel financing the caine. He belongs to a group of yuppie bankers, and they all seem to have made a fortune overnight. I know where one of them hangs out, and I want you to kidnap his ass, put a round in his leg and make him talk. He hates to be in pain. Also, you can't go homeless tonight. The area is an upscale part of town, and you'd be arrested in that precinct area for vagrancy."

"I think I have the right outfit."

"More than the outfit, you had better come up with a damn good facial disguise. I don't want any problems with this one. If I'm right, he'll sing like a canary and we'll end this chapter of our lives."

"What does that mean, Sarge?"

"Simply that we will go on a long, long vacation from being the *edge*. You have less than an hour. I suggest you take my car since you got rid of the wreck."

"Well, driving your car is actually a step down from the wreck."

"Stay serious and stay focused, Larry. I'll be right behind you all the way. When you get his ass, drive him over to the project area and do the work over there. If he tells you everything and confesses, then complete the work on him. His name is Saul Bergenstein."

"What kind of car does Mr. Bergenstein drive, Sarge?"

"It's a white Porsche. Don't forget your gloves."

"Those were the first things that I packed."

Larry arrived in Jenkintown with about ten minutes to spare. He parked the car and surveyed the scene. The Sarge drove around the area in the Jeep and made sure that there were no cops hanging out. Larry parked the car about a quarter of a mile away and walked to the gym. He arrived at 8:00 on the button. Like clockwork, the subject came out of the gym and headed towards his car. Larry had positioned himself near the car, but not too close. As Mr. Bergenstein hit his remote unit for his alarm and opened the door, Larry was on him before he could react. "Open the door and don't make a sound," he ordered. With the barrel pointed at his head, Larry walked around to the passenger side, got in and told him to drive, but not too fast. Saul pleaded with Larry not to hurt him and promised him more money than he had ever seen. Larry told him to shut up and keep driving. After checking to see that he wasn't being followed except by the Sarge, Larry began his interrogation. "Do you know a Mr. Z, Mr. Bergenstein?"

"I've never heard of a Mr. Z."

"Do you know a Mr. Bunbury?"

"I swear to you I don't know either of those people." Larry cocked the trigger on the weapon and said, "You're lying. Mr. Bunbury and you were once partners—once because Mr. Bunbury thinks that you're the weak link in his operation." Mr. Bergenstein paused for a moment and said, "You're crazy. I don't know a Mr. Bunbury."

"Wrong answer." BANG! "Now that's just a flesh wound. The next round will tear your dick off." Mr. Bergenstein pleaded and begged for mercy and Larry said, "You don't show mercy when you sell that caine in the community do you? No, Mr. Bergenstein, you ask for more profits instead. This is your last chance, and I'm only going to ask you once. Don't try to do anything stupid because I'll blow your fucking head off, white boy. Now, do you know Mr. Bunbury and Mr. Z?"

"Yes, I know them both."

"I need an address on the center."

"It's in an apartment building in Penrose Park."

"Big help. What's the address?"

"7701 Lindbergh Blvd, apartment 107A."

"Thank you, Sir. Why would they want you dead? You're a member of the association and you play the game right. Why do they want you dead?"

"I don't know, but if you let me go, I'll pay you a hundred thousand dollars and I'll get the hell out of town."

"I'll do one better. You tell me where I can find Mr. Z and I'll let you go. But first of all, you have to tell me all the names of the members of the association, and who keeps the records and where." Mr. Bergenstein paused and looked at the blood running down his leg. "That wound is nothing. If I put this next round into your dick, then you'll really see a lot of blood," Larry stated.

"The books are kept by Josh Levin."

"Where does he keep them?"

"In his office downtown, in a safe."

"Why does Mr. Bunbury want to cause trouble in the community?"

"Because that's where the profits are. Nig—I mean blacks like caine. Where are you taking me?"

"I'm taking you to the community so that you can see what your product does to the lives of the people who live there, before I let you go. Do you do caine, Mr. Bergenstein?"

"I never do what I sell."

"Would you happen to have some that you didn't sell tonight on you?"

"No, I don't."

"Now, Mr. Bergenstein, if I open that bag of yours and find caine, I'm going to be mad as all hell."

"Okay, wait a minute. I do remember that one of the guys didn't show and I may have his stash in the bag."

"Good, Mr. Bergenstein. Now I want you to slowly reach back into the bag and pull out the stuff. If by chance you think that you are faster than my finger, then I welcome you to try something stupid." Mr. Bergenstein slowly reached into his bag and pulled out what had to be at least ten grand worth of caine. Larry said, "Do you always travel with this much product?"

"Only when I have a buyer."

"Now, Mr. Bergenstein, I'm going to get out of here in a minute. Now pull slowly in that lot over there and cut your lights out."

Mr. Bergenstein did exactly as he was told. Larry hesitated for a minute, but finally placed a round into Bergenstein's temple. He opened the door, got halfway out and then took the caine and threw it all over Mr. Bergenstein's lifeless body."

Larry walked for a few blocks and was picked up by the Sarge. He told the Sarge where Mr. Z was doing his production work and the two men headed for Southwest Philly.

After crossing Lindbergh Boulevard, the Sarge said, "That's the address. Walk around the front, Larry, and see where the apartment is and if anyone is home. I don't want to have the Jeep spotted so I'm going to drive up the street and wait for you there."

By the time Larry had walked around the front, surveyed the premises and started back to the truck, Mr. Z and one of his henchmen were walking up the driveway. Larry recognized him from a picture the Sarge had shown him. Larry said, "Mr. Z this is a long time coming," and fired two rounds into his head and one into his henchman. Larry then ran up the street and disappeared into the night. He caught up with the Sarge and told the Sarge to leave the lights out until they were out of the neighborhood. The Sarge asked, "What happened back there?"

"I ran into Mr. Z and told him goodnight, forever."

"Damn, you're good. Did anyone see you do the work?"

"I'm not sure, but it would be hard to identify me in all of this black shit."

"Let's go home and eat something."

"No, Sarge, not yet. I think that we should try to put a line on Mr. Bunbury and take him out tonight as well. All of the bank records are kept in a safe in Josh Levin's office. Maybe if we stop by a pay telephone, I'll disguise my voice and call the cops and give them that piece of information. What do you think?"

"I think that you're thinking too much, but I like the idea. Let's find a phone and get these turkeys out of the way."

The Sarge found a pay phone and Larry began his act. He insisted that he talk to the watch commander and was turned over to a lieutenant. Larry said, "Just listen because what I have to say is only going to be said once. Bankers are responsible for the caine problem in the area. In the office of Mr. Josh Levin you will find a safe with records of all the illicit money laundering and drug buying." Larry hung up the phone and the two men proceeded to where they could talk and figure out how to get to Mr. Bunbury.

The late news had Lisa Thomas Tora telling about a well-known banker was found dead with cocaine all over his body, replicating the scene from the work of the Shooter. She revealed the possibility that there was a conspiracy and that the banker was a financier of the events. She talked about the death of the infamous Mr. Z and his associate and wondered if there was any connection between the murders.

Mr. Bunbury, after hearing the news about what had happened, called Josh Levin. "Josh, this is Mr. B. Do you think the documents are safe where they are?"

"Not to worry. Our friend had no idea that we kept them in my place, did he?"

"Maybe not, but I don't want to take any chances. I want to move them tonight."

"Do you know what time it is?"

"Josh, I don't give a shit what time it is. Move the documents and place them in the box at our private club. From there we'll figure out a new home. Can't take any chances on Bergenstein; he may have begged for his life, if you know what I mean."

In the meantime back at the station, the Lieutenant had found a sympathetic judge who would give him a warrant to search and seize the records in Josh Levin's office. He instructed two officers to stake out the place and report the comings and goings of everyone who entered the building that night. He also instructed another officer to pull up the driver's record of a Josh Levin. He then told the officer to get all of the license plate numbers on the guy and to send an unmarked to keep an eye on him. No more than fifteen minutes had passed before Josh Levin pulled out of his driveway in a brand new 560SL and headed in the general direction of downtown. He pulled onto the expressway from his house and got off at Broad Street. From there he parked the car right in front of the building, and the guard recognized him and let him in. The boys in the unmarked called the Lieutenant and told him that the subject had just entered his office building. The Lieutenant told them to hold him there until he got there with the warrant.

Twenty minutes later the Lieutenant and two squad cars pulled up and all of the officers entered the building. The Lieutenant showed his badge and asked the guard what floor was Josh Levin's office located. The guard indicated that he was on the 23rd floor. The Lieutenant asked the guard to lock out five of the elevators and to leave one operational. He then assigned an officer at the only exit and told him to stay sharp. The rest of the officers and the Lieutenant caught the operational elevator to the 23rd floor and walked into Josh Levin's office. All of the lights were on in the office. After hearing the sounds of the entering policeman, Mr. Levin cursed them, pulled a pistol from his pocket and fired once, hitting the Lieutenant in the stomach. The rest of the officers opened fire on him and killed him instantly.

Assistance was called for the Lieutenant. An officer went over to the safe and said, "Jesus, this guy has enough drugs in here to supply a battalion of drug addicts."

Thirty minutes later the building was barraged with local police, FBI and Drug Enforcement Agents. They packed all of the records and drugs and carted them off for evaluation. The records would reveal some very impressive, high profile people in this scheme for cash from the sale of caine. It would net some of the so-called city leaders who couldn't resist the kind of return on investment that only the caine business could provide them.

Within thirty-six hours, the pool of law officers would arrest 30 big-name people who made their money off the misery of the poor by supplying the almighty caine. On the run, however, was Mr. Bunbury. It appeared that he had made one last withdrawal from his bank and thanked the many customers that trusted his institution. Somehow and some way, the long arm of the law, or the *edge*, would catch up with Mr. Bunbury.

CHAPTER SEVEN

With two armed robbery charges facing him in Virginia and an attempted murder charge in Jacksonville, Florida, Malik was running out of places to terrorize. Virginia desperately wanted him because during the course of one of his robberies, he pistol-whipped a 63-year-old white woman. The boys there were interested in a hanging.

A hidden camera in Virginia caught Malik in his entire splendor brandishing a pistol and yelling violent threats at his victim. His photo was put on the wire service, and every cop on the east coast was looking for Malik. Therefore, it was only fitting that he made his way back to the alleyways of Philadelphia where he could hide like the rat he was.

In another part of town, the Sarge and Larry were preparing to pick up the ladies and take them to church for some divine guidance. The Sarge was impressively dressed. He wore a gray double-breasted suit and fashionable shoes. He looked this day more like a banker than a part-time Christian. Larry wore a loose fitting double-breasted Armani suit. As the two men were preparing to leave, the Sarge got a call from Smitty. In essence, the call was about Malik. The Sarge turned to Larry and said, "He's back."

"Who's back?"

"Malik."

The men went across town and picked up two of the finest women in Philadelphia. Small talk was in order except when Larry started making innocent fun of Rashida. He asked her, "How on earth did you get into that outfit?" Courtney said to him, "Larry, you're not being very nice today."

He responded by saying, "Courtney, I can pick at her, but no one else had better, not including present company, of course."

"Larry, you're such a pig, but at least you smell good today," Rashida stated.

Church was great! There they stood—a family developed out of need and caring. The Sarge was very proud of his extended family, and all of the members of the congregation could tell. He beamed like a light from heaven. When the minister asked for visitors to stand and give their name and church affiliation, Sarge got up first and said, "Members of my church family, this is my new family. This handsome young man is Larry Holland, my new son, and this beauty queen who is full of life herself is my new daughter, Rashida Brooks, and the Queen of all Queens, my new wife to be, Dr. Courtney Harris." The minister said, "Praise the Lord. Can we say as a congregation, Praise the Lord?" The response from the congregation was awesome. Sergeant Beckmire had made a big hit with the congregation, not by asking them to open their hearts and let his new family in, but in essence, telling them these are the people who he loved. The sermon was great, centering on the need for family in everyone's life. Right on time insofar as the Sarge was concerned. It was a great day for everyone.

After service, the Sarge saw one of the prettier little ladies giving Larry the eye, and he wondered why Larry didn't acknowledge her stares. He asked, "Hey, Larry, did you see that little fox giving you the eye?"

"Sure did, Sarge, but I didn't want to blow my cool."

"Son, forget that cool shit, oops—almost forgot where I was. Forget that cool stuff and concentrate on having some fun and doing what comes natural with the women."

"I'd rather talk about that later. Right now, I just want her to know what she's missing. I think I'm going to join this Church next week." The Sarge smiled and walked over to where Courtney was being asked to consider joining the Church and participating in certain groups, such as the choir.

In the Jeep, the Sarge said, "It's too pretty out here to be going home. I suggest we take a ride out to the suburbs and look at a few houses." Courtney, responded, "Okay man, don't play with me."

"Sweetheart, I'm not playing. The other day I asked you to think about what we're going to do with two houses? Larry do you need a whole house by yourself?"

"Absolutely not, and I don't want to stay on campus either. I want to live with you, Dad."

"Courtney, you see what I've been putting up with. This little criminal drives me up the walls sometimes, but he's the only one I got and I love him. Now, Rashida, do you need a big house for you and the baby?"

"Of course not. I want to live where you guys are going to live. Otherwise, I might as well be carted off to one of those homes for unwed mothers."

"Rashida, don't you ever let me hear you talk like that. This is a truck full of love. There is no way that you're going to be sent away. Am I right, Sarge?" Larry asked.

"Wait, Sarge. I know where I am, Larry, and I sure don't need your big mouth to tell me."

"See, Sarge, I told you she loves me." Laughter erupted. The Sarge told Courtney that he had heard about some homes that had just been built in Fort Washington and that they should take a ride out there and have a look. Everyone agreed and the Sarge proceeded in the direction of the development.

Once in Fort Washington, they saw several different models that they liked initially. The one drawback most of the homes had was that they were situated on about half an acre. The Sarge felt that he would like to have at least one full acre in order to maintain some sense of privacy. As Courtney and Rashida talked with the agent, they were shown lots that had in excess of an acre of land. This caught the Sarge's attention and he became more interested. After more sales pitching from the agent, they received the pricing information and left.

Up the hill and around the corner rested the house that the Sarge liked. It had about 6,000 square feet of space and sat on an acre and a half of land. He told Courtney he liked this model and if she did also, they should seriously consider locking in the rate. She said that she would like to have a serious discussion with him a little later to talk about finances. He told her that he welcomed the opportunity to share how poor he was with her. Larry laughed and walked away.

Heading back into the city, Rashida said, "We're hungry." Larry seconded the motion and they stopped at a restaurant. The service was lax, but the meal was excellent. They ordered two rounds of the salad because the lettuce was so crisp and the dressing was out of sight. They all pigged out and enjoyed each other's company.

On the ride home, the Sarge told Larry that he wanted him to stay with Rashida for a while because he wanted to take Courtney out for a while and spend some quality time with her. Courtney looked at Larry and said, "I dare you."

Larry responded by saying, "Since you dare me, Courtney, I'm going to keep my big mouth shut." He turned to Rashida and said, "Hey kid, are you up for a movie?" Rashida said, "Oh yes, I would really like to see the Crying Game."

"So would I. Well, while the lovers are spending quality time together, we'll just go and get lost so that they can feel at home while we're away. Sarge, I think I'm going to need the Jeep. Rashida, do you have a problem getting in and out of here? We could always drive the other car or even Courtney's car."

"No, Larry, the Jeep is fun."

At Courtney's house, Larry said, "Hey, Courtney, can I have a word with you?"

"Just let me open the door and I'll be right with you."

"Courtney, I know that we haven't spent much time together, but I want to say I respect and honor the Sarge's choice in you as a mate. In other words, it will be a pleasure having you around as a mother and a friend. I love you!" Courtney was speechless, because she thought Larry was going to say something irritating. "Come here, wise guy, and give me a hug." When they entered the house the Sarge said, "What was that all about?" Larry responded by saying that Courtney and he had decided to get married. She slapped him upside his head and said, "You're a real character, but I love you."

"I love you, too, Mom. Can you get used to that?"

"If you mean it, I certainly can."

"Then get used to it, because I mean it from the depths of my heart and soul. Come on, Rashida, before I start crying in public."

Rashida and Larry were about to go out the door when the Sarge asked Larry if he had any funds. Larry told him that it was Rashida's money that he was going to spend. Well, that didn't last long because Rashida didn't have a dime, an issue that Larry would preach to her about to make sure that she always had escape money. The Sarge said to Larry and Rashida as they were leaving, "You both made me very proud of you today in church. Take care of one another."

"Sarge, we owe you our lives, and make no mistake about it, right now, all we can do is make you proud of us." With watery eyes, Larry said, "And that goes for you too, Courtney. God bless us all." They turned and walked out the door.

Riding along, Larry told Rashida there was something that he had to get off of his chest. She asked him what was it and he sighed and said, "Rashida, I love you like a sister. But I must confess, I had sex with your mother. That's why every time I was supposed to come over to see you I would always find an excuse. I feel real bad about it, but it was something that happened to me in another life."

"Larry, I knew that. I don't respect you any less, and as a matter of fact, I love you more for being honest enough to tell me about it. My mother, God bless her soul, made plenty of mistakes and I forgive her for each one. I'm just happy that you and I are a part of each other's life." Larry pulled the Jeep over to the curb reached over and hugged Rashida and said, "Thanks, Sis, I needed that."

"Now, with that behind me, I want to make sure you never walk around with no money in your pocket. It makes no sense for you to be broke when the Sarge and I have funds. Here— take this two hundred and always have a little something hid away for that rainy day. The Sarge is a great guy and I love him. He has made a real human being out of me, and he loves you madly. He wants you to have a healthy baby and to be his daughter. They're going to adopt you when they get married two weeks from now so you have to stay in school and do your very best. That's all he wants from you. I'll help you whenever you need me, but for God's sake, if you don't want to hurt him, stay in school and get good grades. You know, you're about to bring life into this world. Courtney, the Sarge and even I won't always be around. You've got to start making plans for the future of your child and how you want to raise it. He's going to ask you if you want to stop school until you've had the baby. Whatever you say, say no! Tell him that your baby is going to have an educated mother."

"Larry, you mean the world to me. I'm glad you gave me that advice because after the other day, I was thinking about dropping out. I know what I have to do and I know whom I have to please and therefore, I'm all right. But thanks for the advice. It was solid as a rock. You know, Larry, you amaze me sometimes. You pick at me, but it would crush you if I dropped a tear, wouldn't it?"

"Sis, you got me down pat. I never want to hurt you and I won't tolerate anyone else hurting you either. The Sarge is my guardian and soon to be your father and mine as well. That is whom we take our marching orders from the Sarge and

Courtney. Everyone else really doesn't matter, but we'll coexist with them if we have to. Here we are, The Crying Game."

Back at the ranch another kind of discussion was in progress. Courtney and the Sarge were talking about buying a house and the financial responsibility attached to it, as well as her need to pay off over $30,000 in medical school loans. She told the Sarge that currently she made about $78,000 a year. The Sarge told her that he made $57,000 straight time, and with overtime, about $73,000. Courtney said, "That's almost $150,000 a year and I think four people can exist very comfortably on that." The Sarge asked Courtney about the status of her mortgage, and she told him that she owed about $40,000 on the place and could probably get $150,000 if she sold it today. The Sarge then told her that his house was paid for and was worth about $130,000, and that if they sold both places, they could indeed afford a bigger place where all four of them could live. He then asked Courtney if she had a problem helping to support two kids that she had nothing to do with. She told him that she loved him and that he could bring all of the baggage he wanted because all she wanted was to be with him and the two kids. This really touched the Sarge and he said, "Courtney, Rashida is going to have a child, and that will mean five of us in the same place."

"Those houses we looked at could hold ten comfortably."

"I don't want to have ten around, Courtney. I just want what we have so far. But you never know, there may be another little fellah out there that might need our help."

"I'm only going to say this one time, so listen up. If you want me to be your wife, then I want you to be my husband. It was no great infatuation concerning your looks that caught my eye. It was the way you handled a young lady in trouble that made me see how sensitive you were and how much I liked that in you. So you see, if you want a tribe, it's okay with me. I just love you madly and that's all that matters to me. Now give me a kiss."

It was a short kiss because the Sarge wasn't finished with this conversation. He asked her if she would be willing to adopt one or two more children, or would she prefer that they tried to have them naturally. She grabbed him and said, "Let's get busy. If I can have a child, I would be eternally grateful to you. I just thought that you didn't want any more responsibility beyond what you have, or rather what we've already inherited."

"Girl, if you can have children, then damn, let's do get busy. One thing, though, you've never asked me my age and I've never asked you yours."

"One week before our wedding, I'll be 40. How about you?"

"Three months after our wedding, I'll be 48. I've been a policeman for 25 years."

"I didn't ask you anything about being a cop, did I?"

"No, you didn't, but I thought I would let you know."

"Okay, Sarge, before we get busy, I want to recap our conversation. We're going to sell both houses and buy a bigger one, preferably one of the ones we saw today. You want me to have children if possible, is that correct?"

"Absolutely."

"If our family expands by any means then we'll just have to work harder to take care of them, is that right?"

"No, that is not right."

"What do you mean?"

"Courtney, now don't think that I've lied to you, because I haven't. There are a few things that you should know about me." Courtney interrupted him and said, "Like what?"

"I'm going to try this one more time. But this time, I don't want you to interrupt me until I'm finished. Okay?"

"Okay."

"Now, as I was saying, I don't want you to think I've lied to you because I haven't. To make a short story long or a long story short, I can only say one thing. You are one helluva woman and I love you madly."

"Sarge, I know that. You said there were things that I didn't know about you."

256

"Oh yeah. I almost forgot. Anyhow, Courtney, as soon as possible I would like to do a will. You see, I believe at this moment, I'm probably worth close to $4 million."

"Sarge, stop bullshitting and tell me what it is that I don't know about you. You're messing with my mind."

"Yeah, that's bullshit. But before I tell you anything, I want a kiss, and while I'm kissing you, I want to suck on that tongue of yours."

"Naughty boy." They kissed for about a minute and the Sarge began to feel that old dumb organ of his begin to rise. He stopped kissing for a minute and said, "I'd like to finish my story."

"You're going to have to finish it later now. I want to go upstairs while we have the house to ourselves. Come on, no more talking now, just come up here and make love to the woman who loves you to death."

CHAPTER EIGHT

On the other side of town at the theater, the movie was ending and Rashida and Larry as well as everyone else was talking about how deep the movie was. Rashida said to Larry, "Do you believe that crap?"

"Naw, girl. That movie blew my mind. I couldn't believe that it was that way."

As they were making their way through the crowd, a voice said, "Hey chump, is that my baby or yours?" Larry turned to see who it was, and to his surprise it was the devil himself: Malik. Larry, after recognizing him, said, "Naw punk, you got to be a man to make a baby, not a faggot like yourself." Malik responded in his usual way by saying, "Fuck you." Larry retorted, "You're not my kind." Malik got right up in Larry's face. "I ought to kick your ass," responded Malik. "And by the way, I heard you got banged in the ass in jail, faggot." Hearing this set Larry off. He hauled off and knocked Malik to the ground. He turned and told Rashida, "Come on, let's get out of here." Malik got up, pulled out a pistol and fired it point blank into Larry's back. Larry fell to the ground and Malik walked up to him and pulled the trigger again, but the gun jammed. He panicked and ran down the street to find a hole to crawl into.

At this point, Rashida was yelling and screaming for someone to get an ambulance. Larry lay on the ground mumbling, "Get my sister out of here. Please get her home for me." Those were the last words that Larry said prior to passing out on the pavement.

The ambulance and police finally arrived and they rushed Larry to the hospital, where a team of emergency doctors were waiting to try to save his life. Larry had lost an enormous amount of blood, and from the looks of things, he wasn't going to make it. The call from the precinct came as Sarge was getting ready to hit a home run. The officer told him that one Larry Holland had been shot while leaving the movie house and was en route to County General. The Sarge almost hyperventilated. Courtney asked him what was wrong, but he couldn't make a sound. She slapped him with all her might and the Sarge said, "Oh my God, they shot my son." Courtney yelled, "Oh no, not Larry! No not Larry."

The Sarge and Courtney frantically dressed and raced out the door towards the hospital. Courtney asked, "Where is Rashida?" The Sarge didn't have an answer and could only say, "I don't know." She yelled at him, "Don't you lie to me goddamnit! Don't you lie to me! Has anything happened to her?"

"Honey, I honestly don't know. No one said anything about her being shot. I honestly don't know."

When they arrived at hospital, there were cops all around Rashida asking her questions. The Sarge ran up to her, asked if she was all right and told the officers to back off. Courtney ran and got a sphygmomanometer to check her blood pressure. It was not where Courtney wanted it to be, so she told a nurse to give her 1cc of Valium to calm her down. Before she was given the injection, she told the Sarge that on the way out of the movie, she and Larry ran into Malik. He insulted her and Larry hit him in the mouth. Malik pulled a pistol and shot Larry in the back and then tried to shoot him in the face, but the gun jammed. The Sarge told her not to worry and to rest. He thanked God that she was all right. The Sarge turned to Courtney and said, "I'm going to kill that bastard." She turned to him and said, "No, you're not. You're going to be the good cop that you are and not let it get personal. Now go down there and see how our son is doing." It was too soon for the doctors to give any information on Larry. They had been operating on him for only about an hour at this point, and no one was fully certain of the extent of his injuries. The Sarge went into the chapel and fell to his knees and prayed to God. After quieting Rashida down, Courtney came looking for him and was happy to see her man on his knees praying for their son. She joined him and they held each other's hand while they both prayed.

It seemed as though the operation lasted all night. The doctor told the Sarge and Courtney that Larry had sustained multiple injuries, each of which could prove fatal, and that their major concern was that he lost a lot of blood before he got to the hospital. He told the couple that all they could do now was go home and pray. He told them, "If he has the will to live, then he may have a fighting chance. If he's a quitter, then I'm sorry."

About three hours later, the Sarge told Courtney to take Rashida home and asked if she would be able to stay with her tomorrow. She told him that she had the day off, and for him not to worry about her. The Sarge told her that he was going to hang around the hospital for a while and that he would call her if there was any change in Larry's condition.

There was a bed next to Larry's and the Sarge said to Larry, "I said my prayers and I think God heard me. I want you to rest for now, but I want to see a sign in the morning when I wake up that you're going to be all right. I didn't go through all that we've been through for some shithead like Malik to do you. Don't you worry about him. If I have to go into every rat hole in the community I'm going to find his ass, and I'm going to do the right thing to him—a bullet to the base of his skull. Now you just rest, I'm going to be right in this bed next to you. I won't be asleep, I'll just be resting—waiting on you to give me that sign that you love me like you know I love you. Oh, and by the way, your sister is fine, a little shook up, but otherwise she's doing well. I love you, Larry. See you in the morning. If you need anything, just moan and I'll take care of it. Good night, my son. God be with you and I love you."

CHAPTER NINE

Malik made the big time. There was a joint reward offered by the parents of Gina and the new parents of Larry the Wanderer, aka Larry Holland, for information leading to his arrest and conviction. The reward was $25,000.

Malik was not only quick with a gun, but he was quick to get out of Dodge. In a stolen car, Malik headed for Charleston, West Virginia. He had an old freak there, as he called her, who would do just about anything for him, including turning his ass in for the $25,000.

Once in Charleston, Malik fell right into the crowd. He started selling a little caine to make ends meet, but was using more than he sold. After Christie found out that he had a price on his head, she attempted to turn him in. They had perverse sex together, using aids and entering places reserved for the removal of waste. Nightly, he would sex her normally, and then enter her anus. She was a low life, who knew that she had the AIDS virus, but never once bothered to tell Malik to cover up. Christie contracted the HIV virus from her lover, a needle-shooting bisexual who would do anything for a hit.

On this particular night after having perverted sex with Malik, she immediately jumped out of the bed and went into the bathroom. Upon returning, he noticed that she was fully dressed and prepared to leave. Malik might be vicious, but stupid he wasn't. He questioned her about what was going on and found her story to be suspicious. He knew that there was a price on his head and decided that he had better do the dash quickly, but before he left, he was going to make sure that this bitch never did anyone else. He told her he had three grand in his pocket and that he wanted her to get him some more caine. He reached for the pants and pulled out a roll of money. He took half of it and threw it on the bed. Christie reached for the money and he grabbed her. She was fumbling through her bag for something, but he found it first: a straight razor. He slit her throat from ear to ear and then carved a big "M" on her stomach. He got dressed, went down into the basement and crawled out of a window and under a car. He slid along the street like the snake he was and disappeared into the night. He watched from two blocks away as the cops came rolling up in their cars with their lights flashing. He laughed and walked down the street.

As he was walking, he was checking the cars for lights that were blinking to see if they had an alarm system. Outside of a bar, he didn't have to check, because some fool had left a brand new Cadillac running. Malik opened the door, got in, floored the accelerator, drove to the airport and parked. There he broke into a car, hot wired the ignition, and used the parking ticket he received with the Cadillac to get the other car out. He told the attendant that he had forgotten his airline ticket and needed to go back downtown to fetch it. He smugly drove away in a hurry and never looked back.

On the interstate he liked the way the sign to Chicago looked. He reasoned that he had never been there, and therefore, it was as safe as any place for him.

Fourteen hours later, Malik read a sign that said, "Welcome to Illinois." He pulled the vehicle over and decided to take a nap. His nap lasted longer than he had expected. He was awakened by a state trooper. The trooper told Malik that he couldn't stop along this route. Malik told the trooper that he got tired and felt that he had better pull off of the road or risk possibly hurting someone while trying to drive half asleep. The trooper suggested that he drive about two miles down the road and there he would find a truck stop. Malik thanked him and drove off. Realizing that he had a close call and that the cop got the tag number, he decided to pull the vehicle off at a turnaround and head back east. He drove all night and finally stopped

264

outside of Williamsport, Pennsylvania. He reasoned that no one would expect him to be in Philadelphia, and therefore it would be the best place for him. Malik also thought about going to New York and doing Monica. He felt that she really betrayed him and deserved to die. Malik was the kind of guy who the more he thought about something the more determined he was in seeing it through. He felt that his luck was the best thing he had going and it would be a long time before he got caught.

After pulling over and resting for an hour, Malik decided that he would hide out in Philly for a while and then get enough cash to head for the west coast. No one would know me from Adam out there, he thought. He needed cash and he needed it bad in order to make a clean break.

As he turned off of the turnpike and on to 309 South, the sign said, "Welcome to Philadelphia." He realized he had to get rid of the car he was driving; the tags stuck out like new money. He drove straight for the airport so that he could exchange the car for a new one. When he arrived at the airport, he drove into the short-term parking lot, looked around and decided that it might be better just to get new tags, but then he realized that the inspection sticker was different and a dead give away. He sat in the lot for a few minutes until he saw the car he wanted: a sky blue Range Rover, about as inconspicuous as a Rolls Royce, but that's what he wanted. He played with the locks for a few minutes, then the hidden alarm went off. He ran away from the car and walked into the airport corridor. After sitting in the breezeway for about ten minutes, he went back into the garage as though he had just seen someone off on a trip. The truck had quieted down but he abandoned the idea and settled for one of those Japanese cars. He hotwired the car and drove off the lot.

In South Philly, Malik was watching the crowd at Giuiseppe's Steaks. He felt that if he could hit this place, he would have plenty of cash. He waited for three hours, watching and calculating the potential take and then decided to do his number. He walked up and asked for a cheesesteak with fried onions. A big Italian guy asked him if he wanted anything else, and Malik pulled out the pistol and said, "Yeah, the fucking money in the draw." Well, he should have known better than to try to rob the Italians in their own hood. The big guy told him to stay calm as he placed the money in a bag. As Malik started backing away, the big guy dropped to the ground and the entire kitchen started firing at Malik. The lucky sonofabitch fired back, hitting two of the guys, but never caught a bullet himself. He got away once again, with a bag full of money and two people wounded on the other end. This time there was even a better picture of Malik than the one that was placed over the wire. It showed every dimple, pimple, and hair on his face. The sad thing about this robbery for Malik was that Giuiseppe's Steaks would place another $10,000 on his head. Now the total for him was up to $35,000—a lot of money for anyone who could finger this guy.

Malik's picture was shown everywhere. Almost without failure, Lisa Thomas Tora would start her newscast by saying, "And another day goes by with the man in this picture on the run from society and the law." The amount of the reward was beneath his picture and this would certainly get action from anyone who could finger him. Malik was not about to be handed up by anyone. His message to Lisa was, "They'll never catch me. I'm just to damn smart for these dummies."

CHAPTER TEN

It had been two days and Larry had not made a move. The Sarge hadn't made a move either. He was determined to see this thing through and be there when Larry awakened or died. All the members of his new family were praying for his speedy recovery. Rashida knew that Larry wanted her to go back to school, and that was her way of showing her new brother how much he meant to her. She began to excel in the few days since the tragedy and illustrated her conviction that she was going to finish on time and with the best possible grades. She visited the counselor's office and began to review brochures for different colleges and universities.

Courtney, on the other hand, was making preparations to postpone her wedding, unknown to the Sarge. She was sad that her husband to be was in such agony, and it bothered her to view Larry all tubed up and unconscious. She told the Sarge that she had seen many a patient all tubed up, but it hurt her heart to see Larry in that condition.

As she prepared for work and Rashida for school, Rashida told Courtney she had a dream in which Larry died. Courtney grabbed her and told her to have faith, trust in God and try to think positive. She told Rashida that Larry was a strong young buck and that it would take more than a simple bullet to kill him. "Larry will have to kill himself by just giving up. If he fights, he can win." The two women embraced and Courtney sniffled and told Rashida to hurry so she could give her a ride to school. On the way to school, Rashida recounted her conversation with Larry about school and the necessity of being an educated mother. Rashida told Courtney, "Larry said the only thing that you and the Sarge wanted in return for your generosity and benevolence was for us to get a good education and continue to make you guys proud of us." Courtney said to Rashida, "That Larry is some kind of guy. He's just like the Sarge, a carbon copy of him, as a matter of fact. Rashida, Larry told you exactly what we want for you, the baby and for him. Let's keep praying that he'll recover. You have a powerful day and don't worry, Larry is going to make it. I feel it."

In Larry's room, the Sarge was having this long conversation with Larry, who was still unconscious. Courtney opened the door and said, "Good morning, Sweetheart. How is he and how are you?"

"There's no sign of improvement. He just lays there like a vegetable."

"Has the doctor been in this morning?"

"No. The nurse came in and checked out the equipment, but other than that, no one has been here but me."

"Sarge, do you love me?"

"Come on, Courtney, what kind of question is that?"

"I have to know, Sarge. Do you love me?"

"Of course I do. Why are you asking me that at a time like this?"

"Because if you love me, you're going to do as I ask you. I want you to go home and take a shower and change your clothes. Then I want you to go and have yourself a big breakfast. Then and only then can you come back here. I'll keep an eye on Larry. He's as important to me as he is to you."

"Yeah, I guess I could use a bath and a shave. Are you going to leave him alone?"

"Sarge, trust me. I have a few rounds to make and then I'll be back here to sit with him and talk."

"Okay, if there's any change, you call me right away. I mean it, Courtney."

"Sarge, go home and get cleaned up."

"Okay, but don't forget, call me please." As the Sarge got his jacket, Larry made some noise. The Sarge asked Courtney, "What did you say?" She responded jubilantly, by saying, "It wasn't me, it was Larry."

268

Courtney rang the bell for the doctors and attendants and they all came running. She told the doctor that Larry had uttered something and she wanted to remove the breather and pumpers. They all donned their gloves and began to do their jobs. After all of the tubes were removed, the amazing Larry the Wanderer, aka Larry Holland, gasped for air and said, "Courtney, he almost talked me to death." Everybody broke out laughing and the Sarge started crying. Larry said, "Pops, if you hadn't kept up your chattering all night, every night, I think I would have checked out of here for good. I love you, Sarge, and you, too, Courtney. I need sleep now. I'm really tired and don't want to hear his mouth for a while." The Sarge kissed his son and told him that he loved him.

The Sarge went home and cleaned up and then headed to the station for a few minutes. When he arrived, no one said a word for fear that the news he would give would be bad. Smitty walked up to him and said, "How's it going, Sarge?"

"Smitty, it's a good day. Larry is fine."

"Great!" All of the other cops came up and patted him on the back and shook his hand or said, "We were worried." The Sarge had a strong presence in the station. He was a good cop and a good friend.

After looking over his desk, Smitty came over and said, "Your boy did Giuieseppe's the other night. He wounded two employees in the robbery. The good news is that we have a photo of this dude that's clear as can be. Look at this." Smitty showed the Sarge a copy of the picture of Malik. "Sarge, it's only a matter of time before we catch this guy, but I must admit, he is one slippery S-O-B."

The Sarge then went in to see the Captain and gave him an update on Larry's condition. He reminded himself that he had to call the school and let them know that Larry was hospitalized and would probably be out for a few weeks. After talking to the Captain, he told him he was going to take a few days off and stay with Larry. The Captain told him to take as much time as he needed.

After thanking all of the officers for their support, the Sarge told them he would see them in a few days. On his way out, the smartass cop said, "Damn, I'm sorry about what happened to the kid. I feel real bad and hope that everything is all right." The Sarge said, "About the other day, just try to make the best call you can. Don't be macho and you'll turn out to be one of our finest. Thank you for your concern. I think he's going to be all right. You just be the best cop that you can and I won't have to worry about you. Okay?" The guy threw out his hand for a shake, but got the welcoming mat from the Sarge: a man-sized hug.

In the Jeep, the Sarge started listening to a station on the FM dial, 106.1, which played the smoothest jazz he had ever heard. The song that was playing was "Rashida," by John Luciene. It brought his own Rashida to mind. He decided to go by the school and tell her that her brother was all right.

In the principal's office, the Sarge waited and noticed how unruly the kids were. Rashida appeared looking like she was going to deliver any moment and said, "What are you doing here?"

"I came by to tell you that your brother is all right." She hugged the Sarge and started crying. Kids walking by saw the real fruits of love and caring.

CHAPTER ELEVEN

Larry had progressed well and was released from the hospital. Courtney modified the bedroom she used as an office back to a bedroom. The room was just big enough to accommodate the hospital bed that Larry needed. He had worked out a relationship with his professors, allowing him to maintain his studies without falling too far behind. Everything was getting somewhat back to normal, and the wedding had been postponed for two weeks. Rashida was coming near the end of her term and was beginning to really show the effects of pregnancy. She never forgot her new brother. Every morning she would prepare his breakfast and lunch. She carried a beeper just in case he needed her. The Sarge was as proud as anyone could be. He marveled at how the two had become so close and protective of one another. He told Courtney that next to her, the two kids were the most important people in his life.

The Sarge came by as usual to check up on everybody and to eat the dinner Rashida religiously fixed for everyone. She had become a good cook, using books and her own concoctions to surprise the diners. After dinner, the Sarge told Courtney that he wanted to finish the conversation they had started on the day Larry got hurt. She told him that she wanted to speak with Rashida for a minute and then they could discuss whatever he wanted.

In the kitchen, Courtney placed her arm around Rashida's shoulder and told her to sit down for a minute because she wanted to have a word with her. She said to Rashida, "I think that you've done a wonderful job around here, and I appreciate it. You cook, clean and do whatever I'm too tired to do when I get home. However, I want you to stop doing so much. You're coming full term, and we don't want anything to happen to our baby. I'm going to hire someone to come in and cook dinner for us and clean the house once a week. So all I want you to do is just relax and get ready to be a mother."

"I think that's why I'm so busy, Courtney. I'm afraid of being a mother."

"Nonsense. Your problem is that you feel helpless because you don't know what to do yet. Well, let me tell you one thing— after that baby cries, you'll be a pro. I guarantee it. That bag I brought home tonight has some books in it on all about being a mother and the proper care for yourself as well. So you see, I think it's time now for you to take care of the two of you and learn what the so-called experts have to say about raising a child."

"Courtney, let me at least cook. I have no money other than what Larry gave me, and I need to feel like I'm not a burden on you. I mean, you take me in and then you have to take Larry in and then you have to feed the Sarge as well. It won't hurt me to cook, and besides, I want to contribute to this household the best way I can."

"You are so special and precious, Rashida. I love you and you don't have to worry about contributing, because as soon as that baby is born, we're all going to have someone else to care for and love. I just wanted you to know that I don't expect you to do anything, but get ready for "D" Day. If you insist on cooking then I won't stop you. By the way, how is school coming along?"

"Funny you should ask. I get my report card tomorrow and I hope that I don't have to run away because of my grades."

"Don't be silly. If you need help, then go upstairs and see Larry. He's as sharp as a tack. And you know he would be glad to help you. It'll help take his mind off of his problems. I know he's sick of being in that bed. So anyway, don't exert yourself and if you feel funny, forget about cooking. We can always order out."

"Courtney, are you ready to be a grandmother?"

"I'm ready for you to have that baby, but I don't know if I like the sound of Grandma. Sounds a bit old to me."

272

"You're not old and probably never will be. You just have that kind of chemistry. You look good, you don't wear any make-up and your hair is easy to fix. So I wouldn't worry about being called Grandma, because you'll probably have a lot of women asking you for your secrets. I love you!"

"I love you too, sweetie. Just be careful. This is the critical time for you and for us."

Back in the living room Courtney walked over to the Sarge and sat right in his lap. Rashida walked out of the kitchen and said, "Are you guys going to have babies?" She looked at their perplexed faces and said, "Oh well, I guess that's not my business, now is it?" The Sarge stood up and said, "Go check on Larry and make sure he's all right." This only opened the door wider for Rashida, for she asked another of her questions. "Are you guys making it?" Courtney looked at her and just pointed to the steps and away she went. "Do you believe that she asked us that?" the Sarge said. Courtney looked at him and responded, "Yes."

As they sat and watched the news that evening, a picture of their abomination appeared: Malik. Courtney quickly grabbed the remote control unit and switched to another channel. She picked the channel that featured Lisa Thomas Tora as its anchor. She started with the same story, in essence, that their anathema was still without capture. She finally said, "Oh, what the heck. What did you want to discuss?"

"Don't worry. I can't forget that bastard, but he's not going to ruin or hurt my family anymore."

"Sarge, don't talk like that. You scare me when you speak in those absolute terms and with that look on your face. Please don't let that ruin our evening. Please!"

"I'm sorry, baby, but that guy is everywhere and nowhere. Just like the rat he is. But anyway, I wanted to finish our discussion about what to do about our living arrangements. We talked about selling both houses and buying a bigger one before we, or rather you, got horny on me, is that correct?"

"Is which one correct?"

"Come on, Courtney, be serious for just two minutes."

"That is correct, before 'YOU' got horny. That's what we were talking about."

"I have a better idea and one that would probably suit the Queen that you are."

"And what is that, Sarge?"

"As I looked at those houses out there the other week, I found them to be big, but not big enough. I only want to move one more time in life, and I think that we should really get extravagant and go all the way."

"Sarge, nothing would suit me better. Those houses were pretty big, and besides there are only four of us now and a baby on the way. I really don't think that we need anything bigger than what we looked at. Furthermore, I really don't want to be house poor and not be able to furnish it."

"Here's my plan, Courtney. I want to have our house built from the ground up with everything that we want in it and around it."

"Sarge, that's my fantasy, but I'm a realist. We just don't have the money to build from the ground up. I don't want to work all of my life just to pay off a stupid, but necessary mortgage. I've seen too many people bite off more than they could chew and wind up selling, divorcing and being miserable. I love you and I don't want to put that kind of pressure on you or me. So let's just stick to simple dreams."

"Courtney, do you mind fixing me a big snifter of Grand Marnier?"

"That sounds like a good idea. I think I'll have one too."

When Courtney returned with the two hefty drinks, she asked the Sarge, "What shall we toast to?"

"We should toast to our dream house." They touched glasses and swallowed some of the miraculous liquid. The Sarge then said, "I need to tell you something. I hope you won't be mad at me, but I think you need to know a few things about me."

274

"Like what? Are you gay, or seeing someone else?"

"Just one more minute of being serious, please. But to answer your question, I'm not seeing anyone, but you, and I'm not gay."

"Thank God. I think I would still love you if you were."

"Courtney, be serious for just a minute please."

"Okay, I'm serious."

"Before I say what I need to say to you, I want you to tell me how you really feel about me?"

"Stupido, I'm about to marry you. That should tell you something. If you need to hear me say I love you, then ask me."

"Let me hear it."

"Okay. I love you, Ben Beckmire."

"You never call me Ben so I guess that's a good sign. Anyway, I am going to engage an architect to work with you in the evenings to draw up the plans for our new house."

"Sarge, we can't afford to have a house built, and I'm not going to be a slave to it; only to you."

"My dear sweet girl, I love you. And since I love you so much I'm going to have your house built and paid for before you move into it. In other words, I think I have about $4 million in assets as we speak."

"Sarge, don't play games with me. Are you leveling with me?"

"Courtney, I tried to tell you before and I even mentioned the number $4 million. If you don't believe me, then go up and ask Larry."

Courtney got up, ascended the steps and knocked on Larry's door. He yelled for her to come in. "Larry, the Sarge asked me to come up here and ask you a simple question."

"What is it, Courtney?"

"Larry, don't lie to me. Is the Sarge with money?"

"Is Rashida with child? I'm sorry for being funny, but the answer is yes. The Sarge is well off and secure."

"Thanks, Larry."

275

When Courtney arrived downstairs, the Sarge was at the door. He said, "I didn't know how to tell you, but I think we could probably get a big enough house for all of us and maybe for a few more that I'd like to have with you. Give me a kiss so that I can go home and start to look for an architect. You know, I was thinking that we could leave the two houses for Rashida and Larry after they finish college and all. What do you think?"

"I think that you are mad, but I love you and I hope I can handle the fact that I can quit working tomorrow if I like."

"You didn't do all that time in school to lay on your butt, did you?"

"You know better than that. I like my job as much as you like yours. Give me a kiss and go home. Oh, I had my cycle calculated today, and tomorrow we have twelve hours to connect. If we connect we'll just have a little bastard for a few days. Okay, I won't joke like that, but please tell me that you want to try to have our own child."

"We'll try as many times as possible. And yes, I want to have my own child or children, but if it doesn't happen, I don't want you depressed and all. I'll do anything you ask me, because I think we have the nucleus of having a wonderful tribe. Okay, I'm excited now. Call me later and tell me when and where so that I can get away and not feel the pressure of the job. This is great news. I want to sit back down and talk about it some more."

"I want to get a good night's sleep so that fatigue won't be the problem tomorrow. I love you. Now go home." They kissed and held each other for a few moments and then the Sarge left. On his way home he realized how lucky he was. The Sarge lived in two worlds: one of helping, loving and caring and the other—the *edge*.

As he witnessed two men having a street brawl his attention drifted from the positive side of his life and the lives of his new family to those of his bete noire: Malik. He knew it was a matter of time before he was either found or made the mistake that most rats make—getting greedy and careless.

The Sarge had a very restless night and spent most of it looking at old pictures of his deceased wife. The irony of the situation would present itself to him the following morning at work.

The next morning, the Sarge was awakened at 6:00 by Larry. As he attempted to gain his faculties, he asked Larry if he knew what time it was and Larry told him he did. He asked Larry if he was feeling all right. Larry told him that he was fine and that he wanted the Sarge to buy a little stock called Lome Bepot. The Sarge asked him why and Larry gave him the analysis, which he understood. The Sarge asked him how much they should invest and Larry told him if possible, $25,000. That number really got the Sarge's attention, and he asked if Larry had he been drinking. Larry told him it was going to happen and happen fast. The Sarge then told Larry he would think about it and let him know later. The two men told each other that they would talk later.

On his way to work the Sarge listened to the AM news station in the Jeep and heard that during the night a man was decapitated by a truck mirror as he crossed the street on a red light. The Sarge shuddered and said, "Poor bastard. People have to learn what green, yellow and especially red means." As he pulled into the parking lot of the precinct, he ran into Smitty and they went into the station together. Smitty had received a call and knew what the mood was going to be.

As the Sarge entered the building the officers were called to attention by the Captain. As the men stood at attention, the Sarge wondered what the hell was going on. The Captain walked over to a ghetto blaster and played the tape. It was essentially what the Sarge had heard on the radio on his way to work concerning the guy who was decapitated by the truck mirror. He turned to the Captain and said, "I heard this earlier. Why are these guys standing like I'm about to retire or be buried?" The Captain took a piece of paper out of his pocket and handed it to the Sarge. The piece of paper was folded in quarters. As the Sarge slowly opened it, there was a name scribbled inside. The name that was written was Jeffrey Shore. The Sarge looked around the room at the men and the Captain said, "He finally fucked up and lost his head." The Sarge sat down and his eyes watered up. The person who killed his wife and their twins was no more. The Sarge thought to himself, he died too fucking easy, the sonofabitch. He thanked the men for remembering and went about his duties as usual. Smitty walked over and said to the Sarge, "That was a helluva tribute. We all love you, Sarge."

"Thanks, Smitty. You guys know that I love you too, and you all had better show up at my wedding."

"You know that you only have a week left and then you're henpecked once again."

"I'm kinda of looking forward to it."

"Sarge, can I be honest?"

"Never asked me before, so why are you asking now?"

"I just need to say one thing that has been bothering me lately. You know you and I used to go out after work and have a bite to eat and a few beers. Since you met the love of your life and developed a whole new family overnight, you've kinda kicked me to the curb. I'm not trying to make you feel bad or anything, but I was wondering if I did something wrong or if you just got tired of my just talking about women all the time?"

"Oh God, no, Smitty. You are my true friend and you're in my wedding. If I've been a little preoccupied, it's because of Rashida and Larry. You know I'm trying desperately to keep them on the right track, and with her being pregnant and all, she requires a lot of support. How about you and I going out tonight for a few beers? Oh, shit—I can't. I have to do something for Larry. What about tomorrow?"

"I can't, Sarge, I have plans. I can do it on Thursday, I think."

"Listen to us, Smitty. We sound like two jerks that work in one of those offices trying to figure out between our busy schedules when we can do lunch. We have to put an end to that kind of shit. You're my friend and we have to make time. How about just the two of us going out on Friday? I can't think of anyone else who I would rather spend my last night as a bachelor with. Not that you're poofter or anything, but just as two guys bonding."

"Sarge, Friday is tough, but I tell you what—if you can meet me at around seven then it would work well for me."

"Okay, you bum, you're on. Now get away from my desk and catch some lawless types." As Smitty walked away, he gave the Captain the thumbs up sign. There was no way the Sarge was going to get married and not have an illicit bachelor party. He wasn't so smart after all, as he would soon find out.

Back at Courtney's house, Larry was beginning to feel his oats. He had received several calls from the young lady that he kind of met at church. He decided to call her back to ask her if she wanted to come over to study with him that evening and got a resounding yes. He decided that he had better call the Sarge and ask him what he thought of the idea, but decided to go about it another way. He picked up the telephone and paged Courtney. She called and asked if everything was all right and he told her that he was fine. He told Courtney that he had a question to ask her. She queried him on the nature of the question because she knew Larry always had some stuff with him. Larry told her that he wanted to invite the young lady from church over that evening to study and whether or not Courtney would consent to him having a guest in his bedroom. Courtney told Larry that it was the best idea he had come up with in a long time and she had no problem with him inviting her over. She also told Larry that he was at home, and that he didn't have to ask her permission to enjoy his home. He thanked her and told her he loved her and finished his conversation by saying, "I'll see you tonight, Mom," and hung up the telephone. She immediately called the Sarge and told him Larry had sincerely called her Mom and that she was on cloud nine.

CHAPTER TWELVE

Mr. Bunbury wasn't sunning in paradise because what he stole and made from the sale of caine was being spent at an accelerated rate. He was on the run and wanted to maintain a certain anonymity. He knew it was going to cost him big bucks. He knew that if things got bad and he was ever implicated in anything, the first thing the Feds would do would be to seize his accounts. To avoid that problem, he stored millions of dollars in cash in storage lockers throughout the city. In Willowgrove, Mr. Bunbury had stored $3 million in cash in a common locker. This was only one of four lockers in which he had stored that amount.

On a Thursday evening just prior to closing, Mr. Bunbury drove an old car that he kept at a Marina, along with a 34X Express Cruiser, to a storage facility. The boat rarely left the docks, but was always maintained by the dock crew and occasionally test-driven by the mechanics. His boat was his hideaway, but it was not secure enough because people were always admiring the craft.

Upon arriving at the storage facility, he used his keys to open the shed, reached in and gently pulled out a briefcase as though it were an antique. He locked the container and drove back to the Marina and boarded his Yacht. Once on board, he closed the curtains to his forward berth, unlocked the case and smiled at the money he had laying in front of him. His next move was a long, long trip from the Delaware River to Miami, a trip that takes about two weeks cruising during daylight hours.

At five o'clock in the morning, he took a shower, got dressed and installed his radar, loran, autopilot and his VHF radio. The vessel was full of fuel and he was ready to make his move. He knew that the trip would be a grueling one, but with the help of the autopilot tied into the loran, his major concern was hitting something submerged in the water.

Once out of his slip, he gave the long warning blast on his horn and proceeded from the creek to the mouth of the river. Once on the river, he engaged the autopilot and the loran and Mr. Bunbury was on his way. The boat was immaculate and well kept, and he knew that it was just big enough to handle six-to-eight foot seas. The one thing that Mr. Bunbury did not expect was that the first and only modern day water jacking was about to happen to him.

CHAPTER THIRTEEN

Cruising down the Delaware and past the Philadelphia Airport, Mr. Bunbury saw two men hanging onto a capsized runabout. He pulled along side of them, shut down his engines and turned down his swim platform ladder. As the first man started climbing up the ladder, Mr. Bunbury saw that he had a plastic bag in his hand, and it appeared as though the man had a gun in it. He was right. The man took the gun out of the bag and said, "Thanks, sucker. You just made our day. Just sit up there on the bridge and keep your hands where I can see them. All we want is a ride down river. If you fuck with us, I'll blow your head off. So just sit there and keep quiet." As the other waterjacker was busy pulling in a bag, the Coast Guard sent out a mayday, warning all vessels in the proximity of the airport to be on the lookout for two men seen in the water. The jacker with the gun got on the VHF radio and reported that he had helped the two guys out of the water and that they were fine. He was pulling their craft into the shallow water. He signed off and laughed.

Underway again, the vessel headed for Baltimore Harbor, just a wee bit out of the way of Mr. Bunbury's original plans. The large jacker said to Mr. Bunbury, "Haven't I seen you somewhere before?" Mr. Bunbury retorted, "I doubt it."

"You look awful familiar to me, but don't worry, if you do as we say, you'll live to be a hundred. I see you got all of the latest electronic widgets on here. Where were you heading?"

"I was on the first leg of my trip to Florida."

"No shit. You're going to go to Florida all by your lonesome?"

"That's correct."

"Now, how would you like for me and Shortie there to travel with you?"

"Do I have a choice?"

"This is America, man. You can make any choice you want, but you make the wrong choice and your ass becomes the property of the state. Now I'll ask you again, do you want company?"

"I would love to have you two come along for the ride."

"Good then. We have to make a stop in Baltimore to deliver a package and pick up some money. We might even help you buy gasoline for this here fancy boat. Now how do you like that?"

"I think I have no choice in the matter and therefore I'll do whatever you say."

"Do you have a gun on this boat?"

"No, I don't. I have no need for such things."

"Shortie, take a look down there and see if our friend is lying to us."

Mr. Bunbury became a little agitated at the thought and said, "I do have a small pistol down there over top of the stove." As soon as he said that, Slim, the big jacker, punched Mr. Bunbury in the face and said, "The next time we ask you a question, we expect the truth. There's nothing I hate worse than a liar. Now, is that the only gun down there?"

"No, there's a shotgun in the forward berth."

"Where the hell is the forward berth?"

"It's the bed up front."

"You get over here and drive this thing. Shortie, if he even looks stupid, shoot his ass."

Mr. Bunbury was not concerned about these two characters finding the briefcase that was lodged in the rear berth, just forward of the gas tank. He knew that they would find the weapons eventually, but they would never find the money. He also knew that they wouldn't find the two-shot Derringer under the galley table. He calculated that they would be hungry long before they entered Baltimore Harbor, and he would wait for the right moment to blow them to hell. The two waterjackers seemed to be very concerned about the contents of the bag they

284

brought on board the vessel. As Slim came up from the cabin he said, "I know who you are. You're that fucking banker that they're looking for. You're the guy they call Bumbee—something or the other. You're wanted for dealing drugs and embezzlement. Am I right?"

"And if you are, what are you going to do? Turn me in to the police?"

"We just may do that, smartass, or blow you the fuck away."

"May I ask a question?"

"Sure, go right ahead. Don't mean I'm going to answer it though."

"What's in that bag?"

"Don't you worry about that fucking bag. You worry about living through this ride."

"I'm not worried about the bag. I already know what's in the bag. You guys are drug runners and you are carrying a bag full of caine. That makes us pretty much in the same boat, if you know what literally means." Shortie looked at Slim and said, "Do him. He's too fucking smart for his own good." The real boss came to light at that point. Slim said, "Okay, Shortie, but I don't think that I know enough about this here boat to navigate it safely to Baltimore. And besides, this guy wants as little exposure as possible. He's on the run and there's no way he's going to be trouble for us."

"Slim, you got a point there. Now, Captain, are we going to have to kill you or are you going to cooperate and not be a pain in the ass?"

"Since you guys got the upper hand, I have no choice. I just don't want any problems with the cops and I sure don't want any problems with you. I couldn't give a shit about your drug deal. It's so small I wouldn't waste my time on it. If you want to move to the big time, when you're not out stealing boats and selling shit, then we can perhaps talk about how to make real money from caine." This outburst by Mr. Bunbury caught both Slim and Shortie off guard. For a moment, all they could do was wonder whether or not to shoot him or give him his guns back. Shortie finally said, "If you want to help us make this deal, then we'll help you make your getaway. The choice is totally yours. You fuck up we'll kill your ass. You go along with our program and we'll help you get to Florida. After we do what we got to do to these suckers in Baltimore, we're going to have to disappear for a while ourselves. Can we begin a relationship where you don't kill us and we don't kill you?" After thinking about the proposition and looking at the alternatives, Mr. Bunbury said, "Only under certain conditions."

"What might they be?" Shortie asked.

"That you respect my boat and that you take your orders from me as long as you're on my boat. Otherwise, you'll go down with me."

"What the fuck does that mean? I could blow your head off right now and you'd never know the difference."

"You could indeed do that, but you wouldn't live beyond the hour."

"What are you going to do, come back to life and haunt me?"

"No, nothing that drastic. If you would please lift that seat up and then the cover to the compartment, you'll see what I mean."

Slim lifted the seat, pulled the cover off, and to his amazement, there was enough dynamite to blow the Queen Mary to the bottom.

"What the fuck is this?"

"That is my security blanket. You see, I could never do time in jail, so I figured that if the cops got on my trail then I would have to give them my corpse, spread all over the fucking water. I would like for you to hand me my pistol back, because if you don't, we'll all be blown to hell. As you can see, the timer must be reset every hour. I can set the timer remotely or just say fuck you assholes and take you with me to the bottom. What will it be?" Shortie didn't waste a minute. He handed Mr. Bunbury back his weapon. Mr. Bunbury told Slim to take the shotgun into the cabin and put it exactly where he found it.

After ending the Mexican standoff, Mr. Bunbury attempted to take the edge off of the situation and asked them what their plans were once they got to Baltimore. Shortie told him how they had been running drugs, basically reefer, but this time they had a watered-down batch of caine. He told him that they had laced the shit with all kinds of things, trying to improve the potency. Mr. Bunbury told him that they were looking for a short existence and suggested that they sell the product at a reduced rate and confess that they had a weak product, but saleable. Shortie thought that would spell suicide based upon the people they dealt with. Mr. Bunbury told Slim to reach under the seat in the back and hand him a clean rag. After receiving the rag from Slim, Mr. Bunbury told him to stay on course and not try to outsmart the electronics. He told Shortie to come down into the cabin for a minute. He pulled his weapon out, started cleaning it and said, "Never touch my guns. It's as though you were fondling my wife in front of me, and you know what the average man would do to a man if he caught him fucking his wife." Shortie replied, "I got your drift."

Mr. Bunbury, now feeling in complete control of these waterjackers, asked, "How long will it take you to do your deal once we get to Baltimore?"

"I figure it will take us about an hour or two."

"You got two hours exactly from the point we tie up. Once we get to Baltimore, we'll take on fuel and water and head out to the Bay and anchor out for the night. By the way, do you have any cash on you?"

"I have $500 or so," Shortie replied.

"Good. Before you go and do your deal, I want you to do some shopping for us. Have Slim get us some booze, and you go and get us some real food. We're going to need a lot of food and I don't want to stop every minute to feed my face. Do you have a problem with anything that I've said so far?"

"No, I don't. The only problem I have is that we're riding with a bomb on a timer."

287

"Don't worry about the bomb. It resets itself unless I give it a code. Now do you have any other problems that I should know about?"

"No, that's it."

"Do you boys get high?"

"We both drink like fish and we've taken a hit before, but we don't particularly like using what we can sell."

"Good. Now go up there and tell Slim that I'm going to knock the shit out of him for hitting me. And tell him that if he hits me back, you're going to blow his head off."

"Done," Shortie replied.

Like clockwork, the action followed. Mr. Bunbury hit Slim in the jaw and Slim did nothing about it. Mr. Bunbury said to Slim, "I'm glad we understand one another." He realized that these two could bring him good fortune and protection. He was really concerned about them doing their drug deal with a bad product. He asked Shortie, "Did you know a guy who was called the Man from Baltimore?"

Shortie looked at Slim and Slim said, "Yeah, we knew him." Mr. Bunbury said, "He used to be one of my best until some vigilante in Philly blew his head off. How did you boys know him?"

"We ran his weed business for him," Shortie replied.

"What weed business?"

"He had a weed business and made a lot of money from selling the shit."

"Why that sneaky little fuck. I should have had him whacked years ago. I always knew he was into something else, but it didn't hurt my product sales and therefore I really didn't give a shit."

"You mean that he worked for you?"

"Not directly. He worked for my organization. I was the head of it."

Shortie and Slim looked at each other again and Shortie said, "Man, we're sorry for fucking with you, and if you want us to get off now, then we will." The two men realized that they had almost killed the big man in the caine business and that would make their lives worth about a penny each.

"No, you two knuckleheads are going to work for me and be with me every inch of the way. Do you guys have any warrants outstanding against you?"

"I don't," replied Shortie.

"I don't either," Slim said.

"Good. Have you boys ever killed anyone?" There was hesitation and Slim said, "We did three guys who were late on their payments. The Man wanted to send a message to all of his dealers and roadsters."

"You mean to tell me that he had three guys killed for being late with the cash?"

"That's right. He was a motherfucker."

"I hate that word. Please refrain from using it."

"Okay Mr.—ah, what do we call you?"

"You can call me by birth name, Joshua. Maybe later, if you boys are good, I'll tell you the story of a real bad guy, my great grandfather, Mr. Clyde Bunbury. But right now I have a concern I need to discuss with you guys." As Shortie and Slim sat on the circular seat on the bridge, Joshua told Slim to take the helm for a minute. He stepped towards the stern and pulled three beers out of a cooler. He threw each one a beer and then went down into the galley and got a bag of potato chips. As he resumed the operation at the helm, he said, "I'm concerned about what you guys are going to do with that bad product. Personally, I would throw the shit overboard if I were you rather than expose yourself to the wrath of a pissed-off customer."

"Joshua, me and Slim got to do this one. We know the risks, but we think they're minimal. We need the cash and we need to get away from this part of the country."

"Okay, but you need to know my position on this. If you get into trouble, don't come back to the boat. Just hang around and hide out overnight, and if it's clear, then come down to the docks. I'll tie up along the wall next to Arrison's Restaurant and give you every opportunity to get back. But guys, I don't need any more heat. If you bring me heat, then I'm going to be pissed off and that's something you don't want to see. I can use you boys, but you can't cause me any trouble by bringing some pissed-off drug dealer down on me, or even worse, the cops. So I caution you, only do this thing if you can minimize the problems for everyone. Is that clear and do we have a deal?"

"We sure as hell do. We'll get the booze and the food first and then we'll go and do our little job and be out of here in the morning," Shortie replied.

Joshua Bunbury asked, "How bad is that shit?"

"It's not that bad. It's a little weak, but you can get off on it," Slim stated.

"I sure hope you boys know what you're doing. If I were the buyer and you brought me some shit like that, you wouldn't live to see the sunset. Then again, I'm not your buyer, am I? Just don't fuck up and get yourselves hurt, that's all I'm saying."

As the yacht rounded the jetty that leads into the Chesapeake & Delaware Canal, Mr. Bunbury told the guys, "Let's put some power behind this thing. I want to make the harbor by 2 PM." He moved the throttle forward until the tachometer read 3100 RPMs, just short of where the four-barrel carburetors kick in. The yacht was now traveling approximately 26 knots.

The ride was a captain's dream come true. The waves were one to two feet and the boat planed right through them. It was an incredible ride that should have been reserved for a captain and his mate, rather than a caine dealer and two traffickers in junk. Be that as it may, the threesome made awesome time and arrived at Baltimore Harbor in four and a half hours. That was pretty good for a vessel that size, completely loaded with fuel, water and bandits.

Slim was at the helm when the ship began to enter the harbor. Posted on both sides of the entrance to the harbor were signs that read, NO WAKE ZONE—SPEED 6 KNOTS—ENFORCED. None of the six eyes on board saw the signs and they were destined for trouble. The Harbor Patrol was relentless in enforcing the No Wake Zone. As Slim started to realize that he was passing much faster boats, he called out to Joshua and said, "Is there a speed zone down here somewhere?" Joshua replied, "I don't know, but the way those boats are cruising in here, I think something's up. Back her down to 1500 RPMs. Check on the VHF radio and see if there's a speed zone around." Before Slim could reach the radio, a vessel called out the call letters on the craft and said, "Captain, you're entering a No Wake Zone. Six knots are all that are allowed in the harbor." Slim immediately backed the vessel down and watched with great intensity as the Harbor Patrol headed his way. Joshua told Slim to act as natural as possible. As the Harbor Patrol slowed its vessel down and was about to say something to Slim, they got a call that two boats were racing around the harbor near the Aquarium. They told Slim to obey the signs and keep his craft below six knots.

Joshua Bunbury, standing on the landing to the cabin, said, "That was close and we were lucky. I'm glad you asked that question in time, Slim, otherwise we may have caught a ticket and a boarding. We sure as hell don't need that with all of that crooked shit you guys got down there. Slim, see that wall over there at one o'clock? That's where I want you to head. I have to go the john, so just slow down until I can dock us."

"Okay, Mr. Bunbury."

"Hey guys, call me Joshua, please."

Once the boat was tied up, Joshua handed Shortie a list and told him to make sure that he also picked up plenty of ice to store the meats in. He told Slim to hang around just in case someone came looking for docking fees because he wanted to keep a low profile. He also told Slim to get the washing compound out and wash the boat down. He didn't want the salt seizing up on the railings.

Two hours later, Shortie came back with six bags of groceries and told Joshua that he had to go and get ice. He walked over to Arrison's and asked them if he could purchase ice. They sold him enough ice to build an igloo. They stored meats in Tupperware containers that Joshua had on board and placed them in the fish bait wells under the stern seats. Joshua told Slim to pick up two cases of Lite Beer, four bottles of Vodka and two bottles of Grand Marnier. He also told Slim if they wanted some Pluck to be his guest. As Slim was walking away, Joshua said to Shortie, "Catch up with Slim and tell him to get 2 cases of water as well, the 50.7 ounce size."

While Slim was gone, Shortie and Joshua decided upon who would sleep where. There was no doubt about it that Joshua would have the forward berth. Shortie took the rear berth, leaving Slim with the task of turning the dining table into a bed each night. He explained to Shortie that showers at port could be as long as the hot water lasted. When underway, showers would have to be no more than two minutes per person.

It was nearing dinnertime. Slim had returned and worked up an appetite. He said, "Who's going to cook?" Joshua replied, "We'll flip coins and the odd man will have to make preparations for dinner. If I lose then I'll have to cook. I'm not going to go and stand in some restaurant and order food. It's not like pictures don't travel all over the country." Shortie responded by saying, "Oh, what the hell. I'll walk and get us something to eat. I saw a FatBurgers just up the street."

"Good move, Shortie," responded Joshua. "I like a man who cuts through the bullshit and gets the job done."

"My only problem is that I'm running out of money. Slim, do you have any money?"

"I have exactly eighty dollars."

"Don't worry about money. Come here, Shortie. You didn't get that name because you're tall. I want you to climb back near the gas tank and get my briefcase." Shortie made his way over the tank, found the briefcase and handed it to Joshua. Joshua waited until Shortie got out of the hole and told the guys to sit down. As the men sat down, Joshua said, "I know I can trust you guys, and you are now a part of my organization. As such, you should know that I have money hidden all around the country. Cash money." He told Slim to shut the door to the cabin. Joshua then moved the combination locks to their correct location for opening, slid a key into an almost-hidden slot and turned it. The men were flabbergasted by the amount of money that was in the case. Joshua looked at their eyes and said, "Three million cold-hard cash, boys. Do you think that will get us to Miami and set up our business?"

"Hell yes," Shortie replied. Slim just looked at the cash and couldn't open his mouth.

"So you see, that's why I'm concerned about the trash that you guys want to push."

"Joshua, this is the one that gets me and Slim into a lot of cash. We can't back out now," indicated Shortie.

"I understand, but if the deals looks bad, then walk away. I think that we have the beginning of a good relationship. Don't go and fuck it up." Joshua took $4,000 out of the case and gave Shortie and Slim a $1,000 each and put $2,000 in his own pocket. He told them that this was their first week's pay. He also cautioned them about his briefcase because it, too, was booby-trapped. They all broke out laughing. Joshua inquired, "If you guys are ready for another beer, then I'm buying."

After eating the one-pound burgers that Shortie had fetched for them, Slim looked at his watch and told Shortie that they had to make their run. He then told Joshua not to worry because they were going to be partners in every sense of the word. "I'm counting on you guys to make it back without a scratch. I need the both of you," Joshua replied. They left shortly thereafter.

As Joshua watched television, he knew that his face was popular at this time. The only way to change that, he thought, was to change his looks. He reasoned that if he made it to

Miami, he would have to undergo some serious facial transformations. He certainly wanted to get rid of his nose, thicken his lips, build a scar above one of his eyes and shave his mustache and head. He rationalized that he could beat those who think that he is easy to find by modifying not only his looks, but also his behavior. He was correct in all of his assumptions. But that's just what they were—his assumptions. He took a hit of the Grand Marnier and fell off to sleep.

Four hours later, Joshua woke up and realized that he had slept for a long time. His first thoughts were about his new and humble companions. He took another hit of his drink and someone knocked on the side of the boat. Joshua reached under the table, pulled the Derringer down, and peaked out of the window. "Yeah, who is it?" The voice on the other side said, "It's the dockmaster. You have to pay for docking here."

"How much do I owe you?"

"That depends on what size your boat is. I know that you have two electrical lines and they're $4 each. What size is your boat?"

"It's a 34-footer."

"Then it's a dollar a foot plus the $8 for the electric. You owe me $42."

"Be right up."

Joshua gave the dock master a hundred dollar bill and the young guy asked if he had anything smaller. Joshua told him no that was all he had to his name. The Dockmaster reluctantly took the bill and changed it. He gave Joshua the change and his receipt and told him to have a good night. Just as the dock master walked away, Slim and Shortie came back with a look of defeat on their faces.

"What happened?"

"The fucking guys pulled guns on us and took our shit."

"They robbed you?"

"There were four of them. They all just laughed and told us to get our asses out of there before they blew our heads off. I don't like anybody taking shit from me and then telling me that they're going to blow my head off. I want to go and get those bastards."

"I don't think that's a smart move. Just forget about it and get some rest so that we can head out of here bright and early in the morning," Joshua said.

"Joshua, if it had been you, what would you do about it?" Slim asked.

"It wasn't me, so I don't have to consider it now do I?"

After thinking through the question for a minute, he reasoned that Slim and Shortie wanted him to help them do those guys. "Okay you blokes, what on earth do you want to do about it?"

"We want to go and kick some ass."

"How about if I paid you for your losses. Would that satisfy you?"

"No, Joshua. We wanted to do this deal and do it right. You can't take your money and pay us for letting someone stick us up and take our dope. Suppose it was your caine and we came to you with that sorry-ass story? What would you do?" Shortie inquired.

"I see your point. Okay, up the street I saw a parking lot. You guys know anything about stealing cars?"

"Tell me what you want and it's done. We also need weapons. Do you have anything other than the shotgun and your pistol?"

"If I tell you yes are you going to hit me again, Slim? Just kidding boys, just kidding. Yes, open the control panel and hit the accessory switch twice." Slim did exactly as he was told, and a panel opened with machine pistols, 9 millimeters and plenty of ammo. "I'll be damned, look at this," Slim said. "Are you ready, Shortie?"

"I sure as hell am. Joshua, this is our fight—we don't want you to be a part of this one."

"I appreciate your kindness, Shortie, but I'm already a part of it. Get the machine pistols and two clips each. We'll teach those bastards a lesson that they'll remember in hell." As he looked at the three weapons, he turned and said, "This isn't a good idea. Put the Macs back and get pistols and silencers. We can't walk down the street with Macs showing, now can we?"

"Good point, Joshua. We're used to pistols anyway. This shit might just complicate our lives." Joshua locked the boat and hit his remote control unit that set the alarm. He told Slim to go and get a car ready. He didn't want to be standing around while Slim was trying to steal a car.

Later, as they drove to the location where the caine deal went sour, Slim said, "See the guy who looks like he's drunk? Well, that's the lookout guy. He searched us and then let us in."

"Okay, turn at this corner coming up and let me out. Then I want you to drive around the block and drop Shortie off at the corner before the building. Slim, I want you to pull right up in front and park as though you've been there a hundred times. By that time we should be in position. Shortie, when you see me walking, then you come on up. I'll do the guy at the door and then we go in and do whoever is in there. Now listen, I don't want any drugs, but if there's money lying around then get it— but no caine. We leave that shit. We don't need any problems down in Miami. Okay, Slim, let me out now and when we get in, don't leave any fingerprints."

After everyone was in position, Joshua started his walk from one way and Shortie from the other. Slim pulled the car in the front of the building, and the so-called drunk began to put his hand in his pocket. From about ten feet away, Joshua pulled his weapon and fired two shots, hitting the guy in the chest and neck. He told Shortie to pull him in the hallway. Slim got out of the car and they went into the basement, where another guy was standing. He saw Slim, recognized him and reached for his weapon. All three men put rounds into his body. Joshua whispered to Slim to kick the door in and for Shortie to cover from the right, take all his shots to the right and that he would take all the shots to the left. He told Slim that the center was his.

296

After gaining their composure, Slim kicked the door and the mayhem began. Four men and one woman were shot to pieces. He told Slim to get to the car and pick him up where he dropped him off, he told Shortie to wait on the other corner just in case they didn't get them all. As the car rounded the corner, there were no stragglers, just calm and peace. The three men then drove to the docks. Shortie and Joshua got out of the car about a block away and told Slim to wipe the steering column clean and meet them at the boat.

With all three men back on the boat, Joshua said, "That was a piece of cake. We went in, we whacked them and we took their money. Not bad for a night's work, eh boys?"

"Joshua, you are a cold-blooded sonofabitch. You blew that guy away without thinking about it. The broad that you shot was only wounded, and you walked up to her and said, 'Sorry, bitch, it's only business,' and then blew her head off."

"Shortie, what did you want me to do with her? Kiss the bitch?"

"Not at all, but I'll tell you one thing, I never want to cross your ass."

"Then don't and we'll all be better off and rich in the long run. Speaking of money, how much did we get?"

"I haven't counted it yet. Here, Slim, you count like a machine."

Slim counted the money and said, "A paltry $15,000."

"There's no such thing as a paltry $15,000, Slim. You buy the right thing with that and before you know it, you got a $100,000 worth of equity. Shortie, I saw the way you looked at the caine that was there. Did you have second thoughts about what I told you?"

"Not at all, Joshua. I did think for a minute that it could fetch us more money, but then I realized that where we are headed, we don't need the hassle."

"Good man. I would have been disappointed, but I would have understood had you taken the shit."

"Damn, I'm glad we didn't whack you back there near the airport. What a loss that would have been."

"Screw you too, Shortie."

"No, I mean it. In less than twenty-four hours, you've shown us enough money to make a man crazy, you shared your boat with us after we took it from you and then most of all, you helped us whack the shit out of the jerks that robbed us. I mean, Joshua, this is the best. Slim and I haven't had this kind of treatment or been close to equal with anyone. Yet you make us think and you worry about us. That makes me feel very fucking good. I'm your man and I'll do whatever it takes to keep you from jail, and Slim feels the same way, ain't that right, Slim?"

"You said it all, Shortie. The man is upstanding with us. He helped us clean up our sloppy work. Joshua, I'm with you all the way, and Shortie can tell you, when I say that, that's exactly what I mean. I would die for you dude."

"Jesus, guys, you're going to make me cry if you keep this shit up. Let's have a drink and get some sleep. We have a lot of water to cover in the morning. You know guys, I was thinking that maybe we should just head to the Bahamas and lay low for a while, what do you think?"

"When we get to Miami, if that's what you want to do boss, it's all right with us," Slim said.

CHAPTER FOURTEEN

"Smitty, are you ready to go yet?"

"Give me another ten minutes, Sarge. The Captain told me he wanted some files he left on my desk this morning. I think he's losing his mind. He didn't leave any damn files on my desk. Oh shit, wait a minute. This must be what he's talking about. I guess I'm the one who's losing a mind. Okay, Sarge, just give me a few minutes to take these things into him and I'll be ready to go."

"Take your time, Smitty, just do it right."

Smitty went into the Captain's office and asked him if he had he received the call yet. The Captain told him that it had just come in and everything was ready. He told Smitty that he was going to walk out and ask the Sarge if he wanted to have a drink. Then they would begin the sting operation. The Sarge never realized that he was now the subject of a department-wide sting operation that would finally get him caught.

"Okay you guys, I'm out of here. I guess I'll go and have a drink. You interested, Sarge?"

"Sorry, Captain. I told Smitty that he and I would hang out for a little while tonight. You're welcome to come along."

"Thanks, but no thanks, Sarge. I've had enough of this guy for one day."

Smitty said, "Captain, it would be my honor if you accompanied us for a drink and a little food." The Captain thought about it for a few moments and said, "Ah, what the hell, just don't talk too much, Smitty. Come on Sarge, let's go." The three men walked out of the door and Smitty said, "We aren't taking three cars are we?"

"I'll leave mine," the Sarge said. "Captain, you can bring us back here on your way home. Is that okay?"

"Jesus, I'll probably have to pay the damn bill as well. Come on, you jerks."

They drove over to one of the Sarge's favorite restaurants and pulled the car into the garage. The Captain said, "I know why neither of you wanted to drive. Parking is $12 at this damn place."

They walked up the street and into the restaurant, which had been closed for a private party. They told the hostess that they wanted a quiet table for three. As she grabbed the menus and led the men from the reception area to the dining area, there they stood—almost every cop the Sarge had ever worked with or befriended. In unison they yelled at the top of their lungs, "SURPRISE!" The Sarge looked at Smitty and the Captain and said, "You jerks. You set me up, didn't you? How long have you been planning this, Smitty?"

"I haven't planned a thing, Sarge. It was the Captain." The Sarge turned to the man and gave him a man-size hug, and told him that he loved him and kissed the Captain on the cheek. Of course this sent rumors of an illicit love affair going on and the men yelled, "No poofter shit tonight."

It was a grand party and an extravagant one as well. They all drank top shelf, and champagne and ate caviar. The dinner was lobster or filet mignon. Everyone had a marvelous time, and at the end the Sarge said, "Guys, I love each and every one of youse. This has been one of the best days of my life. Actually, I've had a few good days lately. I have a new bride-to-be, I have a daughter who is expecting a child and I have a new son who is on the dean's list at Cruza. It's funny how things happen. Most of you remember when I jumped the broom before, and the tragedy that befell my wife and the twins she was carrying. Well, that sonofabitch who killed my family got his fucking head chopped off. Now that's justice and I feel good for the bastard. But to keep this occasion festive, I want you all to know from the bottom of my heart, I love each and every last one of youse and I will never forget this night as long as I live. Thank you and God bless us all." The Sarge received a standing ovation and tears ran down the big man's face. He realized that he was truly blessed and thanked God for his blessings.

After more drinks and dessert came the nude dancing girls and gifts from the heart and imagination. It was truly a great night for the Sarge, and everyone had a wonderful time. They loved him because he was unselfish and helped everyone when he could.

CHAPTER FIFTEEN

Larry had recovered miraculously. He was up and about, but was plagued by pain. He reluctantly took the Valium that was prescribed for him. As with most young men when their fancies begin to rise, Larry was becoming increasingly attached to the young lady he had casually met at church, Marisa. Marisa was actually the delivery agent for Larry's schoolwork. They had developed a very serious relationship based upon some very fundamental beliefs that over time, relationships eroded as a result of the need for people to amass great wealth and material possessions. Their conversations were more aligned with the great speech by President John Fitzgerald Kennedy. They were true believers that a sustainable society was one where the members of it cared for and helped, those who were less fortunate.

Marisa and Larry had only kissed once, and it had happened when they accidentally butted heads while reaching for the same fallen object. This occurred when she drove him to be fitted for his tuxedo on Friday morning. But on this Saturday morning, his second day out of the house since being shot by Malik, Larry was determined to expand his horizons and investigate the secrets of this woman's lips. Wedding days always tend to make people consider higher forms of existence, and it was no different for Larry. His only hope was that his feelings were shared by Marisa as well.

The Sarge came by to pick up Larry at nine in the morning for a 2 p.m. wedding. As Larry was walking out the door, Rashida asked, "Larry, are you sure you have everything?"

"I'm pretty sure that I do."

"Then why is the bow tie sitting on the floor in your room?"

"Must be someone else's. Can't be mine because I know I have mine in this bag."

"Larry, get your crazy butt up there and get that tie. You'll need it to impress the Princess."

"You might have something there. Hey, Rashida, don't laugh, but do you think she likes me?"

"Fool, who would waste their time on you? But if you really want to know my opinion, I think the girl can't wait until there's some romance."

"I didn't ask you all of that. I asked if you thought she liked me."

"Larry, the woman is ready for anything that you have in mind. Just take it slow and be a gentleman. Personally, I think she's horny as hell."

"Rashida, don't talk like that! It's not becoming of you," Courtney yelled from her room.

"I know, Mom, but if we can't talk about it here and with each other, then who do we talk to?"

"It's not what you said that required my attention, it's how you phrased it. You could have said something like, 'She's all hot and sweaty for you, Larry'."

"Mom, that's despicable for a woman whose about to become a bride. I will tell my father as soon as I get in the truck."

"While you're at it, Larry, tell him his bride can't wait to get him in the sack."

"Mom, what the….on earth has gotten into you this morning?"

"Larry, in case you've forgotten, I'm getting married to that man who's out there blowing that horn like he's about to run away. Make sure that doesn't happen, Larry, or I'll have your butt as well."

"I heard that. See you gorgeous ladies later. Oh, by the way, I invited Marisa. I hope that was okay."

"I called her last night and gave her the official invitation, turkey. Now get out of here before your father decides to come in and cause me bad luck."

"See you later, alligator, after while, crocodile, after supper—ah."

"Don't you dare say the rest."

In the truck an anxious Sarge asked, "Larry, what took you so long?"

"Sarge, I was detained because a certain bride-to-be wanted me to deliver a message to the man who was outside blowing his horn like a wild man."

"What is the message?"

"I was told to tell you—and don't you get mad at me because I'm only the messenger—that she couldn't wait to get you in the sack."

"Did she really say that, Larry?"

"Sarge, I wouldn't lie about a thing like that."

"Good girl, because I'm one horny bastard right about now."

"Sarge, I can't believe I'm hearing this from the man who is supposed to be my father."

"Son, there are somethings that—shit, Larry, you're no virgin. Just shut up and ride before I forget what I'm supposed to be doing today."

"I forgot to tell you that I invited Marisa to the wedding."

"I would have been disappointed had you not invited her, Larry. She's a looker and a fine person along with that. I couldn't have thought of a better place for you two to meet than church. It kind of showed me two young people who had something on their minds besides foolishness and trouble."

"Maybe I'll ask her to marry me today and then we could have a double wedding."

"Larry, don't complicate my life. It's about to become complicated enough without you going out and doing something dumb."

"You're doing it. Are you saying you're dumb?"

305

"Sometimes I could knock the shit out you. But I just say to myself that you really can't help it because you don't operate with a full quid."

"What does that mean?"

"That means that you have less than a full brain, meathead."

"Where did you get that saying from?"

"My great-grandfather supposedly said that."

"Was he Aborigine?"

"No, he wasn't. Believe it or not, he was white. One day I'll tell you the whole story as it was told to me by one of the keepers of the legend."

"Sounds pretty mixed up to me."

"I don't know why. My great-grandmother was Aborigine and my great-grandfather was white. Doesn't sound terribly mixed up to me."

After arriving at the Sarge's place, Larry took his clothes up to his room and asked the Sarge what they were going to do until wedding time. The Sarge told Larry to chill out and have a beer with him. The two men started talking and Larry asked the Sarge to continue the story about what his grandfather had told him. The Sarge told Larry that his great-grandfather was called a Living Spirit, and with that title came the ability to transform into certain animals and communicate with them. Larry questioned the integrity of what the Sarge had told him and asked him for further clarification. The Sarge told him that his great-grandfather was sworn to stop the destruction of the Aborigine people in what was called "BodyBay." It was so named, he told Larry, because the Aborigine lived on valued land and were literally slaughtered by the white man for their land. He told him how complete tribes were tied together and forced off cliffs to their deaths and how the women and children, including little boys, were raped and sodomized, then staked out for the dingoes and the wombats to eat. Larry asked the Sarge what was a dingo and wombat. The Sarge told him that they were animals indigenous to Australia. He likened the dingo to a wild dog and the wombat to a fury little bear with massive jaws and incredible jaw strength.

Before the story continued, the Sarge paused for a moment to go and relieve himself and fetch the two of them another beer. He told Larry it was said that his great-grandfather could turn into the largest saltie known to man and the largest taipan snake as well. He told Larry that his great-grandfather was an unbadged lawman, finding those who conspired against and committed atrocities against the Aborigine people and wreaking final havoc on them. Larry asked how that was accomplished. The Sarge told him that it usually occurred by decapitation, and in quite a few cases, from ingestion by the snake. Larry told the Sarge that he couldn't be serious and the Sarge indicated to Larry that there were many things in the world that had no logical explanation. Larry asked the Sarge if he believed the stories and the Sarge told him yes.

As he continued with the story, the Sarge told Larry that his great-grandmother's name was Marisa, the same as the little lady that he was sweet on. The Sarge then continued on with the story of the metamorphosis that occurred to his great-grandfather and how the legendary Spirits of the Pigeon, Sky Heroes and the almighty Rainbow Serpent talked to his great-grandfather. At this point Larry told the Sarge that he now understood why he was a little off upstairs. The Sarge continued with the stories about the slaughter of the Aborigines and how his great-great-grandfather and great-grandfather put an end to the killing. He told Larry that there was a half-spirit and half-human friend of his great-grandfather's by the name of Wajickee. He told Larry how Wajickee was the wisest of all of the spirits and how he was the most unforgiving. He indicated that Wajickee was hell bent on revenge for anyone who inflicted pain on the Aborigine people.

The Sarge told Larry that it was time for them to get ready and Larry told him after hearing all of those tales that the Sarge

307

should consider going to the hospital instead of the church. Both men laughed, and as they were ascending the steps the Sarge said to Larry, "When I visited Australia and my great-grandfather's village, the people knew me. When I got to the village, a feast had been planned in my honor and they all addressed me as family of *The Great Saltie*." Larry replied, "Couldn't it have been by coincidence that they knew you were coming?"

"The only people who knew I was making the trip were the travel agent and the customs people."

"What did they mean by family of *The Great Saltie*?"

"My great-grandfather was called *The Great Saltie*, because he could turn into a saltie."

"By the way, what's a saltie?"

"It's the largest salt water crocodile in existence. It's said that they range from 7 to 30 feet. *The Great Saltie* was 29.5 feet long and weighed as much as your truck. The Legend keeper told me that my great-grandfather was as vicious or as gentle as the occasion called for. The man who shot my great grandmother in cold blood was savagely decapitated and the rest of his body given to the freshies for dinner. I was told the name of the man who killed her."

"First of all, Sarge, what's a freshie and secondly, what was his name?"

"A freshie is a small fresh water crocodile. Jake Shittaker, was the man who killed my great-great-grandmother and Clyde Bunbury killed my great grandmother. *The Great Saltie* wreaked total havoc on both men and the aristocrats back in east Australia who conspired to kill the Aborigine people for precious metals."

"Damn, Sarge, that was some story. My only question is how much of it do you believe?"

"Son, I believe it all. Now when I tell you this, you are really going to freak out. While I was swimming in this body of water called a billabong, I was suddenly startled by the sounds of members of the village yelling. As I turned to see who they were yelling at, it turned out to be me. The warning was for me to get out of the water. Well, I damn near shit on myself when I saw the head of that thing. I started stroking and the damn thing went

308

under me and just threw me up in the air. It never once hurt me, it just scared the hell out of me. One of the elders in the village said, 'Not you worry, for that is *The Great Saltie*, your great-grandfather'." Well of course I didn't give a shit who it was, all I wanted to do was get the hell out of the water. After playing with me for a minute, it looked me straight in the eye and I swear to you, Larry, it started to cry. At that point, I knew that there was much more to the story and there was some kind of mysticism there which refuted all logic and explanations. Son, I met *The Great Saltie*, and he was my great-grandfather."

"Sarge, I don't know what to say other than that's an incredible story. Maybe one day we can go to Australia, and then perhaps I can have a better appreciation of your family history. It sounds fascinating, but incredulous. Let's get ready—you have a wedding to consummate in a matter of two hours. We'll talk later about that story. I really have an interest in going there. Maybe I'll save some money and go this summer. Will you come with me?"

"Larry, after the honeymoon, and once the new house has been started, I'll see if just the two of us can take a two week bonding trip."

CHAPTER SIXTEEN

The wedding was spectacular. Courtney was dressed in a gown designed by Gianni Versace, and she wore it well. Her maid of honor, an old college roommate, who was unable to come to any of the rehearsals, was also an astonishing-looking woman from New York. Her name was Monica and the two women had no idea their paths had crossed in so many different ways and would continue to cross. Rashida, all of eight months pregnant, was glowing with the beauty of life. Radiant she was in her wonderfully tailored gown with a translucent look that would make God smile down on her. The Sarge was the Sarge, uncomfortable in the tuxedo yet grinning and bearing through every minute of it. He complained to Larry that if he had to ever wear another one of these things, he just wouldn't attend the affair. Larry told him they should go out and have a couple made. That way, they could control the fit. Smitty looked quite unusual out of his policeman's uniform.

While people were eating and enjoying themselves, Courtney said, "Monica, come with me to the ladies room." In the ladies room, Monica said, "Congratulations, Courtney, on your catch."

"Thank you, sweetie. Isn't he great?"

"I think he is adorable."

"You know, Monica, he's with money also."

"Oh, Courtney, you are so lucky. By the way, what do you think of that guy Smitty?"

"He's a cop like the Sarge and probably Sarge's best friend. Why are you asking about him? Do you like what you see, girlfriend?"

"I do kind of like the way he looks, but he makes me feel a little uncomfortable. He won't stop staring at me. He reminds me of a guy I met on the bus not long ago."

"Why didn't you bring him to the wedding?"

"Oh no, Honey, I had to get rid of him because he tried to force me to use cocaine and sometimes got pretty rough when having sex."

"No!"

"I swear to you. I had to get the locks changed and have the concierge throw him out. His name was Malik."

"Jesus, Monica. Where was he from?"

"He was from here, Courtney."

"If it's the same Malik that the entire world is looking for, then you damn sure did the right thing by getting rid of him. Honey, he is one sick sonofabitch. The child Rashida is carrying is his and he also shot Larry in cold blood. He's also wanted for several murders of police officers and a host of armed robberies. Honey, for God's sake, if you hear from him again call the police."

"Courtney, I feel like such a fool. I was so love-starved that I let the guy talk me into dinner. Then when the booze kicked in, he spent the night and then basically lived with me. I need to have my head examined. Let's get out of here. It's your wedding day; you shouldn't be hearing this sad shit about my miserable life. But you know, that Smitty guy looks pretty good to me for a white boy. I'll see what his next move is. He has completely undressed me and can probably tell me if I have any tumors or anything. I mean, he's been watching me with so much intensity. Come on, girlfriend, let's go party."

They say great minds think alike. As the Sarge caught up with Smitty, he asked, "Are you enjoying yourself?"

"I sure am, but I need to know who the maid of honor is. I can't take my eyes off her. I've never seen a woman who just looks like class and has the beauty to go along with it. Sarge, can you get the lowdown for me on her?"

"Why don't you go over and ask Courtney who she is and what the deal is? I really don't know that much about her except she hails from New York and she and Courtney have been friends for over 25 years."

"Sarge, where is Courtney and that lady? What's her name?"

"Her name is ah—Monica. There they are. I see what you mean. She really is a looker, isn't she? Tall, pretty and sexy."

"Sarge, do me one favor and call Courtney over here for me."

The Sarge beckoned to his new bride, and when she arrived, she gave him a seductive kiss and told him, "The best is yet to come and, babe, won't it be fun? Did you want me?"

"Honey, I've wanted you since I met you in that hospital. I'm just glad that Smitty didn't see you first or he might be where I am today. Smitty has a question for you."

"I already know his question, Sarge. He wants to know about Monica. Smitty, she's bright, and makes a lot of money, single, lives in New York and thinks that you should stop staring at her and at least say something to her."

"Damn, Smitty, there you go. The deal's been set. All you have to do is follow through. Now don't embarrass the home team. Go over there and work your magic."

As Smitty sucked in his stomach and proceeded over to where Monica was standing and chatting with a guest, Courtney said, "Malik has struck again, Sarge."

"What do you mean?"

"He lived with Monica for a while until he insisted that she try cocaine. When he continued to insist, she had her locks changed and threw him out."

"Poor girl. That bastard is everywhere and nowhere. How could he seduce a woman like that?"

"Sarge, when you're our age love comes in strange and sometimes challenging ways. She was lonely and needed companionship, and he met her on the bus and that's how it began. Will you tell Smitty?"

"It's not my place to tell Smitty about that. I wouldn't like it if someone had something negative to say about you, because it wouldn't matter. You were my choice and your past is yours and mine is mine."

"God, I love you man. You make the difficult easy and the sad happy. Let's get with the crowd and make our day a joyous one. I love you, Sarge."

"And you know I love you, Courtney. From the moment I first laid my eyes on you, I knew you would be here with me at our wedding. Now go and mix with our guests."

Smitty and Monica were having a pretty good conversation, and it looked as though a relationship was in the cards. She laughed and he laughed and that was something that she had not experienced in a long time—the ability to be silly and frivolous. Smitty apologized for staring at her and gave her the best answer a man could give a woman. She in turn told him that she had told Courtney that he was making her feel a little uncomfortable. The conversation continued and he asked her how long she would be in town. She told him until tomorrow. Smitty suggested that they have lunch before she left, and she reluctantly agreed. The reluctance showed in her face and Smitty asked her, "Am I being a bit too forward?" Monica looked at him and said, "No, not really." Smitty responded by saying, "I thought I detected a little reluctance in your voice."

"Maybe you did, but I didn't mean it. I guess I was disappointed that you didn't invite me to dinner or drinks later tonight."

"Oh, then I can easily rectify that. Would you like to have drinks and dinner later?"

"No, I can't. I'm busy, but I can have lunch tomorrow." Monica looked at Smitty and said, "You know what I'm doing tonight, so why did you have to ask?"

"Again, I don't want to be forward."

"I guess I should ask you if you have plans for tonight?"

"I most certainly don't. I want to be with you and try to get to know you."

"Why?"

"To honestly answer might create embarrassment on my part as well as yours, but I'm going to attempt to give you a flavor of

314

what I was thinking all day. When you walked into the church, I almost had a coronary. I mean, you're beautiful, tall and sexy. You have a brain in your head and you aren't married or engaged. You know weddings make people think about love and you, for the moment, have caught the attention of every cell in my body."

"Not bad, Smitty, I like that analysis. But let me make sure you understand where I'm coming from. I saw you because you wouldn't take your eyes off of me. I don't plan on anything romantic and all. I'd like to talk and get to know you better. I may like what I hear and I may not. Just don't expect anything other than conversation, that's all I'm saying. Don't pressure me and yes, please stare at me. It makes me think that you're interested and I can see whether or not you're sincere or just trying to get—you know what I mean."

"Monica, I'm looking for a friend first and then from there, the sky is the limit. I have no intention of trying anything, and I certainly don't expect anything other than conversation. So you see, I think we're both on the same wavelength."

"Good. There is one thing I will admit to you. I do like you and I think you're fun. Never stop being fun and we'll become good friends."

"I think it's pretty obvious that I like you. I haven't taken my eyes off you since you showed up. Well, I'm going to circulate a little bit and then I'm going to find myself back here with you. I don't want to seem like I'm trying to monopolize all of your time."

"Why not, if that's what you and I want to do? My time is yours except when the bride needs me."

"Good. I would like to introduce you to those guys who can't keep their eyes off of you as well."

Ah, yes, it seemed like a new budding relationship was in the wind.

Larry and Marisa were in one of their deep conversations when Rashida walked up and said, "Can I interrupt for minute?"

"Sure, Sis, what's up?"

"Larry, I'm feeling like shit."

"What's wrong? Are you about to go into labor?"

"You know, Larry, you are so stupid at times. No, nothing like that. I'm sick of people asking me how far pregnant am I and where is the father?" At that point Rashida started crying, and Larry stood up, hugged her and said, "You have the best family support network on earth. You don't have a damn thing to be sad about because we all love you. You know how people are so why do you let them get to you? You stay over here with us."

"Larry, I just feel bad that I met a jerk and got pregnant and didn't even know I was. If I had, I would have had an abortion."

"Don't you ever let me hear you talk like that again. That is life within you. Precious life, and you are the giver of that life. So what? You made a mistake, but the thing that you got going is that you have Courtney and the Sarge and you know what they went through to keep you out of that home. So let's put this thing in perspective. Yes you are fat and pregnant. Yes, the baby will probably never meet his father. Yes, you have a great home, and a mother, father and brother that love you. Is there anything else in life?"

"That's why I love you, meathead. Every time I start feeling sorry for myself, you make me think about how bad it could have been. Thanks, bro. I'm sorry to disturb you and Marisa."

"Rashida, I feel like Larry. I mean, I'm not family, but I feel that we're close enough to consider me a distant cousin or something. Why don't you stay over here with us for a while and then we'll all circulate together," Marisa said.

"I guess I should because Larry isn't going to say anything to you that's important. You know, he asked me the other day if I thought that you liked him?"

"What did you tell him?"

"I told him something like, does a chicken have feathers?"

"Larry, why didn't you ask me if I liked you?"

"See what you did, Rashida? Listen Marisa, I know that you like me but I'm not sure in which way."

Marisa grabbed him around the neck and gave him a kiss that he would remember for a long time. Rashida said, "Well, I guess that answers that." They turned and formed a threesome hug.

The day was a day blessed by God himself. Everything turned out better than expected. The bride and groom were as effervescent as could be. This was truly a marriage made in heaven and sanctioned by all of the spirits of good.

BOOK FIVE

CHAPTER ONE

ONE MONTH LATER

The Sarge and Courtney traveled to Paris for their honeymoon. It was cut short by three days. Rashida went into labor. Larry and Marisa provided all of the support needed and the delivery was a success. She had a girl, weighing 7.5 lbs, who would undoubtedly be the new queen of the house.

The new home that was being built had six bedrooms and would have four acres of land for the new queen to roam around. Rashida named her child LaGina; only God knows where she came up with that name. Her middle name was Courtney, after her new grandmother. The other good news for the family was that Courtney had missed a menstrual cycle.

Smitty and Monica became a hot item. They would alternate between New York and Philadelphia each weekend and were inseparable. Their conversations were serious in nature, concerning what their next steps were. They had discussed marriage and both had agreed, reluctantly, that they needed at least another year or so to really get serious about that subject. Monica had even told Smitty about Malik and how he had touched so many lives in such a dastardly manner. Smitty told Monica that the past is a prologue. This was the first time that she told him that she loved him.

Malik made his way to California and was wanted there for attempted murder and rape. Once again he had slipped between the lines of the law and was en-route to Philadelphia. He made a stop in San Antonio, where he had infected two women with the HIV virus. In Los Angeles, he participated in a caine orgy in which eleven people feverishly sexed one another. In Indianapolis, where he was cut during a fight, his blood mixed with the blood of the guy who sliced him for flirting with his girlfriend. In San Francisco, Malik had seduced a teenager and almost killed the girl between giving her heavy hits of caine and sodomizing her. He took the girl home and told her mother that she was high and had been with his neighbor. The mother was a good-looking woman who had the same problem as her daughter. Malik accommodated her and had sex with her that night also. He committed silent, malicious murder all over the country. When the multiplier effect was added to his known associates, Malik was responsible for committing the largest mass murder in the history of this country. And he never looked back!

For Joshua Bunbury, the great-grandson of Clyde Bunbury, life was not going very well. He had used most of his $3 million to finance a caine deal that went sour. Slim, Shortie and him killed seven people, but never recovered the money. Shortie and Slim had to rob a bank in order to get enough money for fuel to get back to where Joshua could put his hands on more of the money he had made from the sale of caine. Their next port of call would be Philadelphia.

CHAPTER TWO

Life for the Beckmires was as good as it could get. LaGina was the focus and attention of everyone, including Marisa. She was a good baby and rarely cried. Rashida was trying to recapture her figure from the strains of motherhood.

The Sarge had a surprise for everyone this night. As the clan gathered around the table to dine, and after the customary prayer, the Sarge said, "I have a deal for all of you." Courtney asked, "What kind of deal?"

"It's a deal of a lifetime."

"Well, then it must be life itself," retorted Larry.

"No, meathead, it's not life itself, but a way for everyone's life to get better as we approach the future."

"Honey, please tell us so that we can eat."

"Okay. Courtney, first of all, I'm going to buy this house from you at fair market value. I'm planning to turn down that offer that was made on my house and just rent the place out."

"Honey, are we having financial problems?" This got everyone's attention because they all wanted to know how they could help if, in fact, that was the problem.

"No, baby, we are not having financial problems. What we are going to do is give this house to Rashida when she finishes college and my house to Larry when he graduates from college, but until then put the rent money in the bank for them." Courtney looked at the surprised looks on Rashida's and Larry's faces and then looked long at the Sarge before saying, "You are one incredible human being and I thank God that he gave me the wisdom to choose you over the rest."

"What do you mean, choose me? I chose you."

"No, you didn't. I chose you."

"At this point in time, it's not relevant who chose whom. The fact of the matter is that you two nuts are married to each other," Larry said. Rashida never said a word, but the tears streaming down her face were more than enough to show what was on her mind. Courtney said, "I know those are tears of joy and you guys need to get your butts up from the table and give that dude over there a hug and a kiss." That's exactly what they did. The Sarge said, "Courtney, we'll pay your house off in a few days and transfer the money into your personal account for you to tuck away."

"You are such a giving person, Sarge, and it's ironic that you picked this night of all nights to be generous to us. We are not the only one's who will be happy after this day. Pick LaGina up."

"Why?"

"Just do it. Don't ask why. Just do it." The Sarge picked LaGina up. Fastened to her diaper was a little package. He said, "What is this? It's not my birthday."

"Does it have to be your birthday in order for people who love you to give you a gift?" Rashida asked.

"Well, I guess not." As he fumbled with the package and finally opened it, a note on the box read, "You have made all of us happy and we wanted you to enjoy this small token of our love and appreciation for all that you've done for us." The Sarge's eyes began to water. He looked around the room at the anxious eyes that were watching him and said, "You guys are my family and I love you so much. I love you, Courtney. I love you, Rashida. I love you, Larry, and you know that Grandpa loves you, LaGina." He never opened the box, but instead said, "Let's eat. I'm hungry." Larry said, "Well aren't you going to open the box?"

"After I eat, Son." He looked around the table once again and then said, "Yeah, I guess I had better open it and act surprised. I already know what it is."

"I'll bet you your AT&T stock against my entire portfolio," Larry said.

"Well, if you're willing to bet that, then I guess I may not know. However, I think it's that watch I showed you the other day, Courtney."

"Open the box, Sarge, and see," Courtney said. He looked around the room once again and said, "Oh, you people buy a guy a gift then he has to open it when you say so." The Sarge untaped the box and a key fell out of it and onto the floor. As he reached under the table to recover it, Larry said, "I'll get it for you."

Larry then placed the key in the middle of his plate. The key was to a brand new, Trocodaro Red Range Rover. He yelled, "How in the hell did you know what I wanted, and more important, how did you guys pay for it?"

"Because I'm your wife. I'm supposed to know what you want and to try to fulfill your wishes."

"We paid for it with your money, Sarge," Larry jokingly said. Courtney looked at him and said, "Boy, somedays you're like a joke. You never stop trying to make me laugh. Sarge, believe it or not, we paid for it with money Larry made from the market, the money that was in that insurance policy that Rashida's mom had that you found and from my money. We still owe money, but we can easily handle the payments. It's from all of us, and all of us put up money towards it. It's right out back in the yard. Go take it for a spin." The Sarge got up from the table with LaGina in his arms, went to the window and put the lights on in the back yard. There she stood, the brightest red truck in the world—in his eyes—and it was his. Swaying with LaGina in his arms and his lips gently kissing her head, the Sarge began to cry. His family went over to him and gave him hugs and kisses of love. The Sarge said, "Let's eat and be thankful that we have each other. God knows that I'm one happy man." Larry asked him if he was going to take it for a ride. The Sarge told him immediately after dinner they all were going to take it for a ride. As they turned to walk to the table, the Sarge suddenly remembered what this day was supposed to be all about. The doorbell rang and he knew that it was the bearer of good tidings.

"Smitty, come on in. You'll never guess what I got for being a good guy."

"Probably some Maalox to stop you from farting all the time."

"Smitty, you're such a smartass. Take a look out that back window over there."

Smitty walked over to the window and said, "Holy shit! Is that what I think it is?"

"You got that right. It's that Range Rover I've been thinking about. You know, I said I would never buy one because people would begin to talk. However, I never said that my wife and kids couldn't buy it for me. All three of these characters chipped in and bought me that truck."

"Sarge, I've got to say this—years ago when you had that tragedy in your life, you told me you would give it all back for love and a family. Well, you don't have to give anything back because you've brought love to this group and you have a family that would kill for you." Well, those words were certainly true, because after hearing them, Larry walked into the powder room.

"I guess you're right, Smitty. Oh, by the way, did everything go all right?"

"Did you know that this was going to happen?"

"Smitty, I swear to you, I told them what I was going to do with the two houses and before I knew it they had a box pinned to LaGina's diaper. When I opened it the key fell out." He then went on to whisper to Smitty that this was incredible and when he gave Courtney her gift she was going to flip. He told Smitty that this was absolutely a coincidence of the strangest nature.

"What are you guys whispering about?" Courtney asked.

"Oh nothing, dear. Where's Larry? Smitty, stay for dinner because you're the only one who might believe what has just happened." Larry returned from the powder room and looked at the Sarge, who gave him a thumbs up, indicating that everything was all right.

They sat down and began to enjoy the cold meal when the Sarge said, "Everybody got something here except Smitty and Courtney. For you, Smitty and I know that you won't take anything from me but I'm tired of you driving that wreck of yours. You need a car with an airbag, and therefore I'm selling you my car for $100."

"Sarge, you can't do that. That car is worth at least eighteen or nineteen thousand."

"Good. Then I just sold it to you for a $109 and the deal is closed. Courtney, my love, you will never believe what I have for you. The strange thing about all of this is that it's nobody's birthday. I just wanted to do something good for my friend Smitty because I love him and he looks after me. I certainly wanted to do something for my sweet daughter Rashida and my favorite son, Larry. When I was talking to Smitty the other day and asked him what I should get you for a wedding present, we went to this jewelry store, and there it was—the best-looking piece of workmanship I had ever seen. Smitty, do the honors and present my wife with her wedding present."

"I will not, Sarge. You take the box and give it to her."

"Oh, I guess you're right on that one. Honey, it's not much, but when I saw it, I knew it was you." The Sarge handed Courtney the smartly wrapped box. She sat it on the table and said, "I'm hungry, let's eat." Rashida said, "Not you too, Mom."

"Just kidding." She picked the box up and held it close to her face so that no one could see what was in it but her. She opened the box and closed it quickly. In the box was a key with the Mercedes symbol on it. Her eyes opened as wide as new money and she yelled, "This had better not be a joke."

"Let us see!" Rashida shouted.

"Where is it, Sarge?"

"Look out of the front window." Before she could get up, Larry and Rashida were at the window. Rashida yelled, "Holy shit! Larry, look at that bad Benz."

"Rashida, we're going to be riding in style around here. That's a bad motherfucker. Oh shit, Sarge, I'm sorry. Mom, it just slipped. I can't remember the last time I used that word." When Courtney got to the window, she said, "This is a dream come true. Wait until that bitch Marge sees this. Oh shit, I did it too. Okay guys, for the next minute we are going to curse our heads off. Sarge, fuck it, I love your sweet ass."

"Hey, Pops, you're fucking okay."

"Hey, Mom, and Pops, I'm a lady and I can't use words like fuck and fucking, but that's a sweet bitch out there," Rashida said.

"Hey, Sarge, fuck it man, thank you for the car," Smitty replied.

"Hey, Smitty, you're fucking welcome. Now that you people have purged your need to use such terminology around my Grandchild I forbid it to ever be said again in our home."

"Screw dinner guys, I'm going for a ride. By the way Sarge, what is it?"

"It's a 500SL Mercedes Benz."

"Come here you lump and give me some sugar. Boy, can you imagine what Christmas is going to be like around here?"

"I can't," Smitty replied.

"Kids, I've got to go and see what that truck of mine will do. I'll see you all later. Come on, Smitty, I'll give you a ride home."

"No you won't. I'm driving my own car home. You didn't forget that quick did you?"

"No, I didn't, but you didn't pay me the $109 either, did you?"

"You're such a smartass at times, Sarge."

"Sarge, there is something else I have to tell you," Courtney said. "It's rather private. May I see you in the kitchen?"

When the Sarge walked into the kitchen, Courtney turned around and said, "I think I'm pregnant. I'm not sure, but I've missed almost two cycles."

"Oh girl, that's the best news I've heard in a long time. I love you so. You make me so happy and you've taken in those two kids like they are your own and you treat us all like we've been together for a thousand years. Damn, I love you. When will you be sure?"

"I have an appointment tomorrow. I'll let you know."

"Damn, that's good news. Let's keep it a secret until we know for sure."

"Good idea. Can I have a kiss, Sarge?"

"You can have one better than that. How about a big old fat juicy I love you kiss?"

"Suits me fine."

Courtney and Rashida donned jackets and went for a ride with the top down. The Sarge and Smitty left. Larry remained to care for his new niece. He said to himself, *I thank you God for all that you have done for us and I hope what the Sarge and I have done meets with some rationalization on your part.* He then kissed LaGina and she urinated on him. What a night at the Beckmires: two new homeowners and two new car owners. Life was splendid in this house of adoption.

CHAPTER THREE

At the station, things were pretty hectic. The Sarge had his eyes on Jeffrey, another kid who looked like he just needed some loving, and was beginning to show his particular brand of attention to the young man. He even had Larry come down and talk to the guy and try to figure out why this kid was the way he was.

On his third visit to see Jeffrey, Larry stopped by to say hello to Smitty and saw another kid from the projects being brought into the station in handcuffs. Larry told Smitty he knew the kid and would like to find out why he was in trouble. Smitty told Larry that the kid had just shot another kid over some drugs. Larry's eyes began to water. The situation reminded him all too much of where he was before the Sarge came into his life. The Sarge came over to Larry and said, "I know exactly what you're thinking. I want to help him, but when you use a firearm the law becomes less than lenient. Let it go, son, and go back and talk to Jeffrey. Rumor has it he got raped last night. If anyone can sympathize with him, Larry, it's you. Go and do your best. He'll be sent to the big house tomorrow." Larry looked at the Sarge, dried his eyes and headed towards lockup. He was searched as usual and then allowed to enter the cell with Jeffrey.

"So how's it going today, Jeff?" There was no response and he could see that the kid was trembling like he was about to have a seizure. "I heard what happened and I know how you feel."

"You don't know shit, Larry."

"That's where you're wrong, Jeff. You see, I've been exactly where you've been."

"Larry, shut the fuck up and get out of here because you don't know shit."

"Jeff, no need to talk to me like that, man. I've been exactly where you've been, dude. In jail a guy knocked me out, raped

331

me and then wiped his dick across my mouth. So don't tell me I don't know what you're up against."

Jeff looked at Larry and began to cry. "Let it go, man. It's behind you and you don't have to live the rest of your life like that. It has nothing to do with you being a faggot. Trust me, I know all of the things that are going through your mind at this point. Do you want to tell me who did it?"

"No, man. I want to handle this my way."

"Don't get yourself more time than you're already facing."

"I'm not worried about that. I just want to get that fucker in the right way."

"If you do that then you're only going to get yourself in more trouble. If you want to do it and get away with it then let me help you."

"How can you help me? You're out there and I'm in this fucking place. Did you get the guy who did you?"

"No, I didn't, but I had planned on killing his ass. It seems as though someone else who I beat the shit out of for trying to rape me put the word out for no one to fuck with me because I was his. The guy who did me was the Chef at the prison. He didn't follow orders and was found with knife wounds all over his body. I never got a chance to get even. When they put you back in the cell with those guys this is what I want you do. Take your sock off and put that bar of soap over there on the sink in it. After things quiet down they'll probably try it again. Beat them to the punch and you won't have a problem. Aim for the nose, but don't kill them. Just try to break the nose and you won't have any more problems here. I'm going to try to talk to my father and see if he can't get you sent to one of the homes instead of prison. You know you got to do the time, but it's just a matter of where."

"Hey, Larry, thanks man. I'm sorry I acted like such a jerk, but you understand."

"Jeff, I still have dreams about what happened to me, but it's all behind me now. That's exactly what you've got to do—put it behind you but aim for the nose." They both broke out laughing

Larry called for the guard and told Jeff he would see him later in the week after he had a chance to talk to his father.

On the way out Larry told the Sarge, "I'll see you later, Pops. Don't be late for dinner."

"Okay, son. Talk to you later."

The Sarge was looking over some astounding information that caused him great anxiety. He called Smitty over and told him to call the Feds and make sure this report on Mr. Bunbury was correct. The Sarge looked like a man who had met the devil himself. The Captain walked by and said, "Beckmire, are you all right?"

"Yes, yes, Captain. I just ran across some puzzling information on that banker, Mr. Bunbury. It appears as though he has the name of a person that"—the Sarge realized that he was giving away too much information—"ah—a person that may be in charge of a large Florida drug ring."

"Keep looking Sarge, I'm sure you'll find him," the Captain said. Smitty walked over and said, "Sarge, the Feds said the report was correct and if it wasn't we wouldn't have a copy of it."

"Those guys are such prima donnas. Thanks, Smitty. Oh, by the way, I'll get the paperwork on that thing to you as soon as I have a chance to go to the safety deposit box and get a copy of it."

"No hurry, Sarge. Whenever you get the chance."

"You want to have a beer tomorrow after work?"

"Only if you're bringing Courtney. Monica is coming to town a day early. We're going to take a long ride down into the mountains of Virginia."

"Good for you. I'll check with Courtney and see what she has going and let you know."

That evening on his way home the Sarge called Larry and asked him what was he doing. Larry told him that Marisa was over and that they were just playing with the baby. He told

333

Larry he wanted him to take a ride with him and to be ready in five minutes. Larry never questioned the Sarge when he made a point of being that direct. He knew that something was up.

On his new English horn the Sarge blasted away. Larry came running and said, "Do you know you're disturbing the peace?"

"Larry, take a look at this." After reading the document as the Sarge ran his big truck around the corners, Larry said, "No way man. No way. There's no way that there is a connection."

"I won't know until I find the snake, will I?"

"Sarge, there is no way this guy can be the great-grandson of the man who killed your great-grandmother."

"Larry, the Feds ran a check and there's only one Bunbury in this country. His name is Joshua Bunbury and I bet you his great-grandfather's name was Clyde Bunbury. I want to find him, Larry, but not as a cop. I need to have the *edge*. When I read the report, I broke out in a cold sweat. There's one thing I haven't told you or anyone else for that matter, Larry, but don't you dare laugh. There are times when I think I can talk to the Spirits. On my way over here, I stopped in the park, got out and just stared at the trees for a while. I asked if he was the bloodline of the man who murdered my great-grandmother. The wind started blowing hard for a minute or so and a voice said to me, 'The Bunbury's of the world shall be no more. All evil must die and you must see to it'."

"Sarge, you are really starting to scare me with all of this hocus pocus talk. I do believe that there are some things that logic refutes, but Sarge, I don't know about your ability to talk to spirits."

"Larry, I don't blame you for doubting me, but this is the other piece of news that the spirits gave me. I was told that he was traveling along the great billabong and to look in the northeast for him. I know this all sounds crazy, but I got my first information on the market from a spirit, Larry. You can laugh if you like, but tonight I need you to hang around the Delaware in the northeast in about an hour and keep a lookout for any boats that pass the Ben Franklin Bridge. He'll be traveling by night, a thing that many small boaters avoid at all cost."

"Sarge, that's a lot of water. How would I know it was him even if he ran over me with his boat?"

"Son, trust me on this one. If he comes you'll know him as if he was the devil himself. I know you don't believe me, but just this once. If I'm wrong, I'll never mention spirits again. Is that a deal?"

"You're on, Sarge."

"Okay good. I'm going to be near the Neshaminy Creek, and I want you to hang just south of there. If you see any boats coming in, just call me on the phone and let me know. I'll tell Courtney that you and I have some community work to do tonight. That will keep her off of us. I think you need to go by the house and get a piece."

CHAPTER FOUR

It was indeed a long and arduous ride for Joshua Bunbury and his band of two pirates. As if the close quarters weren't enough to drive everyone crazy, the shitter was broke and backed up. The crew used the macerator pump so much that it eventually burned out. Even though they had their slings and arrows, it was still the best way to avoid constant crowds of people that are customary to airports, bus and train stations. Joshua knew there was a large police contingency dedicated to his capture, and he was not about to make it easy for anyone. The one thing he had ignored as a young man was the warnings that his great-grandfather's sins would be his undoing.

One hour and a half out of the Cape May inlet, Joshua yelled, "There's the C & D Canal. We have about two and a half hours of traveling left, and then we'll have enough money for you boys to go and have some fun for a change. We'll have to figure out a good hiding place for me because you know everybody and their sisters are looking for me. When we get to Philly, I'm going to give you guys an address and a key. In the briefcase you'll find $3.5 million in cash. Do not open it, because if you do, it will be nice to have known you guys."

"Hey, Josh, we're with you. Not to worry about any bullshit, because if we know you, you'll triple that amount. You know the one thing I would really like to know is how did you get that name Bunbury?" Shortie asked. "Well, Shortie, I guess you and Slim should know all there is to know about me. My family is from Australia and lived at such a time when you didn't have to pay for land, you just took it. My great-grandfather was a ruthless man and was hired by white settlers to get rid of the Aborigines. He and his gang of men would head out to an area, chain the bastards together and push them off of a cliff or into a river. His name was Clyde Bunbury. Anyway, my great-grandpa was accused of killing as many as 3,000 Abo's. He hated them and would often kill them for the fun of it. They would get drunk and go out into the bush and shoot them as though they were kangaroo. Old Clyde made one mistake when he took on a young white boy named Beckmire. As it was told to me, Beckmire was a demon and could turn into the biggest saltwater crocodile or giant snake known to man. Anyway, the croc ate my great grandpa and placed a curse on the Bunbury family. The curse was that the name would be erased from the face of the earth for the dastardly deeds of my great-grandpa and that no Bunbury would live to be fifty."

"How old are you, Josh?" Slim asked.

"I'm forty-nine, but I don't believe in that bullshit. It was like the story of Christ, and told in so many different ways that you begin to disbelieve it after a while."

"Is there anyone in your family older than fifty, Josh?" Shortie asked.

"That's where I get concerned. No one has lived beyond fifty. I think they panicked and did themselves in. Let me make it very clear to you guys—I have a birthday next week, and I assure you that I am going to be alive and well and not in jail. Ah, look, there's the airport. Slim, slow it down to 2,000 RPMs. There's always a lot of shit floating in the water around here and we sure don't need to hit anything."

Meanwhile, one hour and fifteen minutes away, Larry and the Sarge were making their way up to a less-than-plush marina called Jack's Marina. If you wanted to hide, there was no better place than Jack's. The Sarge positioned himself at the marina's restaurant and ordered himself a grilled barbecue chicken dinner with french fries. He was amazed at the cleanliness of the place and the friendly waitress. When the meal came, he was in awe of it. It was a massive, well-designed plate of food that he would never finish. He pulled his portable flip-phone out of his pocket, called Larry in his truck and told him he was having a wonderful meal and that he would save him some french fries. Larry told him that all was quiet.

338

In the middle of his dinner, the Sarge asked the waitress her name. She said, "Sally." Then he asked if boats normally operated this late at night. She told him now and then a boat by the name of La Marisa would go out and anchor and then come in late. He thanked her and she told him that they had some wonderful desserts. He ordered a deep-dish apple pie with vanilla ice cream. As soon as she came with the dessert, the telephone rang and it was Larry. Larry told the Sarge that for the last three or four minutes someone was flashing lights on the river as though they were trying to see the buoys. He told Larry to call him back if they pulled in where he was. The Sarge hurriedly ate the dessert, and low and behold, a boat pulled into the creek. The Sarge closed his eyes for a moment and decided that it was not Bunbury's boat. He asked for a cup of coffee, picked up the telephone and called Larry to tell him to come over to the restaurant at Jack's. He told Larry that he was sure that this was where Bunbury would be docking.

When Larry got there he asked if it was too late to get something to eat, Sally told him no. The Sarge recommended the barbecue grilled chicken and Larry went for it. He told the Sarge, "I think we wasted our time up here."

"Sometimes I think you lack faith, Larry."

"Sarge, it's not a matter of lacking faith; it's a matter of not going along with the story you told me."

"Larry, for the rest of the night and we made a deal, you'll only illustrate positive feelings. Negative feelings tend to interfere with cosmic waves."

"Now I know you're off your rocker man. What's this cosmic wave nonsense?"

"I said that only because it would get your goat. The truth of the matter is, I will know when he gets here. Joshua Bunbury, the great-grandson of Clyde Bunbury, is very near, Larry. I feel his evil soul."

"Sarge, I'm going to participate in this venture with you tonight, but if it doesn't pan out, promise me you'll not mention spirits and cosmic waves again."

"I already made that deal, Larry. What do you want, blood from a turnip? After all, I'm not a magician. I wanted to watch the New Jersey Nets tonight. I still think that Moe Cheeks is the greatest thief to ever operate in the NBA."

"Yeah he's good, but he's lost a step or two."

"That's all right. The guy is thirty-six years old and can still run with the best of them. I think he'll make a helluva coach, when he finally retires."

"I'd like to see him coach the college game."

"There's no instant money in college. You have to build a program from the bottom and then you can call the dollar shot. But once you go to the college ranks, it's hard to get back into the NBA, so I hear."

Sally brought Larry his plate and he said, "Jesus, am I supposed to eat all of this?"

"Don't worry, you look like you could use a little food," Sally responded.

"Sarge, this is a lot of food."

"Tell me about it, but it's good."

After finishing his dinner, Larry asked the Sarge how much longer they were going to be there. He told Larry not much longer because he felt that things were about to happen. Larry ordered a cup of tea and a slice of cheesecake and watched the Sarge drool over it. Noticeably, the Sarge started sweating and Larry asked, "What's wrong? Why are you sweating like that?"

"He's near, Larry. I can feel him."

Larry looked up the creek and said, "Sarge, there's nothing out there but darkness."

"Darkness is the trading place of the devil, son. Mr. Bunbury is very near. I can feel him." Larry got up from the table, went outside on the porch and shook his head because he didn't see anything. He came back in and said, "Sarge, let's get out of here. There's no one on the river tonight." Sally walked over with the check and said, "I guess that creep is back."

"What creep?" Larry inquired.

"The creep that slips in and out at night and never says a word to anyone. Don't you see that boat turning into the creek?" Larry got up once again, went outside and looked up the creek. He finally saw the running lights on the yacht. He came back in and saw that the Sarge was looking awfully bad and said, "Come on, Sarge, you need some air." Larry paid the bill and walked outside. The two men watched as the yacht passed the restaurant and headed down the creek. The Sarge told Larry to follow him, but not to put his lights on.

On the other side of the marina, the two men took up different positions and talked by car phone. Larry asked, "How do you know it's him, Sarge?"

"Larry, I'm as sure as that full moon above that Joshua Bunbury is on that boat. It's unlikely he'll leave the boat, but we'll wait a while and see.

"Sarge, what are they doing on the front of the boat?"

"They're tying her off and putting out a spring line to keep her from swaying."

"Since when did you learn so much about boats?"

"I was raised around them. I'd like to own another one about that size, but you need to have people who enjoy the water to really own a boat. You don't need a bunch of freeloaders hanging around drinking beer all the time—you need family and friends."

"Well, you got both, so let's look into it."

"Boy, you sure can make plans on my money."

"I love you too, Sarge."

The three men went down into the cabin and the Sarge said, "I bet you this dirty car next to me belongs to one of those guys. I had better move my truck or it will give us away." The Sarge drove his truck on the other side of the creek, pulled out his night glasses and watched the action below. Two men came up the plank and got into the car that the Sarge predicted was theirs.

341

They were having a hard time starting it. The Sarge said to Larry, "Maybe I should offer them a ride. What do you think?"

"Don't be funny, Sarge. If that guy below is who you say he is, then you know these guys are packing and packing heavy."

"Don't worry, I'm not going to do anything crazy." The car finally kicked over and the two men drove off. Larry asked the Sarge if one of them was Joshua Bunbury. The Sarge told him that he would know Mr. Bunbury when he saw him because the evilness of the man would be all over him like the stench from the stagnant pools of water around them.

"Bunbury is on that boat, Larry, and there isn't a thing that we can do. We can't just board his boat unless we want to get blown away, so we'll just wait until the two guys come back, and then we'll use them as the bait. Larry, the boats on each side of his look like they're empty. When and if those two come back, we need to have a plan on how we're going to catch them."

"Why don't I pull my truck near the plank and just lay low. When they come back, you be on the other side of that storage house. When the one on the passenger side gets out, I'll show him this weapon and you can walk up on the other one. Just don't be late."

"Good thinking. I'm going to move my truck now. Do you have any gloves and stockings?"

"I'm always prepared. I once thought about being a Boy Scout."

"Cute. I'll drive over get a pair of gloves and a stocking and position my truck. Now, whatever happens, be careful and don't do anything crazy. If it breaks out into a shootout, get your ass out of here in a hurry. Whatever you do, don't shoot in the area of the boats. There's enough fuel on those things to blow us to heaven."

"Gotcha. You had better come and get ready now."

Another hour went by and the Sarge and Larry became restless. The Sarge thought about calling it off. When he asked Larry what they should do, Larry told him to wait until midnight

342

and then they'd come back another day. At 11:45, lights could be seen coming down the road. The Sarge told Larry to get ready because he thought the two men were on the way back. Sure enough, the car drove up and the two men got out of it. The one on the passenger side was surprised by the barrel of Larry's weapon, and before the driver had a chance to get his gun, the Sarge had his pistol at the man's neck. He told them to walk over to the storage lockers, where he searched them. After confiscating both weapons, the Sarge told the men not to turn around and to place their hands behind their heads. He told them that he didn't want them and all he wanted to know was who was on the boat. Neither man would talk until Larry said, "I guess I'll have to do one of them before the other one talks." Shortie said, "His name is Joshua Bunbury." Larry just stared at the Sarge. "What's in the case?" the Sarge asked. "We don't know. It's locked and we don't have the key." Slim said.

The Sarge pulled Larry aside and told him to sneak down and get on the boat next to Bunbury's. He then told the men to take the case and act normal. He told them if they fucked up, he would blow holes in their heads.

Slim had the briefcase in his left hand and was handcuffed to Shortie's left hand. The two men climbed aboard the boat and called out to Bunbury. He opened the door and said, "I thought you boys had run off with my goods." After hearing that, the Sarge pushed the two men aside and said, "Put your fucking hands in the air! Now!" Bunbury started to make a move and the Sarge said, "You even exhale and I'm going to blow your ass away." The Sarge descended the steps into the cabin pushed Joshua up against the door to the head and searched him. Larry escorted the other two men down the steps. After searching the head for weapons, he pushed both of them into it and shut the door behind them. He said, "Make a move and I'll shoot up that hitter."

After pulling the stocking all the way over his face, the Sarge turned Joshua around and said, "This is not about money or drugs. This is about your past. I'm only going to ask you this question once. What is your name?"

"It's Scott. Why?" With the butt of his pistol, the Sarge smacked the man up against the head.

"Now, let's try it again. What's your real name?"

"It's Joshua Bunbury."

"Now, Mr. Bunbury, that's better. I want you to tell me everything that has been told to you about your great-grandfather."

"What?"

"Which part of the question didn't you understand?"

"Why do you want to know about my great-grandfather?"

SMACK!

"Let me make a point. You answer. I ask. Now what do you know about your great grandfather?"

"I don't know much of anything."

"Then tell me what you know."

"He lived in Australia and was considered a bad guy." The Sarge looked at Larry and back to Bunbury and said, "Tell us more."

"May I sit down?"

"Sure." He looked at Larry and told him to check under the table. After searching under the table, Larry said, "Look what I found."

"Nice looking Derringer, Mr. Bunbury. Is that why you wanted to sit down?"

"No, I forgot about that."

"Just make this night go by quick and tell us what you know about the past."

"Who are you fucking guys, a couple of nuts?"

SMACK!

"Okay, just stop hitting me. He was the leader of a gang that killed a lot of Abo's."

344

SMACK!

"What was that for?"

"They are not Abo's. They are Aborigines. Now finish the story before I put a bullet in your knee."

Josh looked at his watch and the Sarge knew that they were in trouble.

"What are you looking at that watch for?"

"Nothing."

SMACK! SMACK!

A muffled sound came from the head. Larry said, "I'm going to open that door and I want your backs to me. If not, I'm just going to empty this clip in there." He opened the door and Shortie said, "There's a bomb on board that has to be reset."

"Where is the bomb, Bunbury?"

"Find it, motherfucker."

POW! A bullet to knee! Watching the blood gush from his leg, Joshua cried, "Okay, I'll reset it." He reached over to the stove and picked up the remote unit. Larry grabbed it and said, "How do we know to trust this scum?"

"We don't," the Sarge said. "Hey you, in the head, how does this thing work?"

"Just push the red button twice and it will cut it off for an hour," Slim replied. Larry pushed the button twice and then shut the door to the head. He told Mr. Bunbury to open the briefcase. Shortie yelled, "That's wired too. He has to use a key on it."

Joshua, feeling much pain and agony, told them he would open it. He opened the briefcase and the money was stacked as full as possible. The Sarge said, "Blood money. Finish telling me about your family."

"He used to kill people for their land. I was told that he killed thousands of Aborigines for land that had gold and diamonds on it. My grandfather told me that my great-grandfather would tie people together, lead them off a cliff and watch as the animals feasted on them."

"How did he die?"

"I wasn't there so I don't know."

"That almost got your other knee blown off. I'll ask you once again, and then I'll put another round into your other leg if you don't give the right response."

"I was told that he was killed by a white boy that could turn into a crocodile or a snake."

"Do you expect me to believe that, Mr. Bunbury?"

"I swear to you, that's all I know. He was eaten by a boy who could do those things. I don't believe that shit, but that's what was poured into my head since I was a baby."

Larry looked at the Sarge with astonishment.

"Do you know the name of the boy who killed him?"

"They told me his name was Andy Beckmire. What does all of this have to do with anything? Who are you and why are you trying to kill me?" The Sarge leaned over, pulled the stocking off, exposing his face, and whispered in Joshua's ear so that the others wouldn't hear him, "My name is Ben Beckmire." Joshua Bunbury looked as though he had just seen a ghost.

"You're the cause of my anxiety. I knew that I felt the presence of something evil. I know exactly who you are Mr. Ben--." "The Sarge put his hands over Joshua's mouth and said, "My great-grandfather was Andy Beckmire. The woman that Clyde Bunbury savagely killed was my great-grandmother. I have to avenge her soul so that she may stop roaming on Dreamtime." The Sarge put the pistol to Joshua's head and blew his brains out. This caught Larry completely off guard. He said, "Holy shit, what have you done?"

"I did what I had to do. Later I'll tell you why I had to do that, but I doubt if you'll believe me. What shall we do with the two in there?"

"I think we should make them take this boat out of here, anchor it out in the water and let the bomb do the rest. Pull your stocking down before I bring them out."

"Bring them out of there." As the two men came out and saw the blood running from Joshua's head, they started begging for their lives.

"Here's the deal. You know how the bomb works, and if you want to live this is what you have to do. Get this boat out of here and anchor it down river where no one will get hurt when it blows up. After you anchor it, put on life vests and get the hell away from it. I'm going to put enough money in a trash bag to allow you two to get out of town and never come back or look back." The Sarge got a trash bag from under the counter and started shoveling cash into it. He must have put at least $1 million in the bag. "Okay, if you fuck up, the same thing is going to happen to you that happened to this vermin here. You take this money and you had better go straight. Go west, buy yourself a small business and try the legal way of life. If I see your faces on any list, we'll come gunning for you, and we don't miss. Is that understood?"

"Yes sir, we'll do it."

"Where does he keep his guns?"

"All over the place," Shortie said. "Under that counter there are four machine pistols and several 9 millimeters."

"You boys won't be needing them, so make sure when you get off of the boat, you leave all guns behind. Don't fuck up. We'll be watching you, and if we catch one of you with a gun, we'll blow both of your heads off. You people got that?"

"Yes sir. We'll do exactly as you say. And thank you," Slim said.

"You can thank us by doing exactly as we agreed. Look at all of the obvious places that you touched and wipe this thing clean so that no one can trace it to you guys. Take as much time as you need, but do a thorough job. Start this thing up as soon as we're off and get out of here. We'll be down-river watching. Don't fail and don't take anything else that may be onboard. You get off with your clothes and the trash bag full of money. Nothing else."

"We're out of here. Slim, you wipe down the helm and I'll start down here," Shortie said. "Don't fuck up or I'll leave a bullet in your head just like his," the Sarge said.

The two men put the rest of the money in another trash bag and left. The Sarge told Larry to head on home where he would meet him. Larry told the Sarge that he wasn't going anywhere until the Sarge was in front of or behind him.

Both men drove their trucks down State Road and pulled off where they would have a panoramic view of the Delaware River. They waited and waited. Then, like a Roman candle going off on the Fourth of July, a bright flash hit the early morning sky, illuminated by the full moon. The Sarge thought to himself, *Mr. Bunbury, never made it to his 50th birthday party. It was canceled because of death.* The Sarge told Larry he was going to give the money to a Father Flanigan with a note for him to divide the money between OIC, the orphanage and the United Negro College Fund. Larry told him those would have been his picks as well.

At home a worried Courtney said, "I tried to call you but I didn't get an answer." The Sarge just said, "Larry and I were dealing with things from the past that needed our attention. Everything is okay and my great-grandmother can stop walking around aimlessly on Dreamtime."

"What are you talking about?"

"It's a long story, honey. One day I'll tell you all about it. Right now I need to get some sleep, but before that, I need to be loved by you."

Words such as those will always end a night on the right note.

CHAPTER FIVE

Courtney was two and a half months pregnant and enjoying every minute of it. She was pampered by everyone in the house, especially Larry. That evening, she and the Sarge had a dinner date with Smitty, Monica, Larry and Marisa.

Monica and Smitty had really become a constant number. As a matter of fact, they had planned on announcing their intentions of getting engaged. Monica had already made plans to start looking for a job in Philadelphia. It was inconceivable that she would have a hard time trying to find a job paying her the kind of money she was used to. Smitty had offered to move to New York, but Monica told him she wanted out of that city all together and that she only wanted to visit the place.

Larry was about to announce that he and Marisa were going to go steady and would plan to get engaged after he finished his second year of school. Marisa would be a senior at that point, and they were looking forward to struggling for a better life. All in all, this was going to be an important evening for everyone. Courtney was about to tell everyone her good news, so all of them were looking forward to the dinner at Daci's on Broad Street.

In another part of town, Malik was back and looking real bad. He was broke, hungry and unusually dangerous for many different reasons. He had the symptoms of the full-blown AIDS virus and looked like walking death. His only chance of survival was to make small-time stickups. Malik was without fear and was looking for an easy way out of life.

At the corner of Broad and Diamond Street in North Philadelphia, Malik saw his next target—a caine dealer who boasted about never having less than a grand on him. Malik followed him and his two buddies to their crack house, but knew he would never survive trying to do them on their own turf. He waited for about an hour and saw his opportunity. The dealer got into his car and drove to pick up some cigarettes. At the corner Chinese restaurant, Malik caught him coming out and said, "If you even think about going in your pocket I'll blow your fucking head off. Now get in the car on the passenger side." The dealer was caught off guard and didn't have a chance to get away. Malik said, "Give me your caine and your cash or I'll kill your ass." The dealer said, "Malik, are you losing your motherfucking mind? You know you can't rob a dealer and get away with it."

"Shut up and give me the shit." Malik had the pistol in his right hand and a knife that the dealer didn't see in his left. The dealer thought that he could grab the pistol from Malik, but when he tried, Malik stabbed him in the neck, killing him instantly. Malik took the time to go through his pockets and into his shoes and socks where guys tend to hide their money. He found about $400, wiped the knife off on the dealer's clothes and then shot him in the face for trying to take advantage of him. Malik got out of the car as though nothing had happened and walked away. Witnesses told the police that the guy stabbed the man in the car first, then shot him after searching and finding some money and walked away like he was just dropped off from a ride.

Malik walked two blocks, got into his stolen car and drove downtown. As he drove by the Straford Hotel, he glanced out of the window to the left and saw a woman who he thought was Monica going into Daci's restaurant. Malik made a U-turn and pulled up in front of the restaurant in the bus zone. He watched as a couple rounded the corner in the restaurant and got two seats at the bar. He wasn't sure at that point if it was Monica, but he felt it looked a lot like her. He didn't chance getting out of the car. Instead he pulled up a little and got the look he needed to confirm his suspicion. He saw Smitty all over Monica and said to himself, I knew she wasn't nothing but a whore.

350

Malik decided to pull off, but remembered that the woman always kept plenty of cash on her. He looked in the mirror and thought he looked good enough to get in the place. As he was about to get out of the car, he saw a cop walking up the street and he decided to sit for a minute. The cop never looked, and that made Malik feel better about what he was about to do. As he looked around, to his surprise, he saw a guy who he had shot. Malik watched Marisa and Larry enter the restaurant and decided that he would wreak havoc on the faggot. He said, "Motherfucker lived through one of my bullets, but this time I'll just blow his head off." Malik did not recognize the Sarge and Courtney because they weren't people who he was familiar with.

He got out of the car and left it running just in case he had to get away in a hurry. Malik walked into the restaurant and told the hostess that he was going to the bar and that he was waiting for his date. He then asked her where the restroom was. She told him it was downstairs. Malik went down the steps, washed his hands and face and then walked back up the steps. As he turned on one part of the steps, Courtney was descending. She spoke to him, not knowing that he was the guy who impregnated Rashida, shot Larry and who also approached her in the store and asked, "Have you learned to shoot yet?" Once upstairs, Malik hung out by the hostess stand and just looked through the glass at the crowd at the bar. He stared at Larry and then at Monica and knew that he had to do what he had to do. Courtney came back up the steps and the hostess showed the party of six to their table. The group sat down and began to enjoy each other's company.

Malik, on the other hand, was trying to decide who he should do first: Monica or Larry. His choice was made easy when he saw Smitty kiss Monica. Malik walked back down to the restroom, went into one of the stalls and made sure that he had plenty of ammunition in the gun.

In the meantime, Courtney looked at the Sarge and said, "Honey, are you feeling all right?" Larry looked at the Sarge and said, "I know that look. Who is it Sarge?"

"I'm not sure, Larry, but we're in danger."

"Sarge, what are you talking about?" Smitty asked.

"Later, Smitty. Right now I have to ask you if you have your weapon?"

"Of course I do. What's going on?"

"Listen, Smitty, the Sarge has been getting some strange messages lately and each one has been correct. Something bad is about to happen."

"What the hell are you guys talking about?" Smitty asked. The Sarge began to sweat profusely. Courtney became alarmed. The Sarge said, "Larry, he's here."

"Who Sarge? Do you mean Malik?"

"I think it could only be him to cause me this much pain. Smitty, do you have that boot piece with you?"

"Yes."

"Don't ask me any questions, just give it to Larry. Don't anyone move until I say so. We're all in danger."

"Sarge, you're scaring the hell out of us. What's going on?"

"Honey, Malik or someone else who has caused us pain is in this place and he is going to try to hurt us. Please, just trust me."

Smitty handed the boot piece to Larry, and not a minute too soon. From around the corner leading from the restroom came an awesome shadow that looked like Lucifer himself. The shadow caught everyone's attention because it looked scary as all hell. As though in slow motion, each man made ready his weapon.

Having made the decision he was going to off Monica and then Larry, Malik ascended the two steps and headed towards the table with his weapon in his right hand. He passed several tables and then dead reckoned to the table where Monica, Larry and the rest of the group were sitting. As he raised his weapon, aiming it at Monica, Smitty yelled, "No!" Larry, seemingly in slow motion, turned and said, "This is for your daughter, motherfucker," and shot Malik in the chest. The Sarge fired three shots, hitting him in the body, and Smitty fired two hitting him also in various places. Larry fired the final and fatal shot to the head and yelled, "DEATH BECOMES YOU!" Malik hit the floor with a huge THUMP! His body rolled over and over again until it came to rest on the edge of a woman's chair. Her husband frantically grabbed her by the arm and said, "Honey, let's get out of here." She calmly replied, "It's over, dear. This is the scum that murdered our little girl. I feel it and I know it. No, dear, sit down so that we may finish our anniversary dinner. We can't let him have his rage on us as well." It was Gina's mother, and she knew that sweet revenge was at the foot of her chair. People started running out of the restaurant as if it were on fire. Gina's mother just sat there and repeated to her husband, "This is the guy that savagely murdered our little girl. I know it's him. I just know it's him."

As blood ran from Malik's body, Courtney said, "I have to go and see if he's alive." The Sarge said, "Don't you dare soil your hands with the blood of a man that has hurt so many people." She sat there and cried. Monica got up from the table, walked over to where Malik was lying and began to cry. Smitty came over to her and comforted her by putting his arms around her and saying, "He may have loved you in the worst possible way, but I love you in the way that God meant for a man to love a woman." She turned to Smitty and said, "Let's get married soon. I'm afraid and I need you."

The Sarge took the weapon from Larry wiped it clean and then gave it back to Smitty and told him to keep Larry out of it, if possible, but not to lie. The patrons in the restaurant were all gone. Just the help remained at this point.

It would be an easy inquiry. Malik was wanted more dead than alive.

CHAPTER SIX

Life became normal again for the Beckmires, and that's all they wanted. Courtney and the Sarge were the proud parents of a baby girl. They named her Monica Yvette. The Sarge decided to retire at the end of the year so that he could devote his time to his family and the extended family he had inherited. Jeff became a Beckmire and enjoyed the benefits of a true family structure. He went on to become a Rhodes Scholar with an emphasis in economics and was appointed to a Cabinet position as the Secretary of Commerce. Courtney and the Sarge also adopted four other children. Each child was alone, without parents. The new family structure challenged each one to adopt and care for those who were less fortunate than they were. The Beckmire's had inherited, with much love and affection, a large family structure that would endure time and would provide hope and understanding to young people who had gone astray or who had family problems.

Larry and Marisa were happily married and had twin girls of their own. Larry had received a MBA from the Harton School of Business, and Marisa had become the corporate lawyer she was destined to be.

Larry and the Sarge made their trip to Australia, where Larry learned many of the traditions that were held sacred to the Aborigines. He was now a true believer that logic was not always applicable and that there were things in the universe of life that simplified all of the complex questions: FAITH! The one thing Larry would never know was that the banker, Joshua Bunbury, was his biological father.

Smitty set up a financial service business for Monica that she operated from their home. She had employed 37 people and was picking winners in the stock market for all of her clients. Her business was purchased at a high price from a top-ten firm for millions of dollars. She became a successful commentator on GNBC. Smitty labored as a cop, but a good cop. He made Detective and they had a little girl they named Courtney Benet. He became the new Sarge. He set up scholarship programs and was even accused by the Sarge of being the *edge*.

Rashida and LaGina became financially secure early on after Larry taught Rashida how to invest her money, and she spent her days playing the market. Over a period of one year, Rashida had made $450,000 and was well on her way to becoming a millionaire without any trouble. She stayed on with the Sarge and Courtney and continued to rent her house out. She enrolled at Cruza University and was in her third year when she met a young man by the name of Walter. He had custody of his son and the two of them became a hot item. Upon graduation from school, Walter and Rashida got engaged, married three months later and lived happily ever after.

In the community, things were beginning to happen again. Neighbors were meeting neighbors for the first time. They all seemed to share the same sense of thankfulness to the Shooter and prayed that he was never caught or hurt. They were asking each other questions like, "How long have you lived here?" People on the same floor did not know who their neighbors were. Mr. Wilson was the catalyst for a lot of the changes. Just three days ago, two young hoodlums were hanging in front of the building. Mr. Wilson told them to move on and not come back or they might wind up in hell. It was messages like that one which kept a lot of the riffraff away. It felt good to be able to go downstairs and sit on the benches in front of the building without being hassled by thugs near and far.

In apartment 704, Mrs. Jones' son was suspected of dealing drugs. The residents called the law and conducted a sting that netted Mrs. Jones, her boyfriend and her 19-year-old son. The community had become very proactive and refused to be terrorized again. Some of the precious moments shared by the neighbors were in salutations like, "So nice to see you again," or "I saw your grandson for the first time in five years; he's grown to be a fine young man."

People were feeling happy again about being alive and free of the caine traffic. But a new group of caine traffickers were paying close attention to this virgin territory. This group realized that the one thing they didn't have to worry about in the ghetto was the presence of a lot of policemen. They just didn't patrol these areas the way they did other influential neighborhoods. But, the message from the Shooter was very straightforward: DEAL CAINE AND DIE! THE EDGE IS AGAINST YOU!

THE END

About the Author

For over 30 years, Ben has lent his imagination and talents to developing countless innovative programs to steer youth and young adults towards academic success, workplace marketability and financial independence. He is the product of the "mean streets" of Washington, D.C., and escaped the negative influences of street-corner philosophers through his love of education and basketball. When a professional basketball career did not materialize, he focused his attention on helping youth who were at-risk of failure in school and in life. He is a seasoned traveler, avid reader and risk-taker. He spends his spare moments piloting his boat up and down the Atlantic Seaboard. When he is not developing youth programs or boating, he turns his creative juices to his hero of three novels—Beckmire. Be on the lookout for the beginning of the Beckmire trilogy—*BodyBay, The Maiden from Hell's Kitchen and The Edge*.